PENGUIN CRIME FICTION

ONE DEADLY SUMMER

Sébastien Japrisot is the pseudonym (and anagram) of Jean-Baptiste
Rossi. He was born in Marseille, France, in 1931 and wrote and
published his first novel, *Les Mal Partis*, at age seventeen. (Reis-
sued in 1966, it was awarded the Prix de l'Unanimité by a group
of outstanding writers, including Jean-Paul Sartre.) After a period
of work as a film director and scriptwriter and the translator of the
works of J. D. Salinger, Japrisot wrote two more novels, which
first appeared in France in 1962, *The Sleeping-Car Murders* and
Trap for Cinderella; for the latter he was awarded the coveted
Grand Prix de la Littérature Policière, the major French detective-
fiction award. In 1966 he received the Prix d'Honneur for *The
Lady in the Car with Glasses and a Gun*. All of his novels have
been made into films. After a long interval in which he again
worked as a scriptwriter and film director, Japrisot returned to
literature with *One Deadly Summer*, which was awarded the Prix
des Deux Magots in 1978. *The Sleeping-Car Murders*, *Trap for
Cinderella*, and *The Lady in the Car with Glasses and a Gun* are
all published by Penguin Books.

Sébastien Japrisot

Translated by Alan Sheridan

One

Deadly

Summer

PENGUIN BOOKS

Penguin Books Ltd, Harmondsworth,
Middlesex, England
Penguin Books, 625 Madison Avenue,
New York, New York 10022, U.S.A.
Penguin Books Australia Ltd, Ringwood,
Victoria, Australia
Penguin Books Canada Limited, 2801 John Street,
Markham, Ontario, Canada L3R 1B4
Penguin Books (N.Z.) Ltd, 182–190 Wairau Road,
Auckland 10, New Zealand

First published in France under the title *L'Été Meurtrier*
by Éditions Denoël 1977
First published in the United States of America by
Harcourt Brace Jovanovich, Inc., 1980
Published in Penguin Books 1981

LIBRARY OF CONGRESS CATALOGING IN PUBLICATION DATA
Rossi, Jean Baptiste, 1931–
    One deadly summer.
    Translation of L'été meurtrier.
    I. Title.
PQ2678.O72E813   1981   843'.914   80-25170
ISBN 0 14.00.5846 X

Printed in the United States of America by
George Banta Co., Inc., Harrisonburg, Virginia
Set in Electra

The excerpt from the song "Some Day My Prince Will Come" by
Larry Morey and Frank Churchill is copyright 1937 by
Bourne Co., copyright renewed, and is used by permission.

CONTENTS

THE EXECUTIONER   11

THE VICTIM   58

THE WITNESS   96

THE INDICTMENT   112

THE SENTENCE   130

THE EXECUTION   196

"I'll be judge, I'll be jury,"
            said cunning old Fury:
"I'll try the whole cause,
            and condemn you to death."

Lewis Carroll,
Alice in Wonderland

ONE DEADLY SUMMER

THE EXECUTIONER

I said O.K.

I generally agree to things. Anyway, I did with Elle. I slapped her once, and once I beat her. But apart from that, she usually had her own way. I'm not too sure what I'm going on about. I find it hard to talk to people, except to my brothers, especially Michel. We call him Mickey. He carts wood around in an old Renault truck. He drives too fast. He's as dense as shit.

I watched him once driving down into the valley, on the road that follows the river. It's all twists and turns and sudden drops, and the road is hardly wide enough for one car. I watched him from high up, standing among the fir trees. I could follow him for several kilometers, a small yellow dot, disappearing and reappearing at each corner. I could even hear his engine, and the lumber bouncing up and down with every bump. He painted his truck yellow when Eddy Merckx won the Tour de France for the fourth time. It was on a bet. He couldn't even say hi, how are things, without talking about Eddy Merckx. I don't know who he gets his brains from.

Dad thought Fausto Coppi was the greatest. When Coppi died, he grew a moustache as a sign of mourning. For a whole day he said nothing, just sat on an old acacia stump in the snow-covered yard, smoking his American tobacco, which he rolled into cigarettes himself. He went around collecting butts, only American ones, mind you, and he rolled cigarettes the likes of which you've never seen. He was quite a character, our father. He's supposed to have come from southern Italy, on foot, pulling his player piano behind him. When he came to a village or town he'd stop in the square and get people dancing. He wanted to go to America. They all want to go to

America, the Ritals. In the end he stayed, because he didn't have the money for a ticket. He married our mother, who was named Desrameaux and came from Digne. She worked in a laundry and he did odd jobs on farms, but he earned practically nothing, and of course you can't go to America on foot.

Then they took in my mother's sister. She's been deaf since the bombing of Marseille, in May 1944, and she sleeps with her eyes open. In the evening, when she sits in her chair, we never know whether she's asleep or not. We all call her Cognata, which means sister-in-law, except our mother who calls her Nine. She's sixty-eight, twelve years older than Mamma, but Mamma looks the older of the two. All she does is doze in her chair. She gets up only if there's a funeral. She's buried her husband, her brother, her mother, her father, and our father, when he died in 1964. Mamma says she'll bury us all.

We've still got the player piano. It's in the barn. For years we left it out in the yard, and the rain blackened and blistered it. Now it's the dormice. I rubbed it with rat poison, but that didn't work. It's riddled with holes. At night, when a dormouse gets inside, we're treated to quite a serenade. It still works. Unfortunately, there's only one roll left, "Roses of Picardy." Mamma says it couldn't play anything else anyway—it's got too used to that tune. She says Dad once dragged it all the way to the town to pawn it. They wouldn't take it. What's more, the road into town is downhill all the way, but the return journey . . . Dad was exhausted—he already had a weak heart. He had to pay a truck driver to bring the piano back. Yes, Father was a businessman, all right.

The day he died, Mamma said that one day, when my other brother, Boo-Boo, was grown up, we would show them. All three of us boys would set ourselves up with the piano, in front of the Crédit Municipal, the bank in town, and play "Roses of Picardy" all day. We'd drive everybody crazy. But we never did it. He's seventeen now, Boo-Boo, and last year he told me to put the piano in the barn. I'll be thirty-one in November.

When I was born Mamma wanted to call me Baptistin,

after her brother, Baptistin Desrameaux, who drowned in a canal trying to save someone. She always says if we see anyone drowning we are to look the other way. When I became a volunteer fireman, she got so mad at me she kicked my helmet around the room. She kicked it so hard she hurt her foot. Anyway, Dad persuaded her to call me Fiorimondo, after *his* brother—at least he died in his bed.

Fiorimondo Montecciari—that's what's written in the town hall and on my papers. But then war broke out, and Italy was on the other side, and it didn't look right. So they called me Florimond. Anyway, my name's never done me any good. At school, in the army, anywhere. Mind you, Baptistin would have been worse. I'd like to have been called Robert. I often said I was called Robert. That's what I told Elle at first. Just to top it off, when I became a volunteer fireman they started to call me Ping-Pong—even my brothers. I got into a fight over it once—the only time in my life—and everyone went around saying I was violent. I'm not violent, or anything like that. In fact, it was about something else.

It's true I don't know what I'm saying half the time, and I can only really talk to Mickey. I can talk to Boo-Boo, too, but it's not the same. He has fair hair—or light brown—and we're both dark. At school they used to call us macaroni. Mickey would get mad and start a fight. I'm much stronger than him, but as I said, I only got into a fight once. At first, Mickey played soccer. He was a devil! Mind you, he was a good soccer player—right wing, I think, I don't know—his specialty was heading the ball into the goal. He'd be in the middle of a crowd of players in the goal mouth, then suddenly his head would pop up, and head the ball into the goal. Then they all rushed up and hugged him, like they do on TV. Then I hugged you, and kissed you, and lifted you up. It made me quite ill out there on the stand. He was a devil, all right. He was ejected three Sundays in a row. He'd get into a fight over anything—if someone grazed his shin or said something to him, anything—and he always fought with his head. He'd get hold of them by the shirt and bash into them with his head.

Next thing, they were laid out on the ground, and who do you think got ejected? Mickey, of course. He's as dense as shit. His hero is Marius Trésor. He says he's the greatest soccer player who ever lived. Eddy Merckx and Marius Trésor, if you let him get started on those two, you'll be there all night.

Then he dropped soccer and took up cycling. He's got a license and everything. He even won a race at Digne this summer. I went to it with Elle and Boo-Boo, but that's another story. He's nearly twenty-six now. They say he could still go professional and become something. Maybe he could—I don't know. He never even learned to double-clutch. I don't know how that old Renault still goes, even painted yellow. I have a look at the engine every couple of weeks—I wouldn't like him to lose his job. When I tell him to be careful and not to drive like an idiot, he looks all sorry for himself, but really he doesn't give a shit, just like when he swallowed his chewing gum for the first time. When he was a kid—he's five years younger than me—he was always swallowing his chewing gum. Each time we thought he'd die. Still, I can at least talk to him. I don't have to say much—it seems like we've known each other for hundreds of years.

Boo-Boo started school while I was doing my military service. He had the same teacher as us, Mlle Dubard—she's retired now. Every day he went to school exactly the same way we used to—three kilometers over the hill, and at times the path is practically vertical—but fifteen years later. He's the cleverest of the three of us. He's got his junior-high-school diploma and he's now finishing his senior year. He wants to be a doctor. This year he's going to the school in town. Mickey drives him in every morning and brings him back at night. Next year he'll have to go to Nice or Marseille or somewhere. But in a way, he's already left us. He's usually very quiet. He just stands there, very stiff, leaning forward, his hands stuck in the front pockets of his jacket, his shoulders hunched. Mamma says he looks like a lamppost. His hair is long and he's got eyelashes like a girl—he's always being teased about it. But I've never seen him lose his temper. Except with Elle, once maybe.

It was at Sunday lunch. He said something, just a few words, and she left the table and went up to our room, and we didn't see her for the rest of the afternoon. That evening she said I would have to talk to Boo-Boo, stick up for her, that sort of thing. So I talked to him. It was on the cellar stairs. I was sorting through empty bottles. He said nothing, just started crying. He didn't even look at me. I could see he was still a baby. I wanted to put my hand on his shoulder, but he pulled away, then walked off. He was supposed to come with me to the garage to see my Delahaye, but he went to the movies or dancing somewhere.

I've got a Delahaye, a real one, with leather seats, but it doesn't go. I got it from the scrap dealer in Nice, in exchange for a rotten old van I'd bought from a fishmonger for two hundred francs—we then went to the café and spent the money drinking. I repaired the engine, the transmission, everything. I don't know what's wrong with it. It should go all right, but when I take it out of the garage where I work, the whole village is there waiting for it to break down. And it does. It stalls and starts to smoke. They say they're going to form an antipollution committee. My boss gets mad. He says I'm stealing parts, and I spend too many nights there wasting electricity. Sometimes he gives me a hand. But most times he doesn't want to know. Once I drove all the way through the village and back before it broke down. That was a record. When the car began to smoke, no one said anything, no one. They couldn't get over it.

There and back, from the garage to our house, is 1,100 meters. Mickey checked it with the register on his truck. If a 1950 Delahaye, even one allergic to cylinder-head gaskets, can do 1,100 meters, it can do more. That's what I said, and I was right. Three days ago, on Friday, it did more.

Three days.

I can hardly believe that the hours are all the same length.

I went away, then I came back. It was as if I'd lived through another life, and everything had stopped while I was away. What struck me most in town last night when I came back was that the poster outside the movie theater hadn't changed. I'd seen it during the week, coming back from the station. At the time I didn't even stop to see what was on. Last night—it was before the intermission, and they'd left the lights on outside—I was sitting at the café across from it, in the little street behind the old market place, waiting for Mickey. I've never looked at a poster for so long in my life, but I couldn't describe it. I know it showed Jerry Lewis, of course, but I can't even remember the name of the film. I was thinking about my suitcase. I couldn't remember what I'd done with it. And anyway, it was in that theater I first saw Elle, long before I talked to her. I'm supposed to be there all Saturday evening to stop the young boys from smoking. That suits me—I get to see the movies. On the other hand, it doesn't suit me at all, because I get called Ping-Pong.

Elle stands for Eliane, but we've always called her Elle. She came here last winter, with her father and mother. They're from Arrame, on the other side of the pass. It's the village they demolished to build the dam. Her father was brought in an ambulance, just after the furniture van. He used to work as a roadman. Nothing had ever happened to him; then, four years ago, he had a heart attack in a ditch. He fell head-first into the dirty water. Someone told me he was covered with mud and dead leaves when they brought him home. He's been paralyzed in the legs ever since—something in the spine, I think, I don't know—but he spends all his time yelling at people. I've never actually seen him—he stays in his bedroom—but I've heard him shouting. He doesn't call her Eliane, either—he usually calls her Bitch. He says worse things than that.

The mother's German. He met her during the war, when he was doing forced labor. She loaded antiaircraft guns during the bombing raids. I'm not joking. In 1945 they used girls to load the guns. I've even seen a photograph of her wearing boots with her hair wrapped in a turban. She doesn't say much. In the village they call her Eva Braun—they don't like her. I know her better, of course. I know she's a good person. That's what she always says to defend herself: "I'm a good person." With her Kraut accent. She's never understood a word that's been said to her—that's the secret. She got herself pregnant at seventeen by a poor slob of a Frenchman and she followed him. The kid died at birth and all she's found in our beautiful country is a roadman's wage, people who stick their tongues out at her behind her back, and, a few years later—on July 10, 1956—a daughter to put in the cot that had never been used. I have nothing against her. Even Mamma has nothing against her. Once I wanted to get at the truth. I wanted to know if she really was Eva Braun. First I asked Boo-Boo. He didn't know. So I asked Brochard, who owns the café. He's one of those who call her Eva Braun. He didn't know. It was the scrap dealer in Nice, the one who sold me the Delahaye, who finally told me. What can you do about it? Even I call her Eva Braun sometimes.

I often saw Elle and her mother together at the movies. They always sat in the second row. They said it was to get a better view, but they weren't well off, and everyone thought it was to save money. I found out later that it was because Elle never wanted to wear glasses, and if she'd been in the ten-franc seats she'd never have seen anything.

I stood through the whole film, leaning against a wall. I kept my helmet on. Like everyone else I thought she was pretty, but since she'd come to live in the village I'd never lost any sleep over her. Anyway, she never so much as looked at me. She probably didn't even know I existed. Once, after buying some ice cream, she walked straight past me and looked up just enough to catch a glimpse of my helmet. That's all. After that I asked the woman in the cash booth to look after it for me.

I'd better explain. I'm talking about before June, three months ago. I'm talking about how things were then. What I mean is that before June Elle impressed me in a way, but

I didn't really care that much. If she'd left the village I don't think I'd have noticed. I saw that her eyes were blue, or gray-blue, and very big, and I was ashamed of my helmet. That's all. What I mean is...oh, I don't know.... Anyway, things were different before June.

She always went out into the street to eat her ice cream. She always had a crowd around her, mainly boys, and they stood talking on the sidewalk. I thought she was about twenty, or a bit more perhaps, because she behaved like a mature woman, but I was wrong. The way she went back to her seat, for example. As she walked down the main aisle, she knew everyone was looking at her. She knew that the men were wondering whether she was wearing a bra or panties—depending on which part of her they were looking at. She always wore tight-fitting skirts that showed her legs up to mid-thigh and fitted the rest so tightly you couldn't have failed to see the lines of her panties if she'd been wearing any. I was the same as all the others at that time. Everything she did, even when she didn't know she was doing it, put ideas into your head.

She laughed a lot, too, very loudly, great peals of laughter. She did it to attract attention. Or she'd suddenly shake her black hair, which reached down to her waist and gleamed in the lamplight. She thought she was some kind of star. Last summer—not this summer—she won a beauty contest at the festival of Saint-Etienne-de-Tinée, wearing a bathing suit and high heels. There were fourteen of them, mainly summer people. She was elected Miss Camping-Caravaning—she kept the cup and all the photos. After that she really thought she was a star.

Once Boo-Boo told her she was a star for 143 inhabitants—that's the figure given in the census for our village—and she rose to a height of 1,206 meters—that's the height of the pass above sea level—but in Paris, or even in Nice, she'd hardly rise above the street. That's what he said that Sunday lunchtime. He meant she wouldn't stand out and there were thousands of beautiful girls in Paris—he didn't use the word "street" in the vulgar sense. Anyway, she went upstairs, slammed the door behind her, and didn't come down until the evening. I tried to explain that she'd misunderstood what Boo-Boo had said. Unfortunately, once she'd got something fixed in her head, nothing would budge it.

She got along better with Mickey. He's a joker, he laughs at everything. That's why he's got a lot of tiny wrinkles around his eyes. And anyway, the woman in his life is Marilyn Monroe. If they opened his skull, they wouldn't find much more inside than Marilyn Monroe, Marius Trésor, and Eddy Merckx. He says she was the greatest and there'll never be another. At least she provided one subject of conversation with Elle. The only photograph she could bear to see on a wall, apart from her own, was a poster of Marilyn Monroe.

It's funny, in a way, because she was still just a kid when Marilyn died. She saw only two of her films, long afterward, when they were shown on TV: *River of No Return* and *Niagara*. She preferred *Niagara* because of the slicker with a hood that Marilyn wore when she went to see the Falls. We don't have color TV, and the slicker looked white, but we weren't sure. Mickey had seen the film at the theater and said it was yellow. There was a big discussion about it.

Mickey, after all, is a man—it's understandable. Personally, I wasn't crazy about Marilyn Monroe, but I can see what he saw in her. And anyway, he'd seen all her movies. But Elle... do you know what she said? First, she said it wasn't Marilyn's movies that interested her, but her life, Marilyn herself. She'd read a book about her. She showed it to me. She'd read it dozens of times. It was the only book she'd ever read. Then she said she might not be a man—in fact, she certainly wasn't—but if Marilyn was still alive, and it was quite possible she was, it wouldn't take much to make her become one.

She talked like that. It was a very important thing about her, the way she talked. Boo-Boo said an interesting thing: that you couldn't trust people who had such a limited vocabulary— they were often the most complicated people. We were working on the little vineyard I'd bought with Mickey, just above our house. He said I shouldn't trust Elle's way of saying things. She didn't always mean what she said—with so few words at her disposal she had to use the same words to express many different feelings. I stopped the sulfate sprayer and said that anyway, he could use all the words in the dictionary, but he could never say anything that made any sense. It was always Boo-Boo the know-all, but he was wrong, as usual.

I knew very well what he meant. She'd say how upset she was that Marilyn died alone in an empty house, she'd like to have been there, shown her that somebody cared, anything, to stop her from killing herself. But it wasn't true. She always said one thing at a time, as it came into her head. Listening to her was like being hit over the head with a hammer—you just waited for the next blow. In fact, that was the best thing about her. You didn't have to stick the pieces together to get at what she really meant. You could just turn off until the next piece arrived. As for her limited vocabulary, it wasn't just that she had gone to school with her ears plugged up—she spent three years in the same class and finally it was they who gave up, they couldn't take any more—it was that she had nothing to say except that she was hungry or cold or wanted to pee in the middle of the movie and everyone had to know it. Mamma once called her an animal. She looked surprised. And you know what she said? "Just like everyone else," she said. If she'd been treated as a human being, she'd simply have shrugged her shoulders and said nothing. She wouldn't have understood. Usually she didn't even say anything when people shouted at her.

Like her idea of stopping Marilyn Monroe from killing herself—what could it mean to her? She said over and over how wonderful it was that Marilyn died like that, swallowing things, with all those photographs the next day, that she was Marilyn Monroe to the end. She said she'd have liked to know her former husbands and to make it with them, even if two out of three of them weren't her type. She said what was really a shame was that the yellow slicker had probably been left in some closet or burned, but she had to spend a whole day running around Nice and still couldn't find one. That's exactly what she said. Zero, Boo-Boo. Try again.

I get annoyed, but I don't really care. Everything's come back to the way it was before June. When I used to see her at the movies before June, I didn't even wonder how she and her mother got back to the village. You know what it's like in small towns—thirty seconds after the movie's over, the gates are locked, the lights go out, and there's no one in sight. I used to come back with Mickey, in his truck, but I drove. His driving's more than I can stand. Usually Boo-Boo was with us, and we'd pick up a whole lot of kids on the road who got into the back with their scooters and everything.

We once counted how many people were in the back— we'd collected everyone from the town up to the pass. Eleven kilometers. I dropped them off one by one. They stood and waved in the beam of the headlights by dark tracks and sleeping houses. When one of the boys said good-bye to a girl friend who lived higher up, we had trouble getting the truck going again. Mickey said, "Leave them be." By the time we got to the village, the truck was a dormitory. I didn't wake Mickey or Boo-Boo up, I went around to the back with a flashlight. They were all sitting in a line, their backs resting against a rail, good as gold, each with his head leaning against the one next to him. It reminded me of the war. I don't know why, maybe because of my flashlight. I must have seen it in some movie. For some reason I felt happy. They looked so much like what they were, sleeping kids. I switched off the flashlight and let them sleep.

I went and sat down on the town-hall steps. I looked up at the sky over the village. I don't smoke—it affects my breathing—but it was the kind of moment when I'd have enjoyed a cigarette. On Wednesday I was going into training, at the station. I'm a sergeant—I'm the one who makes them all run. I used to smoke—Gitanes. Dad said I was cheap. He'd have liked me to smoke American cigarettes and save the butts for him.

Anyway, just then young Massigne came by in his van, flashing his lights because he couldn't understand why Mickey's Renault had stopped there, and I wondered what he was doing in our village since he lived in Le Panier, three kilometers down the hill. I raised my arm to show all was well, and he went on his way. He drove to the end of the village—I could hear his engine the whole time—and came back. He stopped a few meters away and got out. I told him they were all asleep in the truck. He said, "Oh, I see," and came and sat down on the steps.

It was late April or early May, still a bit chilly but quite pleasant. His name is Georges. He's the same age as Mickey—they did their military service together, in the Alpine Chasseurs. I've always known him. He's taken over his parents' farm. He's a good farmer and can make anything grow out of this red soil of ours. I had a fight with him this summer. It wasn't really his fault. I broke two of his front teeth, but he wouldn't lodge a complaint. He said I was going crazy and that was all.

As we sat there on the town-hall steps, I asked him what he was doing there. He said he'd just taken Eva Braun's daughter home. It struck me he'd been a long time taking her home. I laughed. I can't say how I behaved at that moment, but I do know I laughed as we sat there quietly talking men's talk. I was going to wake the others soon, and if he'd told me he'd made it with the mother instead of the daughter, it wouldn't have affected me one way or the other.

I asked him if he'd made it with Elle. Not that night, he said, but two or three times that winter, when her mother hadn't gone with her to the movies, they'd done it in the back of the van, on a tarpaulin. I asked him how she was, and he gave me the details. He'd never taken all her clothes off, it was too cold. He just took off her skirt and sweater, but he gave me the details.

When we went back to the truck, they were still sitting there, all leaning to one side like ears of corn. I imitated the sound of a bugle, I said, "Get up, all of you in there," and they filed out, eyes only half open, forgetting their bikes, taking them without saying "thank you" or "good-bye," except the Brochard girl, the café owner's daughter, who whispered, "Good night, Ping-Pong," and set off home, staggering around like a drunkard, half asleep. Georges and I shouted insults after them. Finally we woke Mickey up. He stuck his head out of the door, his hair all over the place, and called us every name under the sun.

Then I was alone with him in the kitchen—I mean Mickey, of course—and we drank a glass of wine together before going to bed, and I told him what Georges had told me. He said there were a lot of big mouths around who could get their cocks into the eye of a needle. I said Georges wasn't a big mouth. He said no, that was true. Georges's story seemed to interest him even less than me, but he thought about it as he emptied his glass. When Mickey thinks about things, it's unbearable. To see him concentrating like that, his face all screwed up with wrinkles, you'd think he was about to come up with the formula to make sea water drinkable. At last he shook his head several times very seriously, and do you know what he said? He said Marseille Olympique would win the cup. If Marius Trésor played only half as well as he had been lately, there'd be no stopping them.

Next day, or maybe it was the Sunday after, it was Tessari, a mechanic like me, who talked about Elle. On Sunday mornings one of us, Mickey or I, goes down into the town to place bets on the tiercé at the café. We use a twenty-franc combination for us and a five-franc one for Cognata. She says she's a lone rider. She always takes the same figures: the 1, the 2, and the 3. She says if you're lucky there's no point in complicating things. We've won on the tiercé three times, and of course it was always Cognata who won. Twice in the two thousand francs and once in the seven thousand. She gave some of it to Mamma, just enough to annoy her, and kept the rest for herself, in brand-new five-hundred-franc notes. She said it was "just in case"—she didn't say in case of what. We don't know where she's hiding them, either. Once Mickey and I went through the whole damned house, even the barn, where Cognata never set foot—not to take them, of course, just to play a trick on her—but we never found them.

Anyway, on Sundays, when I've bought my tickets, Tessari or someone else buys me a drink at the bar. I buy a round, then we play a third at the 421, and there's no end to it. That day it was Tessari, and we were talking about my Delahaye. I was telling him how I was going to take the engine apart and start from scratch when he gave me a nudge and looked in the direction of the doorway. It was Elle, with her paralyzed father's five francs, her dark hair coiled up into a bun. She'd leaned her bike against the curb and joined a line of people waiting to place their bets.

It was sunny outside, and she was wearing a sky-blue nylon dress so transparent she seemed practically naked against the light. She didn't look at anybody, just stood there waiting, shifting her weight from one leg to the other. You could make out her round tits, the inside curve of her thighs, and sometimes, when she moved, almost the swell of her cunt. I wanted to say something to Tessari, make a joke of it, something like "You can see more when she's wearing a bathing suit," and "We must all be pretty stupid"—because there were other men at the bar and they, too, had turned around—but in the end, for the two or three minutes she stayed in the bar, we said nothing. She had her ticket punched, she stood again for a second naked against the light, then set off on her bike along the sidewalk and was gone.

I told Tessari I'd like to make her and asked the bartender for another *pastis*. Tessari said it wouldn't be very difficult. He knew several who'd made her. He mentioned Georges Massigne, of course, who brought her home from the movies on Saturday nights, but also the pharmacist in town, who was married with three kids, the tourist the summer before, and even a Portuguese who worked at the top of the pass. He knew all this because his nephew had once been invited out by the tourist with a whole group of people and Elle had been with them. They were all a bit drunk and his nephew saw them at it, Elle and the tourist. I must know how those evenings ended. There were couples in all the bedrooms. His nephew had told him later he shouldn't bother his head about her—she inhaled.

I told Tessari I didn't understand what he meant by "she inhaled." He said he'd draw it for me. Two men next to us heard what we were saying and started to laugh. I laughed, too, to be like everybody else. I paid for the drinks, said *ciao*, and left. All the way home I thought about it, Elle with that man, and Tessari's nephew watching them.

It's hard to explain. In one way I wanted her more than ever. In another way, when I saw her in the doorway of the café, wearing that transparent dress for everybody to see her, I felt sorry for her. She didn't realize, and as soon as she was inside in the shade she really looked quite respectable in her blue dress, her hair in a bun, which made her look taller, and I don't know why, I found her even more attractive, and it wasn't just a question of wanting her. Now I despised her, I told myself it would be easy. She'd be a pushover. Yet at the same time it annoyed me. I was sick of the whole business. Not just of her, either. I can't really explain.

During the following week, I saw her go by several times in front of the garage. She lived in the last house in the village, an old stone house that Eva Braun had fixed up as best she could, putting flowers everywhere. Most times she was on her bike. She was either heading off to buy bread or she was on her way back. Before that I hardly ever saw her. But I can't say she went out less often. It's like those words you notice in the paper for the first time and then see all over the place, and you keep being surprised. I looked up from my work to see her pass, but I didn't dare catch her eye, and I couldn't have said anything. I thought of what Georges and Tessari had said, and since she was concerned neither for me nor for her thighs out in the air, when she was sitting on her bike, I just stood there like a fool watching her ride away. I say "fool" because it had an odd effect on me. The boss noticed once. He said, "Come back to earth. If your eyes were blowtorches she'd never be able to sit down again."

Then one night, in the yard, I talked to Mickey about it. I said a few words, sort of offhand, about how I'd like to try my luck. He said that in his opinion I'd do better to steer clear of a girl like that—she was too much of a rolling stone, she wasn't for the likes of me. We went and filled our buckets at the well. Mamma wanted me to fix up running water in the house—she doesn't know the difference between a mechanic and a plumber. Result? It doesn't work. It's a good thing Dad made Boo-Boo before he died. He's the only one who can repair anything. He pours some chemical into the pipes—it eats them away like acid. He says they'll fall apart one day, but for the time being it works. And when it does work you can't hear yourself speak.

I told Mickey it was help, not advice, I wanted. We stood there next to the well, our buckets filled, for the five thousand years it took him to think about it. My arms were nearly breaking. Finally he said the best way of seeing her was to go to the Sunday dance—she was always there.

He meant a prefabricated shed, the Bing Bang, which moved around from village to village, and which the kids followed around the whole region. You bought a ticket when you went in, and you had to pin it on your chest like a deportee. There was nowhere to sit. There were colored projectors that spun round and round and stopped you from seeing anything, and if it was noise you wanted, you couldn't do better for ten francs. Even Cognata could have heard it from outside, and she never realized we had running water.

I said to Mickey that being in that sort of place at my age, I would look like what I was. He said, "Exactly." I meant an idiot, but he added, right away, "A fireman." If I'd had an extra pair of hands I would have taken his bucket, anything—you mustn't overwork a genius like Mickey. I patiently explained to him that what I wanted more than anything else was that she wouldn't see me there again on duty as a fireman.

In that case, he said, all I had to do was go in civilian clothes. I gave up. I said I'd see, but Mickey had reminded me that there'd be a fireman on duty in any case, and they'd never stop talking at the station about Sergeant Lover Boy. Fortunately, no one in our crew ever volunteered for the Bing Bang. To begin with, Sunday was reserved for the little women, roast beef, and TV. We live in a good place for TV, we can get all the stations, Switzerland, Italy, and Monte Carlo, we can see all the films from the Middle Ages to the present day. Then if there's any trouble at the dance—and there's trouble every time a fourteen-year-old kid feels his moustache growing—a fireman is sent along to stand in for the riot police. One Sunday I had to round up all the men available to go and rescue one of our firemen. He had asked two dancers who wanted the same partner to stop tearing at each other's shirts. If the police hadn't arrived before us for once, we'd have been torn to pieces. As it was, our guy spent three days in the hospital. We took a collection for a present to give him when he got out.

At the training session on the Wednesday before the dance, there were only a miserable half-dozen of us. I asked who would come with me to Blumay. It's a big village fifteen kilometers away, in the mountains, and the Bing Bang was to be set up there the following Sunday. No one volunteered. We went out onto the soccer field next to the station and did some running and jumping. We call it "the station," but it's really an old copper mine. There are several between the town and the pass. They were closed down in 1914, when they became too expensive to run. There's nothing in ours but weeds and stray cats, but we've installed a garage for the two trucks we were provided with and dressing rooms with a shower. As we were getting dressed, I said Verdier was to come with me. He's a clerk at the post office, doesn't say much, and is the only bachelor except me. Anyway, he really likes the job. He wants to take it up professionally. Once he brought back a three-year-old girl with him, the sole survivor of a pile-up on the other side of the pass. He wept buckets when he was told she might die. Since then he's been hooked. In fact he still writes to the girl, even sends her money. He says when he's thirty-five he'll adopt her—the law says you have to be thirty-five to do it. We joke about it sometimes, because he's only twenty-five, and by that time she'll nearly be old enough to marry him.

I look back fondly on that May—especially the days before the Bing Bang. In our part of the world, the winters are terrible, and all the roads are cut off by snowdrifts, but as soon as the fine weather begins, it's like summer. It was staying light later and I went on working on the Delahaye after my normal hours. Or I worked on Mickey's two racing bikes—the racing season had begun.

Usually the boss was with me, because he had something to finish, and after a while his wife, Juliette, brought us *pastis*. They are both about my age—she went to school with me— but all his hair's turned white. He comes from the Basque country, and he's the best bowls players I've ever seen. In summer I play with him against the tourists. When there's an accident or a fire, even in the middle of the night, they telephone the garage—you can't hear the siren in the village—and he drives me himself, at full speed, to the station. He says the day he took me on to work at the garage he'd have done better to break a leg.

I still watched Elle ride away when she passed by during the day, and she still didn't see me, but I had the feeling that something important was going to happen to me, and it wasn't only making love with her. It was like the feeling before Dad died, but in reverse, a pleasant feeling.

Yes, it was a good time. Once, as I was leaving the garage, at nightfall, I went up to the top of the pass instead of going home. My excuse was to try out Mickey's new aluminum bike, but I really wanted to go past Elle's house. The windows were open, the lamps lit in the downstairs room, but I was too far away to see much—there was a yard in front of the house. I left the bike a little higher up and went around by the cemetery wall. At the back, their house overlooked a field that belonged

to Brochard, the café owner. There was just a thorn hedge
between them and the field. When I was opposite the windows,
the first thing I saw was Elle. It came as quite a shock. She
was sitting at the dining table, under a big lamp hanging from
the ceiling, which had attracted a lot of moths. She was leaning
on her elbows and reading a magazine, and as she read, she
played with a lock of her hair. I remember she was wearing
her little dress with the Russian collar, white with big blue
flowers on it. Her face was like I remembered it later, like the
dress, younger, more innocent than she looked outside, simply
because she wasn't made up.

For several minutes I stood there, on the other side of the
hedge, a few meters away. I don't know how I managed to
breathe. Then her father shouted down from upstairs that he
was hungry, and her mother answered in German. I realized
her mother must be in a corner of the room, out of view. I
took advantage of the old fool's shouting to move. As far as
Elle was concerned, he could shout all night—she just went
on reading her magazine, fiddling with the same lock of hair.

Of course I laugh at myself when I think about it now. I
feel quite stupid. Even when I was a kid and had a crush on
a girl—on Juliette, for example, who married my boss and who
I used to walk home with after school—it never occurred to
me to hold my breath behind a hedge to watch someone reading
a magazine. I've never been the village Romeo, but I've had
plenty of girl friends. I'm not counting military service—I was
in the navy, stationed at Marseille—because it was no problem
then. When we were off duty, we just went out and picked up
a girl, and shared her between two or three of us to make it
cheaper. But even before that—and especially after—I think
I've had as many girls as anybody else. Sometimes they'd last
for a month, sometimes for a week, or just one night during
some festival in another village. We do it in a vineyard and
say we'll see them again, and we never do.

Once I stayed for over a year with a market gardener's
daughter, Marthe. We were almost at the point of getting
married, but she got a job as a teacher near Grenoble, and we

wrote to each other less and less. She was blonde and maybe prettier than Elle, though she wasn't the same type. She was really nice. Anyway, we never saw each other again. She probably married someone else. I see her father occasionally, but he disapproves of me and never says anything.

Just this year, in March and April, just before Elle, I was with Louise Loubet, the cashier at the movie theater. Everyone calls her Loulou-Lou. She wears glasses but she has a marvelous body. Only men can understand that. She's tall, and when she's dressed she's not bad-looking—not stunning, mind you—but when she takes her clothes off, you don't know where to put your hands. Unfortunately, her husband is not much help—he's Tessari's boss, and he began to suspect that something was going on, and we had to break it off. She desperately wants to stay in her cash booth, even though their garage brings them in a fortune, just to get out of the house three nights a week. She's twenty-eight and all there. She married him for his money—she doesn't hide the fact—and she says that what with I-can't-tonight and Do-everything-to-me-tonight he'll end up with a heart attack.

When the movie's over it's Loulou-Lou who locks the theater gates—the projectionist says his union won't allow him to, and the manager has gone off to bed much earlier with the money. So she would lock the gates, turn off all the lights except the footlights, so we could at least see what we were doing, while I, so that our affair wouldn't be splashed all over the newspapers next morning, went out the front way and walked around to the back, where she'd meet me at the door and let me in. Usually she was already half undressed by this time. We didn't have much time for love talk. We did it in the auditorium, because the manager's office and the projection room were locked up. We lay down in the main aisle, where there was a carpet, and the first time—I don't know ·whether it was because of her, who was a surprise all over, or because of those battalions of seats around us, and the enormously high ceiling, and us lying there like idiots in that great space where the slightest sound was magnified—I couldn't do anything.

Then we began again Wednesday night—they have only the one show, and I came and kept her company at the cash booth on my way back from the station—and, of course, on Saturday. On Saturday night, Mickey was waiting for me with his truck on the edge of the town. He had a girl friend, too—a girl who worked with Verdier at the post office. They would just be saying good-bye when I arrived. And sometimes I came back alone on my bike, walking the last two kilometers, which are too steep—with my lips burning, what with the cold on the deserted road, it felt good.

Finally her husband started to come pick Loulou-Lou up when she locked the gates, so we had to break up. The night I gave her my helmet to keep, she put a message inside, stuck in the leather band. I found it next day. It said, "You'll only suffer." I didn't know what she meant, and I didn't ask her. She meant what Mickey said that day we were filling buckets in the yard. She'd guessed I was ashamed of my helmet and why. She was more concerned about me than I thought. One afternoon last month—I'd better tell everything in the right order—we were alone, with time on our hands, but it was no better than the first time. It was too late.

On Saturday, the night before the dance at Blumay, I called the garage to get them to send somebody to replace me at the movie theater. We only send volunteers to the movie theater. I think I didn't want to go so I wouldn't spoil my meeting next day with Elle. Or I didn't want to see her go off after the movie in Georges Massigne's van. Maybe both, I don't know. Anyway, I was sorry I didn't go, I nearly did.

As I waited in the kitchen for Mickey and Boo-Boo to come back, I cleaned parts for the Delahaye which I'd brought in wrapped in a rag. I drank almost a whole bottle of wine. At one point Cognata, who I thought was asleep in her chair, told me not to walk around in circles, it made her feel dizzy. Mamma had gone to bed long before. I also took the opportunity to clean and grease our shotguns—we'd left them in a cupboard since the close of the season. This winter I killed two wild boar, and Mickey one. Boo-Boo shoots only at crows—and then misses them.

It was after midnight when I heard the truck come back and saw its headlights sweep across the windows. They'd been to a Western with Paul Newman, and they started playing around with the rifles on the table. Cognata laughed and then got scared because she couldn't hear anything, and Boo-Boo did a death scene like nobody else—bullet in the stomach, eyes crossed, the whole thing. In the end I told Boo-Boo to go die in his bed, and to help Cognata on his way up—she had to be helped upstairs.

When I was alone with Mickey, I asked him if Elle had been at the movies. He said yes. I asked him if she'd gone off with Georges Massigne. He said yes, but Eva Braun had been with them. He looked at me as if he expected me to say something else, but I had nothing more to ask—or too much. He went and put the guns back in the cupboard. I poured him out a glass of wine. We talked about Eddy Merckx and Dad, who'd been a good shot in his time. We talked about the singer Marcel Amont. He was going to be on TV the next night. He's Mickey's favorite singer. When Marcel Amont is on TV, everything has to stop. We have to listen as if we're in church. I said Marcel Amont was very good. He said yes he was, what he did was perfect. It's the big word with him at the moment. Marius Trésor and Eddy Merckx are perfect. Marilyn Monroe is perfect. I said we had to make sure we were back from the dance before the show began. He said nothing.

He's funny, Mickey. Maybe I sounded hesitant—I went on filling my glass at the same time as his—but it wasn't only that. He may be dense as shit, but it doesn't do to treat him like an idiot for too long—he knows how to hit back. We sat for a while and said nothing. Then he said I was to stand behind him at the dance the next day, he would arrange everything. I said I didn't need him to get a girl for me—I could look after myself. Then he said something quite right. He said,

"Oh, yes, you do, you care too much about Elle—I don't. It'll be easier for me."

Next morning, it was that Sunday, we all took a shower in the yard, the three of us. It was brilliantly sunny, and we teased Boo-Boo, who never wants to show his cock, and who yells and screams and wraps himself in the flowered curtain I've set up. The spring water is cold all summer. Your heart stops when it first hits you. We get it up into a cistern with a hand pump and it seems to go on forever. Once you're used to it, it's the height of comfort. Mickey went off to town to place our bets—on his bike, by way of training—and when he came back, I dressed myself up as I'd never done before in my life. At lunch they all stared at me in disbelief—they'd never seen me wearing a tie before.

Verdier was to pick me up in Blumay with the Renault from the station. The four of us—Mickey's girl friend, Georgette, was coming with us—went in my boss's Citroën DS. He always lends it to me when I ask, but every time I bring it back he says it doesn't run as well as before. Verdier couldn't get over seeing me without my uniform. I was wearing my brown suit, with a pink shirt and one of Mickey's red knitted ties. I explained I was with my brothers, I hadn't had time to change into uniform, but if anything happened, my things were in the car.

It was already three o'clock, and there was an ear-splitting din around the Bing Bang, which had been set up in the square. People crammed themselves into the entrance of the huge shed, just to look in—then they never moved for the rest of the afternoon. I told Verdier to stay on duty at the cash desk, and to make sure everybody put their cigarettes out when they came in. He didn't argue. He never does.

They know me. They didn't want me to pay to go in, but I insisted, so I could have my ticket showing like everyone else. It was hell inside. Everything was bathed in red, and the electric guitars, the percussion, and the yelling of those crazed souls were enough to split your head open. But you couldn't see or hear anybody. Outside the sun was beating down on the corrugated iron roof, while inside everyone was suffocating. Boo-Boo went off to look for his pals. Then Mickey pushed me toward Georgette so that I'd dance with her, and he went off, too, through the shadows milling around us. Georgette started rolling her head and wiggling her ass as if in a vacuum— I did the same. The only part of the place where you could see anything was the small circular stage, where the band was letting off steam. They were five young guys in fringed trousers, with faces and torsos striped with all the colors of the rainbow. Later Boo-Boo told me they were called the Apaches and were very good.

Anyway, I danced on the bit of space left for me, with Georgette doing her thing opposite me, for what seemed like ever, and one number followed another. I was bathed in sweat. I really thought it would never end; then suddenly the projectors stopped, the light became almost normal, and the exhausted Apaches strummed out a slow number with their fingertips. I saw boys and girls going to sit down against the shed partition, on the ground, sweat pouring off them. Then I caught sight of Mickey—he had found Elle. She was with Georges Massigne, as I'd feared, but I didn't really care. That's life!

She was wearing a very lightweight white dress. Her hair was plastered down over her forehead, and from where I stood, fifteen or twenty steps away, I could see her chest rising and falling, her lips wide open, gasping for breath. I know it's crazy, but she turned me on so much I was ashamed of myself, or afraid, I don't know which. Anyway, I nearly left. Mickey was talking to Georges. I knew what he was up to. He'd be inventing some fantastic story to get Georges out of the dance and leave the field free for me for a bit. He gestured to me. He said something to Elle, and she looked over toward me. She looked at me for several seconds, without moving her head, without turning her eyes away. I didn't even notice that Mickey had gone out with Georges Massigne.

Then she went over to some other girls—two or three who

lived in the village—and they started laughing. I thought they were laughing at me. Georgette asked me if I wanted to dance again; I said no. I took off my jacket and tie, and looked for somewhere to put them. Georgette said she'd look after them for me, and when I turned around, my hands free, with my shirt stuck to my back, Elle was there, in front of me. She wasn't smiling, just waiting and—you always know when it happens, always.

I had one dance with her, then another. I can't remember what the song was—I'm a good dancer, I never worry about what they're playing—but it must have been something slow, because I held her in my arms. The palm of her hand was moist. She kept wiping it on the back of her dress, and her body through her dress was burning hot. I asked her what she had been laughing at with her friends. She tossed her long dark hair, brushing my cheek with it, but she didn't avoid the question. The first thing she said knocked me over. She had been laughing with her friends because she hadn't particularly wanted to dance with me and, without meaning to, had said something really funny about the fireman and his pump. No kidding.

I know what people are going to say, I've been told over and over that stupid people are more dangerous than evil people—and was she stupid! In just those few words she showed exactly what she was, etc., etc. But it isn't true. It's just because it isn't true that I have to take so long to explain. At the dances all the girls go into squawks of laughter over things they're not allowed to say at home. They certainly know less than they seem to, but they're afraid of looking ridiculous if they don't laugh louder than the next girl. Anyway, I asked the question. I asked why they were all laughing, and she told me. She could have lied, but she never lied unless her life depended on it—it wasn't worth the effort. If I didn't like the answer, then it was too bad for me. I shouldn't have asked in the first place.

Then, as we were dancing, something happened. It's no big deal, and I've already mentioned it, but it's more important than the rest. Her hand was moist. I hate shaking hands with people who sweat, even to say hi to someone passing by. I hate it. But not hers. I said she wiped it on her dress. Anyone else doing that would have disgusted me. But not her. Her damp hand was like a baby's. She brought me close to something I've always liked, I don't know what it is, something that's in babies and children, which brings you back to yourself, to your father and his beat-up player piano, which reminds you in the middle of a dance that you and your brothers didn't go to the bank and play "The Roses of Picardy"—yes, I know what I mean—something that has nothing to do with what is good or bad, but which can just as surely bring you to the situation I'm in or reduce someone like Verdier to tears and prove he's not such a bad guy after all. When people talked to me about her, trying to get me to give her up before it was too late, I always said, "Go to hell!"

As soon as she opened her mouth I noticed she had an accent that was not from our part of the world. It wasn't as strong as Eva Braun's, but you could hear it, even through the din. I asked her if she spoke German with her mother. She said she didn't talk to her at all, either in French or in German—she had nothing to say to her—and she had even less to say to her father. She was smaller than me—I'm almost two meters—but pretty tall for a girl. She was very slim, except around the bust. I could feel her tits against my chest—and I could see them down the cleavage of her white dress. As we danced, her long hair covered her face, and she had to keep throwing it back. It was the most beautiful hair I'd ever seen. I asked her if it was naturally as dark as that. She said, What do you think—it cost her seventy-five francs a month to have that color and it gave her scabs on her scalp. One of these days she'd catch some disease from it.

Suddenly the projectors started to whirl, all blinding reds and oranges, and the Apaches set out on the warpath again. Just at that moment, when we couldn't hear ourselves speak, I asked her if she wanted a drink. She understood all the same—she shrugged her left shoulder and followed me. At the exit I told Verdier to go have a few dances. I'd stay outside for a bit. I didn't say it in my normal voice—he could see I was playing at being a sergeant for her benefit. I don't like doing things like that. He said nothing and went away.

We pushed our way through the mass of people blocking the steps of the shed. We said nothing to each other as we moved across the square toward the café. I took her hand, and she let me, after first pulling it back to wipe it on her dress. At the bar, she had a Vittel-menthe. I had a beer. We were surrounded by people talking about the *tiercé*—I'd lost, and so had Cognata. She looked all around the café, screwing up her eyes to see better. I asked her if she was looking for Georges Massigne and she said no, she wasn't married to him.

It was cool in the bar after the steambath we'd just left, and I felt my shirt sticking to my skin in cold patches. She was sweating, too. I watched a drop of sweat glide from her temple down her cheek, then onto her neck, where she rubbed it away with a finger. Her neck was on the short side, and between her parted lips I saw she had very white teeth. She suddenly realized I'd done nothing but look at her, and laughed. I started to laugh, too. Then she landed me one of her sledge-hammer blows. She said I looked like an idiot staring at her like that, that I did *after all* have a right to talk to her.

There's a hotel on the road to Puget-Théniers, a converted copper mine. They've got a swimming pool and a dining room with red-checked napkins where people eat by candlelight. I don't know how to explain it, but that hotel means a lot to me. I went there once to return a car that had broken down. I always told myself I'd go back and make a splash with my money and have a good-looking, well-dressed girl with me, like the men I saw that day. And before thinking better of it, before recovering from her remark, I said to Elle I'd like to take her out to dinner one night at this restaurant, and probably I'd have gone and told her all the rest if she hadn't cut me short with another remark, even more hard-hitting than the first. I was not to think that just because I took her out o dinner she'd sleep with me—I'd been warned.

I think I laughed. There were all those people around us,

and what with the noise of the slot machines and the Apaches letting rip out there on the square, I knew it was just one of those silly afternoons, with a silly girl. I was knocked out. But she hadn't finished. She blew a puff of air right into my face—not a sigh, she actually blew right into my face—and said she wasn't going to spend all day standing around there: Sunday was the only day she had for dancing.

We went back to the Bing Bang. This time I didn't hold her hand. I couldn't control my feelings—they were written all over my face. When I feel hurt about something I can't hide it. I left her at the wooden steps, where the same people were still stuck together like bees. I said I wasn't going back in. I had to leave. I don't know why I said that—I had nothing to do. I was done for now and regretted what I'd said. I even wanted to make her think I had to meet some other girl, somewhere else, but she didn't give me time to say anything. She just said, "O.K.," and that was it. She held out her hand. She went back to dance, pushing her way through the people sitting on the steps. Anybody, it seemed, could have her. But I couldn't. When she was gone, I remembered I had to go back in anyway, to collect my jacket.

So I returned to the shed. I ran into Georgette, who was dancing with a couple of girls—or by herself. I tried to talk to her, but she couldn't hear a word I was saying. I don't think I wanted to see Elle again. I tried not to look in the direction I thought she'd be, but I saw her all the same. She was dancing with a boy who was finding it difficult to follow her rhythm. She had her arms in the air and her eyes shut. All the movements of her body began in the stomach, with great jerks backward and forward. I got my jacket and left.

I went back to the café and had another beer. For the first time I felt something others have always found it difficult to understand. I don't just mean Mamma or Mickey, or Boo-Boo, but everyone. A few minutes before, when I was leaning against the same bar, customers had turned around to look at us. Simply because she was with me everything had been more

alive, including me. It's silly, I know. I'd never felt that pride
with a girl, that kind of pride—even when I'd been with a
better-looking girl. I was proud of her thick hair, the way she
walked, the way she had of opening her eyes wide and seeing
nobody, and the way she looked like a doll. She was like some
doll I'd seen somewhere when I was a kid, who had grown up
with me. Now I was just a poor guy standing there with a beer.

I went over and sat for a while in my boss's DS, which I'd
parked in the shade. I didn't know what to do. Then Mickey
came over. He'd seen me cross the square. He was carrying
a couple of bowls—he was playing a game with some people
from Blumay. He said he was with Georges Massigne and they
were up three points after losing the first game. He plays bowls
like he drives a truck. He always wants to make a hit, but only
manages to knock his partner's ball away. He said if I wanted
to go home he could arrange with Georgette to use another
car. I said I could wait. He said there was a fair in another
village and when he'd finished his game we could go to the
shooting range there. I asked him who he wanted to shoot. He
shoots the same way he plays bowls. Once he pressed the trigger
just as he was being handed his gun and nearly killed the
woman on the stand.

In the end we decided to go home after his game of bowls
to see Marcel Amont on TV, then go to the fair after dinner.
That's what we did, him, Georgette, and me—Boo-Boo stayed
with his pals. A whole battalion of them came back on motorcycles, but we didn't go to the fair, because we had to play
rummy with Cognata. She lashes out at everybody, and takes
forever to play a card—there's no end to it.

Around midnight Mickey and I took Georgette home, then
came back and left the DS in front of my boss's garage. He
wasn't in bed—he came down to say he wouldn't lend it to
me again. We drank pear brandy on the steps outside, and
they smoked cigars and talked a lot of nonsense. I began to
cheer up. I told myself there wasn't just one girl on the face
of the earth, in fact there were so many you would have to

have millions of lives to get through them all. I said to myself that I'd done well to leave the dance. That much at least was pretty clear—I didn't go running after her.

The following evening Elle stopped by the garage.

When she came in, pushing her bike, just after a storm had flooded the street, I was under a jacked-up car. I could only see her legs, but I knew right away it was her. Her legs moved right up to the car, almost touching it. She raised her voice to ask if anyone was there. I was lying on my back, and when I shifted the trolley under me I saw that, contrary to what everyone thought, she did wear panties. They were white. She looked down at me calmly and said one of her tires was flat, but she didn't budge. I asked her to move away to let me get out. Several seconds passed before she did. I tried my best to act tough like some guy in a film, look her straight in the eyes, nothing else. Finally she took a step backward, and I propelled myself out so forcefully she realized I found her intimidating.

She loved the trolley. She said she'd like to get on it, and did. I didn't even have time to react. I didn't even have time to catch her bike—she simply let it drop to the ground. Anyway, the sillier whatever she wanted to do was, the harder it was to stop her. Lying face-down, as if she was swimming, she rolled from one side to the other for a bit with the help of her hands, screaming whenever she nearly banged her head against something. The boss was out shopping, but Juliette was upstairs in the kitchen, and it wasn't long before she came down to see what was going on.

Juliette didn't like her—no woman, except Eva Braun, could like her—she called her all the names under the sun and told her to go and show her ass somewhere else. I realized the boss must have said the wrong thing to her or something. Juliette is crazy about her husband. She's always afraid some girl is going to take him from her. "Smash that bike up if you like, but get rid of her!" she yelled as she went back up to her kitchen, banging the glass door that separates the garage from the apartment. When there's a pane missing I know there's been a fight.

This time the glass held up. It was no good shouting after Elle—I knew she wouldn't answer. She got up, brushed off her dirty skirt with hands that were even dirtier, and looked at me as if to say, "What's bugging her?" I removed the front wheel of her bike and examined the inner tube. I didn't have to put it under water—it wasn't blown out, but torn, a tear about three centimeters. I asked her how it had happened, but she just shrugged her left shoulder and didn't answer.

I said I didn't have a spare inner tube to replace the old one. I had some at home, some old ones of Mickey's that were still good, but when I suggested she go to our place and get my mother to give her one, she didn't want to. "No thanks!" she said. "I don't want to get yelled at!" She asked me what time I finished work. I said I still had quite a bit to do under the car. She said she'd wait outside. I was stripped to the waist—it was very hot, and a storm was about to break again. She said I was really well built. I'd been less worried about my chances since I saw the tear in her tire, but it was the first pleasant thing she'd said to me. It made me feel good. But I was wrong. She didn't like well-built men. What she liked was slim young boys, thin as a breath.

I finished my work, washed my hands at the end of the garage, put on my shirt, and yelled up to Juliette that I was going. Since she'd seen through the window that Elle was waiting for me, she told me to go hang myself.

Elle was waiting by her bike, sitting on the embankment, her hands flat on the grass, quite still. I've never known anyone who could be as still as her. It was amazing. It was as if even her brain had stopped functioning. There was nothing at the back of her big, wide-open eyes. Once, in the house, she didn't hear me come in, and I stood quite still, too, and watched her. She really was like a doll—a doll you never pick up but leave sitting in the corner of the room. We stayed like that for ages. Finally I had to move. It was driving me crazy.

We walked through the village side by side; I held her bike with one hand and her front wheel with the other. Or, rather, we went down the street—there is only one—and as we went, everybody was out on the doorstep to watch us go by. And I mean everybody, even an infant in a baby carriage. I don't know whether they were there because of that animal instinct that drives people to stay outside after a storm, or whether they were afraid of missing the spectacle of Ping-Pong walking down the street with Eva Braun's daughter. Anyway, we couldn't say anything to each other. Brochard stood outside his café and gave me a vague wave of the hand. The others were content to follow us with their eyes, faces transfixed, without saying a word. Even when I was trying out the Delahaye, I never had this guard of honor.

Our house is a bit outside the village, exactly at the opposite end from hers. It's a farmhouse made of stone and wood, with a big yard. The roofs sag a little, but they could never cave in. Apart from the vineyard I bought with Mickey and some grassland we rent out to campers in summer, we don't have any land. We don't have any animals, either, except a few hens and rabbits. Mamma, who keeps the house very clean, never wanted a dog. Dad left us nothing but the house—that and his player piano. We live off what I earn and what Mickey doesn't spend of his wages in vain attempts to win bicycle races. He denies himself nothing. He has all the equipment of a perfect champion, and if he could get hold of it in town, he would fill his tires with helium like Eddy Merckx. If anyone says a word about it to him, he looks as if he's just swallowed his chewing gum. He makes you feel really stingy.

Anyway, as soon as we were out of the village and we could talk, Elle said I shouldn't have left her like that the day before. She could tell something was bugging me, but she didn't know what. She missed me because I was a good dancer. I said— there was some truth in it—I felt awkward staying with her because of Georges Massigne. She said, Come off it, she didn't belong to anyone. Specially not to Georges Massigne, and anyway, it was over with him. As she walked she shook her head, as if she was repeating to herself what she had just said.

There must have been something in the air that afternoon—the sky looked washed, a dark blue—because when we came into the yard Mamma, too, was standing outside on the doorstep. I called over to her that I had a bike to repair and went straight to the shed, where Mickey's equipment was kept. They said nothing to each other, not even hello. Elle because she had never been taught to, and Mamma because she closed up in front of anything wearing a skirt—including Georgette. I think even a Scotsman in our yard would make her blood freeze.

While I changed the inner tube, Elle went and sat on the wooden tank by the spring, a few meters away. She let her hand trail in the water, but she didn't take her eyes off me. I asked her if she had torn her tire on purpose, so as to see me. She said yes, "with a pair of garden shears." I asked her if she'd come so close to the car because she knew I was underneath. She said yes. She'd known for several days now that I was looking at her legs as she went by the garage. Before coming in, she'd even thought of taking off her panties, just to see the look on my face, but Juliette was watching her from the window and she couldn't.

She didn't laugh or lower her voice or anything as she said that. She said it the same way she said everything else, with her slight Kraut accent. Then I realized I'd put the old inner tube, the torn one, back on her wheel and had to start all over again. I said a girl shouldn't talk like that. She said all girls were the same, the only difference was that the others were hypocrites. I was working with my back to her so she couldn't see the mistake I'd made. I wouldn't have dared to look at her anyway. Then she said, "Ping-Pong's not a name, what is your name?" Without thinking, I said, "Robert."

When I'd finished repairing her bike, she didn't seem in any hurry to get up. She just sat there on the tank, one foot wedged against the rim and the other on the ground so that I could see what she wanted to show me. There was something in her eyes that was more than disappointment, something sad, perhaps because she felt her tricks weren't working any more, maybe I was even getting a bit sick of them. I learned about it later: when she felt she was losing at some game—she was quite good at cards—she got that same look. Finally she straightened her leg, pulled her skirt down over her knees, and got up. She asked me how much she owed me. I shrugged my shoulders. Then she said—not in her usual voice, she almost seemed to have lost her accent—"Aren't you taking me home?" I took her home. She wanted to push the bike back this time, but I said no, it was no trouble; I carried it.

We didn't talk much on the way. She said how much she liked Marilyn Monroe, and how she'd won a beauty contest the summer before at Saint-Etienne-de-Tinée. I said I'd been there with my brothers, and she had won by a long shot. The whole village was out on the doorsteps to watch us go by again, except the baby in its carriage, who must have seen it all before. Brochard made the same hesitant sign, and I waved back. I felt as if it was April Fools' Day, and some trick was being played on me.

I said good-bye to her in front of her house. She took back her bike and shook hands. Eva Braun was outside, at the end of the yard, tending the flowers the storm had blown over. She looked at us but said nothing. I called out, "Good evening," but she might have been a statue. I was about to go when suddenly Elle asked if the invitation to dinner in the restaurant still held. I said of course, whenever she wanted to go. She said, "O.K. What about tonight, right away?" The first thing that occurred to me was that it would be difficult for her to get out of it. She said, "She'll manage." I thought at first she was talking about her mother. It took me some time to understand. I didn't know then that she was in the habit of using the third person when speaking of herself or of those she was talking to. With her, a mere "pass me the salt" became some kind of riddle.

Eva Braun stood watching us, from the other end of the yard. It had struck seven. There were still great patches of sun on the mountaintops, but it takes an hour and a half, what

with all the twists and bends in the road, to get to the restaurant
I wanted to take her to. I couldn't go in work clothes, and I
imagined her, in the candlelight, wearing something other
than a skirt and jersey, not to mention the grease spots she'd
collected while playing the fool in the garage. She understood
all that without my saying anything. I only had to say what
she should wear and she'd be ready in five minutes. I was to
go around to the back—her bedroom looked out over Brochard's field—and she would show me her dresses through the
window. That's why, in the end, I couldn't give her up. She
had a way of putting her foot on the accelerator I'd never met
before.

I nodded. She touched my arm and, with a quick smile,
dashed into the house, letting her bike just fall to the ground.
She ran fast, because she had long legs, but she ran like a girl,
with that special swing of the behind and the legs moving
sideways. I hate to see a girl run like those bulldozers you see
in the stadiums on TV. That really annoys me. I don't know
why.

I walked around their house by the cemetery wall, like that
time the week before, but this time I didn't have to hide. There
was nothing and no one in the field—they bring the cows in
later in summer. From behind the thorn hedge, which was
full of buzzing bees, I could hear Eva Braun talking loudly in
German and Elle answering back. I didn't understand what
they were saying, but I had a good idea. Then it got quiet.

A minute later Elle opened her window. There were three
upstairs windows, and hers was the one on the right. She
showed me a red dress, a black one, and a pink one. She held
a big flower against the black dress to show me, and then a
brooch. She held each dress against her body, and when she
showed me the red one, she kept it up with one hand, and
with the other pushed back her thick black hair from her face.
I gestured no. I liked the other two a lot, especially the pink
one, which was very short, with narrow straps. I opened my
arms wide like a Neapolitan to say I didn't know which one
to choose. Then she took off her turtleneck jersey. She wasn't

wearing a bra, and her tits were just as I'd imagined them, firm and big, pretty good considering how slim she was. First she put on the pink dress. I could only see half of it, because of the windowsill. Then she took it off. She wanted to try on the black one, but there was no doubt. I waved my finger desperately to say that it had to be the pink one. She understood and gave a little military salute. It was a good moment, one of the best in my life. When I think about it, I'd like to start all over again.

I went to the garage while Elle was getting ready. The boss was upstairs, with Juliette, and I came into their kitchen so quickly I couldn't open the glass door, because the refrigerator door had just been opened. You can't open both doors at once—the kitchen's too small. The garage is gradually eating into the apartment; they use every odd corner to keep supplies of oil and documents. Soon they'll be sleeping out of doors.

I told my boss—his name is Henri, we call him Henri IV because he comes from Navarre, like the King—I needed the car. He told me to take the old CV2. He said that because Juliette was there. She must have told him what had happened. I asked him if he needed the DS. Juliette, who was getting dinner ready, didn't miss the chance to put her word in: to do what I was going to do with Elle, I could go to the woods, and not in *her* car, thank you. Fortunately, the boss knew how to deal with her. He said just because Juliette had been out with me when we were at school, she had no need to go around chasing me for the rest of her life. She shrugged her shoulders and went back to her blender and mashed potatoes.

When he opened the refrigerator to get some ice for his *pastis* he gave me one as well. I drank it quickly. He said Juliette wasn't pleased because she wanted to keep the seats of the DS for their own fun that evening. She said, "Oh, you!" and blushed scarlet. But she really didn't mind when he talked like that. He knew how to handle her. As I was leaving, she told me to be careful all the same. I said I was a careful driver. She said she didn't mean that.

I took the DS out of the garage. I realized I had no time left to change before going back to fetch Elle—she'd be ready—so I went straight to her place. She hadn't come out yet, but I drove on to the cemetery so I could turn around, and when I got back to the yard she was waiting for me. She'd done her hair and made herself up. She was wearing a knitted white shawl, and her dress was like the ones you see in magazines.

Eva Braun had come out of the house behind her and shouted something in German. I could hear her father shouting, too, upstairs in one of the bedrooms, but I couldn't tell what he was saying. She didn't turn back. She came up to me with a vague smile and, very, very softly, asked if Elle was as Robert wished. I'd forgotten who Robert was supposed to be. I nodded vigorously. Then she came and sat next to me, taking care not to crease her dress. She told me to drive fast—she had no desire to play the Queen of England through the village.

Unfortunately, you can't drive fast down the street, and we had to take our time. The people who were already outside called to those inside. Brochard wore himself out saying good-bye; he didn't actually wave, but his daughter Martine, who was about seventeen, did wave when she saw her friend in the DS and gave a whistle. Georges Massigne was sitting outside the café with some other customers. He just followed us with his eyes, not showing what he thought, but I felt very uncomfortable. She didn't, of course. She stuck out her tongue at Brochard's daughter.

I parked in front of our gate. On the way she'd said she'd wait in the car while I changed. I did so as fast as I could. Mickey and Boo-Boo were back. I told them I was eating out. They didn't ask any questions. Nor did Mamma, but that was something else again. She didn't open her mouth the whole time I was there.

I shaved in the kitchen. We don't have a bathroom, and Mickey's electric razor isn't any good. Finally Cognata, who was sitting in her chair, asked why I was sprucing myself up. Mickey tried to explain to her, waving his arms around and shouting like a madman. He went upstairs with me to lend

me his eau de cologne and a short-sleeved sweater. He has
some extraordinary sweaters. An Italian who works with him
brought them back from Florence. When you touch them it's
like down. I put on a pair of dark trousers and his black sweater
with white borders, and Boo-Boo came up to give me his shiny
black belt, which goes with my moccasins. They said I looked
terrific. I told Mickey if anything happened and anyone called
me at the station, they could ring me at the Puget-Théniers
restaurant—they'd find the number in my boss's phone book.
As I left I told Mamma I might be back late and she wasn't
to worry, but she went on setting the table as if I wasn't there.

When I got into the car Elle didn't move. She was sitting
up straight on the seat, and the sun had gone down behind
the mountains. She noticed I'd spruced myself up. All she
managed to say was that I looked like Zorro, but from the look
in her eyes and the way she moved over to make room—I had
all the room in the world—I could tell that evening was to be
something special.

On the way she told me her mother made all her dresses,
and that she just shortened them when they were finished. She
never went anywhere without needle and thread, because her
mother kept undoing her hems. She opened a small white bag
and showed me the needle and thread. She said that, apart
from shortening her dresses wherever she happened to be, on
her way to a dance, anywhere, she couldn't do a thing with
her ten fingers. She wouldn't make a good housewife. She said
it with a kind of pride. Then she talked about her father, before
his attack, but I wasn't taking much notice. I was busy cutting
corners to get there more quickly and concentrating on the
road.

When I switched on the headlights, on the road between
Annot and Puget-Théniers, I realized we hadn't talked to each
other for about an hour. She'd moved close to me, so sometimes I felt her shoulder against mine. Outside, the treacherous
brightness of the night was setting in. I asked her if she was
all right. She said nothing, just nodded, but in such a serious,
deliberate way that I thought my cornering must be making

her feel sick. I said so. She said I really did understand girls. It was the exact opposite. She could spend the rest of her life driving around in a car, as she never stopped telling her idiot of a father, who was not even capable of buying one.

I told her I had a Delahaye. She didn't know what it was, but like everyone else in the village, she knew it didn't work. I bet her I would make it work in the end. The trouble was they didn't make the spare parts any more. I bet that one day I would take her on a trip. She asked where. I said she could choose. There was only one place she wanted to go. And as she said that something incredible happened.

I suddenly realized she'd turned completely toward me, her face all excited. She looked ten years older—or perhaps the half-light made me think so. She said, in a rather nervous way—and this time without a trace of accent, I'm sure—that if I ever got that pile of junk going, I was to take her to Paris, to Paris, and I could poke her—that's the word she used—as much as I liked, because that's what I wanted, wasn't it? She held out her hand to me as a challenge. She started tapping my chest, obviously wanting me to shake on it. "Come on! Out with it! You want to poke me, don't you?" I realized that if I didn't calm her down, she'd get hold of one of my arms or something and we'd have an accident, so I pulled up by the roadside.

I've thought about it hundreds of times since, about what we said and all that, and I've never been able to work out what put her in that state. But there was something else, which came as an even bigger shock, if that's possible. When I stopped by the roadside, she jumped out of the car and raised her arms in front of her face as if to protect herself.

I could say nothing. I had no idea what to say. We stayed like that for a few seconds. At first she didn't look at me, just waited, head down. Then she stared at me over her elbows. I had a good view of her eyes. They didn't look sorry or afraid— they were the eyes of someone watching the movements of an enemy, someone who was up on all the tricks. In the end, I turned around toward the windshield and put my hands on the steering wheel. Then she lowered her arms. She pulled her dress down over her knees and brushed back a lock of hair. Still she said nothing. I asked her what on earth I'd said to make her behave like that. She didn't answer. I asked her why she had no accent when she got excited. She said she put it on just to be different. Just like that.

By now I'd calmed down a bit, too, and was laughing. She told me to stop laughing. She said if I told anyone she'd spread it around I'd slept with the wife of M. Loubet, Loulou-Lou. I asked her what made her think that. She said everyone knew— I looked like a secret agent when I walked around to the back of the movie theater. I said if everyone knew she could spread it around as much as she liked, what difference would it make? Without even looking at her, I could sense the same discouragement that later came over her when she began to lose at cards. Lowering her voice, she asked me to swear I would never repeat what I'd heard. I swore. I said the restaurant wasn't very far, but I could take her back to the village, if that's what she wanted. She grabbed my arm, thrust her head and its mass of black hair on my shoulder, and said, "What's wrong with you?" I started up the car. For the rest of the journey, she stayed where she was.

At the Auberge des Deux Ponts—that's what the place is called, it overlooks a stream—some things happened the way I thought they would, and other things, despite what people might say, were even better.

It was pretty full for a Monday night, mainly people staying at the hotel, but we were given a good table, near a window opening onto the floodlit pool. When we went in, Elle took off her shawl. Her shoulders and arms were already tanned. She walked in holding my hand as if she belonged to me, without looking at anyone, as if she was somewhere else and, at the same time, as if she was at home anywhere. The men looked up and stared at her as if to take off the bit of pink material that kept her from being completely naked—and the women looked at me. I know it's stupid, I've already said so, but if you don't understand that special kind of pride I had when we were together you won't understand anything.

We sat down facing each other. We examined the huge menu, and she said it was the first time she'd been to a place like that, with all those candles, silverware, and folded napkins. Once, when she was a little girl, her parents took her to a restaurant in Grenoble, "to show her eyes to a doctor," but it was all oilcloth on the tables and flypaper—awful, awful, except for a big dog named Lucifer, who ate the scraps of meat she gave him under the table, and in the end her father made a scene over a few centimes in the bill.

I don't know why, but she repeated the bit about being a little girl and the big dog named Lucifer, "like the devil," who ate the meat she gave him. Then she laughed and said I was being given the eye by a blonde who wasn't bad at all, in the middle of the dining room, but I mustn't turn around or the old guy she was with would have a stroke. Her eyes weren't in line with the smile on her lips—there was a dark, sullen look in them. I noticed she kept making marks on the tablecloth with the end of her fork. Then she said I wasn't to get annoyed if she asked me something. I said I wouldn't. She asked me to show her the money I had on me.

I took out my money. I've never had a wallet. Before leaving the house, I'd picked up a few notes and rolled them into a bundle. I gave them to her. Under her makeup she was as pale as a corpse. She didn't count them—she just held on to them. When we were in the car, I simply hadn't understood her attitude, but now, silly as it may seem, I thought I understood. She'd just remembered how her father had made a scene over the bill, and she must have been ashamed that day—I know what it feels like—and as she'd gone on talking, a sort of mistrust had come over her. She was afraid there'd be a scene when we left.

When she gave me the money back—she got hold of my hand, opened it, and gently put it inside, without looking at me—I asked her as best I could if that's what she'd been afraid of. Before she answered, I could tell from the look in her eyes.

The color had come back to her face, and an amused twinkle lit up her eyes. She said no, she just didn't know why I was being so nice to her—the other boys had never taken so much trouble over her.

The headwaiter came over—she called him "the conductor"—I stopped asking questions, and we returned to normal. She wanted melon without port, ice cream with strawberries; I can't remember what I ordered. The conductor showed us the long table at the other end of the dining room, covered with thousands of different hors d'oeuvre, and he said Mademoiselle would regret not sampling them. She nodded. He asked me what wine I'd chosen. I looked at Mademoiselle, but her only response was to grin like an idiot. She didn't drink wine. I think that night was the only time I've ever seen her drink a drop of alcohol. She said she'd start crying like a Mary Magdalene and then nothing could stop her. I said, "Champagne." The bastard hit back again: "Which one?" It was she who got me out of it. She got up to go over to the hors d'oeuvre and said with her Kraut accent, "We've been coming here for years and we always have the same one." He nodded and went away as if his brain was working at a hundred kilometers an hour, and I grabbed the opportunity to follow Elle.

In the end he gave us a medium-priced bottle—Elle checked it. She always checked bills at a single glance with incredible precision. That was the only good thing Mamma found to say about her—she was quicker than the cash register in the supermarket—and she'd point out, without a trace of shame, a mistake amounting to five centimes, which proved I was wrong earlier. She'd never heard of Louis XVI or Mussolini—she'd heard of Hitler, of course, because of her mother's nickname—and she never knew, apart from Paris, what city was the capital of what. She couldn't write a single word without managing to make four spelling mistakes, but as far as figures were concerned she was a real Einstein. We'd never seen anything like it. Boo-Boo used to get really mad. He'd say, "What's 1494 + 2767?" and she'd give him the right answer almost before he'd finished. He had to get paper and pencil and she was always right; it drove him mad. One Sunday it took just a minute, watch in hand—we were all there—to explain to her what square roots were. She got it right away, and in no time at all she was much better at them than Boo-Boo. Maybe the bottle of champagne was only middle-range in quality, too, I don't know. When the conductor brought it, along with a waiter in a red jacket, a silver bucket, and everything, she saw that there was gilt on the label and said it would do.

I asked her what had happened to make her want to see my money. She said she didn't know. She said if I wanted to sleep with her I didn't have to put on a show like this, she was ready to start right away, in the middle of the meal, in front of everyone. When she'd come to the village, five or six months before, she had told herself it would be me and nobody else. She saw me the first day she was there. I was wearing filthy overalls, a grease-stained white tee shirt, and a red cap. That's what she said.

She was probably right about the cap—I'd worn one of Mickey's for a long time. He was wearing it when he won his first race, at Draguignan, a sixty-kilometer heat. I remembered the long boulevard in Draguignan, and the multicolored bunch of twenty-odd racers sprinting for what seemed like forever, in a cloud of haze, in the distance under the streamers; then suddenly there was Mickey in his red cap, shooting off with a grin all over his face fifty meters from the line, crouched over his bike, and I yelled like an idiot, I couldn't even see him any more. Despite the heat I had a cold sweat down my back. Then the loudspeakers gave the name of the winner, and it was him, my idiot brother.

She mentioned the player piano in the yard. I can't remember anything more she said. Her face was very gentle, very attentive; then that shadow crossed it again. It made me think of a flight of lost birds, like you see in autumn between the mountains. I think I was just afraid, afraid she would go into one of her trances again—afraid to believe her. I said she was lying. She said, Poor fool. We drank champagne—though she hardly drank any, she poured half her glass into mine—

and we didn't eat anything much. When a waiter came to take away our untouched plates she said without looking at him, "Beat it, we're talking." He went away, wondering, no doubt, whether he'd heard her right, but we weren't saying anything. She took my hand under the table and shook her head to deny she was a liar.

Later I talked about the pool. They turned off the floodlighting. Almost everyone had gone. I wasn't exactly uncomfortable. It was as if I'd never felt anything. She said she couldn't swim and hated water. She ate her strawberries and wanted to give me one on a spoon. I shoved her hand away. I said people had told me who she'd slept with. I didn't say Tessari had told me—just people. She said, "People are stupid." The tourist was true, but nobody had seen her do anything. The pharmacist wasn't true, and the Portuguese on top of the pass still less so. The one she liked best was the Portuguese, because he was slim and "really good-looking." He even asked her to marry him, but nothing had ever happened, except once: to show off in front of his friends, he cornered her against a tree and kissed her on the lips.

I raised my arm to get the bill. She said, "What does it matter, I didn't know you then." I looked at her. I must tell the truth about myself if anyone is to understand. All I could see before me was a girl with false eyelashes and dyed hair, in a creased dress—a tart like all the others. I didn't even want her any more. And she understood, too. Maybe it was the quarter bottle of champagne she'd drunk, but she did what was expected of her. She suddenly put her head on the table and started to cry. It's stupid, but she was my doll, my goddamned doll.

When we came out of the restaurant and she'd been handed back her shawl, I braced myself for the journey home. It was like being in a film, *The Retreat from Moscow*, with Marlon Brando in the snow. The customers were Cossacks in red jackets. For once she hadn't lied—she'd done her best to hide it, but she couldn't. As soon as she started crying, there was no stopping her. If anyone had so much as smiled, I think I'd have smashed everything up—but everything was smashed up in any case, and how—but they all stood at attention at the door. They had that distant look of the frozen steppes. They asked us to come back.

In the parking lot, my boss's DS was alone in the moonlight. I opened the door for her first, then went around to mine. She snuggled up to me, kissing me with moist lips. She said she'd warned me. She was no good, but I mustn't leave her. She said, "You mustn't call it off."

On the way back she cried a lot more, quietly, wiping her cheeks with a little handkerchief rolled into a ball. I could only see her profile, her short neck, and, when another car passed, the highlights in her dark hair. Then I think she fell asleep, or pretended to. I went from one bend in the road to the next thinking of something she'd said: how the first day she arrived in the village she'd seen me wearing Mickey's red cap.

I thought I'd given up wearing that cap long before they moved to the village, that winter, but I wasn't sure. I tried to remember the day they moved in. It's an event that doesn't pass unnoticed in a village like ours, the arrival of a new family. All I could remember was the ambulance that brought her father, which had some trouble turning around in the snow in front of their house, but I knew what bothered me. I just wouldn't wear a tee shirt and overalls in December, unless I wanted to catch pneumonia. She'd made a mistake, or she hadn't wanted to say exactly when the first day was, or even the first ten weeks. She meant this spring, but this spring, I was sure, I'd already given up wearing Mickey's old cap. It was no big deal, except that she'd said something nice and it wasn't quite true.

There was no one around in town, and I went through the streets with my headlights on. When we reached the bridge and took the road to the pass, she suddenly started talking again—like a voice coming out of the night. As if she'd been reading my thoughts, she said the first time she'd seen me was in our yard and there was an old player piano under a big lime tree, with a big *M* painted on it that you could just make out.

She said, "You see, I'm not lying." I explained that it couldn't be the day they arrived in the village, or after. She didn't understand. She said nothing for a bit—I could almost hear her brain ticking. Then suddenly she said she'd told me all that at the restaurant, but I hadn't been listening. It wasn't when they moved to the village she'd seen me, it was last summer, when she came into the village for the first time. They had to leave Arrame, and they were looking for somewhere to live. The piano was out in the yard under a big lime tree—I cut it down later, so she couldn't have made it up. Then she said, "I couldn't have made that up!"

I said no, that was true, but then I didn't understand why the day before, at the dance, she'd said, "I don't particularly want to dance with you." If she'd had her eye on me for almost a year, she'd have jumped at the chance. She said again, like on the way there, that I really understood girls! She was dying to dance with me and everything, but she couldn't show all her friends that, could she? Neither of us spoke until we got to the village. She sat up straight in her seat. I felt she was very far away, and at the same time I knew she was going over a lot of things in her head she wanted to tell me.

When I didn't stop at our house, and she realized I was taking her home, she grabbed me by the arm and told me to stop. I did. Outside, everything was pitch-black—the only light was from the dashboard. She said she wanted to stay with me. I reminded her that only the day before she'd said that just because I invited her to dinner it didn't mean she would sleep with me. She replied that it wasn't the same day any more. I looked at the clock under the steering wheel, and she was right—it was one in the morning. I put the light on to see her face. She started back, because she wasn't expecting it. She looked sort of a mess, but wonderful all the same. Her face was like a landscape after rain. The mascara and lipstick were all gone. Nothing was left but the gentleness, a little sadness or fear or God knows what on her lips. But the gentleness was terrific—there was something stubborn, in a childish way, about her expression. I now think that at that moment she wanted to break it off. A word from me and she'd have burst into tears and asked me to take her home, and nothing would have happened, but I just turned off the light because I couldn't stand her looking at me like that, and said the most stupid thing I've ever said in my life.

I said O.K.

THE VICTIM

I danced with Ping-Pong because Mickey asked me to. It wasn't that I cared that much about Mickey; I didn't. But I didn't hate the sight of him, either. I know when I've got a debt to pay, that's all. Once Mickey saw my mother on the road, and he stopped his yellow truck. It was in February of last year. She told me all about it. He said, "Where are you going in this filthy weather?" She said, "To town"—she had to take all her papers to the Social Security office to collect the few centimes they give her. There was snow everywhere. If you saw a thing like that in a film, they'd be selling Kleenex in the intermission. He said, "Just let me pop back home and I'll take you." She said, "Oh, no! It's too much bother." If you spat in my mother's face, she'd find it too much bother. Mickey drove back home and went up to the house. She, of course, silly idiot, had to get out, even if it meant breaking her leg on the ice. And Mickey said, "No, no, it's no trouble." So he starts trying to turn his truck around and slides all over the place and ends up clear across the road.

Two hours. It took two hours to put together some branches and a pile of cinders to get the truck moving again. Meanwhile Mickey was getting all worked up. He said, "Shit! By the time we get there the Social Security office will be closed." At one point he was so fed up he bashed his head into the door, probably because my mother said, "You see, it is too much trouble." Finally he got her into town, at which point he had to wait the rest of his life, in front of the town hall, till she came out again counting her pension. Then he brought her back to the village. I always know when I've got a debt to pay— for good or ill. Then I'm quits.

In Blumay, Mickey asked me to dance with his brother. He

wanted to play bowls with Georges Massigne. O.K., so I danced
with his brother. He's a tall guy, even stronger than Mickey,
and sweats all over. He said he was thirsty. O.K. So we went
for a drink at the café on the square. It took me ages to understand what he wanted. And when I told him not to try so
hard, I knew what he wanted, he got mad. O.K. We walked
back across the square, without saying a word. He looked as
if his mother had just died. And left me in front of the Bing
Bang and said he had to be going. O.K. Then I danced for an
hour or two, then suddenly Boo-Boo, the youngest brother,
caught me by the arm and said, "What have you been doing
to my brother?" Shit! I told him where he could get off, him,
his brother, and his whole family. He got all mad and started
shouting.

I went outside, onto the steps, with everyone looking at us.
There was Martine Brochard with me, and Gigi, Arlette, and
Moune, and Boo-Boo's pals, and Georges Massigne, and
Georges Massigne's pals, and the whole gang. What a fuss over
nothing. I told Boo-Boo I hadn't done anything to his brother.
"Then why did he go away looking like that?" he yelled at me.
Whenever anybody yells at me, I just turn off. That way I
don't get mad and lose my temper. Otherwise, I might hit
someone or roll around on the ground or burst out crying. I
hate it when people are against me. "Just you wait, you pigs,"
I said to myself. "Just wait till I'm stronger and it's the right
time and place, you'll see what Elle is made of."

I sat down on the steps, my head in my hands, and Georges
Massigne said, "What happened?" and Martine said, "She
didn't do anything, didn't you hear?" A pal of Boo-Boo's broke
in: "She insulted his family, I heard her." In the end everyone
had something to say. I just looked across to the other end of
the square, to the plane trees and the fountain—I couldn't
have cared less. Then Georges Massigne tried to put a hand
on Boo-Boo's shoulder just to calm him, nothing else, but
Boo-Boo jumped back as if Georges had the plague and snarled,
"Don't touch me, you wouldn't if my brothers were here!
They'd smash your face in, my brothers!" He was all red.

Georges shook his head wearily, sat down next to me, and said, "What happened, for heaven's sake? We were having a good time, I never understand what you're up to."

I looked at Boo-Boo; he's tall, slim, and so handsome it should be against the law. And he looked back through his tears of anger. He looked at me with his incredible dark eyes, as if he hated my guts, and suddenly I understood. I don't know how, or where it came from, from my head or what, but I was sure I understood. All this nonsense just because Ping-Pong went off looking as if he'd just been to a funeral, that evil way he looked at me, it was all to hide something else, and to tell me something else. I don't know. Then good-bye. It left as quickly as it had come. Now I didn't understand any more.

Boo-Boo just spun around and went off alone, his hands in his pockets, to the other side of the square. Georges Massigne said, "He must have been drinking. Yes, that's it. Did anyone see him drinking?" I got up and said, "I'll go and talk to him. It'll be O.K." And that was the end of it. I heard them go back to their dancing. Except Georges Massigne, who stayed on the steps of the shed, or perhaps he didn't, because people were looking at him and he felt ashamed. I don't give a shit for people. If I manage to walk on the pebbles without twisting my ankles, it's enough.

I found Boo-Boo standing against a plane tree. He pretended to be watching the guys playing bowls. I said, "You know, Boo-Boo, I did nothing to your brother. I can tell you everything that happened." The heroine in a film. Sweet as honey, just a slight made-in-my-mother accent. He said his name wasn't Boo-Boo, but Bernard. He went over to the low wall that separates the square from the embankment behind it. He sat down. He didn't want to look at me, but I sat down beside him. Sideways, of course, leaning on one hand, because I didn't care for the idea of rolling over and finding myself a few hundred meters below. For ages neither of us spoke. Then suddenly he said, "He's a good guy, my brother. You don't know what he's like." I said that was exactly it, I didn't know what he was like. He said, "He wants to get to know you, but you didn't understand." Then he went on and on, talking about his brother. He called him Ping-Pong, like everybody else. After a while I turned off. I looked at him. He's got fair hair, pretty long, quite a long nose, big eyes, dark with golden flecks, really long eyelashes, a mouth like a girl's that you want to kiss, a pointed, cleft chin, a very long neck, a very long body, very long legs. I said to myself you'd have to do it several times to make love with all of him.

Then, as we were sitting on the wall there, it happened. He went on and on, then suddenly he was talking about a player piano. I said, "What? What did you say?" He said, "What? What didn't you hear?" I said, "You said something about a player piano." He was throwing pieces of gravel into the air behind us. He was turned toward me. He wondered where he'd got to. He said, "Oh yes, Dad's piano. We left it under a lime tree, in the yard. Then, with the rain, it got into terrible condition. In the end I made a fuss about it. That was last year. Ping-Pong took the piano into the barn, and when he came out he looked at the lime tree as if he'd never seen it before. The very same day he got out the chain saw and cut it down. Isn't that something?" I shook my head, though I meant to nod. I don't know. I smiled like an idiot or did something, I don't know. Oh yes, the gravel. I started throwing gravel into the air, too.

When I looked at Boo-Boo again, when my heart had stopped beating so fast, he was watching the bowls players, his eyes all screwed up. He was taking no notice of me. The sun was killing. Great black shadows covered the square. All I could hear was the click of the bowls and my heart beating. I said, "What's the piano like?" Without looking at me he said, "What do you think, after all the rain it's had on it?" I said, "There's an M painted in gold on the front, isn't there?" He turned and looked at me. "How do you know that?" he said. I said nothing. "Our name is Montecciari," he explained. I remember him saying each word very clearly. I remember the dark shadows over the square, the great drop to my right, the red hills in the distance. I remember everything. I said, "Did your father die a long time ago?" He said, "I was five." He's seventeen, so his father died in 1964. I'm the fastest calculator in the world. That and my ass are the only things God gave me. I got up. I dropped the pieces of gravel on the ground one by one to look as if I was doing something. Even though my heart was beating so fast, I managed to say, "How old was he when he died?" And the son-of-a-bitch answered, "Forty-nine, not even fifty." And I said to myself, "Well, there you are! You didn't think it would ever happen, my poor little Eliane." I turned away so he wouldn't see my face. I don't know how I managed to stay on my feet.

That night a whole gang of us went into town for a pizza. I laughed. I kept telling myself how to behave so that no one would notice. At one point Georges Massigne said, "You look pale." I said, "I'm tired." Boo-Boo wasn't there any more, but it made no difference, it was as if I could still see him there, sitting on the wall on the edge of the precipice. All I'd needed to do was to give him a little push, and he would have fallen back, like me in my dreams. He'd be all laid out on a bed by now, smashed up. They'd be making his coffin. The mourning would already be under way.

At midnight Georges and I left the others standing around the motorcycles and cars. We drove for about two kilometers in the van; then Georges stopped in a lane and wanted me to get into the back with him. I said, "Not tonight, I don't feel like it." He wasn't too pleased, but he took me home.

The other fool hadn't gone to bed. She was sitting in the kitchen, making me a dress, her pretty face in the lamplight. The first thing I said was, "Shut up, you bug me," because she asked me where I'd been. The I grabbed hold of the dress, which was made of something like silk, white with a blue-and-turquoise pattern on it, and started to tear it up, the material, the stitches, everything. She muttered some crap in German in her soft, beautiful voice. She just sat there at the table, as she always does, hands joined on her lap, the same tears in her eyes I've seen all my life. "Shit!" I yelled. "Pull yourself together! What have I got to do before you decide to hit me, just once, just once in my life? You understand? I want you to hit me, I want you to hit me, do you understand?" And of course the poor idiot understood nothing, as usual, just stood there like a statue, tears in her eyes, asking herself who I was and what was happening to us. Finally I got her to sit down. I said, "Now, now, come on. Come on! Come on!" I knelt beside her, between her legs, right up against her. I said, "Mother, my own mother!" And as if she was ashamed to do it, she undid the buttons of her bodice and the hook of her brassière. I love her smell. I sucked her right nipple, then the left, then the right, but she didn't look at me. She just stared into the distance and stroked my hair, murmuring something very quietly, and there I was, a little baby, a little baby at my mother's breast.

She's always the first to get up. She always holds on to my head so that my forehead will rest on the chair without getting hurt. I heard her walk away, then go upstairs to her room. I stopped crying. I got up and went over to the sink, turned on the faucet, and splashed water over my face. I looked at myself in the mirror. I was a mess—red eyes, and hair all over the place. "Don't worry," I murmured to myself. "I'm stubborn. I'm more stubborn than everyone else put together. I'll make them pay for it, you'll see." The faucet was still running—cold water springing out like a single column crushed into a thousand sparks. I told Elle, in the mirror, "You're going to calm down. You're going to think about it. You've got to be clever. We have plenty of time."

I woke up. I saw Boo-Boo on the low wall in Blumay. I lay in bed quite still, thinking. A fly came near my eye on the pillow. I lifted a finger and it flew off. I thought of Ping-Pong. First, he's the oldest of the three; thirty, thirty-one? Mickey was too young when it happened. Boo-Boo, forget it, he wasn't even born. The only one who can get me anywhere is Ping-Pong. He's got big strong hands. That's what I remember most about him.

Mother opened the door and said, "I'll bring some coffee up to you." I motioned to her to come over. She came and sat down next to me. She didn't kiss me. She stared into space. I said, "What day was it?" She said, "What do you mean, what day?" But she knew very well what I was talking about. It was in November 1955. She muttered something in German and shook her head. She looked beaten. She wanted to get up. I caught her by the wrist and said, more loudly, "What day was it?" She had a pleading look in her eyes. She didn't want the shithead on the other side of the landing to hear. She said, "I don't remember the day, around the middle of the month. I was a Saturday." I said, "I'll get a calendar for 1955." We just sat there, the two of us, and I took hold of her hand, but she kept staring into the distance. She was wearing her navy-blue apron—she has to do the housework for Mme Larguier in the morning. Then she gently pulled her hand away and left.

A few minutes later I was with her in the kitchen, wearing my white flannel bathrobe, which she'd ordered from Trois Suisses because if she hadn't I'd have thrown a fit. She said, "I wanted to bring your coffee up to you." I put my arms around her from behind, sweet as I can be, and said very quietly, "If I catch them all and punish them, you won't mind, will you?" I love her smell. When I was twelve or thirteen, I got her combinations and a pair of her panties from the dirty laundry and put them on, at night, so I could smell her. I said, "You won't mind, will you? Yes or no?" She shook her head without turning, but I spun her around and she didn't dare look me in the eyes. I said, "You're ashamed? You mustn't be ashamed." She's a beautiful woman, with soft, moist skin and long, fair hair, which she piles up at the back of her head, and which frames her face like a Madonna's. Only her hands give away her age—she's forty-eight. Her hands are wrinkled and rough, because of all the washing she does. I said, "Did you ever see old Montecciari before he died?" She looked very surprised, then shook her head. He died over ten years ago, and we've been in the village only a year. Then she understood. She jumped away from me, with a look of fear in her eyes. "You're mad!" she whispered. "I know Mme Montecciari and her three sons. They're good people." We just stood there, looking at each other. I said to myself I'd better keep quiet and do everything myself, or she'd stop me. "They're good people," she repeated. I said, "I'm not accusing anyone. You didn't understand what I meant." A few words, a little lie, was all that was needed to reassure her. She looked me in the eyes for a few seconds, then turned away. She went over to the stove and filled my bowl with coffee—it is marked *Elle*. She put one and a half lumps of sugar into it, breaking the second lump in her hand.

She was out for the rest of the morning. I thought about how I was going to do it. At one point, as I was taking a bath in the kitchen, a fly landed on the edge of the aluminum bathtub, just near my eye. I put out a finger, and it flew away quickly. I thought about Ping-Pong, with his big strong hands.

O.K. I picked up the garden shears in one hand and front wheel of my bike in the other and said, "Be careful. Once you've done it, you won't be able to turn back." I gave it a great tear and pulled the shears out. It was a massacre.

Then Elle went to see Ping-Pong at the garage to get him to repair the bike. Then he took it back to his yard. Elle had on her flared beige skirt, her navy-blue turtleneck jersey with the little dolphin stitched on the front. She'd put on a pair of her white lace panties so that he could see them right up her skirt. Her legs were already well tanned and her thighs ever so soft. He was so worked up he didn't know what he was doing. He put the wrong inner tube back on. Then, at her bedroom window, she took off her jersey and showed him her beautiful bare breasts. He stood as straight as a toy soldier behind the thorn hedge, and she wondered whether he was just a bastard like all the others or some poor idiot she ought to leave alone. When I weaken, I hate myself—I'd even kill myself. Then there was the drive and the restaurant. Ping-Pong kept moving all the time. When we were going up a hill in Henri IV's DS, he leaned forward over the steering wheel as if he was urging the filthy old car on.

During the meal he did his best to keep up a conversation, but it was always the same story. It wasn't what I thought it would be, "Will she let me poke her or not?" It was something else. I don't know exactly what. I liked it, and it made me sad. What's more, he didn't have the gold bill clip—he kept all his money in one of his trouser pockets. I said to myself, "Mickey must have inherited it, or Boo-Boo, unless the mother's kept it hidden somewhere because it was too valuable. I've never seen the bill clip, but I'm sure if I did see it I'd recognize it. It's a twenty-franc piece with Napoleon's head on it, mounted on two gold circles that close up like a trap. I think I've always been afraid of seeing it.

Ping-Pong is dark. He has broad shoulders and muscular arms. He has a simple face, and his eyes look younger than he really is. I like the way he walks. What gets me most are his hands. I looked at them as he ate. I was thinking that in an hour or so they would be holding me, moving all over me—I wanted it to be repugnant, but it was the reverse. I hated myself. Unless it was the effect of the champagne. I didn't drink much, I can't really drink anything—I start crying and I want to be a little girl again. I don't know.

In the car, on the way back, I got over my tears. I said to myself, He'll stop somewhere on the way, fold back the rear seats, and start. I'd let him do it, then I'd pick up a rock and beat his head in. But he didn't try anything. He was just good old Ping-Pong, who was interested in Elle and tried to understand what she wanted. Poor bastard. At one point he started hassling me with all kinds of questions about Mickey's red cap. It's something Martine Brochard told me once—I don't know what it was all about—I thought quickly. I told him it was last year I'd seen him wearing that red cap, and he hadn't been listening to what I was saying in the restaurant. He swallowed the whole thing. I think he even liked it when I treated him as if he was stupid. He doesn't seem to want to see me any different from the way he imagines me.

Then we went past his house, but he didn't stop—I had to ask him to. Incredible! At last we crossed his yard, hand in hand, and I felt he didn't want to take me into the house, because of his mother and the whole damned family. Both of us said, at the same time, "The barn." It was dark inside. He said, "There's an electric lamp, but it doesn't work." Another century went by and he said, "It's just as well because when it does work you can't stop it. You have to pull out the wires if you don't want to be ruined." Finally he left me there while he went in to get a kerosene lamp from the house.

By the time he got back, I'd found a ladder in the light from outside and a rickety, dusty old bed under the barn roof. As we were going up to it, he said it was his aunt's marriage bed. In the pool of light cast by his lamp as he climbed the ladder, I must have looked like a butterfly above him, in my coral-pink dress. He'd brought a pair of white sheets. When they were kids, he and Mickey—he told me—they used to play in the barn. His aunt's bed was supposed to be a steamboat in America. "On its way up the Mississippi," he said, "it lost two legs and quite a lot of kapok to all the crocodiles around." He took great pains to unfold the sheets, but I just stood there, my hands behind my back. The kerosene lamp was placed on an old chair. Down below, near the double doors, I could see the dark mass of the player piano. It seemed both less beautiful and bigger, heavier, than my mother had described it. I didn't want to look at it—I wanted to forget it was there. I wanted Ping-Pong to kiss me, take me. I was so sad inside me.

Ping-Pong sat on the bed and drew me to him. He raised his eyes toward me. There was so much gentleness in them. He started to say something, then broke off. He put his hands under my dress. I stayed standing and let him feel me. He pulled down my panties, and I raised first one foot, then the other, so that he could take them off. When he put his hands between my legs, he knew very well I wanted it. Then he

pulled me down toward him, without letting go. With the
other hand he undid the zipper of my dress. He felt for my
breasts. Elle is lying on her belly on top of him, her backside
bare, as if she's going to be beaten. She sees herself like that,
exciting and defenseless. And all the time she's moving up and
down, moaning and groaning, I look down at her, from the
stillness of my mind, feeling neither disgust nor contempt,
nothing. I said to her, "Oh! What are they doing to you, my
little Eliane, what are they doing to you?" I wasn't even laughing at myself—it was just like that, mechanical, so that she'd
get to her pleasure and have done with it.

I breathed in the air through my mouth. The barn smelled
of old wood and old plants being dried out. Ping-Pong was
asleep at the other end of the bed, his head turned toward me.
He didn't snore much, just a bit. He had hair on his chest.
He had nice lips, like his brothers. I was naked under the
sheet, like him, and the back of my head hurt. My mother
had probably not slept a wink. I knew her. Never mind the
other shithead. I wanted to pee and I felt dirty.

I got up quietly without waking Ping-Pong. Daylight was
coming in through a skylight. The lamp had gone out. I went
down the ladder without making any noise. Now I could see
it properly—the old player piano was falling apart. It must have
been green at one time, as my mother said: you could still
make out the color in the flaking paint. But it was blackened
and cracked all over from being left outside. Its big handle
must have been gilt, but that was black, too. I could make out
the M engraved on the lid. A very ornate M, with flourishes
on either side; I traced it with my fingertips.

Outside it was a fine morning. Mme Montecciari stood
motionless in her kitchen doorway, wearing a black apron. She
looked at me. We looked at each other for a long time—I was
completely naked. Then I went into the yard, picking my way
carefully over the pebbles. I was a little cold, in a pleasant sort
of way. When I crouched down to pee, against the barn wall,
Mme Montecciari suddenly turned around and disappeared.

A bit later I was lying next to Ping-Pong, and he woke up at the sound of the truck trying to start in the yard. He said, "It's Mickey. He's going to use up the battery before he realizes he hasn't turned on the ignition. It's the same thing every day." Finally, after an eternity, the truck went off. Ping-Pong couldn't see his watch, which he'd put down somewhere during the battle, but he said, "Mickey's taking Boo-Boo to school, it must be eight o'clock or quarter past eight, something like that." He kissed me on the shoulder and said, "Usually I open the garage at half past seven." Then he put on his trousers and went indoors to get some coffee. I got up when he was gone and put on my pink dress. Now it made me feel ashamed. I rolled my panties up in a ball and put them into my little handbag, which I'd carried with me all evening. I don't like putting things on that I've already worn, even if I've only worn them for a few minutes—except my mother's things, that is, when I was a little girl, but they were always too clean, they never smelled enough of her.

Ping-Pong came back with a tray, a single cup, and the hot coffee. He said he'd already had his in the kitchen. I said, "What did you think about when you were getting the coffee ready?" He laughed. He was bare-chested. He said, "I was thinking about you, so there!" I said, "And what do you think of me?" He shrugged his shoulders and sat down on the bed. He watched me fill my cup on the chair where he had put the lamp. Finally, he said, in a funny voice I could hardly hear, "You'll come back, won't you?" I wanted to say I'd see, I'd think about it, but what was the use of that? I said, "If you want me to." I moved toward him, and, like the night before, he put his hands under my dress. He was surprised not to find any panties. He wanted to take me again—I could tell from the look in his eyes. I said no, he was already late. He insisted, but I pushed away his hand and said no. Then he put on his black sweater and took me home in the DS. I stayed in front of the yard as he turned around at the cemetery, and when he went by again, looking at me, I just stood there without moving. I didn't wave or anything.

Mother was in the kitchen, standing near the door, and I was no sooner inside than I was knocked sideways against the saucepans hanging on the wall. It had been three years at least since she'd hit me. Of course it was the first time I'd spent the night out. Before I recovered I got another, then another. She just lashed out at me, blow after blow, saying nothing. I protected myself with my arms as best I could. She was breathing hard. I fell to my knees and she stopped. I don't know whether it was her sweat or mine. The back of my head hurt and my nose was bleeding. "Fucking bitch!" I said. She hit me again, and I was laid out on the tiles. "Fucking bitch!" I said again. She went and sat down on a chair, her chest rising and falling with every breath. She stared at me, making a fist. She must have hurt herself. I looked at her through my hair, without moving, my cheek against the tiles. "Fucking bitch!" I said.

Ping-Pong spent three nights in a row with Elle in the barn. He undressed her, parted her legs on his aunt's bed, and thrust his great thing inside her belly. He put his hand over her mouth to stop her from shouting out. Then, for three days, he floated on a cloud in his garage. He believed what Elle had told him—she'd never had such an experience, and it was too good, she would die. Every morning I went down the ladder before he woke up, and fingered the piano. Mme Montecciari was always waiting there, no matter if it was six or seven o'clock. She stood in her kitchen doorway, wearing her black apron or her white apron. She watched me as I went over to the back wall of the barn, where I crouched down to pee. Then she suddenly turned around and went into her kitchen.

When I got home, Mother didn't hit me any more. She'd be sitting at the table, repairing the dress I'd torn. She knows me—because she loves me. She's afraid for me, but she knows I'm stubborn, that if forced I'll go to the right or the left, but in the end I'll get where I want to. I've never had to prove it to her till now. I must find the other two bastards. I'll be patient. They'll get what they deserve. Their families will suffer.

I said to my mother, "Look at me!" But she didn't want to. She thinks I should have forgotten about it long ago. I put my arms around her from behind and put my cheek against her back. I said, "I think I'm getting along well with Ping-Pong, you know. That's the only reason I'm going with him." I don't know whether she believed me. Upstairs, the shithead heard I was back. He'd been yelling and shouting for the past quarter of an hour. He wanted his soup. He wanted to have his position changed. He wanted someone to talk to him. Anything. They'll be punished, oh yes, and their families will suffer.

It was like that until Friday. On Friday, in the early hours of the morning, we heard Mickey yelling down below, banging on the barn door. "Hey, she's waking up the whole village!" He couldn't have been alone—you could tell from his laugh and his voice. Ping-Pong was on top of Elle, inside her, and he raised himself on his elbows. He yelled down to his brother, "Shit! Wait till I get down there, you'll see what I'll give you!" We could hear laughter. Then Mickey went away and it was quiet again. Ping-Pong gave a few thrusts to finish but couldn't make it. He fell back next to me and said, "Shit! What have I done to deserve this?" I said Mickey was just joking. He didn't answer; he kept sounding off about his brothers.

A little later I dropped off to sleep. He said, "Come on! This is too stupid." I asked nothing, just put on my skirt, my sweater, and my sandals. I rolled my panties into a ball, and we left. He took me across the yard. It must have been about seven or half past. They were all there in the kitchen—Mickey, Boo-Boo, the mother, and Aunt Deaf-and-Dumb. Ping-Pong said, "Hi!" like a challenge. No one answered. "Sit down there," he said to me. I was next to Boo-Boo, who was dunking his bread in his coffee and didn't even look at me. Mother Montecciari was standing by the stove. The silence lasted for thousands of years. Ping-Pong put a bowl of coffee in front of me. He opened the cupboard and gave me butter and honey and jam. He said to Mickey, "If you have anything to say, say it." Mickey didn't look at him and didn't answer. Ping-Pong turned to his mother and said, "And what about you?" She looked at my hand and said, "What has she taken from the barn?" "I haven't taken anything," I said proudly, "it's my panties." I held out my hand for her to see. She made a face and turned around to her stove. "Someone must have missed a few beatings," she muttered to herself.

Ping-Pong sat down next to me with his coffee. He said to his mother, "Listen, leave her alone." "She's staying here?" she asked. "She's staying here," he said. That was the end of it. Boo-Boo looked up at me, then went back to his breakfast. Mickey said, 'We'll have to take off in five minutes!" The aunt smiled at me as if I was there on a visit—she was completely out of it. Ping-Pong buttered a piece of bread for me and spread it with jam. "I'm going to ask her parents," he said.

A quarter of an hour later, he was there in front of my mother, who was standing on the doorstep, already washed and dressed. He shifted from one foot to the other. "Madame Devigne," he said at last, "I don't know how to tell you"—as if the poor woman needed to be told. I said, as much for him as for her, "I'm going to live with the Montecciaris. I'll go get my things. Come on, Robert." We went upstairs, the three of us. He helped me pull out the thumbtacks and take down my photos and my Marilyn Monroe poster from the wall. My room was entirely white—my mother planned it that way. "You won't have all this at my place," he said. I packed some dresses and other clothes in two suitcases. My mother was nearly having a fit, but she didn't say a single word.

As we were leaving the house, I said, "Shit! My bathtub." I went to the storeroom to get it. I said to Ping-Pong, "You can't carry everything." He said, "Can't I?" And off he went, the aluminum bathtub with the two suitcases inside balanced on his head. I said to my mother, "I love you more than anything." She said, "Oh no, oh no, certainly not. I love *you* more than anything. I pardon those who do us wrong because you're alive, and I thank God because I love you more than anything." I was getting annoyed by the whole thing and said to her, holding out my arms, "I'll be there at the other end of the village. You know where to find me, don't you?" She shook her head and said no.

When I walked down the street with Ping-Pong, they were all there, on their doorsteps, supposedly taking the air. Ping-Pong walked in front, my bathtub on his head with my suitcases inside. I followed a few steps behind, carrying my teddy bear, my photos, my book, and my Marilyn poster with an elastic band round it. As we passed the Pacauds, I said, loud enough for them to hear, "You know they really must have nothing better to do if they're outside at this hour." At the garage, Ping-Pong's boss was at the diesel pump and said, "Take the van, it'll be quicker." But Ping-Pong said, "It's all right, I'll be back in a quarter of an hour." Juliette, of course, was at her window, but she just closed up her robe over her fat tits and watched me with her evil eye. Maybe Ping-Pong had made it with her once. Or maybe she thought her husband had made it with me—who knows. I nearly stopped and told her about one night that winter, but he's a good guy, Henri IV, and being married to her, he must have enough to put up with as it is.

The biggest idiot was Brochard. "Moving, are you?" he asked Ping-Pong, and Ping-Pong answered, "As you can see." Then his wife came out of the café and asked Ping-Pong, "Moving, are you?" and Ping-Pong replied, "Ask your husband." And the old bag turned to her husband and snapped, "Why? What have you got to do with it?" I'm telling you, when you want to hear people talk and say nothing in this village, you don't have to switch on the TV.

At the Montecciaris', the mother was nearly having a fit, but no one said anything. We went upstairs, and Ping-Pong threw the two suitcases down on his bed and the bathtub in a corner of the room. There was some awful wallpaper, the furniture was B.C., but it was clean. I shut the door behind me to show the mother, who had followed us along the landing, that her territory ended there. Ping-Pong said, "Well, I'll leave you to settle in. I've got to go to the garage." "I can put my photos up on the walls, and my poster, can't I?" I asked. I seemed so nice and polite with my teddy bear in my arms, he laughed and lifted up my dress to squeeze my ass. He said, "You can do whatever you like. You're at home here." I could tell something was holding him back, something was bothering him. After a lot of hemming and hawing, he managed to get it out. "You see, when you're with me, I don't mind your not wearing panties. In fact I like it. But when you walk through the village like that, you never know, someone might see. It bothers me." I said I didn't have time to put on clean ones. He just stood there, looking stupid. I said, "O.K., I'll put some on right away." He looked really happy. He smiled, and when he smiles he looks younger than thirty. When he's like that I really like him. I was sorry he was the son of his bastard of a father. Then I started to hate myself. I said to myself, "Well, if he doesn't like it, he knows what he can do." But I smiled back all the same, a real convent girl, sitting there all demure, clutching my teddy bear.

I spent the rest of the morning putting up my photos. I emptied a drawer and one side of the wardrobe for my things. I didn't find the gold bill clip among Ping-Pong's clothes or anywhere else. I read through some of his letters—nothing of interest. Army pals, girls... There was one girl, a certain Marthe, a schoolteacher in the Isère. They'd slept together and she wrote endless sentences to describe her memories of him. To say that she thought of him when she touched herself, she took up a whole notebook, and at least four times over, because the envelope was too heavy and Ping-Pong had had to pay the surcharge. Then, in one letter, she said she was beginning to get over it, and she wouldn't write any more. Then there was a whole torrent. I couldn't face undoing the string of the second package. I put my "Miss Camping-Caravaning" cup on the chest of drawers and went downstairs.

In the kitchen the mother and aunt were shelling peas. I said, "I'd like some hot water for my bath." Silence. I expected the mother to say, "Here everyone washes in the sink when there's a wedding or a first communion," but nothing of the

kind. She got up from her chair, without so much as a gesture
or a look, picked up a pan, gave it to me, and said, "Go ahead."
I boiled the water on the stove. I could hardly lift the pan.
She could tell, and without turning her head she said, "You'll
have quite a job, going up- and downstairs to fill your bathtub."
I said that at home I took my bath in the kitchen, but here I
didn't want to be in the way. She shrugged her shoulders. I
just stood there for ages. Then she said, "It'll bother me more
if you get water all over the bedroom floor. I won't be able to
wax my parquet any more."

So I brought my bathtub downstairs, banging the walls as
I went because the stairs are too narrow, and I filled it in front
of the stove. When you turned on a faucet in that house all
the walls shook. After the fourth panful, the old she-ass said,
"It's a good thing we don't pay for the water from the spring."
She said that without turning her head, still shelling her peas.
Then I started to undress and old Aunt Deaf-and-Dumb fell
from the moon and called out, "Merciful heaven! She's going
to wash in front of us!" And she moved her chair so as not to
see me. The mother, on the other hand, inspected me from
top to toe while I was undressed. She shrugged her shoulders
and went back to her vegetables. But she said, "Yes, there's
no denying it, you've certainly got a good body." And that was
all.

As she went out to toss the peapods to the rabbits, she shut
the kitchen door, either out of habit or so that I wouldn't catch
cold, who knows. She came back, went upstairs, and returned
with a towel. I said, "I have my own, in the bedroom." She
said, "I do the washing in any case." And while I dried myself,
standing up in the bathtub, she said, "Your mother's a good
woman. But she hasn't brought you up to work. I can see that
from your hands." She looked into my eyes—hers were wrinkled all around, but not really evil or cold. I said, "My mother
did what she could with me. But she wouldn't like you to talk
to me like that all the time. She'd say that if you didn't want
me to live with you, your son shouldn't have come to get me."

She said nothing else for the four hours it took me to get out of the bathtub and wipe my feet. Then she said, "It won't be for long."

She took the pan and used it to empty the water into the sink. I held back what I wanted to say, picked up my things, and went upstairs to the bedroom. I spent the rest of my life on the bed, staring at the ceiling, calling her all the names I could think of. That was it—before she got rid of me, she'd have to pay for my wedding dress.

In the afternoon, about five o'clock, I went outside and sat near the spring, looking at a copy of *Marie-Claire* that was older than me, eating bread and chocolate. The old bitch went out wearing her black coat. Over her shoulder she yelled, "I'm going to take some eggs to your mother. Do you have any message for her?" I shook my head. I waited five minutes to make sure she'd gone and went back indoors. I knew my mother would give her some coffee and would insist on paying for the eggs, and get her to bring back some silly thing or other I'd forgotten, some handkerchiefs, or my bowl marked *Elle* or my baptism medal, who knows. Anyway, she wouldn't be back too soon. In the kitchen the aunt was asleep, her eyes open, her hands folded on her lap. I went upstairs.

The first door I pushed open led to the mother's room. There was an enormous bed covered with an eiderdown. On the wall was a photo of the old man, in an oval frame. He'd been photographed standing in the kitchen doorway, sporting his moustache and with his rifle flung over his shoulder. He looked like a strong, handsome man, but I couldn't have said how old he was. I wanted to spit at him. I went through all the drawers, being very careful not to disturb anything. She hadn't kept her husband's clothes when he died. The bill clip was nowhere to be found. There were papers and photos of all of them in a big box at the top of the wardrobe, but I couldn't look at everything that time.

Then I went into the aunt's room, which was messier. I didn't find anything there, either, except that there was an old tiled stove, and I looked inside. Then I felt some paper that had been slipped between the back of the stove and an iron plate, exactly in the same place as at home. It wasn't an envelope, like the one in which my mother put money away and on which everything was written, even the hour, and of course the day, month, and year, and the time she took out three francs to buy a pen to write it down with. It was one of those blue cardboard folders you make when you're a kid, out of the bottoms of sugar boxes. I'd never seen so much money at once. There were eight thousand francs inside, in new five-hundred-franc notes. I put everything back the way I found it. I went into Mickey's room, then into the storage room at the end of the landing where Boo-Boo sleeps. They didn't have the gold bill clip, either, unless one of them kept it on him. In a drawer in Boo-Boo's room there was a photo of me out of the newspaper, when I won the contest at Saint-Etienne-de-Tinée. I kissed myself and put everything back where I found it.

When I went down again the aunt looked at me and said, "You're a good girl." I don't know why. "Did you have some chocolate a little while ago?" she asked. "Did my sister give it to you?" I nodded. She said, "I knew you weren't a thief." And she went back to sleep.

Then I went to the cellar, just to look around. It smelled of bad wine, and I could hear vermin running for cover. There was nothing to be seen. When my future mother-in-law came back, I was sitting quietly at the kitchen table, my head in my hands, watching the regional news on TV. She put down in front of me my bowl marked *Elle*, my package of Activarol tablets, which I'm supposed to take before meals, and, of course, my glasses, which I never wear. She said, "I wondered why you always look as if you're smelling something when you look at it." She didn't say what she'd talked about with my mother, but I couldn't have cared less. I'm not worried about anything my mother could tell strangers about me.

Then it was the first Sunday, then the second, then the third, and so it went. We got to June. Once a week Ping-Pong and his brothers went out for the whole day. I came down in the morning wearing my big bath towel marked *Elle* and my pink bikini, and lay down in the sun, near the spring, with Grandma's old magazines from the bar, and my suntan lotion, and my menthol cigarettes. I hardly ever smoke, except to annoy people, and I knew it annoyed old Mother Sourpuss. She came out with her laundry and said, "Where do you think you are, on the beach at the Negresco? I hope you've made your bed at least." When she wasn't looking, I took off my brassière. But maybe she always had her eyes on me, who knows. Not that she bothered me, of course, but I didn't want her to say anything to Ping-Pong about me.

About one o'clock he came in to have a quick bite to eat. We hardly had a chance to talk to each other. Then all afternoon I filled in time. I played solitaire on the bed. I changed my dress three times in front of the wardrobe mirror. I stuck on my false fingernails and polished them. I thought about the people I'd known. Mlle Dieu, my schoolteacher at Le Brusquet, the village above Arrame. She used to say the girls who bit their fingernails were the ones who touched themselves in bed. She said that to make me feel ashamed in front of the class. I answered that with her looks, she must have had to touch herself even more. I got a clout on the face for that! She was crazy about me, and that's the truth. I was the prettiest girl in the class. Everyone said so. At fourteen, even before, I had everything it took. And one day, what did she do? She kept me after school and got down on her knees and begged me for it. Yes, on her knees. And what did I do? I squirted the ink out of the Waterman pen in her face. It went all over her, her dress, everything. What a mess! I was the only one in the class to have ink. Daddy had given me a fountain pen in the hope that it would make me learn better. Stupid ass! Finally I stopped by her place one evening, supposedly to take back my books, after they'd given me a dispensation because they couldn't keep me any longer. She was shaking from head to toe. She must have been at least twenty-six and had probably had less experience than any of the girls in the class. She

certainly saw the world with me. What a show! If I'd asked
her to crawl, she'd have said thank you.

Then, of course, I started thinking about the other shithead.
Because of the pen or something. I stopped dead in the middle
of what I was doing and found myself like that, quite still, an
hour later. Like the time he was walking in the field beside
me, holding my hand, when I was little. Maybe about five.
I can't remember anything about that day, or about any of the
others with him, except that we used to walk in the field, and
I was happy, and there were yellow flowers everywhere. When
I came to again, like that, my hairbrush in my hand, sitting
in front of the mirror—as I said, about an hour later—I had
to go out, I'd had enough. Sometimes I go and collect Martine
Brochard, and we go down to the stream and sunbathe in the
nude. Or I walk through the village to our house, but I don't
go in. I wonder if my idiot of a mother is inside and what she's
doing, then walk on.

Once I stopped by the garage and looked in at the workshop.
Ping-Pong was working with Henri IV on a tractor they were
stripping down. They had grease all over them and were sweating. Henri IV turned around to see who was there, and I said,
"I want to talk to Robert." And he said, as if I'd been there
since the night before, "Who's Robert?" I pointed to Ping-
Pong, whose name isn't Robert. I knew that from his letters,
and his mother had called him Florimond in front of me.
Henri IV sighed and bent over his engine. He said, "O.K.,
just this once, but don't forget what your Robert costs me by
the hour."

Ping-Pong came outside with me and said, "He's right, you
know. You mustn't come during working hours." I stood there
looking at my feet, as if I was holding back my tears, sweet as
honey. He said, "O.K., what is it?" I said, without looking up,
"I wanted to write you a letter and leave it for you so I wouldn't
disturb you. But I make mistakes and I was afraid you'd laugh
at me." We just stood there. Then he said, "I make mistakes,
too. What would you have put in the letter?" He didn't sound
annoyed, quite the opposite, in fact. It's a pity he's the son of

that bastard of a father, and his bastard of a father was born to make me suffer, and I was born to make them both suffer more. I said, "Your mother says I won't be staying long with you. Everyone says so. And anyway, people are saying bad things about my parents in the village, as if I'd become..." He put his hands in his pockets and spun around three times, saying, "Shit! Shit! Shit!" Then he said, "Who's been saying things about your parents? I'll soon teach him a lesson, whoever he is." I said, "Just people."

His blood boiled to see me like that, standing there so miserable before him. He didn't dare touch me because of the grease he had on his hands, and he said, "Listen. I'm not like the others, you know." This time, tears came into my eyes very easily. I said, "Yes, that's just it." I turned and started to walk away. He followed me. Grease or not, he caught me in his arms and said, "Don't go away like that." I stayed where I was. He said, "I don't know yet what we're going to do, the two of us. But I like being with you. I don't give a shit for all of them." I looked him straight in the eyes and kissed him on the cheek, the way little girls kiss. I nodded to show I believed him and walked off. Then I heard him running behind me. He caught up with me and said, "I'll be back soon." At least I knew what awaited me—the same as every evening.

When he came home in the evening, all he wanted was to get into the bedroom as fast as he could. In the beginning he showed me the ceiling before dinner, after dinner, and again in the morning before going to work. And all through the day at the garage, he said, he thought of nothing else but doing it again. His mother's room was next to ours, and when I cried out at night, she banged on the wall. Once Mickey came out onto the landing and knocked on our door and said, "We can't go on like this, we can't sleep!" Ping-Pong put his hand over my mouth as soon as I started coming, but he felt he was stifling me, and anyway, he went at it even more when I cried out. I liked Ping-Pong best, or at least almost got to like him, when he was inside me and was about to come. And also when I was getting undressed and he was impatient, and felt me all over as if he couldn't have enough of me in his hands.

I remember very well what the old bitch said to me. I knew it wouldn't last. After a while he'd calm down like everybody else, but for the moment I had him where I wanted him. I lay on my back and on my belly. I crouched on all fours. The bitch next door banged on the wall like a mad thing. But I could get my own back. For example, one Saturday night, the third I spent with them. I went to the movies, to the Royal in town, with Mickey, Mickey's Georgette, Boo-Boo, some silly girl who was on vacation here, and Ping-Pong, who stood at the back of the auditorium during the first part, wearing his fireman's cape and helmet. During the intermission I went back and said to him, "This is the last time you're going to play the fool when I'm along. I want you to stay next to me and touch me during the film if I want you to." I think his eyes nearly popped out of his head. He looked all around him like an idiot, afraid somebody might have heard, and I said, "Do you want me to repeat what I just said louder, so that everyone can hear?" He shook his head violently and went off at top speed, carrying his stupid old helmet in his hand.

Back home, in the bedroom, he said to me, "You must try and understand." All those bastards want me to understand them. "I provide a service for people. When there's a fire or an accident I'm not playing the fool—I'm providing a service. And it's not for the money, either. They only pay me four francs." I didn't even answer. He pulled me down to sit next to him on the bed and said, "I'll do whatever you want, but not that. I won't give up the job. I can't." I let him stew for a long time; then, as I got up, I said, "I'm only asking you to get yourself replaced with someone else on Saturday nights and to stay with me, that's all. If that doesn't suit you, then I'll replace you with someone else." I could see him in the mirror, and he could see me. He looked down and murmured, "O.K." I came back to him. I stood between his legs. I undid the top of my dress for him to kiss her the way Elle likes it. Then he took her on the bed, harder than any other night, and they banged on the wall loud enough to wake up the old aunt.

Next morning, I think it was the third Sunday in June, I'd had enough—I'd been sweating all week, and it was pouring off me again. First, I left Ping-Pong asleep and went down to the yard in my bathrobe. There were some kids on the porch talking to old Mother Dolorosa. I heard her say, in the kind of voice she'd have used if she'd been on the telephone, "You must ask my son, he's the head of the family." There were two boys and two girls, with a white Volkswagen covered with decals, and a canoe on the roof. After a few minutes they took off. The mother said to me, "They're campers." When she went back into the kitchen, I tried to get the shower working, the one they'd fixed up between the spring and the barn, and the cold water suddenly splashed all over my bathrobe and hair. Boo-Boo and Mickey were watching me out of a window. Mickey was laughing. I knew what Elle ought to do at that moment. I knew very well. But it was still too soon. My photo cut out of a paper—who knows. Suddenly I felt depressed. I gave up and went back to the bedroom. Ping-Pong awoke as I was getting dressed and said, "What are you doing?" I said, "I'm going to see my mother." He said, "But we're going there for lunch." I said, "Well, you can come and join me there later. I'm going to see her right now."

When I got home, I was really nervous. She was upstairs with the other shithead—she has to shave him and change his underwear. I yelled up, "Are you coming down? I've got to see you!" She came down right away. I just stood there against the wall, crying, my forehead resting on my arm. He started yelling and shouting like a madman up in his room. She took me gently by the shoulders and led me to the storeroom like she used to when we wanted to talk quietly. I said, through my tears, "You understand, don't you? You understand?" She murmured sadly, "Yes, of course. You want to be more wicked than you are. That's why you're unhappy." She sat down on the steps and helped me undo the buttons of her dress, my fingers were shaking so much, I could smell her body. I had her moist breast in my mouth. I was in the arms of my darling mother, my darling mother.

In the afternoon, that Sunday or another, Ping-Pong took us out for a drive in his boss's DS. There was Mickey, his Georgette, and me. Mickey was supposed to have gone on a bicycle race, but last time he butted one of the judges with his head over some business about a number he hadn't fixed properly on his back, and he was suspended for two weeks. It was the judge who was in the wrong. Of course.

We stopped for a while by the lake that covers Arrame, the village where I was born. They flooded it to make the dam. They blew everything up with dynamite, except the church, out of respect, who knows, and let the water in. They talked about it on TV. Now it was all calm and there were even people swimming in it. Ping-Pong said it was forbidden but they couldn't do anything about it. He said there were days when, if the sun fell on the lake at a certain angle, you could see the church on the bottom. Not the tower—that was taken away. Just the walls. Then Georgette looked at me and realized I was about to burst into tears. She put her arm around my waist. "It's not very funny," she said to the others and led me off.

We went on to the village called Douvet-sur-Bonnette. I'd put on my dress with the big blue flowers and Russian collar, my hair looked really good, but, I don't know why, I didn't feel up to much. Ping-Pong was as proud as anything to walk with me among all the tourists, with his arm around my waist and fingers that wandered farther down to show the other men who I belonged to. When we'd been around the war memorial for the umpteenth time and I'd learned all the names by heart, Mickey bet a franc with two of the summer people he'd met the year before, and he sent Ping-Pong off for a game of bowls. I passed the time with Georgette over a Vittel-menthe. She tried to get me to talk, of course—but I knew before I cut my first tooth that you mustn't tell girls anything unless you're trying to save the cost of an ad in the paper. She also asked me how things were at the Montecciaris', wasn't it too embarrassing to live under the same roof as the boys since I didn't have a brother, and hypocritical things of the same kind, and whether Mickey had ever seen me naked and compared me to her. The best way of ignoring her is to let her imagine whatever she likes, and that's just what I did.

That evening, after dinner at home, all four of us played rummy with old Deaf-and-Dumb. I won twenty francs and the aunt sixty. While Ping-Pong and Mickey were taking Georgette into town, I said to the mother, who was sitting with me in the kitchen, mending socks or something, "Had your husband always had the player piano that's in the barn?" She said, "He brought it from Italy. On foot, if you want to know." I said, "Why?" She lowered her glasses onto her nose to look at me— she wears glasses when she does mending. After about four hours, she said, "Why what? The piano was what he lived by. He stopped in the villages and people gave him money." Four more hours passed, during which she just stared at me, as if I was some sort of bug, then said, "And why would you be so interested in that piano? From the first morning you came here I've watched you looking at it in the barn, walking around it, asking Mickey about it, and now you're asking me." I put on a puzzled, innocent look. "I asked Mickey about it?" She answered sharply, "You asked him if the piano had always stayed here, or whether it had ever been taken out when he was small. I hope you're not trying to tell me Mickey's a liar."

I swerved to dodge that one and said, "Oh yes. That's true, I did ask him." Four more hours, which dragged on minute by minute, she staring at me over her glasses. When she finally spoke again, it was in a much deeper voice, much more intimate: "Why?" I said, "I thought I'd seen a piano like that in Arrame, when I was two or three." Before I'd finished she said, "Arrame's a long way off. He certainly never went that far. Anyway, the last time he took it out of the yard, you weren't even born." My heart was pounding, but I said all the same, "Maybe you're wrong. When was it taken out?" I could hardly bear her eyes on me like that. I almost came to believe she knew everything, had always known everything. There are guys who tell their wives what they've been up to, but that wasn't it. "You weren't even born," she repeated. "My husband took it into town to pawn it, but they didn't want it. So we kept it." I wanted to ask her more, but I knew I shouldn't. She's a wily old bird. If I said too much, she'd always be suspicious of me. I said, "I must have made a mistake. It's not a crime." I gathered up the cards on the table and started playing solitaire. She went back to her mending for a while. Then I heard her say, "What do you expect, you haven't chosen one of the Rothschild sons. We've been to the pawnshop often enough, I can tell you. Yes, indeed."

Ping-Pong and Mickey came back, with Boo-Boo—they'd picked him up on the way. He hardly bothered to look at me. Mickey wanted to play *belote*, but Ping-Pong said no, everyone had to be up the next morning. The truth was he couldn't wait to get to bed and show me the world. After the battle, we were lying in bed, both of us, the sheets thrown back because it was hot, and I said, "Who brought the player piano back when your father wanted to hock it?" "How did you know that?" Ping-Pong asked, laughing. I said, "Your mother was telling me." Years went by and he said, "I can't remember, you'd better ask her. It was some truck driver, a friend of my father's. I was only a kid, you know." He was just ten, his birthday is in November. I picked up my book and pretended to read. He said, "They drank some wine together and were talking and laughing in the kitchen—that's all I remember."

I let my eyes wander over the pages of my Marilyn book, just looking at the lines. Ping-Pong said, "There was snow on the ground. Anyway, why do you ask?" I raised a shoulder, as if I didn't care, and went back to my Marilyn book. One time I was outside, on the steps of our house in Arrame, with Daddy. I was sitting on the steps. I think he was playing with a cork or something. I wanted to go farther away. I was on the steps. Yes, a cork, tied with a string. I tried to catch it. Daddy pulled the string. On the stone steps. I saw it quite clearly. Ping-Pong said, "What's wrong?" I said, "I don't know, I think I'm going to be sick." He said, sitting up, "Do you want something?" I said, "No, I'm all right now." He looked down at me, a worried expression on his face. I went on staring at my book, all those lines.

On Wednesday afternoons Boo-Boo doesn't go to school. He hangs around in the yard. Once, after the Sunday at the dam, I went into the barn without looking at him. He followed me to the piano. He said, "You should get treatment. You're not normal." I laughed and said, "Oh." He said, "Last week, Mme Buygues's cat was found dead in a field. It had been hit over the head. And this morning it's the Merriots' cat. You killed them." I looked at him. He wasn't joking. He was very tall and very handsome. He said, "I'd been looking at you long before Ping-Pong noticed you." I laughed. I said I knew. We stood by the piano of his very late father; he was behind me. He said, "You know nothing at all. You have no heart, or if you have, you've buried it so deep no one can get to it." I spun around. "Who do you think you're talking about? What do you know, anyway? To begin with, I didn't kill the cats. I can't stand being near animals." I went and sat down on the bottom rungs of the ladder. After a while he said, "Why are you so interested in that piano?" I said, "I'd like to hear it work, that's all." Without another word he went over and turned the handle. Suddenly the whole barn was filled with it. It fell on me like heavy rain. I sang out at the top of my voice, "Tra-la-la, tra-la-la, tra-lala-lala." Then I fell forward, like my daddy—out cold.

When I opened my eyes, the music was still playing, and Boo-Boo was leaning over me, a terrified look on his face. I realized I had fallen head over heels off the ladder. One of my cheeks was on the ground, and it hurt. He helped me back on my feet and got me to sit down. It felt stuffy in there. He said, "Shit, you're bleeding!" I caught hold of his arm and said I was all right, it was just a dizzy spell, it had happened to me before. The piano stopped. I said, "Don't tell anyone. I'll do whatever you like, but don't tell anyone." He nodded, licked his fingers, then wiped my cheek. There was a big bruise there.

That night, when Ping-Pong had come back from the station and saw me at the dinner table, he said right away, "Who did that to you?" He must have thought it was his mother, or one of his brothers, who knows. I said, "It was your aunt with the cheese grater." All hell broke loose. Ping-Pong yelled even louder, "Why did you do that to her?" Even the mother was shouting, "Tell him, you slut! Tell him it's not true!" Ping-Pong got really mad. Everybody got it from him—his mother because she'd called me a slut, Mickey because he said we weren't to shout at his mother, Sono Finito because she wouldn't stop saying "What? What?"—even me because I wanted to get out. Only Boo-Boo kept quiet. At one point our eyes met, but he said nothing. He would have been killed on the spot.

Finally I said to Ping-Pong, who was standing there, helmet in hand, breathing heavily, "If you'd just let me get a word in. I made a joke, that's all." He wanted to land me one there and then, and no doubt the mother wanted to pour the soup over me, but they didn't dare! At last they sat down at the table and listened to someone going on about something on TV. Then, without looking at Ping-Pong, I said, "It was a joke, that's all. Can you see your aunt chasing me around with a cheese grater?" That shut them all up, except Deaf-and-Dumb. To make myself quite clear, I leaned over toward Ping-Pong and repeated, "Well, it's true. What do you want to make all that fuss for? Can you see the poor old thing chasing me around with a grater?" Mickey got up—he couldn't contain himself any longer. He was afraid that if he laughed, his brother would get even more excited. I let them think it was the end of the episode and went on eating. Then suddenly in the silence I said, "I felt faint this afternoon and fell over." Ping-Pong said, "Felt faint? What do you mean, felt faint?" And Mother Suspicion snapped, "Where?" I said, "In the barn. Boo-Boo picked me up. You can ask him, if you don't believe me." They all looked at Boo-Boo, except the aunt, who was watching the images move across the TV screen, and Boo-Boo looked down, all embarrassed, and went on eating. He's as thin as a rake. But he sure puts it away. Then Ping-Pong asked me, all concerned, "Does it happen to you often?" I said, "Never."

A little later Boo-Boo helped his aunt up to her room, Mickey took off to plant his corncob in his Georgette, and I was left alone with Ping-Pong and the mother, who was doing the dishes. Ping-Pong said, "You've been shut up here for three weeks now, with nothing to do but read those magazines of yours and watch movies on TV. No wonder you don't feel well." Without turning around the mother said, "What do you expect her to do? She doesn't know how to do anything." Then she added, "It's not entirely her fault, though. She's never been taught to do anything." Ping-Pong said, "She could do your shopping for you in town. At least it would get her out." They went on like that for about an hour, she saying she had no desire to be ruined by me bringing crabmeat home for dinner, and he saying they were talking about money he earned, and he was now of age and vaccinated, etc., etc. In the end I got up, looking sorry for myself just to annoy everyone, and said, "Anyway, that's got nothing to do with my fainting spell." They said nothing—just looked at each other. Then Mother Dolorosa sighed deeply and went back to her dishes, and I left them there.

In the morning I grabbed Ping-Pong by the arm. I was in bed, and he'd just given me a kiss before leaving. I said, "I'd like to go into town today. I've got to go to the hairdresser's and have my hair dyed." I had about two centimeters of roots showing which were less dark than the rest, and he knew it. I said, "But I don't have any money." It wasn't true—my mother had given me some when I'd left and some more the Sunday before, when we were alone together. She'd said to me, "Go on, go on, I don't need anything." I had 440 francs and the change in the pocket of my red blazer, which was in the wardrobe. Ping-Pong just said, "Yes, of course, I should have thought of it." He took out some notes from his pocket and gave me one hundred-franc note and one fifty-franc note. He looked at me to make sure that was enough, and I nodded. He said, "Just ask me when you need any." He pulled back the sheet to see all of me, sighed, and took off.

About noon I went to get my bike from home. My mother made me hard-boiled eggs and sautéed carrots, which I adore, and we drank coffee, not talking. I put on my tight-fitting sky-blue dress and the band made out of the same material to hold my hair. When I left, she said my dress was too short, that it wasn't fashionable. I said, "It's fashionable enough for anyone with legs like mine—or yours. We've got what it takes, haven't we?" She gave a little laugh. She's really funny when she laughs—you'd think she was ashamed of it and wasn't allowed to show her teeth. I got on my old bike and was off. From the edge of the village to the town it's downhill all the way. First I went to the sawmill to leave my bike with Mickey and tell him to pick me up in the evening. He wasn't there, but his boss, Ferraldo, said he would tell him. Then I went to see old Dr. Conte.

There were a few people in the waiting room, but no one I knew. I waited for about ten minutes, looking at my feet. When the doctor opened the door for the next patient, he saw me and let me go in right away, as if I'd made an appointment. In his office he didn't even ask me how I was. He sat down at his desk and made me out a prescription. I said, "I think I'm going to be pregnant." He said, "What do you mean, going to be? You are or you aren't." I said I'd forgotten to take my pill several times. He said, "Since when?" I just stood there before him like a fool. I said, "Maybe three weeks." He looked up to heaven and said, "O.K. Don't you think I've got anything better to do than to listen to such nonsense? Come back and see me later." Then he gave me the prescription and an ointment sample for my cheek, asked to be remembered to my mother, and let me out. He never charges us.

I crossed the town-hall square and went to the hairdresser's. Moune always does my hair. She's a nice enough kid, but really dense. Her conversation—forget it. Her work's no better. If Mme Ricci, the owner, didn't come over and tell her to get us some tea with lemon from the café next door, and take over my hair, I would come out looking like a feather duster on two legs. Then I went to Philippe's pharmacy. When he saw me come in he got all flustered, like he always does. I showed him my prescription, just to annoy him. Years ago he used to give me the pill under the counter. Ping-Pong said if people were to be believed, I'd slept with Philippe. It's not true. I did want to, but he's a funny guy. I don't know how he ever managed to get his wife pregnant. There were some girls in the shop, summer people with cellulitis, spending their vacation choosing a toothbrush, so he couldn't really talk. He said, "I'll be closing in half an hour, you know." But I said I didn't have time.

I went to the supermarket and without looking bought three balls of wool and two knitting needles. I also bought a can of crabmeat, just to annoy old Mother Tightwad, and a present for Boo-Boo—four copies of my photo taken in a booth. Last time around I shut my eyes and pouted my lips in a big kiss. In the end I didn't like the way I looked and tore them up. I bought a red sweatshirt with *Indiana University* in white letters across the front. I didn't know his size, I just took the biggest—it would be all right. I hate supermarkets. I came out with a splitting headache. On my way to the sawmill I saw the yellow truck coming toward me. Mickey waved at me through the window, and when I got in, Boo-Boo was already there, with his fat briefcase. They both thought my hair looked marvelous. On the way I said of course Ping-Pong or his mother could telephone Dr. Conte, but if they asked what was the matter he would tell them where to get off. Doctors are like priests—they can't open their mouths. Every time we went around a corner—and it was all corners—I was thrown against Boo-Boo. Finally he put an arm around my shoulder to hold me. I felt his warmth. The sun had gone down behind the mountains. Mickey never stopped making us laugh and talking nonsense. He said he could be my brother, and Boo-Boo, too. I wanted

Boo-Boo even more. I hated myself and at the same time felt good.

I waited another week. The most difficult thing came the next day—to hide the fact that I was having my period. I don't mean it was hard to keep from Ping-Pong. So that he would leave me alone, I said the exact opposite. I said it wasn't coming, and I felt sick all over. For three nights he just sighed and went off to bed. I stayed downstairs with the aunt and Mickey, playing *belote* at five francs a hand. When I went upstairs Ping-Pong was asleep. He'd never lived with a girl before, and, as with all boys, the less he had to do with girls' troubles the better. I was much more suspicious of the old bitch, and even of the aunt. I went home for three days in a row, supposedly because the other shithead was sick, and because my mother wanted time to try on my new dress, and I managed.

Of course the poor woman figured out everything. But she didn't say a word. She got my clean underwear—I've never let anyone else wash my clothes, not even one of my hairbands— and she made me hot chocolate, which I adore. It reminds me of when I was a kid. Then she stood in her doorway seeing me off. She was thinking—she didn't have to tell me—that things would never be the same again. I was thinking the same thing. At the gate I turned around, but that made me want to run back to her, because what lay ahead seemed too heavy a burden for me, so I left as fast as I could. I once calculated that I spent three-tenths of my life thinking about her, three-tenths thinking about him, when he was my daddy, the rest thinking about some nonsense or other or asleep.

On Saturday, when I was coming back from home, I met Henri IV's Juliette in front of the garage pumps. She said to me, "Come here, I want to talk to you." I lowered my head, with my basket on my arm like Little Red Riding Hood, and followed her. Ping-Pong wasn't there, nor was her husband. She took me up to the apartment. She asked if I wanted coffee or something. I said I'd already had some. She sat down on a chair facing me and said, "I'd like to be sure you really love Ping-Pong." I didn't even answer. She said, "Are you going to go on living at their house without getting married?" I shrugged my shoulders.

She's fairly tall, with light-brown hair, and was wearing a kid's dress to make her look younger. She's getting a little plump, but she's not bad-looking. I'm sure she cries out, too, when her husband or someone else puts it in. She said, "I knew Ping-Pong at school. His intentions are very pure." I suddenly had the feeling we were in a scene from *Doctor Zhivago*. I nodded and just stood there. I said nothing. In the end she said, "If you have to marry him, I'll let you have my dress. I've kept it in perfect condition. Your mother, with her clever hands, could alter it to suit you exactly." Since I didn't answer she said, "I was slim like you when I was younger." She got up and kissed me on the cheek. She asked, "Would you like to see it?" I said no, it's unlucky. I got up, too—I'm taller than her. I said, with my made-in-my-mother accent, "That's very nice of you. You're not like the others in the village." Then we went down the wooden staircase. In the workshop I said, "Well, good-bye." She looked at me, her cheeks very red. She wanted to say something else, but it wouldn't come, and I took off.

The rest of the time I was really sweet with everyone, as I can be when I want to. For example, I saw Mother Montecciari dragging the great trash can to the gate for the garbage collectors to empty into their truck—they wake us up at five in the morning every Tuesday—and I said, "Let me do that; I can, you know. It's not very difficult. You get treated like an idiot in this house." She said nothing; maybe she felt sorry for me, maybe not, who knows.

I love being with Aunt Deaf-and-Dumb. Once I was alone with her, and I yelled out, "Old bitch!" She said, "What?" I yelled even louder, "Old bitch!" She smiled at me, tapped my hand, and said, "If you like. You're a good girl." I went to the sideboard, took out a chocolate bar, and gave it to her. She rolled her eyes and said, "If my sister could see me." I put my index finger to my lips, to show her that we were pals, the two of us, and she laughed and bit into her chocolate like a little monkey. It's amazing how ravenous you can be at that age. And ugly. I'd rather die when I'm twenty. Or thirty, anyway.

On Sunday morning Mickey went off, with his big calves bare, saying he was going to win, shit. He was in a race somewhere—he wasn't suspended any more. He came back in the evening saying he'd lost, shit. He said it was because of his bike, and Ping-Pong, who takes care of it for him, couldn't understand why. Mickey explained, "I got a good start. I was soon ahead of everyone else. It's that bitch of a bike that weighs ten tons." A strange noise came from Ping-Pong's throat, but he didn't say anything. He loves his brothers as if they weren't his own. For him, Mickey and Boo-Boo are sacred. He yells at Boo-Boo a little for getting up too late in the morning to go to school and for reading science fiction into the middle of the night. He yells at Mickey, too, when he lies about the number of cigarettes he smokes a day, and how he's going to poke Georgette four times a week: "How do you expect to win a race after that?" But it's sacred all the same.

Boo-Boo doesn't look at me, hardly says anything, and avoids me when Ping-Pong isn't there. I went into his bedroom and put my present on his bed. I cornered Boo-Boo on the landing a bit later and said, "I thought you'd like it. You didn't tell on me when I fell in the barn." He stood there, very straight, his back against the wall, not looking at me. He said, "Don't talk so loud, they'll hear you downstairs." I whispered, "Then take it, please." I stuffed the sweatshirt under his arm, and he kept it. He just shrugged his shoulders to show he didn't mind and went back into his room. When I see him like that I want to see him trembling in my arms, kissing my lips till he dies.

So I was sweet with everybody for the rest of the week. Then, on Wednesday, Ping-Pong came back from his training session at the station. We were expecting him for dinner. I was knitting, like my mother had shown me, with my glasses on my nose, glancing at the TV from time to time. The Manageress, who was serving the soup, said to her son, "The campers we saw the other day have come back. They gave me two hundred francs on account. They've settled at the far end of the field." Mickey said, in an angry tone, "O.K., O.K. Can't we have some quiet?" He was watching the film, too. Deborah Kerr was having a nervous breakdown because she'd let some-one kiss her. But the only thing Ping-Pong could see, in that slum of a kitchen, wasn't Deborah Kerr, or Boo-Boo biting his fingernails, or Mickey, and certainly not his aunt; it was me, knitting, sitting quietly in my chair with the glasses I never wore on the end of my nose.

He leaned over, kissed my cheek, which was better by now, and said, "What are you doing?" I sighed and said, "You can see what I'm doing." He said, "What are you knitting?" I shrugged a shoulder and, still counting the stitches in my head, said, "What do you think?"

There was a funny silence in the kitchen after that. All we could hear was Deborah Kerr speaking her subtitled English. Ping-Pong went over to switch off the TV; Aunt Deaf-and-Dumb yelled out, "Now I can read for once." And I felt they were all looking at me. I didn't care. I just went on knitting, like my mother had shown me, thinking of nothing else.

Finally Ping-Pong got a chair and sat down in front of me. He said, "Stop." I looked at him through my glasses. He wasn't annoyed or anything. He said, "How can you be sure?" I said, "I was late, so I went to see Dr. Conte. He said it was still too early to tell, but I know." Then I kept my eyes on my knitting. Nice, regular stitches, like kernels on a corncob. Everything fell quiet again—only the sound of Boo-Boo moving a fork on the table. In the end, it was the old bitch of a widow who opened her mouth first and let me have it. She said to Ping-Pong, in her constipated voice, "Well, you don't have to look any further. This time you may well believe her. She's taken you in, you poor fool."

Ping-Pong got up, pushed his chair back, and said, "Be quiet, please. Nobody's trying to take me in, it's just happened, that's all." I knew he was looking at me, so that I'd agree with

him, but I kept my eyes hidden behind my glasses. I shut up.
Mickey said, "Well, shall we start?" Boo-Boo said, "Be quiet."
Another long, long silence. Finally Ping-Pong said, "You're
not the only one who is fed up with everyone whispering behind
your back when you walk through the village. It's my fault.
Well, we'll soon settle that."

We all sat down and had dinner. I kept my knitting on my
knees. Mickey didn't even ask if he could turn the TV back
on. The aunt said, "What's the matter? Aren't you pleased
with the girl?" Her sister patted her hand to calm her down,
and no one said anything. I think three-tenths of the time of
Mommy, three-tenths of Daddy. I ate my soup. I'm more
stubborn than the rest of the world that's against me. That was
the end of it. I went through with it and signed Eliane Montecciari.

THE WITNESS

She's a good girl. I can tell from her eyes. She doesn't miss anything, and neither do I. Because I can't hear, they all think I can't see, either. She doesn't think that. She knows I can see well, because I watch her. From the first day I knew she was a good girl. She didn't try to take my money. I'm keeping it to bury my sister, and then for my own burial. She found it in the tiled stove in my room, but she didn't take it. She just put the folder back on the wrong side—I knew she'd touched it. I don't miss anything.

The folders were made out of sugar boxes. The good Lord knows how many we made when we were kids in Marseille. Ah, it was a good time. I said to the girl, Marseille is the most beautiful city in the world after Paris. I went to Paris once, for the World Fair of 1937, with my husband. One week. We stayed at the Hôtel des Nations, Rue du Chevalier-de-la-Barre. We had a nice room, with a small stove to make coffee in the morning. We made love every day—it was like a second honeymoon. "Well, you rascal," I said, "Paris certainly has an effect on you." He laughed and laughed. He was ten years older than me, and I was twenty-nine at the time. He bought me two dresses before we left, and he bought me another on the Boulevard Barbès, in Paris, just at the Rue du Chevalier-de-la-Barre. He died on May 27, 1944, during the bombing of Marseille. We lived on the corner of the Rue de Turenne and the Boulevard National, on the fourth floor. The building collapsed with us in it. He was next to me when the bomb dropped. He grabbed my hand and said, "Don't be frightened, Nine, don't be frightened." It seems he was found in the street, under the debris, and they found me in what was left of the second floor with an old woman whose head had been torn off. She didn't live in the building, and no one knew where she came from.

Very often, when I'm sitting in my chair, I think of that last moment, when I held my husband's hand. I wonder how we could possibly have been pulled apart. I tell myself we must have lost consciousness together, and I ought to be dead with him. I've never known another man, or even looked at one. Either before or since. Yet I was only thirty-six when he died, and even though I'm deaf I've had plenty of offers. My sister said to me once, "Find yourself a good workingman of your own age and get married." I cry just to think of it.

She's a real fool, my sister. She never knew another man except her husband, either. And she hasn't got married again! So what's she talking about? And she was better-looking than me. Once, in the barn, Florimond and Mickey found some letters my poor brother-in-law had written to her in 1940, when he was in the army and he'd become a Frenchman for good. All three of us read them when she wasn't there. We nearly died laughing. We couldn't stop. Spelling wasn't his specialty, poor Lello, but he must have missed my sister, because apart from the occasional request to be remembered to someone in the village, he talked about nothing but her. In other words, they were love letters. Later we were a little ashamed about reading them, but even that very evening, at dinner, we couldn't help ourselves, and we were soon giggling away again. He referred to her "alabaster body." He must have read it in the paper or somewhere and made a mental note of it. Lovesick! Then, of course, my sister got mad because she didn't know what we were laughing about. She just dropped everything and went to bed. "Alabaster body"! I wonder where he got that from.

My sister is luckier than me. Poor Lello is buried in the village cemetery—she can go and clean up his grave on Monday afternoon and tell him what's happening—but my poor husband's in Marseille, at Le Canet. During the last ten years, I've only been able to go twice. Once when his brother was buried—he was a jeweler, though he didn't have his own shop, of course—and again when Mickey was in a race at the stadium and Florimond and Henri IV took me and my sister. In the evening, after Mickey had won the race by elimination and piled up goodness knows how many prizes, he took us out for a fish dinner on the Corniche. We came back late at night. We were all very pleased—I because I'd seen my husband's grave, and brushed everything clean, and put flowers there, and the others because Mickey had won his race, though of course I was glad about that, too. We had two bikes tied to the roof of the car, and throughout the trip I was afraid they'd come off.

I'd like to win three *tiercés* again, now that I've made sure the money's there for my burial and my sister's. I'd give all the money from the first to Florimond, because he's the eldest and works the hardest. I'd divide the second between Boo-Boo and Mickey. The third would be for the baby Elle is going to have, but it would be put away in a savings account. I told my sister I hoped the baby would be a girl—we've got too many men in our family, and she'd be as pretty as her mother. Merciful heaven, what a good thing I can't hear—I don't know what I'd have heard if I did. My sister hates the girl. She doesn't think she's honest, and she doesn't like her sassy manners. But most of all she hates her for having taken her son Florimond from her. She says, "If they get married, what will happen to the money? He'll have to share it with her." And I say, "She's a good girl. For thirty years you've been shouting at me, and you know I can't hear. She at least doesn't shout—she talks slowly and I understand everything. Or if it's too complicated, she takes the trouble to go and fetch paper and pencil and write it out for me."

If you'd seen my sister's face—what a horror! You'd think all her blood had curdled inside her. Then of course she shouted even more—because I didn't understand a thing she said. So then she, too, went to the sideboard drawer and got a sheet of paper and, to be revenged, wrote, "Do you know what she calls you?" And I said, "She calls me Sono Finito, she told me." And I laughed and laughed. It's true, the girl calls me Sono Finito, Aunt Deaf-and-Dumb, or Little Monkey. I asked her. She told me. And my sister says the girl isn't honest! Sassy, yes. She walks around naked as easily as others take out an umbrella when it rains. But I think she's unhappy. I mean, her life can't be that amusing all the time, and no one knows, because she doesn't show it as freely as her behind.

I explained what I thought to my sister, but she shrugged her shoulders like the know-all she had already become when she was ten, and I read her lips: "You and your nonsense!" And she made a big gesture over her head to show that what I say is all nonsense. She wrote on the paper, "What did she ask you?" Just to make her mad, I first corrected her spelling mistakes, like I do for the girl—she writes almost in phonetics, it's incredible. Then I said, "Nothing. She likes me to talk to her, tell her things." I read on her lips, "Tell her what?" And I said, "Anything. Whatever comes into my head." She took the paper again and wrote, "The player piano in the barn?" I played the fool. I shook my head. She wrote, "She asked you who brought the piano back when Lello took it to the pawnshop?" I said, "Why do you ask me that?" I remember very well who brought the piano back. It was Big Leballech and his brother-in-law. Big Leballech drove a truck belonging to Ferraldo, Mickey's boss. It was in November or December 1955—there was snow in the yard. When they'd got the piano off the truck, they drank a bottle here with Lello in the kitchen; I can remember it quite clearly. My sister wrote, "Because she wanted to know." I said, "She didn't ask me." That's true. The girl talked to me about the player piano in the barn, but she didn't ask me anything about it that day.

My sister shrugged her shoulders and thought about what she was going to write next. Then she suddenly turned her head toward the glass door, and I knew someone must be coming into the yard. The girl always does the same thing. She set fire to the piece of paper with a match and threw it into the unlit stove. She always makes the same gesture with the poker to lift the cover and put it back in place. When she opened the door, I saw one of the campers who'd put their tent up at the far end of the field, and his girl friend, or wife, a blonde with freckles. I understood, watching my sister go out, that they'd come to get some eggs, or maybe a rabbit.

I was alone and shut my eyes. I could remember very well that winter evening in 1955. Big Leballech and his brother-in-law drinking wine in the kitchen with poor Lello. Florimond was still a kid and kept getting in his father's way. At that time I wasn't always in my chair. I'd walk to the gate, look at the forests, the houses in the village, the road. Sometimes I'd see big Leballech go by in his truck. He had the same job Mickey has now—he carted wood. That evening was the only time I saw his brother-in-law. I still had my hearing aid then and could make out what people said. They explained to me that he was married to Leballech's sister and lived with her over by Annot.

When I'm in my chair I shut my eyes, but I'm not asleep. The others always think I'm asleep. I sleep only at night—and not for long. I spend my time thinking of all those wonderful days. In Digne, when I was a kid, and then in Marseille. The landing pier, which the Germans blew up during the war, and the Rue du Petit-Puits. All that sun. I wonder if we haven't moved farther away from the sun, what with all the rubbish they've invented. The days were longer then, the summers warmer. The World Fair of 1937, in Paris. My sister still has the dish I brought back for her. It's behind me, on the sideboard. There's a view of the World Fair painted on it. My husband said to me, "You'll see! We'll remember this for a long time!"

The girl was sitting next to me one afternoon, and she wrote on her paper, the way she does, "Did you always love him?" I nodded. She didn't laugh or anything. We just sat there. She's a good girl. She's not like the others.

In the morning my sister helps me get dressed. One day it's my legs that hurt, another my arms. She also helps me come down to the kitchen and settle myself in my chair. Florimond and Mickey go to work. Boo-Boo has taken his *"bachot"* in

French, he says he's done his best, and they're waiting for the results. He can read or sleep in his room all morning.

The girl always comes down about nine, after making her bed. She goes out to get her bathtub from the shed, where she keeps it, and prepares her bath. My sister says she'll wear herself out with all that washing. My sister's a fool. She's been good enough to me since my husband died, but she's a fool, always was. I say to the girl, "O.K.?" She puts her head to one side and says, "O.K." The first time she got into her bathtub I was shocked. I didn't even dare look at her. Now I say to myself, "You poor old fool, where do you expect her to wash? She's no different from you when you were young, and your grandmother took no notice." Then she empties the tub, pan by pan, into the sink. She puts on her white bathrobe. Her hair is all wet, her face smooth, and you can see she's not yet twenty.

When she looks at me she doesn't always see me, because she's thinking about something else, but when she does see me I can tell from her eyes that she's glad I'm there. It's something about the way she pouts, or smiles, or shrugs one shoulder as if she doesn't care, because she wants people to believe she doesn't care about anything. I can't hear either the noises she makes in her bath or what she says to my sister when my sister talks to her, though I can see her little nose wrinkle and her blue eyes narrow. But I think I can guess her thoughts well enough. I've never seen her mother—they call her Eva Braun, because she comes from Germany. People are so stupid. I'd like her to come and visit us. I asked my sister to get her to come, but she answered, speaking very clearly to make me understand, "Her mother is like Elle—she's a savage."

After her bath the girl goes out into the yard with her towel and her menthol cigarettes, to sunbathe near the wooden tank by the spring. As soon as she's gone, Boo-Boo comes down in his pajamas. He kisses me every morning—he's the only one who does. He always says the same thing: "You don't change, do you?" Then he fixes himself an assortment of slices of bread, one with honey, one with butter, one with jam, one with peanut butter, and his mother pours him some coffee. When it is ready, he adds one or two spoons of Nescafé—otherwise, he says, it won't wake him up. He swallows everything down, staring ahead of him, as if he's thinking of very important matters, a bit like Mickey does. Except that Mickey never eats so much. Then he washes his bowl, as he has been taught. He hesitates for a moment in front of the glass door, then pulls back the curtain to see the girl lying beside the spring tank. Then he goes up to his room.

I can see what's going on, and you don't have to get to my age to understand what effect the girl is having on him. He gets along well with her, too. I've noticed during meals. He always knows where to find the salt when she's looking for it. She can't see very well. He passes the saltcellar to her, as if he's amused she can't find it. But it's always him who looks after her—the others are watching TV. I think she does it on purpose. One afternoon when we were together, she wrote, "My eyes are just for decoration. I can't even see as far as my feet." I said, "Then why don't you wear your glasses?" She wrote back, "I don't care about my feet." But she knows very well what's going on—even with her eyes. And she likes Boo-Boo to take notice of her.

Last Sunday he came down to dinner wearing a new sweat-shirt. It was red, with *Indiana University* printed on it in white. Everyone said how nice it was, but he acted annoyed and sat down without looking at anyone. Then, a few seconds later, I saw him glance at Elle, just a glance, and she lowered her head with a little smile. You could tell she was pleased, and there was some secret between them. I think she bought him the sweatshirt without telling the others. I think she can't see anything wrong in it, and even if there's less than three years' difference between them, Boo-Boo is just like a little brother. She hasn't got any brothers. I can understand. Anyway, she's very much in love with Florimond. My sister says everybody can hear her at night, when she's with him.

I'd be more worried about Mickey, because he's closer to her age and because his eyes are always where they shouldn't be when she crosses her legs or bends to pick something up. Her skirts and dresses are too short. I told her. She laughed and raised one shoulder, like she always does. When she wears her faded jeans it's worse—they're so tight you couldn't see her backside better if it was bare. But you have to be fair. Girls have a funny way of dressing these days, she's not the only one. Before the war, when we rented the villa at Seausset-les-Pins in summer, I wore trousers, too, but they were baggy all over. It was the fashion. My husband said I looked very smart in them. When we came back from the beach with my nephews and my sister, who was not yet married, we used to sit out in the garden, which was full of acacias, and listen to the phonograph. I can still smell those acacias when I think about it. The record I liked best was that song from *Snow White*:

> *Some day my prince will come,*
> *Some day I'll find my love. . . .*

I can't remember who sang it. It may have been Elyane Célis, I don't know. I'm afraid I'm losing my memories, little by little. I'm afraid of becoming what they all think I am already—senile. My poor grandmother was like that when she died. She laughed all the time, happy as anything. She couldn't remember my grandfather at all—he'd died twenty years before. Nothing, not a single memory. Merciful heaven, don't let me ever get like that! I want to be able to remember my husband right up to the last moment, when he held my hand and said, "Don't be frightened, Nine, don't be frightened." It doesn't have to hurt you, dying. There's no reason why it should. The heart slows down, and then it stops. And on the other side, maybe it's like how I used to think when I was a little girl, and my grandmother told me about it in our apartment on the Rue du Petit-Puits—you're surrounded by all the people you've ever known. It's something I think about at night when I can't sleep. I'm not sure I like the idea, though. My husband was forty-six when he was killed. I'm already sixty-eight. If it's true, all that, and I'll be with him again, next year or in ten years, he'll see me as I am, an old woman. That would be terrible. But the good Lord, if he exists, must have worked all that out, so it doesn't worry me. Perhaps I'll suddenly be like I was in Seausset-les-Pins, during those marvelous summers when we rented the villa. I can't remember the color of the trousers I wore. Yes, they must have been white. It was the fashion. I can't remember what make the phonograph was. That's important—it was a part of those years that went with all the others—now it's gone. There was a dog on the label. Come on now, everybody knows that make. It's on the tip of my tongue. Now I can't remember who sang the song from *Snow White*. Elyane Célis, but I'm not sure. Merciful heaven! I can't remember the make of the phonograph any more.

His Master's Voice.

Now I must be careful. I must think of everything, not lose anything, not let my beautiful memories wander off. When I asked the girl she said, very clearly, "His Master's Voice." I said, "Do they still make them?" She shrugged a shoulder and said, her lips about thirty centimeters away from my eyes, "The mutt is His Master's Voice. Everyone knows that." She said something else, but too quickly, and I didn't understand. I gestured for her to get some paper from the sideboard. She shook her head, repeated slowly, as if I was hearing it for the first time, "You're losing your memory, you poor old thing, you're getting quite senile." I didn't know whether to be sad or not. I was afraid my sister would suddenly come back into the kitchen. The girl was dressed, ready to go out—she had to go get a copy of her birth certificate. Then she said, "Don't let them see you're losing your memory. Ask me." I knew very well what she was saying, as if I heard the words. And she put her hand around the back of my neck and kissed me on the cheek. She said, "I'm not unkind. I'm going senile, too. Get it?" I nodded. Then she went off.

I was left alone for a long time. My sister came back and then went out again. She was busy with her planting or with the boys' vineyard, I don't know and I don't care. I was thinking of the girl. I'm sure that when she talks to me, forming the words properly with her mouth, she isn't speaking aloud—the others don't seem to hear her. She mimes the words in the silence, just for me. She's only been here a few weeks, and she knows how to talk to me better than all the others who've always known me.

Boo-Boo came back first, at the end of the afternoon. He made himself an enormous sandwich, with ham and butter and Roquefort cheese. My sister will yell her head off, as she does every day, when she sees what's left for everybody else. He came back from the swimming pool in town, and his hair was still plastered down. He looked like a twelve-year-old boy. He said something I didn't understand, but it's nice just to see him. It doesn't matter what he says. He went up to his room to read his books on the future.

Soon afterward Elle came back. I saw at once she was not the same girl she'd been three or four hours before. The makeup around her eyes was gone. She looked sad, or worse than that. She washed her hands in the sink. She didn't look at me. I said to her, "Did you get the copy of your birth certificate? Will you show it to me?" She said some rude word, very quickly; I didn't understand, but I knew it was a rude word. Then she looked at me, shrugged her shoulders, took the paper out of a pocket in her red jacket, and gave it to me. It was a copy of a birth certificate from the town hall of Le Brusquet-Arrame. She was born on July 10, 1956, so she'll be twenty in a few days. Her name is Eliane Manuela Hertha Wieck. She is the daughter of Paula Manuela Wieck, natu-ralized Frenchwoman, and of unknown father. I said nothing at first, then she took the paper away from me and put it back in her pocket. I said, "You have your mother's surname?" I'm sure the blood drained from her tanned face. Her eyes were defiant and full of tears. She said, "What's it to you?" I could almost hear the words. I said, "It doesn't matter, but tell me all about it." She wiped her eyes with the back of her hand

and said very clearly for me, "There's nothing to say." Then she left. I said, "Don't go away, I'm on your side." But she didn't listen and went upstairs.

That evening, at the dinner table, she was wearing her tight jeans and her navy-blue short-sleeved turtleneck jersey with a fish stitched on the breast pocket. Florimond was sitting next to her and kept looking at her. Then he started eating and talking to Mickey. He looked at her again and saw she was thinking of something else. He drew her head toward him and kissed her hair. You could tell he loves her a lot. I think he'd seen the copy of her birth certificate and asked her about it. And she, no doubt, just shrugged her shoulder, and he said, "After all, what difference does it make?" Just as I did. When the girl was born her mother wasn't married to Devigne, that's all. Lots of people live their whole lives together without being married. But of course Devigne's name should appear on the birth certificate.

I said, "Florimond, when are you having the wedding?" He said, "On the seventeenth. It's a Saturday." My sister leaned toward me and said something, but I couldn't understand. The girl smiled to see what a fool my sister is and repeated with her lips, "It takes ten days for notice to be given at the town hall." The others looked at her as if she was out of her mind, and I realized I was right—no sound was coming from her lips, she just mimed the words for me. I nodded and said, "His Master's Voice." She laughed and laughed. Then I laughed, too. And the others stared at us, looking even sillier than usual. I said to Florimond, "His Master's Voice." He didn't know what I was talking about, but, seeing both of us laughing, especially her, he started laughing, too, then Mickey, who is always waiting for the first opportunity, and even Boo-Boo, who sat there, his fork in midair, wondering what was going on. Only my sister didn't laugh. And the less she laughs, the funnier it is. Just the sight of my sister's face is enough to make you die laughing. And we just stared at her. She looked like a stuck-up kid. I yelled out, "Alabaster body!" Mickey spluttered out the wine he had in his mouth, all over the table, and

Florimond turned around on his chair holding his belly, doubled up with laughter, and the girl and Boo-Boo didn't even know what I was talking about. They were laughing fit to burst, but they couldn't help it, and I just coughed and spluttered, but I couldn't stop, either. Well, there you are. That's how things are—it's no big deal if Devigne, who I've never seen, got some poor woman with child and didn't acknowledge it. And of course you don't have to get to my age to figure what happened next. The girl suddenly stopped, while all the others were still laughing, and rested her head on her folded arms on the table; I could see her shoulders, from behind, shaken by sobs.

We sat there like statues, watching her, even my fool of a sister, and Florimond patted her hair and spoke to her gently. Then he took her upstairs to their room. My sister, Boo-Boo, and Mickey looked at me as if I owed them an explanation. I just said, "She's a good girl. I want to go to bed, too."

I had to wait two or three days before finding myself alone with Elle one afternoon. When you're old, you get even more impatient than ever. She'd put on a new dress that her mother had just made for her, white with a blue-and-turquoise pattern. The blue exactly matched her eyes. She wanted to go see her old schoolmistress from Le Brusquet; she would take the three o'clock bus. My sister was washing the sheets by the spring tank. Boo-Boo went out after lunch with Martine Brochard and another girl, who's not from here. He said he was taking them to pick lavender in the mountains. Old Mother Brochard, who makes money out of anything, sews up packages of lavender, which she sells to tourists, to put in their wardrobes. I don't know which of the girls, Martine or the other one, Boo-Boo prefers, but I do know he hasn't gone crawling around up there in order to put money in Mother Brochard's pocket. But then that's youth.

I said to the girl, "I've been thinking. I'd like to talk to you before my sister comes back." She was brushing her teeth at the sink, like she does every morning and every night and whenever she goes out. She gestured to show she couldn't answer. She's meticulously clean about her person. She shamed my sister once, as she sat down to dinner. She looked at her glass in the light, turning it around toward the window, and, without saying a thing, went and washed it again. For the rest, what doesn't touch her personally, she couldn't care less. They could leave the dirty dishes in the kitchen for a month; she'd just go outside and eat off her knees for a month. My sister hates her even more than before—which makes me laugh.

I said, "Stop brushing your teeth, and come over here." She looked at me for several seconds with toothpaste frothing all over her lips, glanced out in the direction of the spring, parting the curtain, then rinsed her mouth out under the faucet, wiped it, and came over. I could swear she knew what I was going to talk to her about. I said, "Sit down." She took a cushion from one of the chairs, just a cushion, put it down on the ground beside my chair, and sat on it in this way she has, her arms around her knees. I ran my fingers through her hair, which is heavy and very beautiful. She moved her head away and I knew, without hearing her, that she said, "You're spoiling my hairdo. It's taken me four years to get it like that." I now know how she talks. I'll never know what her voice sounds like, and that will be one more regret for me. My sister told me about her voice. The words she used to describe it were "sharp" and "put-on." She also said the girl spoke with a German accent. That surprised me. I asked the girl about this. She said she did it on purpose, just to make herself interesting. I swear, if she didn't exist she would have to be invented.

I said, "I'm not spoiling your hairdo." She said something like "O.K., you're not spoiling my hairdo. What do you want to talk to me about?" I said, "I want to tell you about my youth, about Marseille, about Seausset-les-Pins. Are you listening? But you're not asking me what you want to know. You must." She didn't move, and she said nothing. I said, "You want to know who the truck driver was who brought the player piano back here, in November 1955, eight months before you were born. I'm not as stupid as you believe. I've got all day to think about things."

She was so still, her head so heavy and so alive under my fingers. I ought to have told her simply what I remembered—I didn't have to make her ask me. I, too, want to be thought interesting. I know that as long as I tell her nothing, I will be interesting to her. I'm afraid that later she'll no longer bother to sit down beside me and listen to me. I could no longer talk to her about the memories that will die before me, one by one in my head. With the others, as soon as I start to say anything, they've got something else to do. My sister has to take care of the rooms, Mickey his bike, Boo-Boo his homework. Florimond is hardly ever there. He earns the money to keep everybody else—he has no time to listen to Cognata.

I said to the girl, "Look at me." I took her face in my hands to make her turn toward me. She looked at me with those blue eyes that seem to go right through you without meeting yours, but she can see you all right, you may be sure. I whispered, "Ask me." She shook her head gently, though she went on looking at me. She was depressed about something, I was sure, but she wouldn't share it with me.

I leaned over and said, "A woman like me, who never had a child, takes more notice of a girl like you, because you're the kind of daughter I'd like to have now." She didn't understand what I meant; she said, proudly, "I've already got a mother." I said, "I know, silly. I simply meant you could trust me." She shrugged one shoulder—she didn't care. I repeated, "Ask me." She mimed the words, "Ask what? Who brought back that old piano? What do you think I care about it?" I said, "You asked Florimond and Mickey. They were too small to remember. You asked my sister. She wasn't even there that evening. She'd gone to Le Panier to help Mother Massigne, whose husband had just died, run over by a tractor. My sister didn't come back till next day, to get the meals ready. That's why I remember it so well. Only I can tell you. And you don't want to ask me."

She thought for a few seconds, without taking her blue eyes off mine. Then she decided. She said with her lips, "I've got nothing to ask you. I want to marry Ping-Pong, that's all." She got up, straightened out her dress brusquely, and added, shaping her lips clearly, "So there!" She left, banging the door, to catch her bus for Le Brusquet.

I got up, supporting myself with one hand on the long table to walk. I cried out, "Eliane!" I didn't see her pass the window—I wasn't sure she was really gone—I said, loud enough for her to hear if she was still near the door, "He's named Leballech. He was with his brother-in-law. Leballech! You hear?" I saw the doorknob turn and the door open again, and she was there, in the doorway. She looked at me with an older face, much older than twenty, and so cold, so heartless. I said, "Leballech. He worked for Ferraldo, Mickey's boss. They drank a bottle of wine in this room. Him, his brother-in-law, and my brother-in-law. It was night, and there was snow in the yard behind you." Instinctively the girl turned to look behind her. I said, "Is my sister there?" She gestured no. I said, "Leballech was sitting at the end of the table, there, and his brother-in-law and Lello where I am now. All three of them had got the piano off the truck. They left it in the yard. Florimond was sitting by his father. They stayed for about an hour perhaps, talking and laughing like men do together. Then big Leballech and his brother-in-law left."

She didn't open her mouth. She stood there in her new dress, her face looking older, as if she no longer had any heart. I said gently, "Come in and shut the door." She shut the door. But she didn't come in. She went out and slammed it. I shouted, "Eliane!" But this time she didn't return. I went back step by step to my chair. I didn't know what time it was, morning or evening. I sat down again in my chair. My heart was racing and I felt breathless. I forced myself to think about something else. She's a good girl and I want her to stay that way.

I thought how pleased my husband was when, in 1938, we thought we were going to have a child. It was summer, like today, but the sun was closer. I was taken to the hospital. It wasn't true, I couldn't have a child, or he couldn't. We went on living and hoping all the same. He had a job with the streetcar company. My sister had gone back to Digne, to work in a laundry. I had my junior-high-school diploma. I'd like to have been a teacher, like the woman the girl was going to see now. You never get what you want in life. They kill your husband. There's nothing you can say. They take your summers away, one by one, till the sun is so far off you feel cold even in July. Hush. It will be Saturday the day after tomorrow, and the girl will be twenty. I can give her two thousand francs from my money. I'll still have six thousand left. That's plenty to bury a couple of widows. I wonder how, on May 27, 1944, I could have let go of my husband's hand when the bomb fell. I don't know, there's no explanation. I can't understand how the bomb could have been stronger than us.

THE INDICTMENT

They arrived about noon—the sun was directly overhead.
There was snow everywhere, on the mountains and on the fir
trees in front of the house, but the sun was warm like in April.
I knew it would be fine until evening, and then the wind would
come from the north and it would snow again. I know the
earth, I know the sky. I am the daughter of peasants. I was
born in Fiss, in the Tyrol. Everybody thinks I'm German, but
I'm Austrian. The French make no distinction. They call me
Eva Braun.

When I was young—about twelve, thirteen perhaps—I
scrubbed floors with my mother and my cousin Hertha in a
big hotel, the Zeppelin, in Berlin, and the porter, an impressive
man who could tap me with a stick when I wasn't scrubbing
fast enough, suddenly cried, "Look out into the street, it's Eva
Braun." We all ran to the tall windows, which reached to the
ceiling. He was pulling our leg. But we did see a young, fair-
haired woman leaving the ministry across from us, with some
ladies and officers. I remember her well-dressed hair, her little
hat, the gentle look about her. There were a lot of gray cars.
But of course it wasn't Eva Braun. The manager, a good man
who was named Herr Schlatter, said, "Come away from there.
Back to your work." It was on the Wilhelmstrasse, the finest
street in Berlin, opposite the Air Ministry. In the hotel lobby,
all along the wall of the main staircase, there was a Zeppelin
reproduced in ceramic, like a huge seventy-five-pfennig postage
stamp. But before that I was in Fiss, in the Tyrol. I know the
earth, the sky, and the mountains.

When they arrived I was outside, on the edge of the woods.
I saw the truck climbing the hill, from bend to bend. It was
a Saturday, in November 1955. I knew they'd taken the wrong

road. There was a fork four kilometers before Arrame, and sometimes drivers took the wrong turn. Otherwise no one ever came up to our house. I was holding a rabbit in my hand, by the hind legs; it had been caught in one of Gabriel's traps, twenty meters from our path. I had on only my combinations under my old American-army greatcoat, and rubber boots. I'd probably just washed up after working all morning in the house. And then I must have gone out, without getting dressed, when I saw the dead rabbit through the bedroom window. As I said, we never saw anyone.

I took a few steps into the snow, in the direction of the truck. There were three of them behind the windshield, but only the driver got out. He was tall, with a crewcut, and he was wearing a lumber jacket with a sheepskin collar. He said, "I think we took the wrong road. Where is Arrame?" I could see his breath in the cold air, yet the sun was as warm as in April. I was twenty-seven. I held my coat closed at my neck with one hand and the dead rabbit with the other. I said, "You took the wrong turn, you have to go left, by the stream." He nodded. He was surprised by my accent and looked at my knees, which showed through the gap of the coat. I don't know why, but I said, "Excuse me." The others were also looking at me from behind the windshield. He said, "That's a fine rabbit you have there." He turned to look at the house and the mountains around us and said, "You're nice and quiet here." I didn't know how to answer. There was a great silence over the snow—all we could hear was the revving of the engine. Finally he said, "Right, thank you. We'll get going, then." He climbed back into his truck. All three sat there looking at me. I waited for them to turn around and pass the house again before I went back indoors.

I'd been alone in the house since the day before: every three weeks Gabriel went to see his sister, Clémence, in Puget-Théniers, and he wouldn't be back until the next day. She would never let him take me along. From the silence of the house and the surroundings, and the way I was standing there, the driver may have guessed I was alone. The idea didn't frighten me. I was very shy at the time, even more so than now, but not particularly afraid of things. I'd exhausted most of my fear during the last months of the war.

I skinned the rabbit and put it in the meat safe in the cellar, where there were already some others; we ate nothing but rabbit that winter. I don't know what I did next. I got dressed about two or three o'clock. As I stood at the bedroom mirror, I thought of the three men in the truck. I thought particularly of the way one of them had looked at me through the window, from the bottom of the path, when I was wearing only my combinations under my greatcoat. I felt my heart beat faster. I can't say it was something else. I'm ashamed to admit it, but it was true. I didn't love Gabriel—except perhaps in the beginning, when we were on our way out of Germany—but I'd never been unfaithful to him. Yet I had this feeling in my heart when a man looked at me insistently and I thought he desired me. Since I was never unfaithful, I said to myself, "It's flirting." I now know I'm like my daughter—or, unfortunately, she has become like me. She thinks men love her because they want to make love to her. I've never told her the whole truth when she has pestered me with questions—I couldn't. No one could. I didn't tell her that when I stood at the mirror, before putting on my dress, I felt a thrill of pleasure in my throat. I didn't tell her that I could have gone down into the village and called on someone and said I was alone and afraid, and stayed with them. They would have called me Eva Braun and looked at me in the humiliating way they do, but if I'd done that nothing would have happened. Instead I tell my daughter, "There you are, you see. I can't regret it happened—otherwise you wouldn't be here, you understand? I don't care what happened so long as you're here." She doesn't understand. She just sits there, her mind fixed on her own thoughts, on the daddy who was taken from her, on another day of horror.

Yes, I remember how, before putting on my blue jersey dress, I stood for a moment stock-still at the mirror, thinking of that man's eyes. Not the driver in the lumber jacket, who spoke to me, or the younger one, who was wearing a Basque beret and smoking a cigarette behind the window. The one with the dark, shining eyes and thick black moustache—the one who knew I was wearing only my combinations under my coat and who wanted me. I saw myself through his eyes in the mirror, and I felt my heart beat faster. Or maybe I'm making it all up—accusing myself to punish myself for other sins. Maybe, after all, it was just anxiety I felt, the fear that makes animals like rabbits stand stock-still just before they're shot.

I was in the big room when they came back. Through the steamed-up window I could see the truck, which, this time, drove up the path to the house. My heart nearly stopped beating. I thought, "No, it can't be." But I knew it was—that was how my life was to be. I went out onto the doorstep. All three of them got out. They didn't speak. Only the youngest smiled, an embarrassed little smile, like a grimace of pain. They were drunk, I could see—they had the studied walk of drunks. They came up to the door, moving apart from one another. They stared at me, saying nothing. All I could hear in the white, empty world around us was the sound of their feet in the mud, on the ground in front of the house where I'd swept the snow.

I let out a cry and ran through the storeroom, which we later made into my daughter's bedroom, into the big room. My legs wouldn't carry me. I wasted time unbolting the door, and by the time I opened it, one of them, the one who had spoken to me that morning, was in front of me. He hit me. He said things I didn't understand. Then the other two were with him. They carried me into the bedroom. They tore off my dress. When I screamed they hit me again. The youngest one said, "You know what we'll do to you if you scream?" I was on the floor, crying. He said, "We'll break your nose and all your teeth with a poker." He left me there, lying at the feet of the other two. He came back, holding the poker. He gave me an evil look and said, "Go on, scream!" The one who had spoken to me threw his lumber jacket onto the bed and said, bending down over me, "You'd better keep quiet. We won't do you any harm if you don't resist." The youngest one raised the poker over my head and said, "Take off your dress, bitch."

I started crying again and said yes. I stood up and took off my torn dress. They pushed me onto the bed. The one who had spoken to me in the morning kept saying, "Be good now, and we'll leave you alone afterward." They made me take off my panties. They all had me. First two of them held my legs and arms while the youngest one was on top of me, but they felt I wasn't resisting and let me go. The one who had dark hair and eyes was next; he kissed me on the lips. The one who'd talked to me in the morning was left alone with me in the room. When he'd taken his pleasure he said, "You're right not to make a fuss about it. It's not worth getting your face spoiled."

He went out to join the others in the big room, leaving the door open. I wasn't crying any more. I couldn't think. I heard them rummaging in the cupboards getting themselves something to drink. Then the one with the dark eyes and the thick moustache came back to me and said, "Come on. They want to eat." I wanted to get some other clothes from the wardrobe, but the youngest one saw and came dashing into the room shouting, "Oh no!" He grabbed my arm and sent me flying into the big room. They'd torn off the straps of my combinations by pulling on them while I was on the bed. And I had to hold them up with one hand to cover my breasts. They laughed to see me like that.

Then they made me drink some wine. Big glasses full. The youngest one held me by the hair and said, "Come on, my pretty, drink up," and he looked at me with his evil eyes. I cooked a rabbit. I didn't know what time it was, except that night had fallen. At some point the one with the dark eyes, the one the other two called "the Italian," opened the door, and I could see the night and the snow. He took a deep breath. The youngest one said to the driver of the truck, "Look at all those stars; beautiful, isn't it?" He wanted me to go out and look at them, too. All you could hear, through the open door, was the cold wind coming from the north between the mountains. I was drunk and had to lean against the wall to stay on my feet.

The driver got me to sit on his knees while they ate and

drank, and he forced me to drink. They said something about music. They laughed. I think I did, too, or perhaps I was crying at the same time—I was drunk for the first time in my life. They put my army greatcoat around my shoulders and made me go out into the snow. They showed me the player piano in the back of the truck. It was a heavy upright piano, dark green in the light from over our door. There was a big gold letter *M* on the front. It was held by two ropes to keep it from moving. They started playing it. I fell to my knees in the snow, rubbing snow over my forehead and cheeks. Snatches of the tune must have been heard in the next village—it was "Roses of Picardy." The truck driver picked me up and wanted me to dance with him. I couldn't. I stood there in his arms, all the strength drained from me. He picked me up and I could feel my head bouncing up and down on his shoulder and my feet trailing in the snow.

Later they drank some brandy, and made me drink some, and the youngest made me stand naked in the kitchen to torment me more. I heard the Italian say, "Stop it. That's enough." But the youngest didn't want to stop, nor did the truck driver. I know I said, "I don't care. I don't care any more." I can remember only a few things about all that. I don't remember how long it lasted. I said I was named Paula. I smoked a French cigarette the youngest one gave me. When I looked at their faces, it was as if I had known them for a long, long time. They brought me back into the room, and had me again, and the youngest forced me to repeat that I was "their little woman." When I shut my eyes it was worse—the whole world seemed to swim around me.

Later still I was sick in the sink. They put my coat around my shoulders again, and the truck driver sat me down on the bench at the table and put on my rubber boots for me. They dragged me outside, saying they were going and I had to bid them good-bye. They kissed me on the lips one by one, and I let them, but inside I didn't want to. Not that it was of any importance after what they'd done to me but because of some idea that came into my drunken head—I was afraid of smelling of vomit. The youngest said, "I'd advise you to keep your mouth shut. Otherwise we might come back. And I'll break your nose and all your teeth." Before climbing into the truck he added, "Anyway, there'll be three of us to say you wanted it." The Italian stayed with me longest, by the truck. He was staggering; I remember his gray corduroy jacket and trousers. He managed to pull out a gold bill clip from his pocket and gave me some money. It was a hundred francs in today's money. I said no, very quietly, but he said, "Go on, take it," and closed my hand over it.

I watched the headlights and red rear lights of the truck descend the hill, then disappear behind the fir trees. I was naked under my coat, and cold. I was glad to be cold. I fell into the snow again before making it to the open door. I dragged myself inside, pulling my coat behind me. When I could feel I was on the tiled floor, I pushed the door behind me with my feet. I knew, through the confusion in my head, that I couldn't get to my bed. I pulled my coat under me and over me. I thought, "The stove is still lit, you must get closer to the stove." I couldn't. I didn't feel hurt anywhere, but there was no strength in my limbs. I heard a sharp, strange sound, which wasn't that of the alarm clock on the mantelpiece. It took me a long time to realize it was my teeth chattering. Then I yelled at the top of my voice and started to sob, hoping I'd be dead next morning.

When he came back, Gabriel found me in the same position, crouching in my coat on the floor. My feet were across the door, and I came to when he tried to open it. He was annoyed because the light had been left on outside all night. I moved my legs, and then he pushed the door and saw me. He also saw the dirty plates and the bottles on the table. He stood there saying nothing. Then he picked me up and carried me to the bed. The sheets and blankets were on the floor, and he picked them up to cover me. He stayed lying beside me to stop my shivering. Then he said, "It's not true. It's not true." The light flooded in through the curtains, and I thought I'd slept for a long time. When Gabriel pushed open the door and I opened my eyes, I was surprised not to find myself in the cellar where I'd slept during the last weeks of the war in Berlin. Yet I'd been in that house for nine years.

He went to make some coffee. I heard him lighting the stove. He must have had time to think about the mess in the room, because when he came back he said, "The bastards! I'll go and get the police." He was still wearing his overcoat and scarf. He drank a large bowl of coffee. My lips felt swollen and strange, and my right eye did, too. I hadn't noticed it the day before, but from the way Gabriel moved his fingers over my face, I realized I must have bruises where they'd hit me. "Do you know who they were?" he asked me. "Are they from around here?" I shook my head. He repeated, "I'm going to get the police." But I knew he wouldn't. I said, to make things easier for him, "Even if they find them, no one will believe me. They warned me. They'll say I wanted it." He looked at me, nervously shaking his head. "They hit you. Anyone can see that." Then I said, "You've hit me, too. And anyone could see that." After a while I said, "Don't do anything. Everyone will know and make fun of us." He struck his thighs with his fists, sitting there on the bed, but didn't answer.

He stayed for a long time like that, without moving. Then, turning toward me, he said, "I'll find them. I'll kill them with my own hands." I knew he wouldn't do that, either. He was thirty-three then, and twenty-three when I first met him. He was afraid of everything. He was proud of being the local watchman and road mender; he felt protected by his badge of office, on which was written THE LAW. But apart from me and a few poor vagabonds, he never quarreled with anyone, except over money. He was even more stingy than afraid, and that's why I didn't love him. I only asked him to marry me once, in 1946, just before the birth of our child. He never did—he didn't want to fall out with his sister, Clémence, who had property from her husband's family, and who had promised to leave him a big inheritance. As far as I've ever been able to find out after so many years, it consists of the house she lives in at Puget-Théniers and a small vineyard.

We spent that Sunday together indoors—something that hadn't happened for a long time. Gabriel had promised to go sweep the snow in front of the town hall and on the path the children used to go up to school, but he didn't. I washed and dressed. In the mirror, I saw I had a dark bruise on one cheekbone and swollen lips on the same side. All around my right eye was swollen, too. Like once in Fiss, when I was stung by a wasp. I'd caught a cold, which didn't bother me—I throw off colds very easily—but when I saw myself like that, I wanted to start crying again. On my arms and legs I had lighter marks, and on my left shoulder there was a bruise from the punch one of them gave me when they caught me in the storeroom. This punch hurt me the longest.

I told Gabriel what had happened, as best I could in a language that isn't my own. All afternoon he marched up and down, pestering me with questions. It only made him worse, and he began drinking wine to convince himself "he would kill them with his own hands." I did the dishes, cleaned up the house, and went to feed the chickens. At one point I felt like laughing, when I saw how life had gone on in the meantime and how, in a sense, nothing had happened. Gabriel, who followed me everywhere, asked, "Why are you laughing?" I said, "I don't know. Just nerves." He looked down. He went on walking around the big room, and then suddenly he went to get his boots and leather jacket and said, "I'm calling the doctor. You don't know me. They're even going to pay for the doctor."

He went out on foot to telephone to the village. Night fell. I went around the house again, with a duster, in case the doctor came. Just then I remembered, like some detail in a dream, that the Italian had put money in my hand before getting back into the truck. I found the two crumpled notes in one of the pockets of my khaki coat. I don't know whether it was fever or fear that everything would turn against me, but I started shaking from head to foot. I threw the notes into the stove fire and waited to make sure that nothing was left of them before putting the lid on again.

When Gabriel came back, three-quarters of an hour later, he said, "The doctor's not at home on Sundays, but they're going to tell him." I thought he hadn't dared to telephone at all or do anything at the last moment, as usual, and I really felt relieved. I was wrong. Dr. Conte arrived while we were eating, and Gabriel burst into tears. Dr. Conte was forty at the time. He ran around the whole region in his rubber boots and big checked jacket, treating children and looking after pregnant women. I had no great respect for him, because I was stupid, and he wasn't just as I imagined a doctor should be, but I changed my mind that evening. He examined me in the bedroom and asked Gabriel to stay outside. Then he said to me, "If you want to lodge a complaint, I'll support you." I said I didn't want everyone to know. He just shook his head, and went out while I got dressed. In the big room he sat at the table to make out a prescription, and I poured him a glass of wine. He said to Gabriel, "She's been beaten, I can certify to that. What are you thinking of doing?" Gabriel said, "Beaten? And what about the rest?" Dr. Conte shrugged his shoulders. "She's been raped, hasn't she?" Gabriel asked. Dr. Conte replied, "She's been raped because she has told me so. And I believe her. Now, what are you going to do about it?" Gabriel sat facing him, on the other side of the table, and said, "What would you do in my place?" "In your place," said Dr. Conte, "I wouldn't have wasted a whole day. They'd have been caught already, whatever the consequences for me. Now, if you like, I'll take your wife to the hospital in Draguignan. I have all the proof we need." Gabriel looked at me, then lowered his head. I said, "It's not Gabriel, *I* don't want to. I'm a foreigner. The people in the village will make fun of us and say I'm a bad woman, they won't believe me."

The doctor hadn't drunk his wine. He picked up his briefcase from the table, and as he got up he said to me, "I don't agree with you." I looked him straight in the eyes; they were blue, with wrinkles underneath, the eyes of a man who did not agree with me or with many other things, a tired man.

I met Gabriel in April 1945, when we fled from Berlin and I was following, with my mother and other refugees, the columns of soldiers going south. It was in a village, early one morning, near Chemnitz. We'd already lost my cousin Hertha, who was three years older than me, between Torgau and Leipzig, because she got into one truck and we got into another. And that morning I also lost my mother. I think she went in a different direction, toward Kassel, to the west, where she had friends, and died on the way.

When I saw Gabriel for the first time, he looked like a stray dog. He was wearing a long black raincoat that had only one sleeve left, and a woolen cap pulled down over his ears. He was drinking water at the fountain in that village—I can't remember its name. I was seventeen, and though he was six years older than me, he looked like all the French, as if he'd been punished for something he hadn't done. I knew right away he was French. I was thirsty, too, but it was *his* fountain. Finally my mother gave him a good shove in the back with her bag.

The three of us walked into the village. I spoke a little French, which I'd picked up from other forced laborers, like him, in Berlin. I understood that he, too, wanted to go south. My mother said she would go get some ham—someone had told her where she could find it. She was like I am now. Forty-five, with fairish hair pinned up at the back. She was wearing her old black coat with an otter-fur collar. That was the last I was to see of her. I didn't know it then, of course, and I was glad to be away from Berlin and to show I knew a little French. It seemed everything would turn out all right. We looked for a truck again, and for once there was enough gas to get us to the Danube. My mother had always said, "When you see the Danube, your troubles will be over." And she was right in a way, except that I saw the Danube far away from where we were aiming for, which was Linz, in Austria, but it's a very long river, and life is long, too, and I was still only a kid.

When the American planes flew over the village and began to machine-gun the convoys of soldiers, Gabriel and I ran through the narrow streets, and an officer pushed us into a truck at revolver point, yelling that he would kill us once and for all. That's where I lost my mother. I yelled back that my mother was in the village, he had to wait for her, but the truck was already on its way and I lost my mother. Since then I've looked at maps of Germany. I can't remember the name of the village. I don't even know what day it was. It was in April, near Chemnitz. The night before, in a barn, she had talked about going in the direction of Kassel, to the west, where she had friends, and she must have thought I'd remember and head for Kassel, too. I don't know. I wrote to Kassel and o Fiss. No one knew anything.

I saw the Danube at Ulm, about ten days later. It's a big, gray river, like any other; Gabriel was pleased because that region was being occupied by French soldiers—there was a blue, white, and red flag on the citadel. I was already wearing my warm American greatcoat, which I'd removed from a corpse in a field. A French officer took Gabriel to one side to speak to him. I stayed in a depot, beside a railway, and just before dawn I walked along the railway and found Gabriel. They'd been beating him because he didn't want to be a soldier, and I said, "Don't cry, don't cry. We'll go to Fiss, where I come from. I know people there."

First we walked in the direction of Fiss, but the French tanks were now arriving everywhere through Württemberg, and in the last week of April, at Kempten, we turned back northward. Gabriel was afraid to stay with his fellow countrymen— he didn't want to be called a coward and get beaten up again. At night we slept in the woods, with other refugees, or on a truck, when we could find one. Food was less difficult to find than a truck, especially when we were with the Americans. They had more supplies than the French and gave us things. I remember the beautiful cardboard boxes that looked waxed on the surface, and all the good things they had inside—meat and vegetables, pineapple in syrup, cheese, crackers, chocolate, cigarettes, and even Dentyne chewing gum—everything a soldier would need for a day.

For several weeks Gabriel worked for the Americans in Fulda, after the Armistice had been signed. We had a room in a shed, and Gabriel was in charge of the German prisoners who were repairing the bridges. We had a lot to eat, clothes, everything. Once an American soldier even put some silk stockings under my window, with a letter in bad German asking me to meet him. I tore up the letter and didn't go, because I was making love with Gabriel and I didn't want to look at anyone else.

We came to France in August 1945, with a big suitcase full of food, and the first town I saw was Lyon. Gabriel sold the food there and we took a train to Nice; then another, much smaller train, with the back of the last carriage like those in the American Far West, brought us to Puget-Théniers. I stayed outside, on the road, while he talked to his sister, Clémence. She opened the front door of her house just enough to see me, but she didn't come out. She didn't even say anything to me. I was three months pregnant, and I was worried that Gabriel would get rid of me because his sister would not want an Austrian girl—and he always listened to what his sister said. I remember I played with pebbles by the edge of the road, black and white pebbles, to discover whether he would keep me or not. I still remember my shadow in the sun, on the road, and the buzzing of the insects in the heat. I was seventeen at the time and had lost everyone; I was used to taking care of myself. If I'd had to go back, I think I would have said nothing, I would have managed somehow. I'm more shy about talking than doing. I'd have gone back to Fiss or somewhere, but I have no regrets. I already loved God, and He knew how things had to work out for me to have my little Eliane.

I lost my first child, who was also a girl, a few hours after her birth. She lived for an afternoon, at my bedside in Arrame, then she stopped breathing. She was dead. She'd only been inside me for seven months, which is not enough, unless I'd been in the hospital and they could have put her in isolation, I don't know. I was sad, of course, but I felt relieved of a certain responsibility. That's perhaps why God punished me and wanted me to pay for the happiness of having my little Eliane, ten years later. She wasn't even eight months inside me, either, but she weighed five pounds and was well formed, right down to her fingernails, and she cried as soon as she left my womb. Dr. Conte delivered her. He laughed and said, "My little lady, children born in July are the most lively, but they are also the most bother, and this one is going to bother you for the rest of your life."

Gabriel didn't want this child, because it wasn't his. He said to me, "Get rid of it, go see the doctor. Explain to him." I went to see Dr. Conte in town; it was in February. He lowered his eyes and said, "I can't do that. I've never done it. It's against life." I was happy. I respected him, and I respected myself. I said to Gabriel, "The doctor thinks it's a bad thing to do, and I do, too." He said, "We'll find a midwife who'll do it." We were sitting on either side of the table, in the big room. I was wearing my American coat and my thick scarf—I'd just come from the bus. I said, "No, I want my child. I don't know who the father is, but I don't care. I'll go back to my own country if you like." He said nothing—and he said nothing all that night and the following day. Then he went to Puget-Théniers to ask his sister, Clémence, what we should do. When he came back he said, "Do what you like, I'll never recognize that child. There's no reason why I should." I said, "No, there's no reason." I went on with the laundry I was doing.

When I had my daughter, it was Gabriel who went to the town hall in Arrame to declare her. He came back shortly afterward, livid. He'd been drinking, and he yelled at me from the big room, "I've had an argument with the mayor—you've got to go see him." I'd asked him several times to let me have the baby in the hospital because we could have declared it where we weren't known, but he hadn't wanted me to. Even the hospital cost too much for him. I got up on the third day, and a woodcutter came to collect me in his van, at the mayor's request. All the time I was gone, I was afraid Gabriel would do my daughter some injury.

The mayor, M. Rocca, was a good man. It was mainly thanks to him, two years before, that I got my naturalization. Now he said, "Devigne doesn't seem to want to acknowledge he's the father. But I want to hear it from you, too." I said, "Devigne is not the father." M. Rocca went all red in the face. He didn't dare ask me who the father was, and he sat there for a long time, biting his lip, without looking at me. I said, "I don't know who the father is." He lowered his head and wrote Eliane on the register. I gave the Christian names—Manuela, because it was my mother's name, and Hertha, which was my cousin's. I don't know where I got Eliane from—I just liked it. I still do. M. Rocca said, "Devigne is a pig." I said, "No, he's not the father, that's all."

Before leaving the little room, just above a nursery school that is in the same building, I said to him, without daring to look at him, "Monsieur Rocca, please. It would be a great shame for me if people knew." He just shook his head and said, "You're very tired. Go home and don't worry about that. I know what's what." He never said to anyone what he'd written in the register. Long before they destroyed Arrame, he retired to Nice. One New Year I sent him a card. I bought it because it was pretty and I couldn't think of anyone I wanted to wish a Happy New Year to. I didn't have his address. I just wrote on the envelope: *M. Rocca, former mayor of Arrame, Nice.* I don't know whether he ever got it.

When she was little, everyone called her "the Devigne girl," and at nursery school she was Eliane Devigne, and at the school in Le Brusquet, too. She never knew that wasn't her real name until we took her to Grenoble to see an oculist.

That was in September 1966; she was ten. She had already been treated in town for her nearsightedness. But her glasses were giving her headaches, and she wouldn't wear them, especially since Gabriel, when he'd been drinking, called her

"Four Eyes." He didn't mean any harm, because little by little he'd come to think the world of my daughter. But a terrible sadness came over him when he'd had too much to drink, and it was no longer clear whether he was teasing the girl or whether he wanted her to love him as he loved her.

With her he even gave up his stinginess. When she was only two or three, she'd toddle after him saying, "My nice daddy," and I never saw him refuse her a single thing she asked for. When he came home in the evening, he'd pull out of his coat pockets whatever she'd asked for, little toys, candy, and later the silver heart she still has. She was very winning and very obedient with me, but for her, her daddy was a god. To impress her he boasted of having crossed Germany and survived everything. She looked up at him with her big blue eyes full of admiration, as she sat on his lap at the table after dinner. I'd say, "We must go to bed now, we have to get up in the morning." She'd wave her hands at me and say, "Be quiet, you. Let me talk with my daddy." He laughed and kissed her. He felt strong with the little thing in his arms, and even I, who knew him too well, saw him as stronger, more like the man I would have wanted. She was also proud, as she grew up, because he was the watchman and her little school friends got quiet when they walked past him. She was proud of everything he was.

One day Gabriel said to me, "I've been asking around about the girl's eyes. We must take her to Grenoble." That's how she found out her name was Wieck. The oculist filled out the form for the new glasses and said, "Eliane Wieck." My daughter said nothing at first. She just took the form before I could get hold of it and looked at it.

The three of us had lunch in a restaurant near a park in Grenoble, and she asked, "Why don't I have the same name as my daddy?" There was a dog that kept running all around her in that restaurant. She gave it scraps of meat under the table. Gabriel said, "It's because of the war. I'll explain it to you when you're older. But it makes no difference." I realized as I looked at my daughter that God was beginning to send me new trials, to punish me for my sins. She answered, calculating quickly, "The war was finished long before I was born." We went on with our meal, and Gabriel, who was unhappy, questioned the bill, just to have an argument, just for the sake of it. Eliane said nothing. If you didn't know her, you might have thought all her attention was centered on the dog, which never left her side. Then Gabriel repeated, "I'll explain it to you. It's not important." She looked at him and nodded. She wanted to believe him—no one has ever seen such a desire to believe, a desire that nothing should change, in the eyes of a little girl. Gabriel said, "Come on. We must be going or we'll miss our train."

It was late when we got home, and the girl, who had said nothing since we left the restaurant, went straight to the bedroom Gabriel had arranged for her in the storeroom. Gabriel went in to see her and stayed for a long time talking to her. He came back into our bedroom with red eyes, saying, "I'm going to recognize her. We have the right." He went to bed. I thought about it for over half an hour. Then I said to him, "You could recognize her if I said it was true. But it isn't true. One way or another she'll have to learn the truth. I'll tell her when she's older." Gabriel said, "You want to keep her for yourself. You don't want to let her be my daughter—that's the truth of the matter!" It wasn't as simple as that in my head, but he was right. The girl was ten, and I was thirty-eight. I'd made love with other men than Gabriel since her birth. I no longer knew what the future held in store for me.

Later I always refused to let him recognize her. It wouldn't have made things any better anyway. He was still her daddy, and she clung to him, sometimes even more desperately than before. But it was as if the anxiety over what she was going to learn one day was already inside her. It was from that time— the visit to Grenoble—that she stopped working at school and began to bite her fingernails. At thirteen or fourteen, she wanted to wear lipstick. Gabriel said, lowering his head, "Let her; you wore it." I had to stop her.

It was already her second year in the same class. She was

good only at arithmetic, by some gift that God had given her at birth, but she didn't even do her homework. She went around with Gabriel all the time when she wasn't at school. She'd sit on the embankment while he was working. He didn't want her to help him fill in the holes on the roads or cut the trees, but little by little she began to do so.

Gabriel's attitude changed once more. A woman knows. When she was washing, for example, he no longer dared to come into the room. He was afraid to see her as anything but his little girl; he didn't yet know it was already too late. Once she said to him, "Daddy, you don't kiss me as much as you used to. Don't you love me any more?" He said, "You're a big girl now." It was true, she was a big girl, and a beautiful girl, and she sensed that her daddy no longer came into the room when she was washing and no longer kissed her like he used to. She wasn't so proud as she used to be that he was the watchman. She had to listen to her school friends making jokes about old Devigne. Once she came in with her hair all mussed up—she'd been fighting with a boy, the son of Pellegrin the carpenter. She said, "I let him have it. He'll remember my teeth." Mme Pellegrin came around to see me next day. Her son was a year younger than Elle. She said Eliane had bitten him on the arms, hands, and even one thigh. I laughed and said her son should be careful what he said about my husband. She said, "Just like a German," and left.

For some months we went on living like a real family, but I knew, I knew something would happen, that life is long and cruel, and you must be ready to bear everything.

On October 14, 1971, in the early afternoon, my daughter went out with her daddy to prune the trees along the path. She was fifteen. They were carrying the big ladder together; she was walking behind him. I can still see them. It had rained a lot during the previous week. It was mild, but everything was soaking wet. She came back two hours later, a wild look in her eyes, crying in great sobs. She said she had struck and struck at Gabriel's head with a spade and killed him.

THE SENTENCE

I banged the door on Aunt Deaf-and-Dumb and crossed the yard. I walked stiffly in my new dress, which rustles with every step, the blood drained from my body. Mother Dolorosa was beating her washing near the spring. Maybe she asked me where I was going, but I didn't answer.

I lost my balance as soon as I was beyond the gate. I leaned against the wall and talked to myself, urging myself to stand up straight, in case some idiot from the village saw me, but the back of my head hurt and there were so many stars in my eyes and tears, who knows, that the whole world was suddenly reduced to the tiny patch of ground I stood on. I seemed to fall forward a thousand years before I found myself again, head over heels.

Then, as always, it passed.

I got up, wiped my knees with my fingers and spit, and picked up my canvas bag, which I'd dropped. I could no longer remember what I'd gone out for. Then it came back to me—to see my old schoolteacher Mlle Dieu in Le Brusquet. I didn't need to now. I'd wanted to ask her to get information about truck drivers who might have come to Arrame in November 1955, but I didn't need to now. Anyway, she's an old fool. I bet she hasn't discovered anything, I said to myself. She's the mayor of the village at the moment, and the only educated person in it, so no one would have thought to go and look into her registers. She must have spent her nights biting her pillow, thinking of what I promised her last time, in exchange for a little information from my birth certificate. But she wouldn't budge—she said she knew what was right and what was wrong, and just stuck to the idea of an unknown father. She was a fool. I didn't even want to think about her any more.

I was walking on my shadow, at the side of the road, under the killing sun, when who should overtake me in his beat-up Peugeot 404 but Merriot, a retired railway worker. He slammed on his brakes, and there he was with his plastered-down white hair.. He spoke to me as if I was the Virgin Mary. I said I wasn't going into town, just to the Massignes'. I got in and sat next to him, all sweet and polite, thank you, Monsieur Merriot, my knees well covered, the whole bit. You have to shout in his car to be heard, and it smells of cats. "So you're going to marry Ping-Pong?" he yelled. I answered, "Oh yes, I can't wait." He said, "What?" Just like Cognata. But since I didn't like him a thousandth or a millionth as much as the old woman, I let it drop. After a while he yelled that his cat had been killed, and he started a whole song and dance on the cruelty of people. I shook my head and said how I sympathized with all my heart, but I wasn't even listening. I was afraid the old fool might think he was still on his rails and miss a turn.

I thought of Boo-Boo, who'd accused me of stoning the animal to death. Why me? He's funny, that Boo-Boo. Because he's dying to make love with Elle, and he's afraid it will happen one day, he accuses her of anything, just to make her seem cheap or crazy or something. I hate touching dogs, cats, or any animals, even with a stick. I wouldn't even kill an ant. I wouldn't have to go back to school to guess who killed Merriot's cat and Mme Buygues's cat, but I'm not a tattletale. Anyway, who cares.

I got out of the car safe and sound, just at the end of the path that leads to Georges Massigne's farmhouse. I said, "Thank you, Monsieur Merriot, give my regards to your wife." He said, "I hope you'll invite us to the wedding?" I said, "What do you think?" Sweet as honey, and my face broke into my Child of Mary smile. All that for a guy who may be in his grave before they set the table for the wedding breakfast, and whose car will probably fall apart at the next corner. I have a soft spot for old men, I don't know why.

At the Massignes', where I'd never set foot before, the earth was red, the walls of gray stone. It was bigger and more orderly

than Ping-Pong's place. In the yard I was met by a barking dog
on the end of a chain, and people came from every direction
to see who'd come: Georges, Georges's three sisters, 114 nephews and nieces, the mother, one of the mothers-in-law, etc.,
etc. I kept my distance because of the dog. Georges came up
to me, wiping his hands on his trousers. It was scorching hot,
and all around the land was dry and desolate.

He said, "It's you?" as if I was an apparition. I said, "I've
got to talk to you. Do you have a lot of work? Could you take
me into town?" He thought for a couple of seconds and said,
"If you like, but we could talk here, no one will eat you." All
the others just stood there staring at me. I said no, I had to
go into town anyway.

I waited at the yard gate while he got out his van from one
of the barns. He gave no explanation to his family. He wanted
to show me that he was boss and he didn't need to give one.
Once I was sitting there beside him, and we'd been driving
along the path leading to the main road, I told him to stop,
and he did. I told him how I'd come to say I was sorry, because
I wouldn't be able to ask him to my wedding. He said he
understood, it was all right. He looked really serious. His hair
was yellow and wavy. And his face square-cut—he reminded
me of an American actor in *Peyton Place*, I can't remember
his name. Georges was wearing a tee shirt and his arms were
the same color as his land. I said, "It's a pity, since the Montecciaris got along well with your family before I arrived on
the scene." He said, "Nothing has changed. It's perfectly understandable that Ping-Pong wouldn't want to see me at his
wedding. Afterward it will all blow over. We'll become friends
again, him and me."

I could have said a lot, just to stir things up a bit more, but
that's not why I'd come, and I sat there for ten thousand years
saying nothing, my knees well covered, a real statue of modesty.
Finally he sighed. Then I sighed. I said, "I've even been told
that Mother Montecciari spent the whole night in your house,
when your father died." He said, "Yes?" Like someone who

was too young to remember. I said, "When did he actually die?" First he said in 1956, then no, it was in 1955, in November. He was five at the time—he was the same age as Mickey. He said, "All Sunday we'd been celebrating my sister Jo's baptism, and the next day, in the snow, he smashed his tractor trying to tear up a chestnut stump and got crushed underneath it."

My heart was beating and my voice trembling somewhat when I said, "It must have been awful," but it suited the situation. So old Massigne died on a Monday, precisely the same Monday, November 21, 1955—and that explained a detail that had bothered me when Cognata was talking to me. The three men in the truck who attacked my mother set out on Saturday night, very late. She couldn't remember the time, or perhaps she never knew it, but it was at least eleven, maybe midnight. When Cognata was talking to me, I thought right away of Ping-Pong, aged ten, still up *an hour or two later*, squatting between his father's legs while the three men drank wine in the kitchen. It just didn't sound right, and that detail bothered me. Now I understood that they were too drunk, and it was too late. They couldn't have brought back the player piano on Saturday, so they waited until Monday, at nightfall.

I said to Georges, "Be a good boy and take me into town now." On the way, from one bend in the road to the next, he told me what a great guy his father had been. Take a boy—twenty-five, thirty years old, any age. Nine out of ten times, he will tell you with tears in his eyes that his father was the greatest guy who ever lived. Nine times out of ten. And for the one who doesn't, the old man has to have killed the rest of the family with a hatchet or something, or you can't stop him from talking about him. They all want to talk about their fathers, for hours on end, until you get to town and they drop you off, with your head full, outside Ferraldo's sawmill.

I thanked Georges, kissed him on the cheek like a good girl, and gave a deep sigh for old time's sake. He looked at me and sighed back. He muttered that I really was a pretty girl, yes, a very pretty girl, but that was life. He wasn't looking at me any more when he said that. A grim expression all over his face, he stared at his own rotten life through the windshield. If they put that scene into a film, there wouldn't be a dry eye in the house.

Finally I took his hand from the steering wheel and put it for the last time between my thighs, under my dress, just so he could sleep quietly that night, and got out. I gave him a sad little wave of good-bye, then turned around, overcome with sadness, the whole bit, and went in to see Mickey's boss.

In the sawmill the noise was deafening. Men covered with sawdust turned around as I walked past, a big truck nearly ran me over, but I emerged in one piece in a small office, with a secretary I'd often seen at the dance or the movies. She was the same age as me and was also nearsighted. Her name was Elisabeth. She wore huge, fancy glasses that turned into bird's wings at the sides. We talked for a while about my dress, my superb hair, and her hair, which is awful. Then she took out a bottle of tonic water for me, from an Arthur Martin refrigerator they had in a corner, and went to get her boss. My mother has an Arthur Martin, too, but it's twice as big.

Ferraldo is a small, rather cold man, with a long pointed nose. He's about fifty, maybe, not much hair left, with sawdust all over his clothes, like everybody there. When he saw me, he thought I'd come to talk to Mickey. He said, "Mickey's not here but he won't be long, sit down." I said no, I wouldn't be long, it was him I had come to see. He asked Elisabeth to go on with her work and took me into his own office, which was exactly like the other one. He's not a man who smiles much, but he's got a kind heart. Mickey said so, and Ping-Pong.

He sat down behind his desk, and I said, standing before him, "Well, I'm sorry to disturb you, I know how it is, but I've come to talk to you on behalf of my father, who is paralyzed." He nodded, as if to say he knew and felt sorry for the poor old shithead. I said, "He wants to know what happened to one of your employees. Maybe he's still with you. His name is Leballech." He sighed and said, "Jeannot Leballech? Oh, that was a long time ago. He was here when my father ran the business   must be twenty years since he left." He gestured for me to sit down on a chair near him, moved his own back a little, and sat down.

He said, "When he left, it was to take over a sawmill of his own, near Digne. I think he's still there. The last time I saw him must have been about five or six years ago, I don't know." Since I kept nodding and said nothing, he looked at me for a long time, as if searching for something to add. Then: "Yes, I think he's still in Digne. On the La Javie road. He's got a good sawmill there. Why, did your father know him?" I said yes but changed the subject. I said, "It's funny, because the Montecciaris knew him, too. It was he who brought their player piano back to the village once. Do you remember?" He shook his head; maybe he didn't even know that the Montecciaris had a player piano. Then suddenly he said, "Wait. What year was that?" "In 1955, November 1955." I almost had the exact day on my lips, but I knew I shouldn't reveal everything— I stopped myself just in time. Without taking his eyes off me, he sat there thinking, his forehead all wrinkled. After a million heartbeats, which seemed so loud I was afraid he might hear them, he got up and went out.

I sat waiting. He came back four hours later with a thick notebook, bound in black canvas, and he showed me, as he sat down, the label stuck on the back: *1955*. He turned the pages, licking his finger, and said, "Yes, I remember. My father made quite a scene about it. A player piano." I knew I shouldn't but I couldn't help it—I got up and went around to his side of the desk, to see for myself. He didn't look up or say anything. At Saturday, November 19, 1955, he stopped; I could see as well as he could, written in fine handwriting in black ink, at the bottom of the page:

> *Leballech/Berliet:*
> *Lumber, Bonnet's building site, La Fourche*
> *Fencing, M. Poncet, Arrame*
> *Piano, Montecciari, Combes Pass*

In the margin there were prices, which seemed to me like a fortune, but they were old francs; then, underneath, in another handwriting:

Pass closed. Piano Monday night.

Without looking up, Ferraldo said, "You see." He turned the page to look at Monday, November 21, but there was nothing except that Leballech was still driving the Berliet and transported some telegraph poles.

Ferraldo was very proud of his register. He said, "My father taught me to keep it every day, and he was right. The handwriting's my mother's. It's really something to look at it again." He closed the book and stroked the black canvas of the cover. I moved away a little, while he took a thousand years to think about his old people. Then he said, "Yes, I remember. Leballech got stuck in the snow and didn't come back that Saturday night. My father didn't like it at all when his trucks weren't brought back at night." He shook his head and got up. "Leballech left us shortly afterward." I said, "They'll be glad to know what happened to him at home. Thank you very much, Monsieur Ferraldo."

He followed me out of his office, and in the passageway I stopped and, looking like some silly woman who'd forget her head if it wasn't well screwed on, said, "Oh, by the way, that's not why I came to see you! It was to invite you to my wedding. I was afraid Mickey might not dare to ask you himself, you being his boss. . . ." He laughed as much as he ever did. "That would be the first time Mickey didn't dare to ask for something," he said. "Whatever he is, he certainly isn't shy." He sighed, probably adding up all the mistakes my future brother-in-law must have made since coming to work there, but he gave up and made a gesture as if to sweep it from his mind. "He's already invited me, so don't worry." I said, "Then please don't tell him I've been here. You know how he is." He sighed again and put his skinny hand on my shoulder, to be fatherly or to see how plump it was, who knows. He said, "In any case, I congratulate you. I think very highly of Ping-Pong."

When he went back to his work, I saw Elisabeth in the office. She was typing, a thick lock of hair over her nose. To bring her up to the right height, she'd stuck telephone directories under her ass, and trying to get the one I wanted nearly caused a riot. She kept repeating, "Yes, yes, Digne, it's in the Alpes-Maritimes." Geography and I disagreed at birth, so I let her do it her own way. In the end, it turned out to be in the next department over, the Alpes de Haute-Provence. She said, "Oh, not by very much, not by very much." I tell you, you could say anything to Elisabeth—what mattered for her was that the conversation should last until closing time.

I looked up Leballech in the directory. I drank the tonic she had given me earlier right from the bottle—it was still cold. She never took her eyes off me from behind her owl glasses. I did my best to keep her from seeing that all the letters were blurred for me, that I was God knows where when I thought I was at Digne; finally I gave her the book back, asking her to look it up for me while I called home.

I called Henri IV's garage. Juliette answered. "Juliette? It's Eliane. Am I disturbing you?" Sweet as honey, just a little accent. No, I wasn't disturbing her. I said, "My mother is altering the dress. I wanted to thank you. It's very, very beautiful." For the next ten years she went on about her own wedding, but I wasn't even listening. Elisabeth gestured that she had found Leballech, and I said into the telephone, "Juliette, listen. Tell Ping-Pong I'm having dinner with my schoolteacher in Le Brusquet, and she'll bring me back, and he's not to worry." She said O.K., then she made me repeat it about fourteen times, the last time without an accent because I thought it might be the accent that was making her so stupid. Finally I said, "You'll see. I'll do your dress justice. It's marvelous."

When I hung up, Elisabeth was holding out to me the bottle of tonic, which I hadn't finished, and the open directory. I tore out the page she was showing me. "Oh!" she said, and laughed. I said, "You know I'm getting married." She nodded gravely, the trace of a smile around her eyes. I said, "That won't stop us from being friends, though, will it?" I suddenly wanted to love everybody, I don't know why. I folded the page from the directory in quarters and put it in my canvas bag. I looked at my watch, which my mother had ordered from Trois Suisses for my birthday, which was two days later. It's a modern watch, but it's got roman numerals, which makes it look more expensive. Nearly five o'clock. "Well, will it?" I repeated. She said, "Not as far as I'm concerned." We both laughed, and I took off. I used the rear exit, to avoid meeting Mickey in the yard.

I went straight to the bus station. There was nothing for Digne until six, even if I crushed my nose against the glass over the timetable. I thought it would be better to set off on foot. If no one picked me up on the outskirts of town, there'd still be time to catch the bus. Usually, for me, the first car stops. I think people must feel sorry for me—I'm not pretentious.

I crossed the square and went into Philippe's pharmacy to telephone Mlle Dieu. His girl assistant was with him—a real cure for love, that one—and I didn't want to speak in front of her. He took me to the storeroom at the back where only last year he used to get me to undress once or twice every couple of weeks. It was enough for him just to look at me, or, on rare occasions, just to make me even crazier—I was ready to be locked up after each session—he'd stroke my breasts or my belly with his finger tips. I tried everything—I made fun of him, begged him—but it was no use. All he wanted to do was look at me. Yet in the end I was more in love with him than anyone. Twenty-four hours before our date I'd have butterflies in my stomach. Try to figure that out.

Even now, standing at the wall telephone, surrounded by the same medicine-filled shelves, in the same orange light from the ceiling, I felt all nervous. Philippe had gone back into the shop—he loses all control, too, when he see me—and I rang Mlle Dieu, first at the town hall, then at home. When she answered, her voice sounded as if she was at the other end of the world, Australia or something, or the North Pole—it was so icy. She said I'd promised, she'd been waiting for me all afternoon with her cakes and cookies, she'd even made some ice cream and had a birthday present for me—I had to shout to interrupt the flow. She stopped talking; I imagined her biting her lower lip, looking at her feet, wearing a bright yellow pleated skirt, which she'd put on because last time I told her she looked good in it. I said, "O.K., listen, Calamity." That's what she used to call me when I was in her class, and that's what I call her now. I said, "Get your car and come pick me up in Digne." She nearly choked. "In Digne!" She's thirty-one and has had her driver's license for ten years, she's got a little car in which you don't have to change gears, but only three times has she ever had to go beyond the boundary of her district. I said, "Yes, it's very important. You must come. You've got plenty of time. You don't have to be there until about eight." After all the whys—"I'll explain"—and all the hows—"by the road, of course!"—she said nothing for a thousand years, just to allow the idea to sink in, then asked, in a plaintive voice, "Where at eight o'clock? I've never set foot in Digne." Neither had I, so we were bound to meet.

I told her to hold on for a second. I went to see Philippe in the shop. He was serving a customer I knew by sight, who made room for me at the counter. I asked where I could arrange to meet someone in Digne, so the poor girl wouldn't have to go around in circles till this time next year. Between them, they found a place.

When I got back to the telephone, Mlle Dieu wasn't on the line, but she hadn't hung up. I waited with the patience that is one of my most attractive qualities. I looked at the locked safe where Philippe puts his poisons and dangerous products. At first I'd pursued him only to get him to explain certain things to me and to find an opportunity, between two divine ecstasies, of opening that bitch of a safe. When the opportunity did come, and I got what I wanted—just the day before my nineteenth birthday, almost exactly a year ago—I went on seeing him, because I still hoped for those ecstasies, or, more than likely, because I'm a bit of a maso. He said, "Narcissist, not maso. Narcissist, with two s's and a lovely behind." I don't think he saw what I'd taken, and anyway, I didn't care if he had.

Calamity came back, all out of breath, and said, "I went to get a Michelin map! Do you realize what I've got to do?" I said, "Exactly eighty-three kilometers via Saint-André-des-Alpes." You can't trip me up on my addition—as she knew only too well! She was breathing heavily. She must have gone upstairs, to what she calls her study. It had been her mother's bedroom. She's lived in her mother's shadow all her life, etc., etc. The old bitch died five years ago—quite a character, that one, she'd have taken a bone from a dog. Ever since, Mlle Florence Dieu has lived alone with her fantails and fourteen tons of books. At her place you have to walk over the books. She only had it once in her life, when she was twenty-five, in a car, with a traveling toy-salesman, and—this is her version, of course—she was *so afraid, it hurt so much,* it was *so sordid,* that she never wanted to try again. Human beings disgust her. Except for me, of course, because I am *so strange.* She says she can do very well without those things.

I explained on the telephone that she was to meet me at eight o'clock at the Café Le Provençal, Boulevard Gassendi, in Digne. She couldn't miss it, even if she drove with her eyes shut. But she's a real case, I'm telling you. Do you know what she said? She said, "I'll never find it, I know I won't. It's no use trying to explain to me!" A schoolteacher with fourteen tons of books—and she's actually read all those pages. When I squirted my Waterman's ink in her face, during that year of shit, she looked at me with her terrified eyes, looked at her skirt, her bodice, which were both ruined, and burst into tears. I said to her, into the mouthpiece, "You know what, I've never known such a silly cunt in all my life!" She said nothing, lowered her eyes, bit her lower lip—I could see her as if I was there. For the last time I repeated, with the infinite calm for which I'm noted, where she would find me. I said if Ping-

Pong called before she left, she was to say we were having dinner together, but I wasn't in the house, I'd gone next door or was in the garden, anything. I said, "Calamity, are you listening?" She said, "Yes, don't be cruel, don't shout at me." I blew her a kiss and hung up.

Then, for the rest of my life, I stood stock-still against the wall, filled with hate for myself, for others, for everybody. I think three-tenths of the time of Daddy, three-tenths of Mommy, but it was the idea of seeing Leballech with my own eyes that very evening that got me moving. Philippe was in the doorway, in his white coat. He said very quietly, as if we were in church, "I could hear nothing but you. What's going on, are you in trouble?" I shrugged a shoulder, shook my head, and left.

On the road, the first car to pass was a big steel-gray sedan with a black roof. I can usually recognize the makes, but I didn't know that one. The guy at the wheel, well past thirty, was wearing a white turtleneck sweater and had hair too long for his age. He opened the door for me, I got in, saying thank you, sweet as I could be, and off we went. I said it was a little chilly inside and he said it was air-conditioned. I nodded to show I understood. He was a lawyer and was going to pick up his wife and son, who was five, in Sisteron. He was a Parisian. He'd rented a house with a window that didn't shut, and it was a nuisance at night, because it banged in the wind. His wife kept thinking there was a burglar. He'd also rented a color TV, but it had been there ten days and the bastards hadn't put up the antenna yet.

We drove through Annot. There were already posters for the Fourteenth of July up on the walls. The guy turned on the radio. Jean Ferrat, whom I adore. He was singing "Nous dormirons ensemble." To show me it was stereo, the guy fiddled with a knob, which made it come out first from one side, then from the other. I said, "No, no, leave it alone, let me listen." He got annoyed and left it off until we got to Barrême. There he offered to buy me a drink, by the roadside, in a small place for tourists. He told me his life story, then his wife's—she was very beautiful, sort of like Princess Grace—and his son's. Then we left, and the conversation pursued its fascinating course until we got to Digne.

It was half past six when he dropped me off in a big square, where, it seemed, all the cars, trucks, and motorcycles in the department had arranged to meet. The first street I took, which was wide, long, and full of cafés and shops, was the Boulevard Gassendi. Even Calamity would find it, if she got that far.

She'd panic when she got to the Café Le Provençal, because you can't park in front, but she'd find somewhere to leave her car. Inside it was like a railway station, and just about as noisy. There was sawdust on the floor, which stuck to the soles of my shoes. The owner's wife sat at the cash desk. You could tell by the suspicious way she handed out the change that she was the owner's wife. I said, Good evening, madame, I'm not from these parts, the whole bit, and then, "Do you happen to know M. Leballech?" Yes, she knew him, he had a sawmill on the edge of town, straight ahead. She handed a customer a pack of Gitanes, gave him change from ten francs, counting it out twice, and said, "Yes, that's right." She'd already forgotten I was talking to her. I said, "I'm looking for his brother-in-law." She said, "Touret, the real-estate agent. He's M. Leballech's brother-in-law." I said, "Oh, I see." I must have sounded stupid or something, because she added, "Since Leballech has only one sister, I presume he has only one brother-in-law." Customers were beginning to pile up around the cash desk. She said, "It's a little higher up on the other side of the road." I thanked her, but she was no longer listening to me or looking at me. She set to work like a mad thing, trying to catch up.

I crossed the boulevard without getting run over, through a traffic jam and a deafening concert of car horns. On the sidewalk, it was like at Nice or Cannes, except it was narrower and there seemed to be a million people there just to stop you from moving. Everyone was wearing shorts, and fat mammas with plastic earrings seemed to be taking up all the room. I looked at the shop signs and, after four hours, found the real-estate agent's. If for no other reason than to get out of the sun and the noise, I pushed open the glass door and went in.

Inside it seemed dark, and I couldn't see. An electric fan was going around and around on one wall, but the air it sent out was not really cool. Through the stars in my eyes I could make out a black girl coming toward me. A few seconds later she wasn't black any more, just coffee-colored. She must have been about twenty-five, with a mass of frizzy hair around her face, and she was sweating in a red dress with straps I'd seen before, in Trois Suisses, or La Redoute's catalogue, who knows. Otherwise, she talked like you or me, but with a southern accent. She was M. Touret's secretary. M. Touret wasn't there. She asked me to sit down, but I said no, I would come back a little later. She said that, unfortunately, she'd be closing in ten minutes. Then she said she liked my dress. She smiled all the time, because she had such extraordinary white teeth. I showed her that mine weren't exactly dirty, either, and smiled back, sweet as honey, saying, "I've come from Nice, and I've been transferred here. I'm looking for a small furnished apartment, something not too expensive. I'm a schoolteacher, so you can imagine I haven't got a lot of money to throw around."

She was looking through a pile of papers describing various dream apartments for me when Touret came in. My first glimpse of him when he took off his sunglasses was enough— I knew at once he was one of the three bastards who'd threatened to smash my mother's teeth in with a poker. His eyes went straight to what interested him in a woman. Only after undressing me and weighing my tits, as if he was dying for it, did he deign to catch my eye. He made a little bow and put on his shopkeeper's smile.

He was about forty or forty-five now and didn't look any younger, despite his light-colored alpaca suit and his young man's manner. He was thin, average in height, with eyes that seemed to be gray-blue, as far as I could see, but there was something shifty about them. My heart, of course, was beating as if it was about to burst, and I couldn't open my mouth.

He called me "mademoiselle," then, very quickly, "my little lady." He asked Suzy—the coffee-colored secretary—how far we'd got, what I was looking for, how much I was willing to pay. He had *exactly* what I was looking for. He took Suzy's place behind the big metal desk. She said nothing and moved away. My glance caught her big black eyes for a moment, and I realized I could abandon the idea that her boss was making it with her, as a kind of exoticism, before, during, or after working hours. Her eyes told me she didn't think much of him. But who knows.

When I finally managed to get a word out, I said I'd like to see it right away. He looked at his big watch, one of those where you have to press a button for it to show the time. Georges Massigne has a similar one, but less vulgar-looking. And he said, "It will be a pleasure. It's quite near here." I sat down in front of him with my legs crossed, just so that he could look at them, but it disgusted me when he did. I put them back as they should be and pulled down my skirt. He's not stupid. He noticed it, and, no doubt, I lost a point. When I'm like that, I could kill myself.

He picked up a piece of paper and said, "Could you give me your name, little lady." "Jeanne Desrameaux." It's Cognata's maiden name. "And you're from Nice?" I said, "Thirty-eight, Rue Frédéric-Mistral." I didn't know if it even existed, but almost every town has one. "Schoolteacher," he said, and wrote it down. He was wearing a flat gold wedding band; his fingers were thick for his height, and sunburned. I said, shyly, "As a rule I live by myself, but I want an apartment with privacy." He looked at me, and I knew I'd scored a point. I looked down, then up again, and smiled; our eyes met. He imagined me being poked in that apartment, which he knew like the back of his hand; he had a foothold. He said, "It's a shame to live alone, a pretty girl like you."

He gave the office keys to Suzy and told her she could lock up and go home. I'd barely heard the glass door shut behind us when he took hold of my arm with his hairy fingers, supposedly to help me through all the traffic. We turned onto a side street, then onto another, without hurrying, and I just let him ramble on. By the time we got to the small decrepit building, I knew that business was bad, that he was married to Leballech's sister, who was named Anna, that they'd been married for over twenty years and had two children. I even asked their ages. He went on about his car, a CX with electrically controlled windows—we hadn't taken it because the apartment was so close. I said as little as possible, first because I didn't want to make any mistakes in grammar or say anything else that would give the game away, and then because the less I said, the more difficult it would be to find me later.

The apartment was on the fourth floor and overlooked a yard. There was one room, four meters by four, a tiny kitchen, and an even tinier bathroom, with a shower and a toilet. It had been redecorated. It was all very artistic—the walls were white in the main room, a glossy red in the rest of the apartment, and the furniture was modern. I didn't dislike it. He said he had had everything redecorated himself, but I didn't believe a word. As I looked around he sat down in a chair and lit a cigarette. He offered me one, but I said no thank you.

For a thousand years we kept silent. Even my heels made no noise on the carpet, and he was happy enough just sitting there examining me. I looked out of the window, into the yard, then turned around and asked, "How old did you say your children were?" He hesitated just long enough to let me see he was lying and said, "Seven and thirteen or fourteen, I think." He laughed. "You get so involved with work, you don't notice them grow up."

I stood before him, thinking hard, then said, "Look Monsieur Touret. I can't decide definitely this evening. I like the apartment. Very much. It's just what I'm looking for. But I don't think I can pay eight hundred francs a month." He went into a great song and dance about how sorry I'd be not to take it, the pleasures of a shower, the telephone, the Scholtès cooker, which cleaned itself, and—just think of it—a wardrobe that was the perfect thing for a woman, huge, a real ballroom. Well now, what about that, how could his little lady resist it, yes, how could she? I looked down and said obstinately, "I can't make up my mind this evening, Monsieur Touret. Perhaps you could show me something else, less expensive." His eyes opened wide. "Now?" I said no, another time, I could come back. He sighed and said, "As you wish."

I went down first, while he locked the apartment door. I felt better being out in the street alone. There was still sun on top of the walls. It was half past seven. I'd never thought things would happen like this. I would have to change my plans. Unless Leballech was just as I'd imagined him all these years. Either one of them—it made no difference for what I intended doing. Actually I'd told Touret the truth—I couldn't make up my mind that evening.

He tried to take my arm again when he caught up with me, but this time I moved away. Not annoyed, just a bit straitlaced; after all, I was a schoolteacher. He walked with his toes turned in. If he'd gone on wearing his Basque beret—I'd always remembered the bastard with his Basque beret, the way my mother had described him—it might have stopped his hair from falling out. It was pretty thin on top, and the sun must have burned his scalp, but with my eyes, I couldn't see well enough. He said Digne was a good town when you got to know it. I'd like it. Which school was I going to teach at? Oh, the bastard! I was already hesitating, and he noticed it. I had to turn it to my advantage. I said I was under an obligation not to reveal it yet. He said, "Oh, I see." And dropped the subject. I went back to it myself after a while: "There's a lot of jealousy, you know."

We left each other in a great square that cuts the Boulevard Gassendi in two. I repeated its name—Place de la Libération—and that of the street the apartment was on, Rue de l'Hubac. I said I'd come back and see him the following week, Wednesday or Thursday, and I'd probably be living in Digne from August on. He seemed put out at having to let me go so soon and said, "You surely have time for a drink with me?" I said thank you, next time, I had an appointment and was already late. "Would you like me to take you there in my car?" I held out my hand. He took it and held it in his. It was the worst moment of that bastard of a day. Before looking away, I said, "No, it's very near, good-bye," and my hand slipped away from his. I walked straight ahead, without looking back, but I knew he was still standing there watching me.

I found a taxi at the corner of the square. Some men were playing bowls, and I went to ask who the driver was. It was a little old man wearing a beret, who was watching the game. He wasn't very pleased at having to leave it, but he probably figured the sooner he got me to my destination, the sooner he would be back. He took off so fast I could hardly keep up with him. The others, like the idiots men are, shouted out remarks as he left, such as, "Hey, let us know if you need any help!" Things like that. Anyway, as long as it's not Touret, Elle adores it when men look at her and think of all the things they could do to her. In fact, it's the only thing that gives her a lift.

I got into the back seat of the car. The little old man just about remembered how to start the engine and asked me where I was going. I said, "Leballech's sawmill, on the La Javie road. Could you wait for me outside? I won't be long." We drove on, left Digne, and three or four kilometers later parked at the roadside by a great open gate. Everything was quiet except the birds. As I got out my heart missed a beat, because there was a sign, right there, indicating that we were near a village called Le Brusquet. Obviously it wasn't the same Le Brusquet as mine, but it gave me a terrible shock. It was as if, at that moment, my mother's God really did exist up there.

Not to mention the silence—the workers must have gone home—Leballech's sawmill wasn't much like Ferraldo's. It was very small, with a workshop, a shed, and a modern house at the far side of the yard. Apart from a black Peugeot, there were no vehicles around. The still air smelled of lumber and resin. There was sawdust everywhere.

A dog barked in the house as I approached, and the door was opened by a girl holding the collar of a big German shepherd, just like Lucifer. The girl was a bit older than me.

Fairish, kind of plump in her tight jeans. Sweet as honey, I
asked for M. Leballech. She said, "Of course, which one? My
father or my brother?" She turned around, laughed, and said
something I didn't quite catch to someone I couldn't see. Obviously the brother, who came to the door. He was about a
head taller than her and younger than me, a funny guy, also
wearing jeans. He had long hair like Boo-Boo, but he wasn't
as slim or as good-looking. The girl said, "My father's in his
office." She pointed to the workshop. I said thank you and
walked in that direction.

He was standing in a small room made entirely of glass,
which looked out over the silent machines. He said, "Yes?"
and came out to meet me. My heart was beating even faster
than when I saw Touret appear, because I already knew he
would be the one I'd have to manipulate, he'd be the less
difficult to bear. He was tall, perhaps taller than Ping-Pong,
heavily built, pepper-and-salt hair. His sleeves were rolled up,
but he was wearing a tie, loosely knotted. He, too, had blue
eyes, a little like mine, but I know that means nothing, my
eyes are too much like my mother's. I get my eyes from her.
My voice wobbled all over the place as I said, "Monsieur
Leballech? Excuse me, I'll probably be renting an apartment
from your brother-in-law. I'm a schoolteacher." He waited for
me to go on, and I made a great effort to look him in the eyes,
to swallow the big lump I had in my throat. He was the driver
of the truck. He was the one who'd worn a lumber jacket. If
my mother had described him correctly, he must have been
about fifty now. I said, "I would like to know how much you'd
charge to make some bookshelves for me. I've got fourteen tons
of books." He raised his eyebrows, then realized I didn't really
mean fourteen tons. He said, "You see, I'm not a carpenter;
I would provide the wood, perhaps, but that's all."

We stayed like that for a million years, I looking as if the
bottom had dropped out of my world. Finally he said, "Wait
a minute, I'll put you on to someone." He went back into his
glass-walled office, and I followed him. Life had given him
a calmness, in his walk, in his face, that others probably found

reassuring. I knew he was the one who had hit my mother first. He was probably the calmest of the three that day. He probably hit her calmly. But it was the bruise from that blow she carried the longest.

He gave me his business card, after writing an address on the back with a felt-tip pen, in careful, primary-school handwriting. Even I write better than that. His hands were still thicker than Touret's, but his went with his size. His gold wedding band cut into his finger, puffing up the skin on either side; he could never have taken it off. He asked me, "Which apartment is it?" "The one on the Rue de l'Hubac." I found it really hard to look at him because his eyes were so calm and there was no cruelty in them. Touret's eyes were hard and narrow, even when he tried to be the good guy selling dream wardrobes to shitty schoolteachers. Leballech said, "I see, your bookshelves won't be very big, then. You'd do better to buy them ready-made at the Nouvelles Galeries." He moved his great body toward the door, to make me understand that I should now leave. But for me, when I don't want to understand, it can go on a long time, even if a taxi is waiting for me outside. I studied my false fingernails, leaned my behind against a table, and looked upset. I said, "Actually I may not rent the apartment. I told your brother-in-law it cost too much." There was nothing for him to say, of course, but all the same he said, "That apartment is his. You'll have to sort it out with him. The less I have to do with my brother-in-law's affairs, the better." This time he went out into the workshop, expecting me to follow him, which I did.

In the yard I held out my hand, and he shook it. I said, "Thank you anyway." He said, "How old are you?" I added on two years. He said, "And you're a schoolteacher?" I could see I looked as much like a schoolteacher to him as he looked like the Pope. But quick as a flash I said, "Come and make my bookshelves for me and you'll see." Just relaxed enough for him to believe me, just Elle enough to make him think of things. I walked to the gate. The setting sun was in my eyes. At the last moment I couldn't help turning around, and there he was, standing in the same place, tall and solid, and he was looking at me, and I knew I was stubborn. I knew everything would be just as I'd always imagined it, never letting it slip my mind for more than an hour at a time, day after day, for the past five years. He was looking at me.

The little old taxi driver opened the door for me without comment. On the way there, he'd begun to give me a list of all the peasants in the region who were tearing their hair out because of the drought. He now picked up where he'd left off. It was twenty past eight by my watch, and twenty-five past by the clock on the dashboard. I felt something painful dying down inside me. I sat back, relaxed at last. I watched the countryside go by. I said, "Your clock is fast." He said, "No, your watch is slow." I was glad to annoy him.

Calamity was waiting for me, not on the terrace or inside the café, but outside. She'd been walking back and forth on the sidewalk since last year, among people who must have thought she was some kind of spin-dryer. She wanted to keep an eye on her car—she was afraid someone might steal it. She was wearing her bright yellow pleated skirt, as I'd been sure she would, and a frilly, transparent blouse, which didn't go at all with the skirt, and her fair hair piled up on her head and tied in a thick yellow velvet ribbon. I tell you, if a bird seller had seen her he would have put her in a cage.

Predictably, the first thing she said was that I was a bad girl, a very bad girl indeed, to make her walk back and forth on the sidewalk where passers-by might think she was who?—she asked me. Then she exploded, What is this all about? I told her, to shut her up, "You know you can be really stunning when you want to be. Have you dolled yourself up like that for me? Isn't that something!" She shrugged her shoulders and looked sulky, but she was blushing to her earrings, which were yellow, of course, as were her shiny plastic bag, her shawl, the whole show. I took her arm, and we walked along the sidewalk. She said, "But what about my car?" I said, "It won't run away. Let's eat first, I'm hungry." She kept looking over her shoulder, desperately anxious, as if her bitch of a mother was dying in that car.

We found a pizzeria on a little side street, almost at the corner of the boulevard. We both chose *scampi* and a pizza with anchovies. I wanted to pee, wash my hands, and fix my face a bit. When I came back, she'd put a square package on my red napkin. It was tied with a gold ribbon. I smiled, and she smiled, too, looking a bit pale. I opened the package without saying anything. I could have dropped dead. In a yellow-and-blue box was a bottle of Waterman's ink.

I had just enough time to recognize what it was before tears came to my eyes. The only thing I could see—and it was all so clear, I don't know how I stopped myself from howling and rolling around on the floor, how I even managed to bear it—was him, him, *him*. He was wearing his old leather jacket, and I was near the blue enamel stove in Arrame, and I watched him fill the pen he'd just given me. He had curly brown hair, and he raised his eyes toward me, leaning forward, and he had dimples in his cheeks as he always did when he smiled, and he said, "Who knows? Maybe you'll work better now?" At almost the same time—the same second—there were the trees in the forest. I could smell the dead leaves and the sodden earth. I knew I had the spade in my hands, and the horror was about to happen. I cried out.

I cried out.

Everyone at the other tables turned around to look. My blood was beating in my head like a torrent. Through my tears, I could see Mlle Dieu—her face was all red. I felt my tears run down my cheeks, and I wiped my face in my hands, not thinking of anything. Mickey. Yesterday, or the day before, he'd said he would be racing at Digne sometime—it would be an opportunity for me to come back. One evening I was taking a shower in the yard and left the curtain half open on purpose so that he could see me. Once I'm married, I'll get Mickey to screw me. I want it especially when I'm knitting on the steps, or in the kitchen, and his eyes are fixed at a point between my legs and he thinks I haven't noticed. And Boo-Boo. I melt just to think of it. But I don't suppose he knows much about it, except feeling up that tourist girl—unless I'm very much deceived—or giving himself a good time at night, thinking of me. I once asked him, very quietly, on the landing upstairs, if it was true, but he only shrugged his shoulders and said nothing. I die just to think of it—my little brother.

My head was still in my hands; I said, "Excuse me." Calamity didn't answer until the resurrection of her mother. She then leaned toward me, across the table. She smelled of some Dior thing, the same as Mickey's Georgette. I said, "It had nothing to do with you. It was something else." I looked at her. She removed that bastard of a Waterman's ink bottle from my sight. She nodded and smiled anxiously, as if she understood. She understood nothing at all, of course—she's an idiot.

I looked around me, but we weren't interesting any more, people were talking and eating. I said, with what enthusiasm I could muster, "Well, let's eat. It will get cold." After a while she whispered, "You know, it wasn't your real birthday present. The real one is in my bag. But I'm afraid to take it out now." I said, sweet as I know how, "Come on, show it to me." The back of my head hurt. It was a Dupont gold cigarette lighter, with *Elle* engraved on it. She'd written a few words on a card slipped into the case, and at the last moment she was ashamed of it—there was a whole scene about it. She'd written, "To have a little piece of your love."

I thought it was completely idiotic, of course, but I reached across the table and kissed her on the cheek. I said, "Later, in the car, I'll kiss you better." At least that brought the color to her face. I love it when she blushes and gets all embarrassed. I can just imagine her with her toy salesman, on the back seat of an old DS, legs in the air and her dress over her head, gritting her teeth and hoping it would be over soon. Sometimes she makes me die laughing.

When they brought the *scampi,* she talked so much about what she'd got ready at home for my birthday that I was no longer hungry. I didn't feel sick, either. I watched her eat and pretended to be listening to her. She ordered a bottle of Chianti, and since I don't drink she'd end up knocked out. She asked me why I was in Digne, and I told her to hush—there were certain things I'd wanted to break off before my wedding. She pretended to understand, sighed, and burst her lace bra. You could see it through her transparent blouse. Apart from her blonde hair the best thing about her are her pale breasts, but she's always ashamed of them, since her stuck-up mother said they were too big. Now I'm the only one she wants to show them to. If I'd gone to her place, as arranged, she would probably have worn no bra under her blouse and been as excited as a flea but scared shitless before coming to the door. She's a real hypocrite, Calamity, but I like her. The same kind of way I like Ping-Pong. I don't see what they have in common, but that's how it is. If I'd gone to her place, as arranged, she would have beaten around the bush for four hours, served tea with trembling hands like when I was fifteen, and wanted to try on dresses so that I could advise her, and talked of "that marvelous actress" and "that marvelous *chanteuse*" who likes only girls—"yes, yes, honestly, everyone knows that"—or Marilyn, for that matter. So that I'd get all wet to be in such company. I swear to God, no matter what we've done already, each time she lays herself out she'll press her hand to her forehead, roll her eyes, the whole bit, and implore the good Lord to tell her how this could have happened to her.

She said to me, over her strawberry ice cream, "You aren't listening." I said, "I was thinking of you." She wouldn't believe me. "And what were you thinking?" I said, "I can see your bra under your blouse. I'm sure you wouldn't have worn it if I'd gone to Le Brusquet." She blushed and said nothing. Then, leaning across the table toward her, I said, "Have you found out anything about those truck drivers?" She nodded without looking at me. I waited, the suspense nearly killing me. Stirring her ice cream, she said, "In November 1955 they took some fencing to M. Poncet. He kept the bill. They were men from Ferraldo's firm." All right. People aren't as dense as I think, O.K. She looked up and asked slyly, "Why did you want to know?" I said, "There used to be other rolls with the piano, apparently. A box of them they must have left somewhere. I just wanted to know." She paused, spoon in the air. "Twenty years ago!" I looked down at my lemon sherbet and said, "Yes, I know it's silly. Oh well." After a while I smiled at her and said, sweet as honey, "Do me a favor, for my birthday. Go to the ladies' room and take off your bra." She blushed. "You're crazy!" she whispered. "There are people here." I put my hand on hers and said, so sweetly, "Please." She looked at me, her face deep red. She desperately wanted to do it, to show me how modern she was, but she couldn't. She said, "I warn you, I'll do it." I said nothing. I went on eating my sherbet and looked at her, as if to say what a fool I thought she was. She suddenly got up from her seat, blushing to the roots of her hair, and walked over to the ladies' room.

I went on eating my sherbet. I wanted to drop the whole thing—Leballech, Touret, Calamity, Digne. I thought of Philippe undressing me in his pharmacy storeroom. Then, of course, the other fool taking off her torn dress, crying, and saying yes, because there were three of them and she was afraid of being hit or disfigured, who knows. And then of *him*, very quickly, just for a second. The blue enamel stove. I said to myself, "Stop! Now! Stop!" I pulverized what was left of my sherbet and pushed it away from me.

When Mlle Dieu came back she walked very stiffly. Her face was as red as a beet, and her big white tits swung visibly under her blouse. Apart from one of the red-vested waiters, no one took any notice of her anyway: I was just about the only one in the whole place who wasn't more or less stripped to the waist. But she must have imagined that all eyes were fixed on her tits as she put one leg in front of the other like a duck that had had its head cut off. I don't know how to explain what I felt, seeing her there like that, the poor fool; but, feeling it, I hated myself. I could have killed myself. She knows what is right and what is wrong, she does. I begged her to write *Gabriel Devigne* on my birth certificate. I promised to let her do anything she wanted with me, and even if it made me want to laugh I would pretend to be in paradise. I swore to her I would cry out like a lunatic, calling her my love, the whole bit. But no—father unknown! That was the end of it. I lit a menthol cigarette with the lighter she had just given me.

In the car, on the Annot road, she drove as if she'd passed her test just the day before, screwing her eyes up, looking for headlights in the night. I was half asleep. Occasionally, when she was sure she had at least fourteen kilometers of straight road in front of her, she'd put one hand on my knee. She said, "I think about you all the time. You don't know what it is to love as I love." Things like that. She wasn't jealous of Ping-Pong—she didn't even know him. She was glad I was getting married, glad I was happy. She said how proud she was to have shown herself "to everybody" without her bra, just to please me. I said, "Next time, you must show them your ass." She said "Oh!" and laughed nervously. I didn't know whether it was what I said or the Chianti, but the car was hardly moving by this time. I said, "Try and drive a bit faster or we'll never get there."

After we'd driven through the deserted town and passed the bridge, she stopped the car by the roadside and got out to pee behind the fir trees. When she came back she looked at me and gave a deep sigh. She dropped me off at the Montecciaris' gate. I kissed her on the lips—incredibly, she kisses very well—and I promised to telephone her from Brochard's café. She kissed me again, digging her fingers into my ass and sighing a whole lot more. I got out. I said, "I'll have to go back to Digne sometime. Will you come and fetch me?" She nodded, looking sad. Her face was all flushed and her yellow hair-ribbon hung to one side. I pulled it off, rolled it into a ball, and gave it to her. I said sweetly, "Calamity." She gave a sad little smile, and I was gone.

When I went into the kitchen, Ping-Pong was sitting at the table, under the lamp, which he had pulled down to head level. He was cleaning spare parts with gasoline. He hardly looked up. It was a quarter to midnight by my watch.

I said, "Are you mad at me?" He shook his head. I stood next to him for a while, but he didn't speak to me. Then he said, "I rang Mlle Dieu about seven. She wasn't there," I said, "She took me out to dinner in a restaurant, for my birthday. She gave me a Dupont lighter." I took it out of my bag and showed it to him. He said, "She seems to be very fond of you." There'd been a lot of forest fires, almost every night since the beginning of July, and he hadn't been sleeping much. I said, "The one time you could have slept, and you had to wait up for me." He said, "I can't sleep when you're not there." I bent down and kissed his disheveled hair. We looked at each other, and I said, "Let's go into the barn tonight." He smiled, stroked my ass through my dress, and said, "O.K." We went out quietly to the barn to make love, and he made me forget who I was.

Then one day I woke up and I was twenty.

I drank my coffee in the kitchen, with Aunt Deaf-and-Dumb and Mother Dolorosa. I went and teased Boo-Boo in the shower in the yard, to get him to hurry up. I followed him in, washed, and went back up to my room. I put on my white shorts, my white turtleneck sweater, and my sandals. I would go and see my mother.

She tried the wedding dress on me. It was unrecognizable as Juliette's old dress. There was lace all over it, the way I wanted it. In the full-length mirror downstairs in the dining room I looked tall, very slim. I was really pleased with how I looked. The poor fool had tears in her eyes, seeing me in that dress. She found one or two little things to do to make my ass even more beautiful, and as she worked away at her sewing machine she said, "I've got something to ask you, but I don't want you to get mad." She'd been thinking about what I'd said to her when I first met Ping-Pong, and she was worried. Mme Larguier, whose housework she did, had described old Montecciari to her. In short, she wanted to see a photo of him.

We sat there saying nothing after that. My heart was in my throat. She even stopped sewing. I said, "Old Montecciari had nothing to do with it, I'm sure now." She said, "Only I can be sure so bring me a photo." When she's like that, I see red.

I said, "Shit! You're not going to start all that and spoil my wedding, are you? What are you going to think up next?" She said, without looking at me, eyes cast down to her worn hands, "If I have the slightest doubt, I won't let you go through with it. I'll tell everything. I've vowed it in church." I got up from the table, put on my shorts, my sweater, my sandals, and, with my hair all mussed, I went out, slamming the door behind me.

About five minutes later I was at the Montecciaris'. I found Sono Finito alone and asked her for a photo of her husband, who was buried in Marseille. She said, "Why? Why?" I said it was to show it to someone in town who would do a painting from it. It was the present I wanted to give her for my twentieth birthday. She started sobbing and crying. She said, "Only you would think of something like that. You're a goodhearted girl. You think with your heart." I took the photo down from the wall in her room. I didn't even remove it from its gilt plaster frame, but went into my room and found a supermarket bag big enough to put it in. Then I went back down to comfort the old fool. I said to her, "Don't tell anyone. It's a secret between us." She kissed me on the cheek with her dry lips and squeezed my hand till it hurt. I said, "Shit! You're hurting me!"

As I went past Brochard's café, I saw my future mother-in-law talking with two other village girls. She looked at me, and I gave a broad smile. But I might as well have been smiling at the war memorial. Just to cap it all, Ping-Pong was out in front of the garage and saw me. "There are some alterations to be made to the dress," I shouted; "everything O.K.?" He said yes. He doesn't like me wandering around in shorts—he's already told me. What he would really like me to do is wear armor till our golden wedding anniversary.

Twenty minutes had passed by the time I got back home. The shithead upstairs was off again. He wanted his soup, he wanted his newspaper, or he'd heard me coming, he knew I was there. I've never seen him since he was paralyzed, I've never spoken to him, even through the ceiling. When he feels like it he insults me. Mother says he's still got his head on straight, but I don't know.

She was sitting in the same place, at her sewing machine, waiting. Besides myself, I know no one who can wait as long as she can. If you told her you'd be back and you came back a year later, she'd still be there, just the way you left her, her hair in perfect order around her face, her hands folded in her lap. She was born on April 28—she's a Taurean. I don't know much about it, but I've been told that Taureans are crazy about Cancerians, they're the only ones they can get along with.

I said, "Look what I've got here!" She took the frame from me cautiously and studied the smiling face. He had carefully combed dark hair, a sharp pointed nose, quite attractive, very dark eyes. He looked really sure of himself—he wasn't bad at all. My mother said, "Is that old Montecciari? Mme Larguier said he had a moustache." I replied, "Oh don't start. There are times in a man's life when he has a moustache, and there are times he doesn't. He didn't have one then, that's all." She didn't look at the photo for very long. She said, "It's not the Italian, in any case." The worst thing about it was that she didn't seem very relieved. Or she realized she wasn't sure she could recognize the bastard, after all those years. Who knows? I said, "If it had been him, you'd have recognized him right away. Even without a moustache." She shrugged her shoulders. I put the photo back in the supermarket bag and said, "If Ping-Pong knew we suspected his father, he'd pull both our heads off." She looked at me and smiled. I can't stand it when she smiles. That was the end of it. Then she made the alteration on my dress, and I tried it on in front of the big mirror, and I looked as divine as ever.

In the afternoon Ping-Pong took me into town in the garage's 2CV, so I could take care of the list of presents. I was wearing my jeans and a white tee shirt. He went straight back to the village—he wanted to make the best of his afternoon off working on his Delahaye. He'd brought back the remains of a Jaguar the week before—three dead, it was in the paper—which he'd

bought for practically nothing. He explained to me that the
engine was still in good condition, and he was going to put
it in the Delahaye. In town he had to go pick up another
mechanic, Tessari, who works for M. Loubet, Loulou-Lou's
husband. As I was going down the sidewalk of the square I
said, "And don't use this as an excuse to see her and stick that
thing in her again." He laughed like an idiot. He likes it when
I pretend to be jealous.

I took the photo of Cognata's husband to a boy I know,
Varecchi—everyone calls him Vava. He works in a printing
plant, and in the summer he does portraits for tourists on the
café terraces. He agreed to do it for a hundred francs, because
it was me, and for the following week. Or if I posed for him
in the nude, it would cost nothing. He was joking, of course,
and I said we'd see. We talked at his door, on the top floor—
there were people in his room. I told him to make sure he did
a good job on the coloring—it was for someone I loved very
much—and to be careful of the wretched frame. Then I went
down again, like an old woman, clinging to the stairs, because
I have a horror of slipping on waxed stairs and breaking a leg.

After that I did the list of presents. I went into three shops
and chose, without troubling myself too much, what they suggested. Except one or two idiocies my mother wanted, and
which I'd give her—then perhaps she'd talk about something
else. I went to the post office at four o'clock, but Georgette
was behind her counter, so I couldn't telephone from there.
I said hi, how are things, and bought ten stamps for my in-
vitations. I went to telephone from the café opposite the Royal
movie theater.

There was one booth, full of instructive things drawn on
the walls. Leballech was outside the workshop—they'd go and
get him. I recognized his voice on the other end as if I'd known
it for a thousand years. I think I missed nothing during that
rotten afternoon; the voices and faces, the slightest detail, I
kept everything in my head. I said, "Excuse me, Monsieur
Leballech, it's the schoolteacher, you remember?" He remembered. I asked him if I'd left my little silver heart on a chain

while I was there. He said, "I found it in my office, I thought it was yours. I asked my brother-in-law for your address, but I couldn't find your telephone number." "I don't have a telephone. I'm calling you from a café." He said, "Oh, I see," and I waited ten centuries. Finally he said, "Would you like me to mail it to you, or will you come pick it up?" I said, "I'd prefer to come for it, you never know. It means a lot to me. And anyway, it will give me a chance to see you again, won't it?" Ten more centuries. He said, "Yes." That's all. "Yes." I said, "I'm glad you found it. I know it's silly, but I was almost sure it was you." There was a touch of nervousness in my voice, just enough. There was none in his, which just got lower, more hesitant: "So when will you be coming to Digne?" I said, sweetly as ever, "What day would suit you?" If he doesn't back off now, I've got him. He didn't. He kept silent for a long time. I said, "Monsieur Leballech?" He said, "Tuesday afternoon? I have to go to the bank in Digne. I could give it to you somewhere." This time I kept silent, so he would understand that we understood each other. Then I said, "I'll be waiting for you at the corner of the Place de la Libération and the Boulevard Gassendi, at four o'clock. There's a taxi stand there, right? I'll be on the sidewalk across from it." He agreed. I repeated, oh so sweetly, "Four o'clock, then." He said yes. I said O.K. I waited for him to hang up first. Neither of us said another word.

I came out of the booth, my legs almost giving way under me. I felt drained and cold inside; my cheeks were burning. I drank a cup of tea with lemon at a table, pretending to busy myself with my wedding list; I was adding up all the prices without thinking. I was thinking of nothing. The boss's son came over to speak to me—I knew him. It was nearly five when I left the café. I walked for a long time in the sun. I took off the little red scarf I had around my neck and tied my hair in it, looking at myself in a shop window.

I went to Arlette's, then to Gigi's, but neither of them was in. When Leballech said "Tuesday afternoon" on the telephone, I realized it would be the thirteenth, and his story of having to go to the bank was a lie. I walked past the Crédit Agricole to check. They close at noon on the thirteenth. The Société Générale did the same. I'll get him. I'll make his family weep tears of blood.

I didn't know what else I could do in town to get me out of myself. I went to the swimming pool—sometimes I go when I expect Boo-Boo to be there, or Arlette, or Gigi, or whoever— but it was full of a million summer people I didn't know, and the noise was killing. Outside the sun was beating down. I walked on my shadow. I said to myself, "After Tuesday you'll be finished with them. Both of them!" I'll know what to do— I've been thinking about it for the last five years anyway. The woman at the cash desk of Le Provençal, coffee-colored Suzy, Leballech's daughter and son. No, no one will think of me, I'm sure. They'll never find me. Ping-Pong himself isn't responsible, neither is Mickey or Boo-Boo. I want to make them pay, of course, as a debt inherited from their lousy father, but I've never thought that the punishment would be the same for them as for the other two. I don't know. The other plan I've had ever since I've known Ping-Pong would take time—three or four weeks perhaps—but I'd keep my hands clean. I'd just use what God gave me. I don't know.

I thought of Tuesday afternoon with Leballech, and other afternoons later. Suddenly Elle was almost as real as if she was walking next to me. Elle doesn't care what has to be done. In a way she even wants to do it. It's the kind of thing she likes doing. She wants to put her arms around your neck, she wants to be kissed, to make love, and to become nothing and nobody. She is me, but not really—I have to think of everything for her. She'll never grow up. She's more unhappy than if she was dead. She woke up howling when I was at the pizzeria with Calamity. I felt her stir just now in the telephone booth. She digs her fingers into me, wrings my heart, makes me feel like I need air, makes the back of my head hurt.

I say to her, "On my wedding day, I'll go and see *him* in my beautiful white dress. I'll pluck up the courage. You know how brave I am." He'll be sitting in his armchair, all thin and

old—what will he be like? When we left Arrame, I ran away
so that Elle wouldn't have to help with the moving. I wandered
around in the snow on the hills until evening. When I arrived
in my new home, my mother was lost among the furniture,
boxes of dishes, and all the other rubbish we brought. She said
to me, "You've got no heart. You left me alone on a day like
this." I replied, "I didn't want to see him. If you'd been alone,
you know I would've stayed to help you." I undid the top of
her dress as we both sat on the sofa, which we hadn't yet taken
upstairs, and I said, "Let me, please," because she is always
ashamed and thinks it's wrong, but then Elle goes to sleep at
last, quiet for that day anyway, in the arms of her beloved
mommy.

I was at the river's edge, without even remembering how
I got there. I sat on a rock, near the clear water rushing over
the pebbles. My tee shirt was stuck to me with sweat. There
were people on the bridge not far away, so I couldn't take it
off to dry. It was about six, but the sun was still beating down.
I looked for candy in my canvas bag, but there was none left.
I lit a menthol cigarette with my Dupont lighter.

I decided that on Tuesday I would take with me the tiny
tinted-glass bottle on which I'd stuck a nail-polish label. It was
in my red blazer pocket with my money. After lunch Cognata
asked me to help her up to her room. She told me to get the
cardboard wallet in the porcelain stove, and she gave me four
new five-hundred-franc notes for my birthday. I was amazed.
I put this money with the rest, in my red blazer pocket, and
I felt the bottle in my fingers. I think I wanted to break it, get
rid of the powder, I don't know. I wept without tears because
of that old fool, I felt gentle and warm inside, and touching
that bottle was like touching a snake's skin. Now that I'd decided to take it with me on Tuesday, I wanted to hold it, right
away, and keep it with me all week. I would take it along. I
would see whether I needed to use it.

I walked out to the road to meet Ping-Pong, who was coming
back for me about seven. Then, who do you think caught up
with me, wheezing like a seal standing up on the pedals, with

his red-and-white jersey and his calves bare? He said, all out of breath, "Shit, I've had you in sight since the bridge and it's taken me three turns to catch up with you. Tomorrow, at Puget-Théniers, I'll finish the course after they've taken down the streamers." He got off his bike. You could make out his whole bazaar under his black shorts. It was the first thing he scratched, in fact, without concerning himself whether it bothered me or not, then his neck, moving his head backward and forward.

We sat down on the grass by the roadside, and he wiped his face with his cap and said, "I'll wait for the roadsweeper with you. I'm beat." I asked him how many kilometers he'd gone, and he said, "As far as my brothers are concerned, a hundred. The truth is I've only done fifty, and I've drunk three bottles of beer." He shrugged his shoulders, then said, resignedly, "What do you expect, that's the way it is." We lay there on the embankment in the shade of the trees; it felt good. I looked up at the sky. At one point I looked at him, and he was sitting up, his arms around his knees, his forehead all creased, thinking. "What are you thinking about?" I asked. "I said the Olympique de Marseille would win the cup, and they have. Now I'm saying I'll win a race. I sense it." I said, "Where are you racing after Puget?" He gave me his program up to the Apocalypse. He'll be running at Digne on the twenty-fifth, a week after the wedding. A race around the town, twenty times up the Boulevard Gassendi, and if he goes faster than the others each time, he'll win extra prizes. If he wins the race, he'll be given something in metal with his name on it, and some shitty bike he can sell for five hundred francs. I'd like him to win. He said, "If I stay with Deuffidel and Majorque on the way up, I've got a chance. I've shown them my backside at the finishing line at least twenty times."

I pulled my tee shirt out of my trousers and lay down on my back, moving the cloth up and down over my chest to ventilate it. Mickey smoked one of my menthol cigarettes. He said, "Ping-Pong said we're having a celebration tonight." He didn't look at me. I said yes and shut my eyes. I imagined us both going into the woods behind us. I stroked my left breast under my tee shirt, as if without thinking. It was all hot and swollen, and my heart was beating underneath. I don't know whether Mickey noticed. I imagined we were in the woods, and he was stroking my breasts. Then Ping-Pong arrived.

He was with Tessari in the 2CV. He stuck his head out of the window and said, "I'm just taking him home—I'll be back in a few minutes." I got up all the same, went over to the car, and gave him a kiss. I gave Tessari my left hand to shake. I said, "Excuse me, but it's the hand of my heart." I knew Tessari's nephew and hated him—he's a dirty little peeping Tom. I said, "Well, does the Delahaye go?" Tessari laughed. Ping-Pong said, in all seriousness, "It will go. But we don't need the Jaguar engine. It will go with its own engine." Mickey came up and put his arm around my waist. He said to Tessari, "How are things?" And, like me, he put his left hand through the window.

The car moved on into town, and we went back to the embankment, where he'd left his bike; he still had his arm around me. He let me go to sit down. I kept standing, looking at the sun going down behind the mountain. Mickey said, "There'll be daylight for a long time yet." He wanted another cigarette, and I lit it for him with my Dupont lighter. He has fine, tiny wrinkles around his eyes, because he's always laughing. I dropped down beside him, really depressed. Mickey must have felt it because he said, "It's sad seeing the sun go down." I said yes, but it wasn't so much the sun as Ping-Pong, and him, and Boo-Boo, and feeling at home with them and everything.

When we got back that evening, with Mickey's bike tied to the back of the 2CV, my mother was in the Montecciaris' yard. I hadn't been told she was invited to my birthday party, and the first thing that came into my head when I saw her through the windshield was that she might have been taken on a tour of the house and seen the true bastard with the moustache in the Queen's bedroom. I felt all on edge until she kissed me. Her Madonna smile reassured me.

I said, "You're staying for dinner, aren't you?" "Oh no, of course not! I'll just stay for the apéritif. I can't leave him alone for too long." She took me by the shoulders. She was happy to be there, happy to see the whole blessed family, and happy about my twentieth birthday. She'd really dressed herself up, a cream-colored summer dress that she'd altered with braid. She was made up just right, and her hair looked beautiful. Mickey said she looked like my sister. I wanted to kiss them, her, Mickey, and everyone, I was so happy. Even Mother Dolorosa had gone to the expense of a dress with little mauve flowers.

We took the big table out into the yard, and I helped Ping-Pong serve *pastis,* Cinzano, and Clairette-de-Die. Cognata, who came outside for the first time in ages, told my mother all about Seausset-les-Pins. I drank water with a little Cinzano to color it. Then Boo-Boo came out of the kitchen with a tray, and there were twenty small candles lit on it. Everyone laughed at how surprised I was, and sang "Happy Birthday" to me, and clapped. Since my mother couldn't stay for dinner, they had put the candles not on a cake, but on an onion tart, which is one of my mother-in-law's specialties. Boo-Boo had made the candles, because there weren't any at Brochard's, and Mickey, who forgets everything, had forgotten to buy them in town. Ping-Pong put his arm around my waist, and I said, "Watch, everyone!" I took a deep breath and blew out all the candles in one try. Ping-Pong said, "Well, that's it. There's no doubt about it! You'll be married this year!"

Then, when Mickey had come back from taking my mother home in the 2CV—still wearing his racing outfit—we ate outside as night was falling. The mountains were red. You could hear the animals coming back. I was the only one not to drink wine—Mother Montecciari doesn't drink much, either—and they all got very merry, even Cognata, who laughed so much she kept coughing and spluttering. Ping-Pong kissed me several times on the neck, and in my hair. He told us all about his military service in Marseille. Boo-Boo told us about his mathematics teacher, a forty-five-year-old virgin who wore stockings rolled down just above the knees, and all the tricks they played on her. Mickey told us about a race he'd lost, or won, I don't know. I was thinking of my mother describing to the other shithead all the details of the three seconds she'd spent here, and how she'd brought a piece of onion tart back for him, all that. I was still laughing, of course. I know how to behave.

When we'd finished, the young ones all went up to change. In the bedroom Ping-Pong took out the pink dress I'd worn the first night I went out to dinner with him. It reminded me of the box on the ears I got the next morning when I came home. He set out the dress on the bed, and there was a package on it. As I undid the paper, he stood behind me, lifted my tee shirt, and stroked my breasts. "If you do that," I said gently, "we'll never get going." But it disgusted me just then, and I wanted him to leave me alone. He'd bought me the red bikini I'd shown him once in a shop window. He didn't like it, because it was really the minimum, but he bought it for me all the same. I didn't turn around. I said, "You're really sweet." He took his hands off me and got ready.

We spent the evening in town then, in Puget-Théniers, where Mickey was to race next day. He said he'd have to tie a dog to his bike to show him the route. There was Ping-Pong and me, Boo-Boo and his tourist girl friend with the funny accent, Mickey and his Georgette. Boo-Boo's girl was naked under an almost transparent long dress—you could just about make out her pubic hair, and Boo-Boo behaved like an idiot. He looked at her as if she was a China vase and started trying to talk like she did. She kept kissing him. He opened his shirt; I heard nothing of what they were saying to each other, but the slut kept putting her hand on his chest as if he was the girl, and they made me want to leave them all, there and then, the shitty music, the revolving lights, the glasses half knocked over the table, everything.

O.K. In Puget, at some club where there was a guitarist

playing, I said to myself, "Don't get hysterical. He knows that pisses you off. He does it on purpose, just to annoy you." I danced a Joe Dassin number with Ping-Pong, the sweat pouring off me. Ping-Pong was all right, I felt him against my belly, but Boo-Boo wasn't even looking at me. He just sat in his seat smoking, his head back, his girl friend's mouth buried in his skin just below the neck, and he was talking, talking to her all the time, without stopping, his eyes fixed on the ceiling with its pictures of Spain or Italy. You could put all the words I've heard him say since I met him in any one of his sentences to her. Maybe that's what upset me most about him. Then it passed. I felt stupid in my hundred-year-old pink dress, which was too short, but I didn't care any more. I went over to the table to get my cigarettes and my Dupont lighter, then out into the soft night. I walked over to a fountain.

Ping-Pong, of course, came after me. I said to him, "I had to get some fresh air. It's all right, I feel better now." He was dressed in black, like the first time we went out together. Me in pink, him in black, it was his idea, he seemed to like it. He said, "If there's something bothering you, you can tell me, you know. You don't have to wait till we're married." I shrugged a shoulder and didn't answer. He said, "Just now, when we were dancing together, I realized what you saw in me." I looked at him, and his face seemed so gentle, so innocent, I felt even angrier. I said spitefully, "And what did you realize? Go on! What did you realize?" He held my hands. He said, "Calm down. You felt all alone in town this afternoon. I know what it's like. Then you go home, and there's your mother and the candles, all that. It's too much. I'm beginning to understand you." He felt he could let go of my hands, and he did. He said, "Just now, you were thinking of us and the baby. You were afraid of the future. You felt nothing could be like it used to be." We stood there by the fountain for a thousand years; then I said, "O.K. You understand everything. Let's go back." He followed me into the club, his hands in his pockets, looking sad. O.K. I waited for him and took him by the waist. I said, "Roberto. Roberto Fiorimondo Montecciari. Eliane Manuela

Hertha Wieck marries Montecciari." I laughed and said, "It sounds good, doesn't it?" He said, "Yes, not bad."

In the car—we'd exchanged the 2CV for Henri IV's DS—we were all crushed together, I between Ping-Pong, who was driving, and Boo-Boo, because he was the slimmest. We left Boo-Boo's girl in town, and Boo-Boo got out, they kissed and said they'd see each other the next day, etc., etc. A bit farther on it was the same thing for Georgette and Mickey, except they made less fuss. They disappeared into the night for over three quarters of an hour. God knows where they went. Georgette once told me, eyes cast down, that he put it into her anywhere, and she was always afraid someone would surprise them. One evening they did it on the cellar stairs at the Montecciaris', while Ping-Pong, Boo-Boo, Cognata, and I were playing rummy. She could actually hear our voices through the door. No kidding.

At last we got back to the house, I was half asleep in the car. Boo-Boo and Mickey were joking in the rear. Ping-Pong said, "Stop your nonsense back there, will you?" They stopped. While Ping-Pong was taking the DS to Henri IV's garage with Mickey, Boo-Boo and I crossed the yard. It was a full moon, and all we could hear was our own footsteps. The kitchen door was locked from the inside. Boo-Boo said, "It's no use waking Mamma. We'll have to wait for Ping-Pong."

We stood there, saying nothing, till the end of the world. I forgot I was angry with him and took his hand—I said I was afraid. I said, "Talk to me." I felt he wanted to take his hand away but didn't dare. He asked me why I'd left them like that, at the club in Puget-Théniers. I said, "You know very well." He shrugged his shoulders. I said softly, "I was jealous seeing you with that girl, I wanted to cry." He didn't take his hand away—he said nothing. I said, even more quietly, "Do you find her more attractive than me?" He shook his head; that was all. I don't know how I managed not to put myself in front of him and kiss him to death. I said, "Talk to me, Boo-Boo. Be nice." He told me that his girl, who is named Marie-Laure, was a medical student. She was two years older than him. She was a good kid to have around for the summer, and that was all there was to it. I said, "Good. I'm glad." I squeezed his hand. It was a very big hand, and it made me think he was older than me. Finally he took his hand away and tapped on the window to wake his mother. I didn't have time to stop him. "Mamma!" he shouted, "it's us!" We said no more to each other.

Mother Dolorosa opened the door, wearing her thick cotton nightgown. "Why didn't you knock right away?" she asked Boo-Boo. He said, "We didn't want to wake you. We were waiting for Ping-Pong." She shrugged her shoulders and said sourly, "You know very well I don't go to sleep until everybody's back."

I went up with her, but Boo-Boo stayed downstairs waiting for his brothers. In the bedroom I took off my dress and put it on a hanger. I felt my little bottle in the pocket of the red blazer before closing the wardrobe. I got into bed naked and thought of Boo-Boo, the hand that had held his between my legs.

When Ping-Pong got back, there was only one thing he wanted to do, of course, and it wasn't to read his newspaper. I tried to say I was tired and he should go to sleep, because I was disgusted at the thought that Boo-Boo might hear me that night. I came right away and again and again, my mouth crushed into the pillow to stifle my cries.

Then it was that horrible Sunday. In the morning I met Boo-Boo in the yard. He didn't speak to me and avoided looking at me. Wearing my red bikini, I blocked his way to say hi. He leapt away from me like a savage—it was a miracle I didn't throw myself on the ground, with my suntan lotion, my menthol cigarettes, my glasses, and the whole bit. He said, "Leave me alone!" His dark eyes looked mean, and they would hardly rest on me. I said, pleading, "Boo-Boo!" But he dashed into the house without turning around. I thought about him for the next fourteen years, totally miserable as I lay there near the spring. I don't know whether he regretted taking my hand the night before, or whether, on the contrary, he was furious and wounded because he'd heard me making love with Ping-Pong.

I thought, "That's what you wanted to do, after all, create trouble," but it made me feel depressed anyway.

At the table it was worse. We had lunch early, because Mickey had to go to race at Puget. Boo-Boo said nothing throughout the whole meal, except at the end, just to show me up in front of everybody. We were talking about the movies with Mickey. I said, in all innocence, that if I'd wanted to I could have been an actress, too—there were worse ones than me. God, did I get it! First, I was an ignoramus. Second, I was pretentious enough to parade myself around a village where no one saw anybody but two-hundred-year-old grandmothers. Third, in Nice or Paris I'd be no more than average among the girls who walked the streets. I don't answer when I'm yelled at. I threw my napkin into the middle of the table and went upstairs. When Ping-Pong came to talk to me, I locked the door. I wouldn't go with them to Puget, that was that. I didn't want to calm down. I wanted to be left alone.

The afternoon was hell. They'd all left, except the two merry widows, and each minute lasted four years, each hour a lifetime. I didn't want to watch TV with Cognata. I opened the bedroom window to get some fresh air, but I shut the blinds. I didn't even want to go see my mother. Finally I got my little bottle, full of white powder, from my blazer. I lay on the bed holding it tightly in my hand, trying to remember something I'd done with my daddy. I was in the kitchen in Arrame. I was seven. What happened? Maybe we were playing dominoes. He let me win, on purpose. He smiled, with his dimples. He said what a clever girl I was. I was always the most beautiful, the most intelligent, the most everything. Not for one second did he stop talking to me, telling me I was his little darling. I could have spent the rest of my life thinking about that, clutching my little bottle in my fist, to get my revenge on both of them, Elle a little girl with her adoring daddy. What did Cognata say? "Ah, it was a good time!"

Later I fell asleep, or lost the thread, and the bottle disappeared. It was under the pillow. I'd crushed thirty tablets— five or six were enough to kill a man in two hours—in a napkin by rolling a bottle over them. "The heart bursts," Philippe had said. It bursts with the first attack. I put a little of the powder on my tongue with a finger to taste it. It was bitter; peasants use it to put their dogs to sleep, two tablets crushed and sprinkled over their food—that's what Philippe said—and the poor animal eats it all the same. Half a tablet is used as a medicine for some serious illness or other. Five or six and you've had it. I'd have about two hours to get lost without anyone's thinking of me. It would be known, of course, what they'd died of, but between feeling sick and dropping dead they wouldn't have time to say who they'd been with.

I looked at the papers in town. It's not the same edition as in Digne. The only person who could suspect me was Philippe. But I'd taken the tablets out of several different boxes, and even if he'd noticed, and even if he read the paper—which would surprise me—no one's going to say much about two poisonings in the next department over. Those bastards are dying all the time.

Night was falling when I heard them come in downstairs. I lit the lamp on the bedside table. I put the warm bottle in my blazer pocket. I put on my blue-flowered dress, with nothing underneath, and my white shoes, and arranged my hair and everything in the mirror. I'd been crying a lot, but I didn't care who saw. I went and unlocked the door, then lay on the bed. Ping-Pong came in almost at once. He'd caught the worst sunburn ever.

He sat down next to me and said Mickey was an ass. I said they were all the same in his family. He laughed. He said Mickey didn't finish the race until the winner, a guy from Toulon, had already gone home. O. K. He could see I hadn't calmed down. He said, "Boo-Boo didn't mean what you think." I said, "I know. I thought it was a compliment, but since you mention it, I do know he more or less called me a whore."

Ping-Pong was really in a fix. He didn't want to be mad at his brother, and he didn't want to be mad at me. Finally he went to talk to Boo-Boo and asked him to apologize to me. I melted, just at the idea. I imagined Boo-Boo, all downcast, asking my forgiveness. There's no harm in dreaming. When I went down to dinner, he wasn't even there—he'd gone out to meet his girl.

Cognata and Mickey were very nice to me, as usual. We watched a movie on TV. I didn't say a word the whole filthy evening. If I'd known where Boo-Boo was, I'd have gone there, even if it meant getting it in the face from his Marie-Laure. But I didn't know where he was. So that was the end of it. Mother Dolorosa brought my knitting and put it in my lap. She said, "You ought to do something instead of sitting there biting your nails. You wouldn't want your baby to wander around all naked, would you?" I put the knitting under my chair; I didn't even have the heart to answer.

Monday the 12th

In the afternoon Mother Dolorosa went to the cemetery. Cognata was asleep in the chair with her eyes open. I went up to Boo-Boo's room—there he was, on the bed, in his flowered swimming trunks, reading. I stood leaning against the closed door. I said, "What's the matter? Don't look at me like that." He was looking at me as if I was the devil. He said, "If you don't get out now, I'll throw you out." I shrugged a shoulder to show I didn't care and said, "Are you mad at me for what was said the other night? Are you sorry about that?" He didn't answer. He just stared obstinately at the wallpaper. I said, "I'm going down to the stream. I'll be waiting for you. If you don't come, I don't know what I'll do." He turned toward me to say something, but in the end he looked down and said nothing. I went up to him and touched him on the cheek. I said, "Please come, Boo-Boo."

I left him there and went into my room to put on my red bikini under my dress and to get my canvas bag. Then I went downstairs. Cognata was sleeping quietly. I didn't take the road, but went through the fields, at the back, by the little path that goes down to the stream. I hopped on the big stones and rocks till I got to the place we call Palm Beach. That's where I go and sunbathe with Martine Brochard. There are two huge, flat rocks to lie on, and a fir forest behind. Except on Sundays in summer, there's never anyone there.

I took out my bath towel from my bag, lay down on it in my bikini, and waited. After about an hour, or a bit less, Boo-Boo came, by the same route I'd used. He was wearing canvas trousers, and a printed tee shirt with my portrait on the front. Yes, my portrait—my head, my hair, my smile. It was all photographed in red on his tee shirt. Incredible.

He stood there, two meters away from me, smiling, a little embarrassed, his hands in his pockets. I said, "Shit, where did you get that?" He said, "In Nice. A pal of mine brought it back for me last week. I'd given him your photo." He took off the tee shirt and gave it to me. He said, "It's for you. I think it's too big." I knelt down and put it on. I said, "But where did you get the photo from?" He said in my room—he'd chosen the one he liked best. The tee shirt was a little too big, but marvelous all the same.

I held out my hand and he took it to pull me up. We looked at each other for a few all-too-short seconds, perhaps a thousand years, then he said, looking down, "You're going to marry my brother. It's as if you're my sister. You understand?" I felt he was going to turn away and leave, and I said, "Boo-Boo, don't go. Please don't go." He said, "I just came to tell you that." I said, "I don't care. Stay with me."

In the end he stayed. I lay down in my red bikini, and he did, too, in his flowered swimming trunks. He said nothing else. He was very slim and suntanned. Not much lighter than me. After a while he dived into the cold water. I saw he swam well. Anyway, whatever he does, I adore looking at him. He was killing me. I felt he was killing me. I gave him my towel when he climbed up onto the rock, and I dried his back. I said in his ear, pleading, "Just once. Just once. No one will ever know." He shrugged his shoulders, without turning around. "I'd know," he murmured. I put my lips on his back, and my arms around his body, and said very quietly, "It will happen anyway." He moved away and stood up. I stayed on my knees, looking into the distance. I could hear the stream. I realized

I was acting with him like Calamity did with me. It was incredible. I nodded without looking at him, then I got up, too,
dressed, and took off.

I left him on the path. I put the tee shirt in my canvas bag.
He was stripped to the waist. I tried to smile—it was a disaster.
I said, "I'm going to see Ping-Pong. I don't want to go back
with you. If your mother starts criticizing me, on top of every-
thing, I won't be able to bear it." It was stupid, I know, but
I couldn't help it—I held my mouth out for him to kiss me.
He kissed me on the cheek and went away.

Tuesday the 13th

Late in the morning I went to Brochard's. I called Calamity.
I told her to come get me at the same place, at the same time.
Do you think she understood? She understood nothing at all.
I couldn't speak to her because Brochard's mother had nothing
better to do than to clean and polish her end of the bar, just
next to me, while I was telephoning, but the poor fool yelled
into the receiver, "In Digne? Is that what you said, in Digne?
What's the café called? I can't remember." I said, "You'll find
it. See you soon." I hung up in the middle of her whining.
I wasn't even sure whether she'd come or not. I couldn't care
less. I got the package of laundry powder Mother Dolorosa had
asked me to fetch, and as I paid I pointed out I'd been over-
charged ten centimes. Then I went to talk to Martine on the
terrace. Martine is a few months older than Boo-Boo. She's
got a round face with laughing eyes and brown hair cut like
Mireille Mathieu's. I'd often seen her naked, down by the
stream, and she's chubby all over and very sweet.

I said, "Do you think he sleeps with that girl?" She turned
toward the bead curtain across the door to make sure her
mother's ear wasn't stuck in it. She said, very quietly, "You
bet! When they come with me to collect lavender, they go off
by themselves, and Marie-Laure comes back all flushed."
said, "Have you ever seen them?" This time she blushed. She
hemmed and hawed and hesitated for a thousand years. I insisted. "Once," she whispered. "But it was by accident. I hadn't

tried to see them, and I left right away." She really annoyed me—I wanted to take her by the hair and shake her. I said, "But what were they doing?" She could hear in my voice how annoyed I was and blushed even more. She looked again at the bead curtain and said, "It was Marie-Laure who was doing it." That was all. She drank her coffee and ate her sandwich.

I said, "O.K." I left her at her table and went home. I tried not to hear the crap thrown at me by the Manageress because I'd brought back the wrong brand of laundry powder. I went up to my room and slammed the door. If I hadn't needed to find my reflection in it next day, I'd have smashed the wardrobe mirror. I wanted to smash everything. I lay on the bed without moving, to the end of my days, trying to think about nothing. I'd felt crushed, every minute a little more, since the moment he'd let my hand go. I could no longer see the point of going to Digne. I wouldn't be able to go through with it. I wouldn't be able to go through with anything. I was just what he said I was, a pathetic, silly ignoramus. I mean nothing to him. A bag of bones like Marie-Laure was a dream next to me. Even with his thing in her mouth, she probably managed to say intelligent things. I was really fed up. Really.

At lunch I kept my head down, so as not to see him. I picked at the fried potatoes on my plate—I wasn't hungry. Ping-Pong asked, "What's wrong?" I said, "Shit!" He shut up. Of course, they all thought I was in a bad way because of the baby. When Boo-Boo, who had so far said nothing, suddenly started talking about the Tour de France, I left the table and went up to my room to get ready.

I put on the outfit in which I'd planned to bring Leballech down in flames. I didn't even believe in it any more but just pretended I did. My sky-blue dress, which is low-cut, and gathered under the breasts. Not too short, but light, close-fitting. It billows out when I turn around, and you can see me in outline against the sunlight. My shoes with thin straps. White lacy panties. I took out my white leather bag, I put into it my money and the small bottle with the nail-polish label on it. I pulled my hair up in the band made out of the same

material as the dress. I put on a little lipstick and a touch of
eye makeup and went out.

To Ping-Pong, who walked with me to the church and who
thought I was seeing a lot of my schoolteacher, I said, "It's
better than wanking myself off every afternoon in the bedroom." That shut him up, and it's a good thing it did, because
this was just the day of the year to get a handbag in the face.
He left me at the bus stop. He didn't say good-bye—but that
was the least of my worries.

I went into town in a bus full of summer people heading
for the swimming pool. No one said anything. I just caught
the two-thirty bus to Digne. There was a guy next to me reading
a magazine, and after a long while, during which he must
have learned it by heart, he gave it to me. The drought. Gis-
card. Poulidor. The pollution on the beaches. The Montreal
Games. Elizabeth Taylor. There was a page of funnies, but
all I could read was the headlines. I tried to make out the
rest—the guy must have thought I wanted to eat his paper.
Anyway, I don't understand the funnies. Or one out of ten,
perhaps. You'd have to tickle me at the same time to make
me laugh. As we neared Digne, my heart began to beat really
fast.

The bus left me on the Place de la Libération, at ten minutes
to four by my watch. They were getting the dance ready for
that evening. There were fairy lights everywhere. It was even
hotter than on the road. I was sweating and already felt dirty
and tired. I went and stood across from the taxi stand. I stared
into space, my ears full of the voices of the bustling crowd.
Then suddenly Leballech's black Peugeot stopped by the sidewalk. It was exactly four o'clock when I got in and sat down
next to him.

I said politely, "You're very punctual." Just seeing his eyes
on me calmed me down—I went up in my own estimation.
It was the subject for a film that had never been made—the
fifty-year-old guy, on the road to perdition, arrives for a date
with the misdeeds of his youth. I was sure his heart went on

beating madly when I shut the car door and sat down next to him.

He spoke in a funereal voice about this and that. Everyone knew him in town. It wasn't like him to go around with a girl who wasn't even as old as his daughter. He hadn't thought I'd come, etc., etc. He was wearing pale-gray trousers, well creased, and a slightly darker turtleneck sweater. He had a boxer's arms, like Ping-Pong's, the color of scorched earth, with fair or maybe white hair on them, I don't know. He smelled of some cologne I knew, but I couldn't remember the brand or who else wore it. He looked at me once or twice as we went down the boulevard, which was all decorated in red, white, and blue, and I repeated to myself that my eyes were like his, but even more like my mother's, that I got them from her. My hair, its color and thickness, came from the Montecciaris, I was sure; so, too, did the length of my legs in proportion to my torso, the same as my three brothers'.

After the traffic circle, which was where I'd got off the bus, we crossed a river. The sun was setting in the distance at the other end of the bridge. Leballech said, "It's the Bléone." We drove along the Bléone in the direction of Durance and Manosque, according to a sign. I asked where we were going. He said he didn't know—he didn't want to stay in town. He said, for the sake of form, "Perhaps you'd rather I gave you your piece of jewelry back, and we said good-bye right away?" I looked through the windshield and said no. We drove on. He didn't speak for the next thousand kilometers. His Peugeot wasn't new—there was no lid over the glove compartment— but it drove smoothly, without much noise. I love driving around in a car and saying nothing, just looking at the trees. Then he said, very quietly, "I don't understand." I said, "Oh." I knew very well what he didn't understand. I may be an ignoramus, but this sort of thing is on my level. He couldn't understand why a filthy old woodcutter should be presented with something like me on a plate, without ever having asked for it. He said, "I've thought about your telephone call a lot.

You talked to me as if something was already decided between us. As if we'd already known each other for a long time." I repeated, "Oh."

We stopped at a sort of castle set back from the road. There were horses, a swimming pool, and a millon half-naked people sweating in every language under the sun. Inside, in a hall with walls built out of big stones, with a chimney for walling up useless old grandmothers, it was cool. We sat down at a low glass table. I had tea with lemon, and he had a beer. He hardly took his eyes off me now, and he could see that the tourists were looking at me, too.

He gave me my silver heart and chain and said, "Are you taking my brother-in-law's apartment, after all?" He leaned his bulk over toward me, with his pepper-and-salt eyebrows and hair. He could crush me with one hand. I lowered my eyes, like some idiot who didn't dare ask where the toilets are, and said, "I haven't given it serious thought. If you want me to take it, I will." A century went by, and I kept my eyes on the table. I let him swallow his saliva, then added, "You know, the other day, when I came to see you, I wasn't expecting much. But I've been thinking about our talk on the telephone, too. I don't know how to explain. I was afraid, yet I felt good." I raised my big eyes to him, all innocence, as I know how except with Boo-Boo, and he nodded twice, with a faint smile, as if to say he understood, it was the same for him. Yes, you never know what life has in store for you. I looked down at the table again, at the patterns on the red carpet underneath it. If the face I made was shown in a movie, everyone would rush out to adopt an orphan.

After that I didn't look up again. At the end of a long silence he said, "You aren't a teacher, are you?" I shook my head. "Well, what do you do?" I raised one shoulder and said, "Nothing." He stared into space—or at my cleavage, I don't know. "Jeanne," he murmured. I smiled sadly. Tears were coming to my eyes, I could tell, and so could he. He put a hand on my bare arm and said, "Let's not stay here. Let's go back to the car and drive around. You have time?" I said, "Until eight o'clock or half past." He slid his hand along my arm and said, "You haven't finished your tea." I drank my tea, he drank his beer, and we held hands between our two chairs, without saying a word.

In the car, as he was driving, I moved closer to him and rested my head against his shoulder. He said, "Jeanne, why did you come to Digne?" I said, "I don't know. Any town would have done just as well, but I'm glad I came to Digne." Boo-Boo may make fun of me, but I'm a pretty good actress. In school plays my heart beat too fast. "Articulate! Articulate!" Mlle Dieu used to shout. She said I didn't speak naturally. In real life I can speak naturally, especially when I don't believe a word of what I'm saying. Or if it's only partly true. I don't know. Like having my head on his shoulder, for example. Even if it's a guy I'll end up killing or having killed.

Gold for Men. I suddenly remembered—that's what he smelled of. Gold for Men. Philippe sold it in his pharmacy. It was a Portuguese, Rio, who put it on his face and neck. I was crazy about him, two years ago. He once kissed me on the lips as I stood against a tree. He lifted my dress to stroke my legs, but I pulled it down again; that was all. He used to shave out in the fir trees, before going to the dance. He'd take out a bottle from a gold-colored cardboard box and spread the cologne all over himself. Gold for Men. Nothing ever happened between us except that: he kissed me standing up against a tree, just to impress his pals, who were building chalets at the top of the pass. I said, "Let's go back to Digne. I'll take the apartment."

Leballech parked by the roadside, on the dry grass. He took me by the shoulders and looked at me for a long time. I could see myself in his eyes, far away in the distance. I breathed short, rapid breaths like I know how, fear and desire mixed, all that crap. Then he did it. He kissed me on the mouth and stuck his filthy tongue between my lips, and then . . . Elle came back. She was there, seven or twelve or fourteen years old, and

she looked at me lovingly. She knew I would never forget—
I'd kill them both, as I'd promised her.

We stopped at the first café we came to, and I telephoned
Touret. He wasn't there. Suzy answered. I reminded her who
I was and told her I wanted to rent the apartment. I'd be there
at about seven to sign the papers. Leballech, who was standing
next to me, shot me looks of approval at everything I said. He
put his hand on the back of my neck when I hung up. I smiled
at him, with the air of a brave little soldier who had done his
duty. He, too, smiled, and shook his head. He had another
beer at the bar; I drank nothing. I went to the door for a
moment so he would see me in outline under my dress, and
so the other customers would see me, too. Then I came back.
I laid my head against his shoulder and let him imagine that
the other men envied him because I was his. Then we went
back to the car and set off for Digne, thirty-one kilometers
away.

As he drove he said, "You know, I've had my adventures,
like most men. But for a long time I've been a good father and
husband, thinking only of my family and my work. It's really
extraordinary that this is happening to me." I had to stop myself
from saying that what was happening to him was my ass under
a blue dress, but it's not my style to use vulgar words. I let
him recite his catechism. It's always the same with those rotten
guys, you'd think they'd all learned it from the same priest.
It's just the wife's first name that changes, that and the kids'
names. Once I'd learned that the saint of a wife was named
Fernande and the angels Estelle and Hubert, there was no
point in listening any more. I looked out at the road, at the
trees. I thought of what I was going to have for dinner that
evening. When he'd finished with his nonsense, or even before,
I said, "I understand. It's not your fault. It's no one's fault.
That's just how it is." He put his protective arm around my
shoulders and went on driving, holding me close to him.

In Digne, he left me at a mean little street, parallel to the
Boulevard Gassendi. "It's only a few meters from the agency,"

he said. "I've got to just pop home, but I'll pick you up here in an hour." I looked at my watch and said, "I won't have much time then." He said, "I want to see you before you go, if only for a few minutes." He put a hand on my knee, then climbed a bit farther, pushing back the hem of my dress. I didn't move. I said nothing. I stared at what he was doing, looking almost as if it was hurting me. He said, in a funny kind of voice, "I've wanted you ever since I saw you." I said, "I know." I sighed. He stopped when he got to the beginning of my white panties. He dragged his fingers back over the softest part of my skin and pulled my skirt down after them. He said, "Go quickly. I'll be waiting for you."

I got out, went down a narrow street that led to the boulevard, and found myself almost directly across from the Touret agency. He was sitting behind the metal desk when I pushed open the glass door. The ventilator was still throwing out warm air. Suzy wasn't there. I said, "Good evening, Monsieur Touret." He got up, all excited, and shook my hand. As usual, he held on to it. He said, "I was expecting you." He was wearing the same alpaca suit and the same Big Bad Wolf smile. His eyes fixed on my cleavage, he explained how he was going to do me a special favor. Usually, besides the first month's rent in advance, you paid an additional month's rent as a deposit— to cover the cost of any damage. Well, he wouldn't ask me to pay the deposit. "No, my little lady." I said thank you, it was very kind of him.

Eventually he let my hand go to sign a paper. I didn't read it, first because I would have found it very difficult to without glasses, and second because I didn't care anyway. I signed *Jeanne Desrameaux* or, rather, *Jeanne* illegible. He asked me for my date of birth and I added two years on, as I had done with Leballech. I said I was born in Grenoble. He filled out the rest of the form for me and stuck it in his pocket. He got the apartment keys from a drawer in his desk and said, "I'll go along with you to take the inventory." He shifted his weight from one foot to another, his eyes on my cleavage, as if he couldn't wait to jump me—or wanted to pee, or something.

This time he took me to the Rue de l'Hubac in his new CX. I said I was thirsty. Before going up to the fourth floor, we went into a café a little farther on. Like Leballech, he drank beer, except that he pushed the button on his watch before deciding. He explained that he never drank before half past seven. We hadn't even been served when he took out his money. I gripped the bar with both hands, my heart missed a beat, and I don't know how I stopped myself from shouting out. I'd known I'd recognize it, I'd been afraid of seeing it, but it was even more terrible than I'd thought it would be—there it was! Exactly as my mother had described it. It froze my blood. It was a gold coin mounted on two circles of the same metal that closed up like a trap.

"Check, please." I heard Touret's voice from far away, and then he said, "Are you all right?" I took a deep breath, and my heart started to beat again. I said, "It's the heat." We got our drinks, and I sipped my Vittel-menthe slowly. The bartender gave him his change. I watched him fold the notes carefully. I said, as naturally as I could, "It's nice, your bill clip. It must be valuable." He showed it to me, in his hand. He said, with a smile, "It's Napoleon." That was all. I thought he might get suspicious if I went on, but I couldn't resist saying, "Where did you buy it?" He made a gesture over his head and said, "I've had it for years! A friend gave it to me, an Italian." The words stopped dead in my ears as he looked at the object, remembered, and drank a mouthful of beer. He said, "We made a deal together. He's dead now, poor guy."

He shook his head and put the money in his pocket. I looked at his beer. Instinctively I reached out for my bag, which I had placed too far from me, and put it on the bar. My bag reassured me. I wanted to kill them both that evening, but I knew that was the last thing to do. The coffee-colored secretary, whose name I could no longer remember, would describe the customer who had telephoned her boss. I had to be patient and give her time to forget me.

And yet the bill clip had suddenly made everything impossible. I could no longer bear to be alone with him in that apartment and have to push away his hairy paws. I knew I'd pick up the spade and hit him on the head and go on hitting until he lay there, motionless in the mud and dead leaves. I tried to grab hold of something with my left hand. I heard a cry.

Then I was on the floor, in a bar, and there were all these people standing over me. Someone said, "Don't touch her. We must call the police. Whatever you do, don't touch her." He wasn't dead, my mother said, he wasn't dead. He couldn't move, he couldn't speak, he wouldn't say anything to the police. I was with him in the forest, that was all. He fell from his ladder while cutting branches off a tree. We had to wait. At the hospital, they told my mother we would have to wait. I was on the floor in a bar. I knew where I was. In Digne. I said, "Where's my bag? Give me my bag." My dress would be all dirty. Elle mustn't cry. Elle mustn't cry. I was sure I was going to get up.

It was nearly eight when we left the bar. I must have looked like a drowned cat. My hair was plastered to my forehead and temples. They tried to get me to drink some brandy, but I spat it out. They gave me some very strong coffee. The back of my head hurt. The world was no longer turning around me. I said, just like my fool of a mother, "I've given you a lot of trouble." He said, "No, not at all." I'd just given him a scare. Did I often have this kind of attack? I said, "No, it was the heat. Taking the bus, all the excitement." I put one leg in front of the other, like Calamity when she came back from the ladies' room after taking off her bra. Suddenly I would have given anything to be with her, right away.

We stopped in front of the decrepit building, and Touret said, looking all concerned, "Will you be able to climb the stairs?" I nodded. I grabbed hold of the banister rail and he let go of my arm. He walked up behind me, but I don't think he had the heart to concern himself with my legs. He must have had plenty of time to think about the whole business, and the hundred and fifty people with him when I was lying on the floor in the bar. I stopped at the third-floor landing, to get my strength back, and he said, "Don't rush yourself, take a deep breath." Finally we reached the apartment door. We went in, and I headed straight for the toilet.

I'd had no lunch, so I just brought up liquid. I cleaned the sink and washed my face in cold water after taking off my dress. I dried myself with my handkerchief, did my hair, and put on fresh lipstick. I'd lost two false fingernails from my left hand. Probably when I was grabbing for something to hold on to, at the bar, before falling. I shook my dress and rubbed it with my damp handkerchief to remove what stains I could.

When I went back into the room, Touret was sitting in the same chair as the week before. He said, "Ah! Do you feel better now?" I managed to smile. He said, "It certainly is a crazy summer. Apparently they can't keep track of the number of people who're dying of sunstroke." I sat down on the edge of the bed. It was wide, even for two people, and covered in red velvet. It was arranged as a sofa with big cushions. I felt my damp dress under my thighs.

I looked around me, and Touret said, getting up to put out his cigarette, "Don't worry about the inventory. We'll make an arrangement if you break any dishes. O.K.?" I didn't care— I didn't even know what he meant. I said, "I'll pay you for the first month." He stood up and said, "If you like. But it can wait." I opened my bag and took out one of Cognata's five-hundred-franc notes and three of my mother's hundred-franc notes. I said, "Is that right?" Again he said it could wait. He would have to give me a receipt, and he didn't have one on him. I said, "Oh dear, I thought I would have the keys this evening." He said, "Oh, I can give you the keys."

He'd opened the window while I was in the bathroom. In the distance I could hear an open-air band and a woman shouting at her husband. He shut the windows again and said, "Anyway, it's hotter outside than inside." I felt the bad moment was about to happen, just from the tone of his voice. I got up and moved away from the bed. After a thousand years, he said, "Have you arranged to meet someone here, tonight?" I didn't look at him but just nodded. "A boy friend?" I raised my shoulder slightly and didn't answer. He said, "I don't want to be indiscreet. It's understandable, after all." When I looked at him he was rubbing his chin with the back of his hand. I smiled as if I was embarrassed and said, "It's not what you think." We must have looked like a real pair of fools, standing there facing each other. I went over to the bed to get my bag and said, "I have to go out. I've arranged to meet someone else first."

I knew he would catch me by the arm and would want to kiss me—the whole bit. But I was as tall as him, in my high heels. And he didn't have two other bastards with him to hold me down. He did nothing. He just sighed. I went slowly toward the door with my bag. He said, "Just a minute. I have something to ask you." I turned around, and he lit another cigarette. He asked me if I'd known his brother-in-law, Jean Leballech, before coming to Digne. I said no and shook my head. "I needed some shelves for my books, and I was told to go to him." He said, "He called me to get your address." I said, "I know." He wanted to ask another question, but in the end he just looked at me, then down at the carpet.

The tone of his voice changed. "I hope you won't be annoyed if I say I've rarely seen such a pretty girl as you?" I laughed. I said, "That's always nice to hear." We looked at each other for a thousand years, I with my big round eyes. I said, "I hope next time I see you I won't fall around all over the place like a fool." He laughed, too. He said, "Well, it had its charm, I suppose." I presumed he was referring to the color of my panties. I shrugged my shoulders with my Child of Mary look, all ashamed of myself, but in fact I couldn't have cared less.

Outside, on the sidewalk, he offered to take me back in his car. I shook his hand and said no, I didn't have far to go. I had the keys of the apartment in my bag and was relieved to have got out of his clutches without any trouble. That must have brought the color back to my cheeks. He said, "You're looking better now. When shall I see you again?" It seemed impossible to get my hand back—he'd probably decided to keep that as a deposit. I said, "Next week. I'll let you know when I come back, and this time I'll give you a drink in *my* apartment!" He said, "Wonderful," then, when I gave a tug on my hand, "Excuse me," as if he hadn't been holding on to it intentionally.

I walked on. Night was falling, and I caught snatches of music from the dance. Ping-Pong had wanted to go dancing in town with his brothers, but I'd said no, I hated the Fourteenth of July crowds. I couldn't bear to have to watch Boo-Boo and his Marie-Laure all evening.

Leballech was waiting for me in his car, at the place he had suggested. No sooner was I sitting next to him than I tore into his brother-in-law: "He just wouldn't let me go!" Then I said, "Are you annoyed with me? I was really getting desperate. I was afraid you wouldn't wait. Then, on top of everything, I got sick. It must have been the heat, or the excitement, I don't know." He tried to calm me down by stroking my breasts through my dress. I said, "Please, not here, not now." Sweet as honey, I said, "Look." I held up the apartment key. He smiled, all serious, and we sat there, like a women's magazine story, our eyes on the windshield, thinking of our great love and the good time we were going to give each other in that little nest.

Then I put my knife in. "He's quite a ladies' man, your brother-in-law." I felt him bristle without even looking at him. He said, darkly, "Did he make a pass at you?" I sighed and said, "A pass? I was scared stiff, yes. I don't know how I managed to keep him quiet. He's a sex maniac, that guy." I let him grind his teeth, then added, "Forgive me for talking about your brother-in-law like that, but really, I've been alone with him twice now, and both times I was scared out of my wits." He said, "I'm not surprised. No, I'm not surprised." He took me in his arms again and started rubbing my back as if I was cold. That was as far as it went. It was a quarter to nine by my watch—the clock on the dashboard wasn't working. Calamity would be having a fit.

I said, "I really must go now, darling." Sad and everything. He went on kissing me for a thousand years, I sighed enough to burst my dress and got out. I looked him straight in the eyes and said, as if really bushed, "I can't see you before next week. You won't forget me, I hope?" He didn't even bother to answer but asked, "When?" I said I would telephone him, just to hear his voice and to fix a date. I'd be very careful—I'd only talk about the bookshelves. I'd be expecting him in the little nest. Tuesday at the latest, I swore. When I left him, it was so beautiful, so moving, I almost believed it. I swear, my breast was filled with sighs, and my throat was dry. Once I'd finished with them both I would go to Paris and act in the movies.

At one o'clock in the morning by my watch, Calamity pulled up her Innocenti-something-or-other-matic in front of my fool of a mother's gate. She was crying. I said, all patience, "Shit, that's enough, you're no use to me crying like a Mary Magdalene." I pulled her by the shoulder and turned her toward me. She looked at me with big red eyes. She said, "I can't . . . help it. I can't help it . . . ." I turned off the car light. I held her in my arms for a thousand years or more. She went on crying and hiccupping stupidly, and whenever I wiped her face with my hand, she cried still more. A thousand years.

Finally I said, "You know very well I don't get out here. I live with Ping-Pong." She looked around her crazily and sniveled some more. We'd just come from Le Brusquet, where she'd made an omelette and a salad. She'd started crying before we left her house. She'd hardly stopped since I told her I was at the mercy of two bastards who could disfigure me, injure me for life, or kill me, as they liked, and who forced me to do you-know-what. She didn't know, of course, the poor idiot. When I explained to her that they provided me with an apartment to receive men in, her hand went to her mouth, and the tears poured out of her eyes. It was a miracle she managed to drive so far without the windshield wipers; as it was, she had to stop five times along the way. She cried and cried, her head resting on the steering wheel. I cried almost as much, in fact.

I'm like a monkey. If someone does something, I have to do it, too.

We were sitting on the sofa in the living room, on the first floor, when the idea came to me. She'd taken off my dress and my panties and was doing this and that to me. I was about to come—not really, I hardly ever do with her, I just pretend to. I hardly have to do anything to her—you just have to touch her and she comes. I really like watching her when she's coming. She doesn't shout out, she shudders as if with pain, but her face changes. It's incredible, she gets more and more beautiful until she falls back as if all her nerves were snapped. And every time, when she opens her eyes, you'd never guess what she says: "My God, I'm so ashamed!" I swear, that's what she says. What's more, she has the tiniest feet—almost like a child's—and when she comes, all her toes curl up.

I took her in my arms on the blue sofa and talked to her in the same voice she used when she was my teacher. First, she must keep it a secret. Once I was married, the two bastards would probably leave me alone. Otherwise... She looked up, her eyes red with crying. She looked terrified. "Otherwise what?" I said, "Otherwise, I'll get rid of them, one way or another. Or I'll tell everything to Ping-Pong, and let him do it."

In the car I said, "Calamity, take me home. I won't be able to explain why I've come back so late." She nodded her head several times, swallowing her sobs, and we set off. We drove through the village. There was still a light on at the Larguiers', and in a room over Brochard's café. There was a light on upstairs at my mother's, too. I tried to fix my hair before arriving. Then I told myself it was useless—Ping-Pong would see how I looked.

Calamity pulled up at the open gate. I let her turn around before I got out. The headlights swept over the yard, and I saw a cat dash across. If Dolorosa saw it near her rabbits, that would be the end of it. I said to Calamity, "I trust you. If you repeat anything I've said, you can't imagine what will happen to me." She threw herself at me and kissed me as if she'd never see me again. She said, "My darling, my child." I took her by the shoulders and forced her away. "It's no use going to the police, do you understand? They wouldn't believe me. They're both respectable married men, not at all the pimps you might think. They've both got wives and children, and plenty of money, and if they kill me, no one would find my body. It's happened to others."

She put her hand to her mouth again. She stopped crying, but it was even worse. She looked at me as if I was already chopped up in pieces. Pure horror! I didn't know how she would manage to get home. I said, "O.K. I hope for my sake you understand. If things go badly, the only person besides you I'll say anything to is Ping-Pong." I put a finger on her forehead and said, "Let it stay there." I got out of the car, and she tried to grab my arm. She sprawled across the front seat, trying to hold on to me, a mad look in her eyes. I said, "Don't worry. I'll be careful." I pulled my wrist free. When she was sitting up again, I slammed the door. I headed off toward the house. She shouted after me, "Eliane!" I turned and said, quite loudly, "Come and see me tomorrow afternoon. I swear everything's all right now. Go back home now. See you tomorrow afternoon."

In the kitchen, it wasn't Ping-Pong waiting up for me but the mother-in-law. She was standing by the table, wearing her ancient nightgown. I leaned against the wall after shutting the door. She was angry, but perhaps more surprised than angry when she saw me. She said, "What happened?" I shut my eyes. I heard Calamity's car move off. I said, "I fainted at Mlle Dieu's. I was very sick." A century went by in the dark. I heard her breathing and my own. She said, "They've called out all the firemen. There are terrible fires above Grasse." I said, in the dark, "Poor Ping-Pong."

When I opened my eyes, I saw she had come over toward me in her slippers. She looked at me—not in an evil way, but not with love, either. Her face was brown and wrinkled. Her eyes had lost their color. I said, "Come on. You must get some sleep." We went upstairs. On the landing, before opening the

bedroom door, I kissed her on the cheek. She smelled like
Cognata. She said, "I've put an old bill on your bed. The truck
driver who brought back the piano was a man my husband
knew, he was named Leballech."

I thought of Calamity missing a turn on her way home.
"What do you think I care?" I asked wearily. She didn't look
annoyed. She said, "I thought you were interested. I spent all
afternoon looking through my things to find that bill." I looked
down and said, "I thought I'd seen your piano when I was a
little girl. My childhood is very important to me." She said
nothing for a moment, then, "Yes, that's true. That's one thing
I can understand about you."

When I was in the bedroom, I picked up the paper from
the bed, put on my glasses, and looked at it. It was an old bill,
in old francs, with *Ferraldo and Son* printed at the top. It was
dated November 19, 1955, and signed in ink, in very careful
writing, *Montecciari Lello.* The name of the truck driver was
written in by hand, like the rest, probably by Ferraldo's mother:
J. Leballech. At the bottom you could make out *Paid in cash,
11/21/55,* and a signature. I took out of my bag Leballech's
card—he'd written an address for my bookshelves on it. He
hadn't made much progress in twenty years. I was thinking
more of Calamity than him and all that. I'd made up my mind
once and for all in Le Brusquet, after hesitating for several
days. Now I was tired.

Before falling asleep, I smelled Mlle Dieu on me, mixed
with that Dior thing. It's funny, someone's smell. My daddy—
stop that. My mommy. I like her smell best. Boo-Boo. I ban-
ished the thought that he was at the dance. I told myself he
was sleeping at the other end of the landing. I wasn't annoyed
with him any more. I'd make love with him as sure as I'm
alive. And again, and again, and again. I still had in my mind
the sight of the road unfolding in the headlights. Our Father,
who art in heaven, make sure that idiot gets home safely.

I woke at dawn, drenched in sweat. I'd had a horrible dream.
I hadn't closed the shutters, and a cold light was gradually

invading the room. I heard Mickey getting his coffee ready downstairs, just below. Ping-Pong hadn't come back. I got up and went to the wardrobe to make sure the bottle was still in my red blazer pocket. I took it out and looked at it to make sure it was the same one. In my dream, it was my mother who was poisoned as I looked on, at the bar in Digne. I knew she was going to die, and I cried out. Then they started pulling handfuls of her hair out, and her face was covered with blood. Mlle Dieu was there, and Ping-Pong, and Touret, but not Leballech. Someone said he was coming, and everyone laughed and forced me to eat my mother's hair.

I don't know how long I stood in the room, naked. I heard Mickey in the yard, trying to get his truck going. I went to the window. I asked him what he was going to do so early on the Fourteenth of July. Maybe he'd brought Georgette back with him last night. I couldn't see whether she was in the truck. I watched him go off, then put on my white bathrobe with *Elle* embroidered on it and went down into the kitchen. There was no one there. I made myself some coffee, turning around several times because I had the feeling someone was behind me. Finally I went out with my bowl and sat down on the stone seat near the door to drink my coffee, which steamed in the first rays of the red sun, between the mountains.

Things got better, as always. I walked barefoot in the yard, going as far as the fields behind, where the grass was soft and damp. I had no idea what time it was. The campers' big tent was silent at the far end of the field. I didn't go any farther. I wet my feet in the stream, but the water was icy, and I took them out right away. I sat down on a big stone, trying to think of nothing. When I think of nothing, I always think of the same crap. This time, I saw myself coming on the blue sofa in Le Brusquet, Calamity's head between my raised knees. She said it was so strong I pulled on her hair without realizing.

After a while one of the campers—the taller of the two— came out with a big bucket to get water from the stream. He was wearing rather threadbare shorts. His body was tanned brick-red, and the hair on his chest was bleached by the sun.

He said, "Good morning, you're up early." We'd never spoken to each other before. He told me his name was François, and I showed him mine, embroidered on my bathrobe. He said, "That's not a Christian name." I said, "No? Well, that's one more illusion you've lost." He asked me if I'd had my coffee. He said, "Come and have another cup with us." I said O.K. and followed him.

We both walked barefoot to the tent, and he told me they were all from Colmar, in the Haut-Rhin department. I had no idea where that was, but I said, "Oh yes," as if I'd spent all my life there. He asked me where my accent came from. I said, "My mother's Austrian." He tried to speak to me in German and I repeated, *"Ja, ja."* I understood a bit, but not much. Finally he dropped it.

His friend and the two girls had just woken up. The friend was wearing canvas trousers, one of the girls old jeans cut off at the knees, and the other a slip with an open hand printed on the behind. They both wandered around with their tits showing. They were well tanned and healthy-looking and all that. I was introduced to Henri and shook hands with him. He wasn't as good-looking as François, but not bad, except that he hadn't shaved for a long time. The blonde girl, in cut-off jeans, was named Didi, and the other one, the prettier of the two, who had small, hard, well-rounded tits, Mylène. They made coffee and we drank it sitting on the ground in front of the tent. It was really quiet there. No one ahead of them, no one behind them. Didi told me they didn't have enough money to get to Sicily, so they'd decided to stay there. Both the boys worked in a bank in Colmar. I said, "Why didn't they open a safe?" But they only smiled politely and said nothing. I saw the air mattresses inside the tent. There was nothing between them, and I asked, "How do you manage fucking?" But they didn't have an answer for that, either. Finally I realized they were beginning to find me a bit vulgar, and not at all what they'd thought, so I shut up.

I'd been there four thousand years, and I knew every detail of their boring lives, including the dates of their baptism, when

we heard someone coming, and who do you think it was? A
guy with dirt all over his face and hands, wearing a soiled shirt,
crumpled trousers, filthy boots—he looked done in. But he
looked as pleased as Mickey's favorite racer when interviewed
on TV. In fact, he resembled him in some ways, but was about
twice as well built. He waved his hands around at everybody
and said, "Excuse me, my hands are dirty." To me he said,
"Are you up already?" I didn't have to go back to school to
realize he'd be sulking all day because I had nothing on under
my bathrobe, and everybody must have realized. The fact that
the other girls had their tits bare didn't seem to matter. In all
fairness, he didn't even look at them, just at me. I got up, said
good-bye, and thanked them for the coffee and all that, and
the two of us walked back toward the house through the field.
I said, "Listen, Ping-Pong. It's just by chance I happened to
be there." He said, without looking at me, "I'm not criticizing.
I'm just tired." I walked three or four more steps quickly to
catch up with him and took his arm. He said, "Anyway, don't
call me Ping-Pong."

When we got to the house, Boo-Boo, Cognata, and Mickey,
who had come back, were in the kitchen. Boo-Boo, in his
pajamas, was eating his way through twelve thousand slices of
bread. He said, "Brochard came over a while back. Your
schoolteacher called to say she got home safely." A lump came
to my throat at once—it seemed a great proof of love that she
should have thought to do that. But I said, "How can you
swallow all that?" He shrugged his shoulders and smiled. I die
when he smiles. I kissed Cognata and went upstairs.

In the bedroom Ping-Pong got undressed and lay down on
the unmade bed. He said, "I've got to get some sleep. Tonight
we'll go out dancing together, just the two of us." I was sitting
next to him. He hadn't bothered to wash, and he smelled of
smoke. He kept his eyes open for a while, then shut them and
said, "Verdier has a broken collarbone. You know, the young
guy who was with me at the Bing Bang when I met you?"
"Yes, I remember." "He's broken his collarbone."

I was pleased Mlle Dieu had called. That was a real proof

of love, or at least I thought so. It's the greatest proof of love
when people are concerned about your worrying about them.
Everybody—except my mother—thinks that if someone is concerned about me, I don't care. It's not true. I just don't want
to show my feelings, that's all. Telephoning Brochard is a
greater proof of love than the one she thought she was giving
me the night before, in Digne, when I got into her car. She'd
been there a long time, waiting for me, across from the Provençal. When she got through with all the complaints about
how late I was, the first thing she said to me was, "I went to
see your parents on Saturday afternoon. Your mother showed
me your wedding dress. I took them a request for recognition
of paternity for your father. I didn't manage to persuade him
to sign it, but you'll see, one day it will be part of your family
file."

So there you are. Saturday afternoon, when I was wandering
around town, not knowing what to do to pass the time. After
calling Leballech, I'd been weeping inside like that idiot could
cry outside. She'd gone to our home. She thought she would
make me happy and everything would be marvelous and I'd
finally understand that she'd loved me, as she said, since I was
fourteen or fifteen, from the first moment she set eyes on me.
I did understand, in fact, I wasn't *insensitive*, certainly not.
I'm not *insensitive*, or *asocial*, or of *a perverse character*, as
some shit of a social worker typed out after some idiotic tests
they made me take in Nice. And there was a doctor with her
who almost wanted to lock me up. And yet, and yet, what
went through my head when Calamity told me about her good
deed was not that she loved me, or that I should jump for joy
and split my head open on the roof of her mini. What went
through my head was that she had seen him, *him*, talked to
him, gone into his room, and I hadn't. I hadn't—that was it.

I was standing at the window, my forehead against the glass.
I was in the sun. I told myself I'd go see him in my white
wedding dress, on my wedding day, when they were all drinking
and laughing and telling their idiotic stories. For the first time
in four years, nine months, and five days. And then, before

the end of July, Ping-Pong would see his family fall apart as mine had done. He would lose his brothers, as I had lost my father. Where was my father? Where was he? It hurts me when I think of my fool of a mother with those three bastards, that snowy winter's day, and I hate them for what they did to her. But the truth is, I don't really care. I don't care when I think of what they've done to us, to her and to me. Where is he? I hit some dirty guy over the head with a spade, but he wasn't my daddy, he was some guy I didn't know. You must stop, now, stop. He used to say to me, "I'll give you money. I'll take you on a trip—to Paris."

The sun was hurting my eyes.

I would tear Ping-Pong to shreds. He would get one of his filthy father's rifles, and I would say to him, "It's Leballech, it's Touret," and he'd kill them. I will be Elle. Wiped out. I shall come to my daddy and I shall say to him, "All three are dead now. I'm cured, and so are you."

I realized I was on the stairs, sitting on a step, holding the banister. My cheek was resting against the polished wood, and at times I could see the kitchen below, the brightness of the window. There was no noise, nothing, just my breathing. I'd had to pull off my false fingernails, one by one. I felt them in my other hand, which I held tight against my mouth. I cried when I thought of his face. He came along the path to our house. He stopped a few paces away from me so that I could run and jump into his arms. He laughed. "And what has Daddy brought back for his darling little girl?" he shouted. "What has he brought back?" Nothing and nobody could make me understand that that was *before*, I wanted it to be now, and to go on forever. Forever.

THE EXECUTION

It was a summer of fires.

At night I couldn't sleep. I remembered the pine trees burning on the hillsides, the planes flying low over the fires, the sheets of water beating against the ground like cannonballs, glittering in the sunlit clearings, through the smoke.

I remembered the wedding, too. Elle in her long white dress, altered with so much loving care by her mother that it seemed like a second skin. The veil she took off in the yard, and tore up to give a piece to everyone. Her smile that day. In the church, as I was putting the ring on her finger, I saw in her that same shadow I'd seen before. It reminded me of the flight of lost birds, in autumn, between the mountains. Her smile, just at the corners of her lips, was so hesitant, so delicate, I felt sorry for her, yes, sorry for her. I'd have given anything to understand her and help her. Or maybe I'm making it all up now, I don't know.

There were thirty-five or forty of us for the meal. Then more people came, then more, from the village and from elsewhere, and by the middle of the afternoon, when we were dancing, there were perhaps twice as many of us or more. I opened the dance with Elle, a waltz, to please her mother— and mine. She held her dress in one hand, so as not to dirty it, and she kept turning and turning, and finally she let herself fall against me, laughing, and lost her balance. She said very little to me during the morning, but once she said, "Isn't it marvelous, isn't it marvelous...?" I hugged her to me. I had my arm around her waist as we went back to the tables, through all the guests, who were giving me great slaps on the back. Even now I only have to think of it to feel in my hand the softness of her body through her dress.

Later I watched her dance with Mickey. He was best man, and at lunch he had gone under the table and removed from her leg one of my grandmother's blue garters, the only one we could find to keep up the custom. They'd all taken off their jackets and ties, and even in shirt-sleeves my luckless racer of a brother looked like a prince, because he was dancing with a princess. I said to Boo-Boo, who was sitting next to me, "Just look at them!" He put his arm around my shoulders and gave me a big kiss on my cheek for the first time since he'd got it into his head that it wasn't manly to kiss his brother. He said, "It's a marvelous day!"

Yes. The sun on the mountains around us, people laughing at Henri IV's jokes, the flowing wine, the records being played alternately to please the young and the old so they could both dance—yes, everything was fine. Eva Braun was there; I'd found a nurse in town to look after my paralyzed father-in-law until eight o'clock. Sometimes our eyes met—hers are blue, like her daughter's—and she smiled at me, to show me she was pleased. I'm sure she really was pleased; we've talked about it since. She knew more than I did about what Elle had in store for us.

At one point, standing all by myself at the barn door, I could hear music and shouting, and I started to laugh out loud. I thought, "Well, this is my wedding day. I'm married now." I'd had a lot to drink, and the sound of my laughter didn't enter my ears as it usually did. I seemed to be laughing in another world. The people dancing in the dust weren't real. It wasn't really our yard, the one I'd always known.

It was shortly after that, as far as I remember, that I began to look for Elle. No one knew where she was. Boo-Boo, who was busy in the barn looking after the stereo a pal from school had lent him, said, "I saw her go into the house five minutes ago." I went into the kitchen, where a lot of people were laughing and drinking. She wasn't there. I said to Mamma, "Well, I've already lost my wife." She hadn't seen her for some time, either.

I went upstairs. There was no one in our room, and I looked

again, out of the window, at the couples dancing in the yard. Eva Braun was sitting at a table with M. Larguier. Mlle Dieu was sitting by herself near the spring, a glass in her hand. I also saw Juliette and Henri IV, Martine Brochard, Moune the hairdresser, and other friends of Elle's whose names I didn't know.

I hadn't seen Mickey, so I went and knocked on his door. Georgette shouted out, terrified, "No! Don't come in!" And I realized I was disturbing them. Whenever I knock on a door, there's Mickey behind it with Georgette, getting ready to lose his next race.

I went back downstairs. I walked around the yard again, looking for her. I went as far as the road to see if she was outside with someone. Then I had a word with Eva Braun. She looked around her anxiously and said, "I thought she was with you." I found Mlle Dieu in the barn selecting records with Boo-Boo and his pal, the owner of the stereo. She'd had a lot to drink, too—there was a glazed look in her eyes, and her voice sounded odd. She said she'd seen Eliane going down into the field, "to invite the campers, but that was some time ago." Except for Eva Braun she was the only one to say "Eliane," and, I don't know why, it irritated me. I'd only met her once. She'd come on the afternoon of the Fourteenth of July, three days before—and I knew right away I wasn't going to like her. It would be no use now trying to explain why. It's my stupidity as much as hers that's to blame for everything.

I crossed the yard, forcing myself to walk naturally so as not to upset the guests, but I couldn't help running down the field. The campers' Volkswagen was not there under the trees, and the tent was empty. I was breathing heavily. I don't know what I imagined had happened. I thought of the Fourteenth of July, when she'd come back so late—half past one in the morning, Mamma said—and I found her there, naked under her bathrobe, when the sun was hardly up. I stayed for a moment in the tent, thinking. I looked around and saw the inflatable mattresses, the clothes all over the place, the unwashed plates and things. There was a smell of cooking and rubber. I had that feeling again that things were not quite real, but I wasn't drunk. I told myself the campers would be leaving at the end of the month, and if they wanted to stay longer in our field, I could find some excuse to say no.

On the way out I almost bumped into Boo-Boo, who had come to find me. "What's going on?" he asked. I shrugged my shoulders and said, "I don't know." We walked on to the stream, and I splashed cold water on my face. He said I'd had a lot to drink, and when you had had a lot to drink, you saw everything distorted, even the simplest things. It was quite possible, after all, that Elle had wanted to be alone for a while. It was a big day for her. He said, "She's very emotional, you know." I nodded several times. I adjusted his bow tie for him, and we walked slowly back through the field. When we reached the yard I found that everybody was wondering where I'd got to. I danced with Juliette, then with Moune, then with Georgette, who had come down from Mickey's room. I forced myself to laugh with everyone. Henri IV went to get some wine from the barrel, which was set up outside the bicycle shed, and I drank a glass in one gulp. It was our own wine—not a big yield, but it's good.

Every now and then I looked at Eva Braun. She managed a broad smile whenever anyone walked by her, but I could tell she was getting more and more worried. Mlle Dieu was at another table, looking very sorry for herself, with an empty glass. I saw her get up and refill it. She was making as much of an effort to walk straight as I was to look as if I was having a good time. She was wearing a very low-cut black dress, the material of which had got caught in the cleavage of her buttocks, and she kept pulling on it. I thought she looked ridiculous, but I was glad, in a way, that she did.

At seven o'clock Elle had still not come back. When people asked me where she was, I answered, "She's gone to lie down for a while." I realized, more and more, that no one believed me, and that the guests fell quiet when I walked by them. Finally I went and had a word with Mickey. I led him over to the gate and said, "We'd better take Henri IV's car and drive around—she might be on the road somewhere."

We drove through the deserted village—everyone, or almost everyone, was at our place—and stopped at Brochard's café. Mother Brochard hadn't wanted to close, in case she missed selling a safety pin to some tourist whose trouser zipper had broken, but she was determined to see the wedding all the same and had left her husband to look after the café. He was alone inside, sitting over a beer and one of those magazines he didn't dare look at when his wife was there. He hadn't seen Elle since she'd come out of the church on my arm that morning. He said how good I'd looked, and the bride, too.

We went to Eva Braun's. It was the last place I expected to find her, since her mother was with us, but Mickey said "There's no harm in trying. You never know." We knocked on the door window, but there was no answer. We went in; the whole house was quiet. The kitchen wasn't a living room, like at our place, but was separated from the main room by a partition. Mickey had never been inside. He looked around with curiosity and said, "Well, they've certainly done a good job with it." "Is anyone here?" I called out. I heard someone moving around in the room upstairs, and the nurse I'd hired, Mlle Tusseau, came down, a finger on her lips. She said, "He's asleep now."

She looked exhausted—I could tell something had happened. Her eyes were red, as if she'd been crying. She pulled a chair toward her, sat down, and sighed deeply. "My poor boy," she said. "I don't know who your wife is, it's no concern of mine, but I've had a terrible time." She looked me straight in the eyes. "Terrible."

I asked her if Elle was upstairs, and she said, "Good heavens, no! But she has been here." Mlle Tusseau was about forty. She wasn't really a nurse, but she could give injections and look after the sick. That day she was wearing a white apron over a blue dress, and it was torn. She showed it to me and said, "She did that." Then she shook her head, her eyes full of tears. She couldn't speak.

I sat down, and Mickey did, too. He was embarrassed at being there and said that if I liked he could wait for me outside in the car. I said no, it would be better if he stayed. I didn't know whether I was drunk or not. Everything seemed even more unreal than at home. Mlle Tusseau wiped her eyes with a little handkerchief rolled in a ball. We had to wait for a long time before she managed to tell us what had happened, and even longer to get to the end of it, because she kept going off on tangents to make quite sure that everybody had a good opinion of her in town, knew that she'd helped a lot of people, etc., etc. Mickey was less patient, or less drunk, than I was and kept saying, "O.K. What happened then?"

That afternoon, said Mlle Tusseau, Elle arrived about five, alone, in her wedding dress. She didn't bring a piece of wedding cake or a bottle of wine or anything. She just wanted to see her father, to see him. Elle was "very emotional"; that was obvious, you could tell from her voice. Mlle Tusseau thought it was very nice of her to leave the wedding to show her paralyzed father that she was thinking of him. If she herself had never married, it was because of the health of her parents, when they were still in this world. "O.K. What happened then?" Mickey asked.

They were both going upstairs when it happened. The old man, from his room, recognized his daughter's footsteps and started shouting and insulting her. He yelled that he didn't want Elle to come in. But before Mlle Tusseau could stop her, she'd run across the landing and gone in.

He shouted even more loudly that he didn't want Elle to see him. He fidgeted in his chair, his arms over his face, as if he was going mad. But she went up to him, pushing Mlle Tusseau aside, "with incredible savagery." It was then she tore the apron. Tears were streaming down her cheeks, and she was breathing heavily. She stared at her father. She couldn't speak. She stayed about a minute, standing there before him while he tried to hide his face. You could tell she was making a terrible effort to say something, and then she dropped down onto her knees and put her arms around his dead legs and clung to him. She, too, was shouting, not words, just a long cry.

Then Mlle Tusseau had tried to pull her away, threatening to call the police, but Elle "fought like a wildcat," and it was dangerous because she might have pulled her father out of the chair with her. The old man had stopped shouting. He was crying. She, too, calmed down after a while and just lay there, her head on his legs. He whispered, "Please, please"—all the time, like a litany. In the end the old man said, still hiding his face, "Go away, Eliane, go and get your mother. I want your mother."

She got up without saying anything. She looked at him for a long while, just standing there, then said, "Soon we'll be the way we used to be. You'll see, I'm sure of it." At least that's what Mlle Tusseau understood her to say. The old man said nothing. When Elle had gone, he went on crying, alone in his chair. His pulse was "very alarming." Mlle Tusseau gave him a sedative, but it was an hour before his heart slowed down and he fell asleep.

There was something else. There was always something else with Elle. When she came back down into the kitchen to leave, she went to splash some cold water on her face. She looked at herself in the mirror over the sink. She saw that Mlle Tusseau was watching her. Without turning around she said, with her usual frankness and in the words that came most easily to her, what she thought of old maids, and what they ought to try instead of meddling in other people's affairs, and, if I understood her correctly, something else that Mlle Tusseau found particularly "terrible," because she didn't even know it existed.

Without being asked, Mickey took over the steering wheel when we went back to the car. He didn't start up the engine right away. We sat there in front of the gate, which Eva Braun had decorated with climbing roses, smoking a cigarette. Then he said, "You know, you can't believe everything women say. They always exaggerate." I said yes, of course. Then he added,

"Anyway, he's obviously senile, the poor man. Every day shut up like that in a bedroom. Don't you think?" I said yes, of course. In his opinion, it was quite a simple matter—there were things like that in every family, but they passed. When Elle had come to live with me without getting married, her father had sworn never to see her again. I should put myself in his place. And she had thought, because she was a good girl really, that her wedding day would be a good opportunity to make peace with him. And that's how he treated her, and in front of a stranger. I should put myself in her place. I said yes, of course. He said couldn't I say something else, just to vary it a bit. But in his opinion Elle was probably hiding in a corner somewhere, just like a kid, not wanting to see anybody. I had to realize that, for all her fine airs, she was really only a kid.

I looked at him, my brother Mickey. Sweat and sun had made his hair stand every which way. He had our father's hair, real Rital hair. I thought he was right about everything except the most important thing—that incredible scene between Elle and the man she always referred to as "the old shithead," or "the other shithead." In other words, he was right about nothing. But I said, "O.K. Let's go and see if she's come back."

She hadn't come back. Mickey took Eva Braun home to relieve the nurse, and night began to fall. I said nothing to Eva Braun—she'd find out soon enough. I kissed her on the cheeks and held her tight in my arms. She said, very sadly, in her German accent, "Don't be angry. It's not her fault. I swear it's not her fault." I had a terrible question to ask her. I nearly did ask it, then I saw her blue eyes, her trusting face, and I couldn't. I wanted to ask her whether, five years earlier, Elle had had anything to do with her father's accident. There are times when I'm not so Ping-Pong as people think.

Many of the guests had gone. Others were getting into their cars. They all thanked me as they left, with a gaiety I felt to be false. The yard was littered with empty bottles, empty glasses, and shreds of Elle's veil. A cloud of dust seemed to hover just above the ground. In front of the barn, around some trestle tables, a few people were still listening to Henri IV's stories. There was Boo-Boo and his school pal, Martin Brochard, Georgette, Tessari and his wife, and some other people I knew only by sight. Juliette and Mamma were setting one of the tables. Mamma said, "We're going to eat something anyway."

Mlle Dieu was sitting in the kitchen, next to Cognata's chair. She said to me, "Don't be angry with her when she comes back." She added, "You'll only regret it later, when you know her better." Cognata wanted to know what we were saying. I waved my hand at her to tell her to be quiet, and I said to Mlle Dieu, "Why? Do you know her better than I do?" She looked down, because I spoke quite loudly, and said, "I've known her longer." She looked as if she was sobering up, and she'd fixed her hair. Her breasts, in the clevage of her black dress, were white and of a size you couldn't fail to notice. She felt I was looking at them, and she put her hand there. I don't know why, but I no longer felt any animosity toward her. I said, "O.K. You were her schoolteacher, after all."

I took a bottle of wine out of the cupboard and filled the three glasses without asking. The blonde of my dreams took the glass I held out to her and gave a little nod by way of thanks. I clinked Cognata's glass, then said, "Your health, Mlle Dieu!" She said, "You can call me Florence." I said her pupil always called her Mlle Dieu. She laughed—not a lot, but it was the first time I'd seen her laugh. She said, "Oh no! Do you know what she calls me? Calamity. She has no respect for me at all." While she was drinking, she put her hand over her cleavage again. We looked at each other for a moment; then I said, "She's got no respect for anyone."

Later Mamma served outside what was left of the wedding breakfast. Boo-Boo had strung up a wire from the barn to a lamp over the table, but the electricity on that side of the barn only works when it wants to, and the wire wasn't long enough to reach the kitchen. After discussing the matter for quite some time, we reached the conclusion that it would be too difficult to move the table nearer the house, so we lit some kerosene lamps and candles. Cognata agreed with Juliette and Florence—Calamity—that it was "fairylike."

In the end there were about fifteen of us. Boo-Boo's pal and Martine Brochard ate in silence; apparently it was love at first sight, and just as everybody was saying good-bye, they'd managed to summon up courage to speak to each other. Henri IV was asking riddles, which made Mickey burst out laughing, and which Juliette and Georgette were determined not to hear, and which I couldn't listen to. The air was warm, my throat hurt like when I was a kid, and I didn't want to look like a blubbering cowboy.

I shook hands with Mlle Dieu, who was going home. I shook hands with a couple I didn't know. At one point Boo-Boo said to me, "Next Sunday Mickey is going to win at Digne. It's just his race, you'll see." I don't quite know how to put it, but it seemed to me to be obvious enough that neither Elle nor I would see next Sunday.

It was nearly eleven when Elle came back. I was sitting with my back to the gate, on purpose, so as not to see her when she came back. I could tell when she'd come from the look in the others' eyes. Everyone fell silent and looked at me, wondering how I'd react. I turned around, just for a second, as she stood there without moving, in her white dress, the hem all soiled, her long hair spread wide, her face indescribable—or maybe just tired. I looked at my plate. She came up; I heard her behind me. She stopped quite near; she bent down and kissed me on the temple. She said to me, just loudly enough for everyone to hear, "I didn't want to come back until you were alone; I thought everybody would have gone home."

Boo-Boo, who was sitting next to me, got up, and she took his place. She looked at what remained on the plate in front of her and started to eat. I'm sure it was more to have something to do than because she was hungry. She was never hungry. She'd eat bread and chocolate from time to time. She never drank, either—just a Vittel-menthe when she was out. Otherwise, water from the spring, in her hands. To break the tension Mickey said, "They won't be calling you Eliane any more, but Désirée." She smiled, her mouth full, and took my hand under the table without looking at me. When she'd swallowed she said, "I'm a nuisance to you all."

She said it in such a way that after a moment of surprise, everybody preferred to laugh. Cognata, who hadn't heard, had it explained to her. She, too, laughed and said to me something that has always remained engraved on my mind: "The girl doesn't even know what words mean. She says anything, just to show she's there, like someone might play on a piano without knowing the notes—at least it makes a noise."

No one had ever heard my aunt speak in this way except Elle, I think, who continued to pick at the vegetables on her plate without seeming concerned. Cognata said, "Listen to me! You've got ears, haven't you?" She tapped on the table with her fingertips, and I understood what she wanted to tell me before she said it. She stared at me with her washed-out eyes. What she had to say was for my ears. Three dots, three dashes, three dots. Laughing, she said with her thin, old woman's voice, "I'm right, aren't I? I'm right, eh?" I said nothing. The others didn't understand, and she said, still laughing, "I was a captain in the Guides when I was a girl. That's all I remember of Morse code." She was still laughing. "You see, if that's all I remember, it proves there must be a lot of us who want to say the same thing. We make different noises, that's all."

It was Elle who put the finishing touch to that day. Still holding my hand under the table, she spoke to Cognata without making her voice leave her mouth, just with her lips, so no one heard anything. But Cognata started laughing again, coughing and spluttering, so much so that Henri IV and Mickey got up to slap her back. Of course everybody wanted to know what Elle had said, but Cognata opened her eyes wide, trying to breathe normally, and shook her head, just shook her head. Then I turned to Elle, and I spoke to her for the first time since she'd come back. I said, "What did you say to her?" She squeezed my hand. She replied, for everyone, "I said I wanted my wedding night, I couldn't wait any more, and all your chitchat was keeping me up." Honestly, that's exactly what she said. There were still several others around the table. They can confirm it.

She'd stayed for several hours by the river, at a place called Palm Beach; then it was too late to come back without having me make a scene in front of everybody, so she waited until she thought the guests would be gone. The later it got, the more afraid she was I'd beat her, and that hardly encouraged her to come back. It was not so much the beating that frightened her as being beaten in front of people.

That's what she said next morning. There was no one at home except Cognata, downstairs, and we could talk in peace. I was lying in bed, as I do every Sunday morning when I was married the day before, and she was sitting next to me, naked, her feet on the ground, with my fist between her thighs—she said she found it easier to talk when my left hand was in its place. It was her own form of yoga.

She didn't mention her visit to her father until she found out I knew about it. First she said, "Shit," staring at herself in the mirror, and then, looking at me, she said it wasn't important, she couldn't care less about that old shithead who smelled of piss. Whatever that bitch of a nurse had told me was lies. Couldn't we talk of something more amusing?

I asked her why, if she thought so little about him, she bothered to go and see him. She said without hesitation, "He promised he would recognize me if I got married. I want his name on my papers." She had a kind of genius for shutting you up with the one reason you weren't expecting. Nevertheless, I asked her why she was still concerned about having her father's name, when she now had mine. She said, again without hesitation, "Just to annoy him. If she croaks before him, I'll inherit the property from his sister, Clémence. At least I'd be able to compensate my mother for the life he's led her. And that, believe me, would annoy him." I didn't even know such a sister existed, and if she hadn't brought her mother into it, I wouldn't have believed her, because it wasn't like her to be concerned about an inheritance. She may have had her faults, but she wasn't grasping. Even Mamma had to admit that. Again she asked if we couldn't find a more amusing topic of conversation, so I dropped it for the time being.

I talked to her about Mlle Dieu. She laughed. "You see, I'd be jealous if you put your thing in M. Loubet's Loulou-Lou, or in Marthe, who wrote you letters. But if you like Mlle Dieu, I really don't care what you do to her, provided I can look." She was watching me in the wardrobe mirror, and I must have been making a face, because she laughed even harder and fell back onto the bed. All I could find to say was, "You've read my letters?" She became serious again, put my left hand in the place that gave her courage, and said, "Not all of them—they're too stupid." Then she said, "She was a schoolteacher, too." She thought for a long time, looking at herself in the mirror, sighed deeply, and said, "Move your hand, I want myself."

In the afternoon we both went to Brochard's café. I played bowls on the square, with Henri IV as my partner, and we won a hundred francs each from some young tourists staying at a hotel near Allos. She was wearing her sky-blue nylon dress and watched us from the café terrace, sitting with Martine and old Brochard. With her long tanned legs, her heavy dark hair, which she always tossed back with a single movement of her neck, her pale, slow-moving eyes, like two points of light from another world, she was the most beautiful woman I'd ever seen, and mine, she was my wife, she even put me off my game.

I had so many questions to ask her. A whole life wouldn't have been enough to understand her, but there was at least one thing I had understood, the night before, standing in the campers' tent, and that was that sooner or later I would lose her. I didn't accept it, no. I told myself I would never accept it. I would rather take down one of my father's guns. Oh, I don't know—I don't know anything any more. But I'd come to realize I was going to lose her, because others—a camper from Colmar, let's say—were more attractive than I was, and she was too young, too much of an animal, and the more I asked questions, the more quickly she'd get sick of me, the more stupid she'd find me. I had no chance. On the square, as I let Henri IV, all by himself, relieve of their money some guys who'd learned to play bowls in Paris, I repeated to myself that I had no chance.

Later the two of us went to have a look at the Delahaye. It still couldn't be driven, but it would be ready soon. At the beginning of July I'd got the idea of replacing the engine with one taken from an old Jaguar I'd brought back after an accident on the other side of the pass. Up till then, I'd made at least fifty parts from scrap, in eight months. I made each of these parts two or three times. Only my boss or Tessari could understand the work that means. Finally I discovered that the Jaguar engine wasn't worth bothering with. Tessari said so, even before we took it apart. You're wasting your time, he said. He sees things with his ears. He helped me take it apart, because that's what he'd come for, but he was right. It was incredible. The guy who'd been driving the Jaguar—all three died in it—even if he hadn't missed the turn, the engine would have blown up in his hands a few kilometers later. The bearings had worn away to nothing.

I'd cleaned up the body of the Delahaye, which was originally beige, and the inside, too, to show her, and she was quite impressed. She didn't say much except "shit," of course, but I could see in her eyes that she liked the car. She stroked the mahogany dashboard and the leather seats. She whispered the word "Delahaye." She looked at me in the way I liked best, at once innocent, sweet, and serious, and said, "You make a funny husband, you know." We stayed there for about ten minutes, and she asked me where the car came from—I'd been told it belonged to a minister in the old republic, but who knows—and then Juliette came down and Henri IV arrived on the scene.

We had an apéritif with them and stayed for dinner. I was surprised to see that Juliette spoke to Elle with a kind of quiet gentleness, as if they were old friends. The four of us played *belote*, and before eleven o'clock we'd won a hundred and fifty francs from them. As I've already said, Elle was good at cards—she could remember every card that had been played. Mickey joined us a little later. We all sat out on the wooden steps, and, just to please them, I smoked one of my boss's cigars. It's a strange thing, smoking. And being like that, sitting on the wooden steps, on a summer's night, with your voice sounding different because Elle is beside you, resting her head on your shoulder, and you think, "I might lose her. No, she loves me for good, me and no one else." And knowing you're going to walk home through the sleeping village, with Mickey in front marking out his aims in life with pebbles, and Elle next to you, sweet and warm under her dress, in your arms.

It was Sunday night, July 18. I lost her on Wednesday, July 28. Our marriage lasted eleven days, including the wedding day. Then I did what you mustn't do. You have to live through your hell without opening your mouth. Instead I went around everywhere, asking questions, trying to find her. It was grotesque. I found her again on Friday, August 6. I went and got one of my father's guns. A Remington automatic, two cartridges in the magazine, one in the chamber, 270 caliber. It was the gun I'd used to kill two wild boars the winter before. I went to the garage to saw off the barrel. I thought again of that Sunday evening when I'd sat smoking a cigar, with my love sitting beside me.

There was no question of my taking a vacation in the middle of summer. Henri IV and I had decided I'd take two weeks off at the end of September, when most of the summer people would have gone home, and also—which was important for me—when the drought was over and there'd be fewer fires. Since the beginning of July I hadn't spent three nights in a row at home.

I'd told Elle we would go on our honeymoon then, in the perfect Delahaye, as I'd dreamed. We hadn't picked where we'd go, to Switzerland or to Italy. I saw she wasn't interested. She said, Wherever you like. I'd have liked to go to southern Italy—to the Mezzogiorno, as my father called it—and see the place he came from, Pescopagano, about a hundred kilometers south of Naples. I looked for the name on a road map; it was printed in about the same size as, say, Barrême or Entrevaux. I thought it wouldn't be difficult to find our relatives there, relatives we'd never seen, his sister's children, who'd stayed there. In the sixties, at Christmas, we still used to get a New Year's card, signed by everyone—Peppino, Alfredo, Giorgio, Gianbattista, Antonio, Vittorio—with a stamp that Cognata steamed off for her brother-in-law in Marseille, who collected them. But Elle just shrugged her left shoulder, not even listening. She wasn't interested. Anyway, September was too far off. She knew better than I did that we wouldn't get that far; I understand now.

On two nights during the week before the wedding, she came back very late, driven home both times by Mlle Dieu. She was always the same, at least to Mamma or anyone who didn't pay much attention: one moment she'd be very nice, another unbearable; one day she'd laugh about nothing, another she'd shut up like a clam. I knew, from the first night we had dinner together, that she could move from one mood to another without showing the slightest sign on the outside. She was like that. I would leave her after lunch depressed over something she wouldn't tell me about, and that evening, when I found her again, she made fun of everything and everybody, and she'd say vulgar things just to provoke me and Boo-Boo—and we couldn't help laughing.

In bed it was the same. Not that she'd ever refuse to make love—except once or twice, perhaps because she was really in bad shape—no, it wasn't that, she always wanted it. But not in the same way. Some nights love was gentle for her, like a refuge; when she was like that, she really won my heart. I must admit she was usually like that, but then, without any warning except her silence at dinner, or just a sudden stubbornness, a determination to be proved right in some argument about nothing at all, another woman was in my arms who was not her, but a terrible, sick woman, which hurt me, because everything sick hurts me. One day she said, "All this crap about sex, it's not dirty or anything. It's like eating or drinking. No matter what you do, you want it again the next day." Maybe I didn't understand what she meant, but there was something despairing about the way she put things, like when she talked about love as "all this crap about sex."

Yes. Mamma, or Mickey, or even Cognata, who came to adore her because Elle had given her an oil painting of my uncle made from a photo, or even Boo-Boo, who had managed somehow or other to get her face printed on a tee shirt—everyone saw her as she had been the first day she came into our house. We knew her a little better, that was all. Even I, who obviously paid more attention to her than anyone, noticed no change I could define. Her eyes were blue or gray, depending on the light, as they'd always been. They just seemed a bit paler, a bit slower-moving, they looked more than usually like two cold, alien spots of light in a face I'd got to know better than my own. But after all, the sun had been accentuating the contrast between her eyes and her skin since May. As for her moods, it was the same thing. It seemed to me her carefree periods became shorter, and those when she said nothing, and did nothing except sit around looking gloomy, longer and more frequent. But the heat affected everyone—except Cognata, who grew old in the shade of the kitchen—and I still believed Elle was pregnant.

On the Tuesday after our wedding, I got back from work and was told by Mamma that Elle had taken off early in the afternoon, without saying where she was going. She was wearing her red dress, which buttoned all the way up, and had her white bag. She left no message for me. She seemed preoccupied, no more. When Cognata asked her where she was going, she answered with her favorite gesture—she puffed up her cheeks and blew out straight in front of her.

I said, "O.K." Neither Mickey nor Boo-Boo was home yet. I went up to our bedroom and changed. I felt around in the drawer where she put her underwear, without any definite idea, but feeling guilty about it. I looked through the photos she kept. Most of them were of her beauty contest at Saint-Etienne-de-Tinée. She was wearing a two-piece bathing suit and high-heeled shoes, and her legs looked very provocative, as did the rest of her. I've never liked those photos. There were others, from when she was a kid in Arrame. They didn't seem to be of the same girl, except for the brightness of the eyes. Two dots that disturbed you because the irises hadn't taken on the paper. She always seemed to be with her mother. There was no photo of her father; I will probably never know what he looks like. One day she told me she'd torn them all up.

I lay down on the bed and waited, my hands behind my head. After a little while Boo-Boo and Mickey got home. Boo-Boo came up to see me. We talked of this and that, but my heart wasn't in it. Then we went down and started dinner without Elle, and we watched a film on TV. We were about a quarter of the way through the story, which I hadn't managed to follow, when Henri IV came into the yard in the DS. The others all got up with me, except Cognata, who hadn't heard or seen anything through the window. It's funny, because they were used to seeing Henri IV arrive, especially that year, to tell me they'd received a telephone call at the station, but we all thought it was about Elle, and that something had happened to her, I don't know why. Henri IV said to me, "The girl's in town. I told her to take Cazenave's taxi, but she didn't want to. She wants you to go and get her." They were all standing around him at the door. I asked him if she was all right. He looked surprised and said, "She's annoyed about missing the bus. Why? Why shouldn't she be all right? She's already set out to meet you." Mamma gave a great sigh. Mickey and Boo-Boo went back to the film. Henri IV said, "Take the car. I'll wait. I had to turn off the set when William Holden found his girl again, when she was about to marry the other guy. Did she finally make up her mind?"

I drove into town, cutting all the corners. I nearly smashed into a Peugeot 504 full of people, and the driver, once he'd got over the shock, honked his horn like a madman. She was waiting for me just before the bridge, standing by the roadside. I stopped and got out. When she saw me coming toward her she stepped back several paces, saying in a frightened voice, "Be careful. The day you hit me, you won't see me again." I went up to her all the same and pulled down her arms, which she'd crossed over her face, and hit her several times, holding her up with one hand to stop her from falling. Only her head had fallen back. Suddenly she started crying, and after a moment, eyes cast down, she whispered, "Shit! Shit!"

She was breathing with difficulty. Without letting go of her, I asked her, "Where've you been?" She threw her head back and said, "I don't care if you hit me." Her cheek was marked by my blows. She stared back at me with an evil look in her eyes that suddenly reminded me of what Mlle Tusseau had said in Eva Braun's kitchen three days earlier. I let her go. I wiped the sweat off my forehead with my forearm, crossed the road, and went to sit on the embankment. I, too, was breathing heavily. My heart was beating fast.

She also crossed the road, much farther up. She sat there without moving for ages, in her red dress, holding her handbag. The sun had gone down behind the mountains a long time before, but there was still daylight, and the air was warm and smelled of fir trees. I was annoyed with myself for hitting her— it was the last thing to do if I wanted her to talk to me, and anyway, it wasn't like me. I hadn't hit anyone since I was in primary school. Finally I said, "O.K. I'm sorry. Let's go home." She said nothing but came over to me.

She dropped down beside me and put her arms around me. She said, "I've lost a heel." Just like that, as natural as anything. She put her head against my chest and said, "I went to Digne to look at the shops. I missed the seven o'clock bus. Otherwise I'd have come back long ago." I said, "You went shopping and didn't buy anything?" "No, I didn't need anything. It was just to get out of the house. I get so bored with your mother and your aunt, I'm growing wrinkles."

Two cars heading up to the pass overtook us. She drew apart from me, just because I moved to let her do it. You only have to be a bit above her to see her tits in that dress, and she never fastened the lower buttons. I said, "Button up your dress. Don't you think it's short enough as it is?" She obeyed, without sighing or anything. I was crazy at the idea that she'd been wandering around all afternoon without me in the streets of Digne, dressed like that, with all the men undressing her with their eyes. I imagined some of them nudging their pals to point out the spectacle—and I imagined what they said to one another. Maybe one of them had tried to approach her, thinking she must be an easy lay to show herself off like that. I stared at the road, the sweat breaking out on my forehead again, but it must have been fairly easy to guess what I was thinking, because she said quietly, "I'm sick of this dress, too. I won't wear it any more."

I brought her home. Nobody said anything. She ate a bit, looking at William Holden with one eye and the false fingernails of her left hand with the other. Only then did I notice she wasn't wearing her wedding band.

When the film was over, everybody got up except the two of us. She wanted to wash in her bathtub before going to bed. I said to her, "Have you lost your wedding band?" She didn't bat an eyelid. She simply replied, "I washed my hands when I came in. I took it off." It was true that she'd washed her hands. I looked over to the sink, but she let out a weary sigh, picked up her small bag, which was hanging on her chair, took out the ring, and showed it to me. Then she said, "If you ever put your ring on that filthy old sink, you'll have to demolish all the pipes to get it back. I look after things."

She went out to get her bathtub from the storeroom. When she came back, I put some water on the stove, in the big pan. We could hear Boo-Boo talking to Mickey upstairs. She sat quietly at the table, her chin in her hands. I said, "Does it cost a lot to go to Digne by bus?" She didn't answer. She sighed again, but with annoyance, and picked up her bag. She didn't poke around in it—she always knew exactly where she put things. She simply pulled out two bus tickets and put them on the table. As she got up she said, "You really are getting to be too much."

When her bath was ready—just lukewarm—I sat down and

looked at the tickets. Digne, round trip. I remembered that my mother and Cognata had been born in Digne, and also that Mickey would be racing there the following Sunday. She undid her red dress and took it off, facing me. She threw it into my arms and said, "Your mother can make rags out of it to clean shoes." Her body was almost equally tanned all over; her behind was only a little lighter when she took off her panties, and that, too, made me feel sad, jealous, and stupid. When I'd remarked on it earlier, she said she went alone or with Martine Brochard to a special place by the river where nobody goes. In a village like ours, if you know a place where nobody goes, it's because you never lived there.

I watched her wash. She often washed twice a day, as if she worked in a mine. There was something abnormal about the care she took to soap, rub, and soap herself again. I said, as I'd said before, "You'll wear your skin away one of these days." She said, "Why don't you go to bed? I hate it when people watch me washing." I made sure that she had a towel near at hand, picked up her bag from the chair and the two bus tickets, and went upstairs. I was only on the third step when she called out, "Don't be silly. Leave my bag." She sounded gentle, a bit sad, like when she'd forgotten her accent. I said, "Why? Are you afraid I'll find something inside? You read my letters, after all." She turned her back on me in the bathtub and shrugged one shoulder. That was all. She said nothing more. I continued up the stairs.

My brothers had closed their doors, but there was still music, at low volume, coming from Boo-Boo's at the end of the landing. He listens to Wagner while doing his mathematics homework during the school year. During the vacations, it's rock and science fiction. He gave me one of his books to read once. It was about a man who got smaller and smaller and ended up the size of a mouse, or even a spider. A cat tried to catch him. A real nightmare. That night I felt a bit like that myself, I didn't know why.

In the bedroom I looked at the bus tickets again, then emptied the contents of her white bag onto the bed. I set aside all of the women's things—the tube of lipstick, a comb, a box for eyelashes, a bottle of nail polish, Kleenex, a pack of needles and thread, and even a toothbrush and a sample tube of toothpaste. She always carries a toothbrush around with her. Very particular. I also put to one side the money she had—just under three hundred francs. She didn't spend a lot of money, and she never asked me for any, except for her hairdresser or odd trifles. That left a piece of paper folded in four, her Dupont lighter, her menthol cigarettes, her wedding ring, a photo of her as a child on the back of which someone had written, "The prettiest girl in the world." In faded blue ink. I thought it might be her father or mother. Her father, probably, because women don't have that kind of handwriting.

I unfolded the sheet of paper. It was taken from a Total advertising pad I'd brought back from the garage, which was kept in the sideboard downstairs. On two lines, written with so much care and so many spelling mistakes you'd think she'd done it on purpose, Elle had written:

> Well, what have you gained
> by going through my bag?

I didn't laugh, I didn't find it particularly funny. On the contrary. I imagined her at the kitchen table, writing the two lines with a fountain pen while I was outside getting her bathtub. It was the only time I'd left her alone. If she'd already known I was going to go through her bag, she could have taken out what she didn't want me to find. Anyway, even if she'd arranged it so that I'd never find anything on her that I wasn't to see, and even if that message had been written long ago and was always kept in her bag, it showed she was suspicious of me. When you're suspicious, it's because you're afraid for one reason or another. Unless she just wanted to keep me guessing, to touch a raw nerve; but why?

I put back her things and lay down. I didn't hear her climb the stairs and was surprised when she came into the room, naked, her face all serene. She hung her towel on the handle of the open window, and her panties, which she had just washed, on top of that, and came and lay next to me. We stayed like that for a long time, without saying anything. Then she stretched out an arm and put out the light. In the darkness she said, "My cheek still hurts. You hit me hard." I didn't answer. She said, "If someone wanted to hit me like that, would you defend me?" I didn't answer. After a while she sighed—a deep sigh—and said, "I'm sure you would defend me. Otherwise, you wouldn't love me." She groped for my hand and put it between her thighs, for courage. Then she went to sleep.

Next day, at work, I made one mistake after another. If Henri IV noticed, he didn't say anything. Each time I just did over what I'd forgotten to do or done badly. I could think only about Elle and what she might be hiding from me.

In the afternoon I couldn't help myself. I dropped everything and went home in the 2CV. She wasn't there. Cognata said, "She's almost certainly gone to sunbathe. I suppose she has a right to go out when she wants to." I ran down to the tent at the bottom of the field, but it was empty. Again. I walked along the river to Palm Beach. There was no one. I walked back to the garage, along the path that leads to the cemetery. On the way I walked past Eva Braun's house. I didn't dare go and ask if she was there.

I must say something I'm ashamed of, or people won't understand me. On the night of the wedding, when she was asleep, I got up to examine her white dress. I found stains of resin on the back. She must have been leaning against a fir tree. I remembered the Portuguese she'd mentioned that first evening at the Auberge des Deux Ponts, who'd kissed her against a tree. I got back into bed and thought about it for a long time, like a fool. She hadn't bothered about her dress because it had already been torn during the scene with her father—that was obvious. But nevertheless I imagined her leaning against a tree with someone. In her wedding dress. Someone must have said to her, "I want to see you on your wedding day." And she must have said yes and gone to meet him. Sometimes I'm even more Ping-Pong than people think.

That Wednesday evening, as usual, I had to go to the station, in town. When I went to get the 2CV from the house, Elle still wasn't back. Mamma said, without looking at me, "If you start torturing yourself, there'll be no end to it." I shouted at her, "What? What do you mean?" The blood drained from her face. She said, "Don't speak to me in that tone of voice. If your father was still alive, even at your age you wouldn't dare." She realized I was sorry I'd shouted and said, "My poor boy. Now ask her what she's been knitting. Ask her." I could see no hate in her eyes for Elle; she was just sorry for me. I went out with my helmet and got into the car, then waited for quite a while before driving off. I hoped to see her suddenly come home. Finally I drove to the station.

It must have been about eight o'clock when I arrived. Elle was there. There were about a dozen firemen with her. They were tossing her into the air like a crêpe, her skirt lifted above her waist, on a canvas sheet, found God knows where, which had been given us to catch people jumping out of seventh-floor windows and which we never used, because there aren't any seventh-floor or even sixth-floor windows, and not very often third-floor windows, in our beautiful part of the world. She was laughing and shouting enough to terrify the whole town. She was laughing as if in a dream, and as they tossed her up, they laughed almost as loudly. Believe me, Ping-Pong was proud of his wife. When they'd stopped and sat down on the ground, Renucci said to me, "We weren't doing any harm." I could easily have spat in his face.

I didn't stay with them. I drove her home. I overtook Mickey's yellow truck going up to the pass. He honked, but I didn't feel like answering. She waved at him through the window. She said, "Come on. It's over now. Don't be like that." I said, "I'm sick of having all my friends see my wife's ass." She shut up, leaned her shoulder against the door, and said nothing until dinnertime.

There were six of us for dinner, and she didn't eat anything.

Mamma said to her, "I'm beginning to think you don't like my cooking." She said, "You get the brass ring! As a matter of fact, I do like my mother's better." Boo-Boo laughed, and so did Mickey. Mamma didn't make a scene. Cognata had heard nothing and went on stroking the girl's hand, smiling in her senile way. I said, "By the way, you haven't been knitting much lately." She said nothing. She looked at Mamma. Then she said to Boo-Boo, "You should give me some of your appetite—I'll give you something in exchange." I said, "What? What have you got to give him?" Everyone sensed I was beginning to lose my temper and looked at me. She poked the food in her plate, as if she was looking for a fly in it, and said, more quietly—I sensed she was playing at being tough but was afraid of getting what she'd got the day before, on the road— "A bit of what you don't want your friends to see." As if nothing had happened she added, "I've gained a couple of pounds since I've been here. All in the behind. Then your mother tells me off because I don't eat." Boo-Boo and Mickey started to laugh. I was thinking only that she hadn't said anything when I asked her about her knitting.

I waited till I was alone with her in our room to ask her again. She went on undressing, then, without looking at me, said, "I'm a terrible knitter. It would be better to buy everything." She hung up her skirt, and I caught the expression on her face in the mirror as she shut the wardrobe door. It showed what she thought of me. Controlling myself, I said, "You think it's a good idea for a pregnant woman to carry on like you did today at the station?" She didn't answer. She heaved a deep sigh. She put on her white bathrobe and started washing her panties in the china bowl we use as a washbasin. She always washed her panties as soon as she'd taken them off, or her pantyhose, on the rare occasions I saw her wear them—when she put on her black dress to go out, she thought it was smarter to wear pantyhose. I said, a lump rising in my throat, "This baby's an invention, isn't it? Answer me." She paused for a moment without turning around, just put her head to one side and said nothing. I walked over to her and hit her, with my open hand.

She cried out at once, trying to regain her balance, and I hit her again, but the blows fell on the top of her head or on her arms. I shouted, too. I don't know what I said. Maybe I just told her to answer me. Or that she was a bitch, that she didn't need to invent something like that to get married. My brothers, whom we had left downstairs, suddenly came into the room and dragged me off her. I wanted to get back to her and make her speak. I threw Boo-Boo across the room; then Mamma came rushing in and tried to get hold of me. Mickey kept repeating, "Don't be stupid. Shit! Don't be stupid."

She was on her knees in the middle of the room, her head in her arms, sobbing, her whole body shaking. When I saw there was blood on my hands, and on her bathrobe, my anger suddenly vanished. I felt drained of all my strength. Boo-Boo knelt down in front of her to examine her head. She realized it was him and put her arms around his neck, shaking and sobbing. You could see there was blood all over her face.

Mamma got a wet towel and said, "Get out, all of you. Leave me alone with her." But Elle wouldn't let go of Boo-Boo. She started shouting again, holding him tightly in her arms. In the end she stayed like that, clinging to him, while Mamma wiped her face. She just stared at me, her big eyes filled with tears. There was a surprised, imploring, almost childlike look in them, but no bitterness, as one might have expected. Her nose was bleeding, one of her cheeks was swollen, and she could hardly breathe for sobbing. Mamma said, "There, there! It's all over now. Calm yourself." Mickey took me by the arm, and I followed him out of the room.

Much later, Mamma came down and joined us in the kitchen. She said, "She won't let Boo-Boo go." She sat down at the table across from me and put her head in her hands. She said, "And you, you were the quietest and gentlest of all.

I didn't recognize you." She wiped her eyes and looked at me. She said, "You hit her all over, even on her chest." I couldn't say anything. Mickey said it for me: "He didn't know what he was doing." She said, "Yes, that's just it!" and she put her head in her hands again.

The three of us just sat there for a long time. Cognata had gone to bed. We heard talking upstairs but couldn't make out what they were saying. Then Boo-Boo came down. His shirt was all stained with blood. He said, "She doesn't want to sleep in your room tonight. I'll let her have mine, and I'll sleep with you." He filled a glass with water and went back up. We heard him take her into his room; then, after a while, he came down again. I asked him if she'd calmed down. He shrugged his shoulders. He looked at me for a moment and said, "It's you who should calm down." He looked very shaken by what he'd been through, pale under his suntan. He said nothing more and went out into the yard.

I didn't drop off to sleep until morning. Boo-Boo was breathing regularly next to me. Lying in the dark, I waited for the hours to pass. Then I slept a bit. That's all I remember of that night. My ideas were confused. I kept seeing her smeared with blood, clinging to my brother. After what Mamma had said, I was afraid I might have done some serious damage, something permanent. I remembered her washing her panties. She didn't take off her ring to put her hands in the soapy water. Suddenly I realized she'd been lying the night before, when I noticed she wasn't wearing the ring, and the expression I'd seen in the wardrobe mirror seemed to say, "Poor bastard!" Then my arrival at the station, to find her being tossed up and down. And that sunny Sunday, right at the beginning, when I was standing at the bar with Tessari and some other guys, and we could see her body through her nylon dress. And what Tessari had told me that morning. What Georges Massigne had said, one spring night, sitting in the village square, while all the kids were asleep in the truck.

I got up and went down to wash in the kitchen. Mamma was already awake. She made my coffee, as usual. We didn't speak to each other, except as I left I said, "See you soon." I walked to the garage and worked all morning with the same confused ideas in my head.

At midday, when I went home, she was still in Boo-Boo's room. He'd gone up to see her a while before. He said, "Be nice to her. Leave her alone for a bit." I asked him if she was badly bruised. He said, "Her cheek's swollen up." We had lunch without her, and I went back to the garage.

In the evening, about seven, she was in the yard, wearing jeans and a turtleneck sweater, playing bowls with Boo-Boo. I went up to her. She smiled nicely, with a smile that was terrible to see because of her swollen cheek. She said, "You won't be able to take me as a partner tomorrow. I'm still at zero." She wiped her hands against each other and let me kiss her. She whispered, "Be careful, it really hurts when you press on it." Then she went back to her bowls, and I played a game with them. Our eyes met less than usual, that's all.

She came back to our room that night, and we stayed for a long time lying side by side, without moving, in the dark. She started to cry, almost without a sound. I said, very sincerely, "I promise you, I'll never hit you again, never, whatever happens." She wiped her eyes with the sheet and said, "I wanted to stay with you. Everyone tried to tell me you would drop me, when you didn't want to any more. That's why." We spoke in whispers. Her voice was like breathing—I could hardly catch the words. I said I didn't care that we wouldn't be having a child; in fact, I'd rather we didn't have one, I didn't want anything to come between us. But I was afraid she was hiding something or someone from me, and that drove me crazy. She said nothing for a bit, maybe a minute, maybe more. Then she put her arms around me in the dark, rested her good cheek on my chest, and whispered, "If I am hiding something from you, it's not at all what you think. It's something that's got nothing to do with you and that I can't tell you about, not yet anyway. In a few days, it will be settled. If I have to tell you what it is, I will tell you."

She could feel I was stretching out my arm to turn on the

bedside lamp, and she stopped me, saying, "No, please." I asked her in the dark if it had anything to do with her health—the first thing that came into my head—or maybe with her relations with her father, but she whispered, "Please, don't ask any questions. Because I love you."

I think I'm more or less like other people, and we are funny animals. I felt as if a weight had been taken off my shoulders, even if what she was waiting to have "settled" was the result of a blood test or a malignant tumor or worse. Yes, I wasn't proud of myself, but it was true. It was like a weight taken off me. I whispered, "O.K." I kissed her hair. I had a lot of sleep to make up, and I dropped off quickly.

Mamma woke me just after dawn. She said the red Renault from the station was in the yard, and Massard was waiting for me. The fires had started up again above Grasse. I dressed quickly and went out. In the evening I was able to telephone Henri IV from a police car to warn him I wouldn't be back that night—the fires were raging over several kilometers. He said he'd seen the fires on TV, and I was to take care.

Massard brought me back to the village on Saturday evening, just before nightfall. Elle stayed with me while I took a shower, by the spring. She still had the bruise on her cheek, but it was turning brown and blending in with the color of her skin. Or she'd put on a lot of makeup. I don't know. She looked sad, but she said, "I was worried about you. But then I'm always like that when night falls."

All day the sun had been beating down as if we were in Africa, and the air was hot and dry, but for me, after the oven I'd come out of, it seemed mild and bracing. She was wearing a red bikini, the one I'd bought for her birthday, without much enthusiasm, because it was just a scrap of material that showed more than it hid, but that evening it merely made me want her all the more. I told her to come behind the shower curtain with me, as she had done one evening, but she didn't want to, except just to get slightly wet and dash out again.

We ate outside; the boys were also wearing bathing trunks, and Mamma made polenta. No one was very hungry, because

of the heat. On the other hand, we couldn't fill the glasses fast
enough, and I had to warn Mickey not to drink so much
because he was racing next day. He said he wasn't worried,
he was sure to win. There was a big hump on the circuit, and
although he wasn't that hot going up, he knew he would be
able to shoot ahead on the way down and fire off like a champagne cork fifteen meters before the finish line. We ended up
believing him. Mamma must have had a talk with Elle while
I was away and sorted something out, because she talked to
her a little more like Cognata did. Even when she remarked
that her bikini didn't cover half of what the good God had
given her, she laughed and gave her an indulgent little tap on
the backside.

We stayed outside for a while, in the night, sitting around
the table, which Elle, believe it or not, had helped to clear.
Mickey was talking about Merckx with Boo-Boo, who still
claimed that his reign was coming to an end, that Maertens
would take over. There was a real argument about it. Elle sat
next to me, I had my arm around her waist. Her skin was
burning hot. She joined in the conversation at one point to
ask who Fausto Coppi was, because Boo-Boo and I, maybe for
sentimental reasons, out of respect for our father, never failed
to attack Mickey on the subject and say that he was the greatest.
Mickey as usual launched into a complete list of Eddy Merckx's
victories, from his first amateur race on. No one could deny
that it took four hours to get to the end of it, and then we all
went to bed.

I made love with Elle for the last time that night. Something
had already gone. I didn't know what it was yet, of course. I
just thought it was too soon after our fight for her to forget I'd
hit her. She shuddered in my arms, she let me do whatever
I wanted; but I felt she was anxious, preoccupied, and when
she finally came, after a very long time, she didn't cry out or
move more violently, she just pressed her wet face against my
shoulder, her arms around my neck, with a kind of sad, childish
gentleness, as if she knew it was the last time.

*   *   *

Next day we had lunch in a restaurant on the Boulevard Gassendi in Digne while Mickey went off to join the other competitors, an hour before the race. Besides Elle and me there was Boo-Boo, Georgette, and Georgette's ten-year-old brother. We were near a window and could see the people beginning to gather behind the metal barrier along the sidewalk. There were a lot of advertising streamers, and supporters walked up and down, wearing on their paper caps the name of the local competitor, Tarrazi. There was a fanfare, too, which we heard through the open doors, and a lot of talk.

Elle was wearing her white summer dress. You could no longer tell I'd hit her. She seemed pleased to be there. Boo-Boo teased her, then made up for it by saying she was the most beautiful girl in the world. She even talked to Georgette's little brother. Over dessert I left them at the table and went to help Mickey get ready for the race. I checked his bike and his spare tires one last time. When the starting shot was fired, he was positioned in the middle of the pack. I followed his red-and-white jersey for a while, then walked down the boulevard, through the crowd, back to the restaurant. I had just enough time to eat some ice cream before they announced that the first lap was about to begin.

Boo-Boo and I dashed out to the sidewalk, and we saw Mickey in the pack, next to Deuffidel, Majorque, and the guy from Toulon who'd won the race at Puget-Théniers two weeks before. He looked like a pasha; Boo-Boo was disappointed he hadn't gone all out for the first sprint so he'd get the prize, but I said that he had nineteen to go and that, anyway, it was the last that counted.

It took them about ten minutes to finish the first lap. On the second lap, we were still at that table. Now we had to fight our way to get to the barrier. Mickey was still behind the same three, pedaling easily, his hands well up on the handle bars. To start with, at least, he wasn't making faces like he did after a climb, which always took it out of him. I said to Boo-Boo, "We're going to win. You'll see." I said the same thing to Elle when I went back into the restaurant. She said, "I hope so."

I looked at her face again. She was no longer, for many reasons, the girl I'd known at the Bing Bang less than three months before, but I felt a little of the same thing at that moment. I can't really explain it. She seemed to have found again what I've always liked in children. They look at you with their frank, trusting eyes—they know at once who you are, and they know you love them. Usually they don't care. Or maybe it was because, in her eyes, I had become once again the guy she danced with for the first time one Sunday in May. I don't know. I understand some things now, but not everything.

During the afternoon we mingled with the crowd on the Place de la Libération to watch the competitors cross the line, and our Mickey, who, from the eighth or ninth lap on, won all the sprints. He set off each time, on the right or left behind Tarrazi, who rode fast, and he overtook him in the last few meters, like a cat. The loudspeakers kept repeating along the boulevard, "First, Michel Montecciari, Alpes-Maritimes, number 51," and the prizes he'd won, donated by various shops in the town. Or they'd announce to us, while he was out of sight, that he'd fallen back at the top of the hill and hadn't made up for it on the way down. It was the kind of nonsense the announcers use to make the race seem more exciting, but we could be sure, when the first competitors took the corner at the traffic circle in the distance, under the streamers, Mickey's red-and-white jersey would be just behind Tarrazi's green jersey, and all the people in Digne around us would start yelling what a bastard my brother was—"You'll see, he'll do the same thing to him again!" It was while arguing with some guys, after a sprint that was exactly like all the others except that their Tarrazi had tried to hold my brother back by the jersey, that I'd taken my eyes off Elle and lost her in the crowd.

I looked for her for a while, and so did Boo-Boo; Georgette had gone to buy some ice cream for her little brother, and that didn't help, because I was afraid of losing that kid as well. When Georgette came back, the competitors were arriving at the circle for the fifteenth time. She said, "She must have gone to the bathroom in the bistro. She's a big girl now, you know."

We watched Mickey grimacing, showing his strength to the others, then, mission carried out, straightening up and dropping gack into the pack to relax. I had a fleeting thought that he was letting himself coast, that this would be the ideal moment, when he had just won a sprint, to close in on him and pull him way in front, but it was an unpleasant thought, and I let it go.

I walked through the crowd to the bottom of the boulevard, glancing into the cafés as I went. She was nowhere to be seen. After an interminable argument with the stewards, I was allowed to run across the road and go up the other sidewalk to the Place de la Libération. I was too preoccupied to follow the race. I wasn't even listening to the stream of words coming out of the loudspeaker.

When I got back to Georgette, she told me it was the eighteenth lap, and Mickey, like the rest of the pack, was slackening. After winning the sixteenth sprint, he had recovered enough to rest, very pleased with himself, and three competitors, one of whom—Arabedian—had won at Puget, took the opportunity to spurt ahead. I was already worried on account of Elle, and this depressed me even more. Boo-Boo wasn't there. He must still have been looking for her. I said to Georgette, "They'll come back," but I no longer knew, really, whether I was talking about Mickey and the pack, or Elle and Boo-Boo. Georgette said, "No one wants to lead, so Mickey is doing all the work."

In fact, Arabedian and his two teammates passed the line at the end of the eighteenth lap, and Mickey, leading the field, was more than forty seconds behind. He had that stupid grin on his face, as always when he's exhausted, and his jersey was wet through. I called out, running along the sidewalk; he heard me, he told me later, but he didn't respond. To those who didn't know him, he seemed cheerful and carefree, but I could see that he was done in.

At one point I saw that Boo-Boo had joined us, in the midst of the crowd. He looked wrecked. "Have you seen Elle?" I asked him. He shook his head. He didn't even look at me. I thought he was wrecked because of Mickey. Now, I'm very sure of what I'm saying. I can describe everything exactly as it happened, without pretending I was smarter then than I really was. I said to my brother Boo-Boo, "I can get eight hundred francs for the bike they're giving the winner. If Mickey doesn't put a spurt on, he'll never make it." A bit later the loudspeakers announced that Mickey and Spaletto, a track racer from Marseille, had detached themselves from the pack and were closing in on Arabedian. Everybody started shouting, and Georgette jumped up and down excitedly and kissed me. It was then that I saw Elle.

She was on the other side of the square, on the edge of the sidewalk. She seemed to be sleepwalking—yes, sleepwalking, that was the first thought that came into my head. She walked and paused, as people moved to one side to let her pass. She was looking at the ground. I realized, with every fiber in my body, that she didn't know where she was or what she was doing. She was obviously lost. I realized that, I swear, and yet she was over a hundred paces away from me, just an outline in a white dress, so small, so alone, and I pushed everyone out of my way and ran across the road, despite a barrage of police whistles, shouting "Eliane!"

When I caught her by the arm and turned her to face me, her eyes were full of tears and seemed even bigger and paler than I'd ever seen them. I said, "What happened to you?" She slowly shook her head and said, in an unrecognizable voice, "The back of my head hurts, it hurts." I led her away from the crowd to a little side street, where we sat down on a step at the entrance of a building. I said, "Keep quiet, don't move." She repeated, "The back of my head hurts." Two deep furrows, which I'd never seen before, dug into her face from her nose to below her lips on either side, and her eyes were wide and empty, as if there was no light in them. She seemed dazed.

I held her to me, with my arm around her, for a long time. I heard the shouting in the square as the racers went by, I heard the loudspeakers. I heard nothing they said. I didn't dare move or do anything. I felt her in my arms, inert and far away from everything. She was breathing through her mouth, as she usually did when upset, but it wasn't like that, she seemed more dazed than upset. She stared ahead of her, seeing nothing, and she breathed through her mouth in a regular, almost natural way.

When she began to come to herself and moved away from me, she whispered, "It's all right now, it's all right." I didn't want to ask her right away what had happened, so I just helped her get up. I brushed down her dress. I asked her if she wanted anything to drink. She shook her head. She looked at me. I saw the tears flood into her pale eyes again. Then she took my hand, and we went back into the crowd.

The race was over, and Mickey had won. Georgette and her little brother were jumping up and down, fists clenched, shouting. They were too overjoyed to take any notice of us. Boo-Boo gave us a smile of relief when he saw Elle with me. Later he said, "Mickey wants you to know that Spaletto is as good as his word."

I went to talk to the bicycle salesman who was offering a racing bike to the winner. He took me into a café and gave me eight hundred francs instead. I found Spaletto eventually and shared the money with him. Elle and Boo-Boo followed me around like my shadow. I noticed that she shivered every now and then, but she seemed pleased that Mickey had won, smiled when the name Montecciari came out over the loudspeakers. Boo-Boo held her hand, as I had done earlier. He seemed pleased, too, but I know my brothers: he was anxious and sad when he looked at her.

We went back to the village in the DS, without Mickey, who'd been invited to dinner by the organizers, and without Georgette, of course. On the way we talked of nothing but the race. I dropped off Georgette's little brother in front of his parents' door, and there were just the three of us left in the car. Halfway up the pass, she asked me to stop—she had to be sick. I went with her to the embankment, but she gestured to me to stay back. I returned to the car. I said to Boo-Boo, "It's sunstroke. Definitely." He nodded and said nothing. She came back to the car, her face pale, without a word. She just made a gesture with her fingers to tell me to start the car again, she wanted to get home.

When we arrived, she whispered, "No. To my mother's." I felt, as did Boo-Boo, that she couldn't say anything else, that she was about to vomit again or faint or something. I drove through the village. People were still sitting on Brochard's terrace. We drove into Eva Braun's yard, and when I stopped in front of the house, the sun hit us head-on, dazzling us from between the hilltops. I helped her get out. Her mother said nothing when she saw her, but the blood had drained from her face.

In their kitchen Elle stayed on Eva Braun's knees for a long time, without moving, without saying a word. Upstairs the old man was yelling like an idiot, and I yelled back at him through the ceiling to be quiet. Boo-Boo took me by the arm and said, "Come on, let's not stay here." I brushed him off and bent over Elle, who was clinging to her mother, both arms around her neck, and I said, "Eliane, speak to me. Please, speak to me." I couldn't see her face at all, under her hair. Eva Braun said gently, in her Kraut accent, "Your brother's right, let her stay here tonight."

And that's how it turned out. Or nearly. Who can say exactly how things happen? You only see what you see. I couldn't see her face. I was so concerned to see her face I didn't see her mother's, or Boo-Boo's. I had a feeling her mother and Boo-Boo were against me—because I'd hit her a few days before, I don't know—and I felt I'd been rejected by Elle and by them and by everybody, that I was alone. I said to Eva Braun, "We'll talk about it tomorrow." I touched Elle's hair, very gently, and left.

That night, at home, I stayed outside in the dark till Mickey came back. A car dropped him off at the gate. I called out to him as he crossed the yard, and he came and sat next to me. I told him what had happened. He said, "She's been depressed ever since she had that fight with her father. Then there was that fight with you. And the sun this afternoon. The tar was melting, I can tell you." I asked him how his dinner had been. "Not bad," he said. A lot of people had advised him to go professional. He said, "I've got all summer to think about it." In fact he didn't want to talk about himself.

He said nothing for quite a while, sitting there next to me, then went to get a bottle and two glasses from the kitchen. As we drank he said, "I don't know what's bothering her, but she'll tell you in the end. I'm sure of one thing, though: she's got nothing to reproach herself with since she's known you." I pretended I didn't understand—I understood very well, he had the same idea as I did—and he explained, "Let's say she'd been with someone before you, he wouldn't leave her alone, had threatened her or something. These things happen. Just read the papers." I said, "If someone's threatening her, why doesn't she tell me about it?" He said, "Maybe someone's threatening her to hurt *you*." He said that as if it was obvious. I'd never thought about it that way. More and more I suspected she'd seen—or been forced to see—"someone she'd known before me," but I imagined she'd done so quite willingly, because of some feelings that still remained, to lessen the pain.

I got up and walked out into the dark yard. I said to Mickey, "If that's the case, she met that guy in Digne this afternoon. And last Tuesday, when she was supposed to be shopping. He must live in Digne." In the cool air that was blowing down on us from the mountains, I felt my forehead sweating. Mickey said, "Listen, it's just an idea, no more. Don't get all worked up. Maybe she'd be more likely to talk to you about it if you stopped getting so excited. Instead of that, you beat her up." It was incredible that Mickey should talk to me like that, but he was right. I couldn't wait for the next day, when I'd be able to take her in my arms and tell her she could trust me, that I wouldn't get worked up any more.

I couldn't make out Mickey's face as he sat on the stone seat near the door, so he couldn't make out mine, either. I said, "Poor Mickey, the one time you win, everyone's worrying about something else. We should all be celebrating with you, and look what happens." You'll never guess what he said. He said, "I've got wine in my glass. And I'll win other races."

Again I slept very little and badly. It may be that my lack of sleep during those weeks in late July and early August would account for certain things. Next morning I looked at my face in the wardrobe mirror. I was neither good-looking nor particularly bad-looking, but I was too strong, too heavy, and I didn't like the way I was. I didn't intend to go to Elle's—her mother's—before noon or one o'clock. I wanted to find her rested, and talk quietly with her, and get back her confidence. And I saw this husband in front of me, in the mirror. Over thirty, all muscle and fat, 87 kilos—not her type at all. I washed, shaved, and took a clean shirt and trousers with me, so that she wouldn't see me in overalls.

I did what there was to be done at the garage, as best I could with the ideas I had in my head. Mickey, who was taking a load of wood into town, stopped by the pumps at about ten o'clock. We went for coffee at Brochard's. We didn't talk, except to say how hot it was, or that it wasn't a good idea to repaint the brickwork on the church, that it looked better with the patina of age on it. I knew he'd changed his whole itinerary in order to see me, and he'd get told off by Ferraldo again. He's like that, a real idiot but dependable.

When I arrived at her parents', Elle was sitting on a bit of ruined wall at the end of the yard. She was wearing a red-striped dress I'd never seen her in before, which she must have found in the house. She was staring at the ground, her arms at her sides; she had that look of a doll that's been left in a corner. When she heard my footsteps on the ground, she turned her head and gave a big smile. Her whole body seemed to come to life as she ran toward me. In my arms she said, "I was expecting you, you know. I've been expecting you since . . . since . . ." She couldn't say how long she'd been expecting me. I laughed. I was happy. She turned her face toward me—no makeup, no mascara, nothing—and said, "I hurt you.

Forgive me for everything, right now. It wasn't my fault." I laughed. She said, "Come on, let's go in. Mommy's got lunch ready. You'll see. She's a good cook." I'd already had lunch on several Sundays at Eva Braun's, and knew she was a good cook. What Elle said made a terrible impression on me.

She led me by the hand to the kitchen. She said, lowering her voice, "Mommy is with Daddy upstairs. He's ill, you know." She saw I was stricken, watching and listening to her, and suddenly she became once again the woman I knew. That's just the way it happened. She said, "Yes. You think I'm crazy, don't you." She didn't smile. Just a slight look of disappointment. She said, "You're wrong, you know."

She took out a bottle of apéritif from a cupboard, some cheap vermouth, and poured me a glass. "Will you be coming back tonight?" I asked. She nodded several times. She sat down across from me, her chin in her hands, and said, with a touch of gaiety, "We're married now. You won't get rid of me so easily." I've always liked her face when she has no makeup on. At that moment I loved it more than everything, more than my own life.

I had lunch with Elle and Eva Braun. Elle saw me to the gate. We hadn't said much in front of her mother. She walked slowly, an arm around my body. She seemed very tender, very gentle. I didn't want to spoil that moment, so I told myself I would question her later about what had happened the day before, during that eternity when she'd disappeared.

I worked as best I could again, getting everything wrong because time wouldn't pass and I was growing impatient. Then at last I went to wash and change, at the end of the garage, and I was about to go when the station called to say that Renucci would come fetch me, that a number of fires had started up again above Grasse. I wiped a hand across my face, trying to contain the anger I felt. "O.K." I said, and hung up.

I ran over to her mother's to see her, but she'd already gone. She was waiting for me at our house. She was with Boo-Boo and Cognata in the kitchen. They were playing rummy. She was wearing jeans, and the big tee shirt with her face printed in red. She'd pinned up her hair, but she still wasn't wearing makeup. I found her adorable like that, and I felt even worse about having to leave her.

She went up to our bedroom with me. As I got ready she said, "I don't want you to go feeling worried about me. I'm fine today." I asked her what she'd been doing the day before in Digne, for almost an hour and a half. She said, "Nothing. I felt I was going to faint, in the middle of that crowd. It was the heat. I wanted to get out of it for a while. And then my headache became so bad I didn't even know where I was any more. I think it's because I spent so long in the sun." She looked me straight in the eyes. She seemed to be telling the truth. It was just that I'd never heard her say so many words so quickly. I said, "Yes. It was probably the beginning of sunstroke. You should have covered your head."

I kissed her on the lips, and her mouth on the photograph on her chest, before going out of the room. She laughed. I felt her bare breasts under the tee shirt, against my cheek. I wanted to kiss them, too, by lifting the material. She moved away. She excused herself by saying, "No, please. I couldn't bear to finish myself off alone." This was just the kind of thing she would say, but all the same, I left more unhappy than ever.

Between Le Loup and L'Esteron, at an altitude of over a thousand meters, the hills were aflame. There was no road to reach them, no water supplies nearby, nothing but fire. It was the most exhausting call we'd had that summer. The army had been called out—they'd finally got used to doing a job they hadn't been trained for—but the real work was done by the planes going back and forth over the Massif des Maures. We couldn't save a quarter of what was threatened by the fire.

I got back to the village on Tuesday night. Mamma came down in her cotton nightgown to unlock the door, and she stayed with me while I washed in the kitchen, and gave me something to eat. I learned that Elle had said scarcely a few words during the whole day, but she hadn't been unpleasant. A bit preoccupied, in her dreams. She'd straightened up our room. She'd helped do the ironing. Not very well—she didn't know how to iron. She'd waited up for me until midnight. I said to Mamma, "What do you think of all this?" She shrugged her shoulders and said, "You can't understand her. Yesterday afternoon, while you were at the garage, she wanted to go with me to your father's grave. She stayed there with me only a minute, perhaps less, and then she left." I said, "She wanted to do something to please you. But she can't bear cemeteries. She told me so once herself."

When I went into our room, very quietly, Elle was fast asleep. She was lying in her half of the bed, nearer the door. She couldn't sleep on her heart side. I looked at her in the light from the landing. When she was asleep her face was totally different from when she was awake. Her cheeks were round like a child's, her mouth slightly swollen. She breathed so gently I had to bend down close to hear it. She'd thrown the sheet back. She was naked, her legs folded, her left hand slipped between her thighs. It was a beautiful, touching sight. I moved my fingers over the short curly hair on her belly. I'd have liked just to wake her up and take her, but I didn't dare. As soon as I was lying in bed myself and the door was shut, it occurred to me that I'd never visited my father's grave, and I fell asleep.

I opened my eyes very late, yet I didn't feel well rested; I'd had unpleasant dreams, which I couldn't remember. I never can remember my dreams—I only know if they're pleasant or not. She wasn't in bed. I looked out of the window and saw her lying on her belly, near the spring, wearing the bottom half of her red bikini. She had her glasses on and was reading an old magazine she'd found in the barn. I called down, "O.K.?" She looked up, hiding her breasts with one arm. "Sure," she said.

I went out with my bowl of coffee and sat down next to her. She was lying on a towel. I said, "Don't you think you're tanned enough already?" She explained that she wanted to stay tanned all winter: "I'm saving it up." She asked me about the fires. She wanted some of my coffee. Then I asked her to put on her bra, because Boo-Boo was coming out of the kitchen and walking toward us, in his flowered shorts. She breathed heavily and said, "Your brother's already seen me, you know, since I've been living with you." But she sat up, turned around, and put on her bra.

She walked with me part of the way when I left for the garage. She hopped barefoot among the stones on the roadside. I asked her what she intended to do during the day. It was that Wednesday, July 28. She shrugged one shoulder and made a face. I said, "If you stay in the sun like that, you'll end up consumptive, and anyway, you must wear a hat." She said O. K. She held out her lips, closing her eyes, for me to kiss her. I watched her go back, hopping over the stones toward our gate, in her red bikini, her hands outstretched, more than half her backside showing. It was the last time I was to see her before August 7, last Saturday.

At midday I went with Henri IV to tow in a truck that had broken down near Entraunes. We stopped for a sandwich on the way. When I got back that evening, Mamma said Elle had gone off in the afternoon, with her big canvas bag and a suitcase, and hadn't wanted to say where she was going. At the time Boo-Boo was at the swimming pool in town with his friend Marie-Laure. Mamma couldn't stop her.

I went up to our room. She'd taken her white suitcase, the smaller of the two, her toilet and makeup things, some underwear, and, as far as I could see, two pairs of shoes, her red blazer, her fawn skirt, her dress with the Russian collar, and her sky-blue nylon dress. Mamma said that when she went she was wearing her faded jeans and her navy-blue turtleneck sweater.

I went to the Devignes'. Eva Braun hadn't seen her since the day before. "But didn't she say anything to you?" I asked. She shook her head slowly, her eyes cast down. I said, "Haven't you got any idea where she might have gone?" She shook her head. I was breathless and sweating. Seeing that woman, so silent, so calm, I wanted to shake her. I said, "She's gone off with a suitcase full of clothes. Aren't you at all worried?" She looked at me right in the eyes and said, "If my daughter hasn't said good-bye, then she will come back." I couldn't get anything else out of her.

At home, Boo-Boo was back. He could tell from my face that I hadn't found her at her mother's. He looked away and said nothing. Mickey came back half an hour later. She'd said nothing to him. He had no idea where she might be. I went back to the garage with him in the yellow truck and called Mlle Dieu. I let it ring for a long time, but no one answered. Juliette put her hand on my arm and said, "Don't worry. She'll come back." Henri IV looked at the ground, his hands in his pockets, a table napkin stuck in his vest.

I waited till one in the morning in the yard, with my brothers. Boo-Boo didn't talk. Neither did I. Only Mickey made suggestions as to where she might be. She'd had one of her fits of depression and gone to see Mlle Dieu. They'd both gone out for dinner in a restaurant, like they did for her birthday. Or this or that, none of which he really believed. I knew she'd gone for good, that she wouldn't come back. It was a certainty I felt in my blood. I didn't want to break down in front of them, so I said, "Come on, let's go to bed."

Next morning, at eight o'clock, I called Mlle Dieu. She hadn't seen her. She knew nothing. Just as I was hanging up, she said, "Wait a moment." I waited, I could sense her breathing as if I was in the same room. Finally she said, "No, nothing. I don't know." I shouted into the mouthpiece, "If you have anything to say, tell me!" She didn't answer. I heard her breathing more quickly. I said, "Well?" She said, "I don't know anything. If she comes back, or if you get any news, please let me know." If you get any news! I told her she could count on me, it would be my main concern, and hung up without saying good-bye.

At midday I went back to Eva Braun's. She was sitting outside, her eyes red, holding her garden shears. She said, with that accent that reminded me of Elle, "I'm sure she won't

leave me without letting me know. I know my daughter." I
said, "And what about me? What am I in all this, a dog?" She
looked at me, then looked down. She said, "There's nothing
stopping you from being sure, like me, that she will let you
know." It was the same logic as Eliane's—a logic that was
beyond me. Which shut me up, perhaps, but by breaking me,
by leaving me each time a bit more unsatisfied, a bit more in
the dark. Standing before her, I said, "She's gone to see some
lover. I'm sure of it. And you know who!" She looked up. She
gently shook her head and gave a little sigh, to show me the
idea was absurd. She said, "If it was that, she would have told
you to your face, as you know very well."

She made me stay for lunch that day, too, but we didn't
say much to each other. I realized for the first time how much
her daughter, physically at least, resembled her. The short
nose, the pale eyes, a slowness of movement and gesture.
Before I left she said, "One day, if she allows me, I'll tell you
what a good little girl she was, and how she has suffered." She
made an effort not to let the tears flood into her eyes, but I
felt she would cry her heart out as soon as she was alone. I
asked, "Have you told your husband about it?" She shook her
head.

Next day, in the later morning—or the day after, I don't
know—Eva Braun came to see me at the garage, wearing her
apron. The mailman, whom I'd seen go by in his yellow 2CV
and who had nothing for me, had just brought her a postcard
from her daughter. It showed an early model of a motorcar,
no landscape. It had been postmarked on July 29. It came from
Avignon. That was the first thing I looked for, where it had
come from. My mind was unhinged.

It was written with a fountain pen, with her own peculiar
spelling, and with no commas or periods:

My darling Mommy
Don't worry I'm well and will be back soon I don't know what
to write to Ping-Pong so show him my card he's not stupid he'll

*understand Above all tell Cognata I'm well and the others too I
have no more room so I must stop Don't worry Kisses from your
daughter*

She'd crossed out her signature—Elle, I presumed—and
written out in capital letters, at the end of the last line, which
ran under the address: ELIANE.

I sat down on the running board of the truck I was repairing.
I'd taken the card between my two index fingers so as not to
dirty it, and I turned it over. I then read, under the picture
of the car:

1930. Delahaye. Type 108.

I wouldn't have recognized it.

I asked Eva Braun if she knew anyone who lived in Avignon.
She shook her head. After a long while she asked me if I'd
understood what her daughter meant. I said I did. She asked
me if she meant well. I nodded.

I now know what Elle had to do in that town where she'd
never set foot before. Through her poor stubbornness and lone-
liness she'd taken the time, in some department store or to-
bacconist's, to choose precisely this card, or perhaps she'd only
thought of buying it on seeing it. Doesn't that prove she loved
me?

My Delahaye is a twenty-horsepower, six-cylinder, three-
carburetor, righthand-drive convertible, and was designed to
reach a maximum speed of around 170 kilometers an hour.
It will probably never do that again, but it's still a good car,
and it helped me a lot to get through the long week that
followed. I worked on it half the night to postpone the moment
of finding myself in the empty bedroom, and two or three times
I actually slept at the garage. I didn't even want to talk to my
brothers. What could I have said?

On Sunday my boss lent me his DS, and I went to Avignon.
I left the car along the ramparts and walked into the city center.

I went into several hotels, picked at random, to ask if she was there. A horrible afternoon. People jostled me on the sidewalks. I saw young lovers, girls the same age as Elle in the arms of boys who were more at ease in life than me. I was alone. I was hot. In any event, I later learned Elle was no longer in Avignon that Sunday. She'd gone on her way. I got back into the DS at nightfall and sat there for a long time looking at the stones of the ramparts through the windshield, then turned on the ignition and left. I had the postcard on me, which her mother had let me keep. I stopped on the way near Forcalquier, to have dinner in a restaurant. I looked at the card again. I didn't have to reread it—I knew it by heart.

On Wednesday night the Delahaye engine worked for the first time. Henri IV was with me. He said, "We'll have to check everything, but you're at the end of your labors." Like me, he heard some misfirings in the exhaust and put his hand over the pipe. I said, "If that's all it is, it's easily fixed." I slept in the workshop. In the morning Juliette came to wake me. A call had come from town, for another fire, they didn't know where. I told them on the telephone that I wasn't going. Each day I hoped Elle would come back. I wanted to be there when she did.

The night before, I'd walked down to the station and bought a package of aspirins at the pharmacy so as to get a closer look at that Philippe who had known Elle. He was about forty and my height. He was slim, the way she said she liked men. He looked like an overaged student—an intellectual, if you like— and he spoke abruptly, looking away because he was shy. I said I was Elle's husband. He knew. I asked him if he'd seen her recently. He shook his head. He said, "Excuse me," and went to serve a customer. I saw that his assistant, a girl of about thirty with short hair and a permanent frown, was getting ready to go home. I waited for her a bit farther on down the street. I asked her about Elle and got no answer except a threat to call the police.

Then I went past the Royal movie theater. As I said when I began telling you about all this business, I looked at the poster of a Jerry Lewis film that would be showing over the weekend. I saw Loulou-Lou arrive for the evening's screening. She said she'd be free the following afternoon, and I arranged to see her at four o'clock, on the edge of town.

On Thursday, then, at four o'clock, I saw Loulou-Lou in the 2CV. News travels quickly where we live, and I didn't need to tell her much to bring her up to date. She said, "My husband's in Nice. Let's not stay here, come home with me." She lived in an old house on the Puget-Théniers road. She gave me a bottle of beer and we talked. She said, "That girl wasn't for you. It's not that I have anything against her, I don't know her. But you don't know what kind of man she might have been with before coming to the village. You know nothing about her." We talked for a long time, going over the same old ideas—the same ideas that kept me awake at night.

At one point—I'd drunk several bottles of beer by this time—I put my hand under Loulou-Lou's skirt, as I sat facing her in her kitchen, and said a lot of nonsense like, "You understand me, don't you?"—all that. We went up to the bedroom, and she got undressed. I was ashamed to see her naked; I can't explain it, but I felt despicable, both for Eliane's sake and for hers. I said, "Sorry, it's no good." She saw me to her door. Before I left she said, "Have a word with your brother." I didn't understand—it was so far away from me. When she said "your brother," I thought of Mickey. She added, "The younger one. If she left on Wednesday the twenty-eighth, he knew before you did. I saw them together that afternoon, near the swimming pool."

I'm telling you exactly as it happened. I said suspiciously, "What am I supposed to make of that?" She said, "Nothing, except that I saw them together, and they were pressed up against each other, behind the swimming pool, and they looked very sorry for themselves." I said, "You bitch!" I wanted to slap her across the face, but my hand was shaking. I seemed to be shaking from head to toe.

I dashed out to the 2CV and went back to the village. Boo-Boo wasn't home, nor was Mamma. I yelled at Cognata,

"Where's Boo-Boo?" She didn't know. Trying to get out of her chair, she said, "My God! What's the matter with you, Florimond?" I slammed the door, but she opened it again behind me and shouted, before I could get to the car in the yard, "Boo-Boo hasn't done anything wrong, that's impossible!" I turned around to answer her, but I realized she couldn't hear me, I couldn't make her understand. I made a gesture, telling her to go in and not to worry. I was still shaking or so it seemed. I'd never been in such a state.

I left the car on the square and went into Brochard's. I pushed aside the bead curtain, and the sun from outside reached right up to the bar. I saw Georges Massigne with some other guys. His brothers-in-law, I don't know. I felt my shirt sticking to my back, cold. I heard someone say, as he went out through the bead curtain, "There's Ping-Pong looking for his wife again." Maybe not that exactly, but something like it. I went up to Martine. She was sitting at a table, across from the guy she met at our wedding, the one who lent us the stereo. I asked her if she'd seen Boo-Boo, or if she knew where he was. She didn't. She looked at me, half surprised, half afraid. Mother Brochard said something I don't remember—I know she said something, that's all—and I turned to Georges Massigne. Everyone who was there will tell you he didn't say or do anything to make me madder than I was already. That's true. Maybe they'll tell you I went into Brochard's on purpose to pick a fight with him, but that isn't true. I didn't know he'd be there.

I said to Georges Massigne, "You find it amusing to see me like this?" He said, "Come on, Ping-Pong, nobody finds anything amusing." I told him not to call me Ping-Pong any more. He shrugged his shoulders and looked away. I said to him, "Maybe you're going around boasting that you had my wife before I did?" He looked straight at me; there was anger in his eyes. He said I was to get one thing straight—the one who had taken her from the other was me. He called her Elle, and me Ping-Pong. I put my fist in his face. I've already said I'm not in the habit of fighting, and that was the only time in my adult

life I've been in a fight. I don't know how to fistfight, but then
I've got my height and my weight, and Georges Massigne fell
back, his lips cut open. He threw himself on me as soon as
he got his balance back, even before, and I hit him again,
almost as a reflex, to push him away.

Then the people who were there separated us. I felt all
empty inside, but my heart was beating wildly. Georges Massigne was bleeding from the mouth. They gave him a towel
from the bar, and someone said he had some teeth broken.
Mother Brochard suggested calling the police. Georges said
no, I was crazy. With blood running down his chin onto his
shirt, he said, "Can't you see he's going crazy?" I tried to go,
then realized that someone was holding me; it was Boo-Boo.
I hadn't seen him come in.

We both got into the 2CV. He'd just come back from the
vineyard with Mamma when Cognata told him I was looking
for him. I didn't want to have an argument with him in the
house, so I took him to the vineyard. It's just outside the village
and overlooks the road. It can only be reached by a dirt track.

In the car I asked him, "Is it true you were with Elle
Wednesday afternoon, behind the swimming pool?" He
seemed surprised I should know, but he said yes. He looked
down and said, "Don't start imagining things." Although he
was as tall as me, maybe a bit more, I've never stopped thinking
of Boo-Boo as a kid. I said, "I'm not imagining anything. It's
up to you to tell me about it."

He sat down on an embankment, at the edge of our vineyard. I remained standing in the evening sun, my shadow over
him. He was wearing old canvas trousers that were too short
for him, and which he'd put on to work in, and a shirt with
thick blue and green stripes. His long hair fell over one eye.
He said, "Last Wednesday I tried to stop her. But it was no
use." I said, "If you saw her go, why didn't you tell me?" He
said, "That wasn't possible, either." He pushed his hair back
to look at me and said, "She didn't want me to speak to you,
and, seeing the way you're behaving, I'm glad I didn't. She
was afraid—and she was right." He looked straight at me, his

head raised; his eyes looked sad and defiant. "She didn't want you to speak to me about what?" I asked. He shrugged his shoulders and looked down. He didn't answer.

I sat down next to him. I said, "Boo-Boo, you can't leave me like that, without knowing anything." I said it gently, without turning to look at him. For a long time he said nothing. He broke up a lump of soil in his fingers. Then he said, "She talked to me, the night you hit her, and next day, too. Do you remember what Cognata said to us the night of the wedding? It was true. She's calling for help." All I wanted to know was why she'd gone, where she was, but I sat still and waited. I sensed that if I asked another question too quickly, he might not tell me anything. I know Boo-Boo. He said, "Will you swear you won't leave this village? You'll wait for her to come back, if I tell you about it?" I swore on our mother. I didn't really intend to keep my word—after all, what is a word—but I swore all the same.

He said, "Last summer, when she was still living in Arrame, she used to spend the afternoons at a clearing in the middle of the woods, above Le Brusquet. Sometimes she went with friends, sometimes alone—to sunbathe. One afternoon she was alone, and two men came up without her hearing them, and they caught her." A lump rose in my throat, but he said no more, so I asked him what he meant by "they caught her." He shrugged his shoulders nervously and without looking at me said, "They were the words she used. I didn't have to have them explained to me. They caught her."

After a long silence he went on. "Two or three days later, they came prowling around her house. She told no one, because they'd frightened her, and anyway, in her village no one would have believed her. She was even more terrified seeing them near her house. So she went back with them to the woods." "Of her own accord?" I exclaimed, incredulously. He turned around quickly toward me, his face twisted with anger, his eyes full of tears. "And what's that supposed to mean, 'of her own accord'? Do you know what kind of bastards she was dealing with? Do you know what they said to her? They said they'd break her nose and all her teeth with a poker. They said they'd do the same thing to her mother. They'd pull her mother's hair out and make her swallow it. They told her what they'd had done to other girls like her, by guys who were paid to do it, especially to one girl they'd crippled and made a permanent invalid because she thought she'd be clever and go to the police. Do you understand now?"

He was holding me by the shirt. He was shaking me as if to get into my head every word that was coming out of his mouth, and tears were running down his cheeks. In the end he let me go and wiped his tears with his arm. He turned away, coughing, as if he was going to suffocate.

Gradually he calmed down. The light was failing. Everything was frozen inside me. Boo-Boo said, very quietly, in a voice drained of all emotion, almost coldly, "Another time they took her to a hotel, in a car. Then she never saw them again. The dam over Arrame had been finished. First she went to live with her parents in a châlet the town hall had lent them. That winter, when she settled here, she thought it was all over. Sometimes she was afraid when she thought about it, but in the end she believed they'd been terrorizing her just for their own amusement, that they weren't looking any further ahead." He paused for a few seconds. He added, "Then last month they found her again."

I said, "When?"

"Two days before her birthday. She went out to dinner with her old schoolteacher in Digne. One of them, the one she said was the worse of the two, was at the restaurant."

"They live in Digne?"

"She didn't say. They found her again, that's all. They forced her to come to Digne another day, the day before the Fourteenth of July. She told herself that since she was getting married, they would leave her alone. But not at all! They showed her a horrible photo. It was of the girl they'd had crippled. They said they would leave her in the same state. They said someone would come here right away to get you if she told you about them. Those were the words she used."

I couldn't see his face, and his voice was toneless, almost without expression. He wiped his eyes again with his arm. I didn't move. I don't know whether it was the stupefaction I felt, or the difficulty I had in imagining things so far beyond my experience, but I said, "It can't be true, all that." He said, "That's what I thought."

I tried to remember July 13. Where I'd been, what I'd done. At the time nothing came back to me. I asked, "What did they want from her? Did she say?" He said, even more quietly, "For them she represented money. That's all she said." I was beyond everything, beyond pain, beyond hate. This came as a more terrible blow than the others. I thought of the scene she'd had with her father, on the day of the wedding. I thought of the words Mlle Tusseau had repeated: "'Please, please.'" I thought of the inheritance she talked about the following day. I found it very hard to sort out my ideas. In the end the most important thing was to find out where she was, and to get to her as quickly as possible. "Do you know where she is?" I asked. He shook his head. "When you talked to her, behind the swimming pool, did she tell you where she was going?" He said, "She told me to forget all that. She said she could put an end to it once and for all, on her own. Then, since I didn't want to let her go, she said she'd made it all up, that the two men had never existed."

Neither of us said anything for a bit. Then I asked, "You didn't believe her?" He shook his head again. "Why?" He said, "Because I've seen them." It's funny, but it was only from then on, not really before, that the whole thing became real for me, words became images, this horror became part of my life. I said, "What do you mean? What do you mean?"

In Digne, the Sunday of the race, when she'd disappeared, he'd been looking for her at the same time as I had. In a narrow, deserted street he'd seen her inside a car drawn up by the roadside. She was sitting in front, next to the taller and older of the two men. The other one was in back. They were both talking to her at once, angrily, then more calmly, as if to convince her of something. Boo-Boo had stood stock-still

on the sidewalk as soon as he'd noticed her. He couldn't see
her face because she was turned toward them, her head down,
but he could tell from certain movements she made that she
was crying. They talked to her for a long time; then suddenly
she opened the door, and the one who had been sitting next
to her caught her by the arm. She looked crushed. The man
said something Boo-Boo couldn't hear, but in a hard, spiteful
way, and he let go of her arm roughly. She started to run down
the street, straight ahead, and Boo-Boo couldn't follow her
because the car was between them, and because he feared for
her safety if he showed himself. He tried to catch up with her
by making a detour via the boulevard, but he lost her.

I remembered how upset he'd seemed when he came back
to me. I thought at the time it was over seeing Mickey so badly
placed at that point in the race. I remembered how, later, he'd
followed me around with Elle, holding her hand, looking sad
the way he did when he was with her.

The blood was flowing once more in my veins. My ideas
sorted themselves out, because, in a way, I'd already decided
what I was going to do. I got up. I arranged my shirt—Boo-
Boo had pulled off a button when he'd tugged on it a few
minutes earlier. I asked him to describe those two men. The
taller and stronger was between forty-five and fifty. He hadn't
seen the man standing, but his build would be about the same
as mine, with a bit more added on for the difference in age.
His hair and eyebrows were gray, his eyes blue. There was a
successful look about him—he was someone who'd bettered
himself in life. The other was at least five years younger, slim,
with a big nose, thinning hair, and nervous movements. He
was wearing a lightweight suit, cream or beige, and a tie. Boo-
Boo could think of nothing else to say, except that he looked
more disreputable than his brother-in-law. I asked how he
knew they were brothers-in-law. "She told me," he said.

The car was a fairly old Peugeot 504, registered in the Alpes
de Haute-Provence. He remembered the figures 04 in the license number. He'd tried to remember the whole number, but
he'd been so upset he'd forgotten it. I asked him if Elle had

told him their names. He shook his head. There was nothing else he could remember. He thought for a bit, then said, "The name of the street. It was the Rue de l'Hubac." He thought again, then shook his head, disappointed at not knowing more.

Then I asked, "Why did Elle talk to you?" He looked up at me and said, "Because the night you beat her she couldn't stand any more. She had to talk to someone. Next day she told me everything, from beginning to end. Then she wanted never to talk about it again. She didn't even know I'd seen her with them in the car." We looked at each other for a few seconds in the fading light. He said, "I'm not hiding anything from you. If you really want to know, nothing ever happened between her and me." He was holding back his tears. I could tell from his voice. At the same time there was a certain pride about him, like that of a young cock. I shrugged my shoulders and said, "That's all we'd have needed."

I walked over to the 2CV and waited for him at the steering wheel. We sat without talking. In the yard I saw Mickey's yellow truck and said, "We've got to keep all this to ourselves."

We went straight in to dinner. Mickey and Cognata both looked at us but said nothing. Then I asked, "Is there a film on tonight?" I got up and turned on the TV. We ate in silence, glancing at the screen from time to time to follow something or other. Then I said I was going back to the garage, to work on the Delahaye. Boo-Boo asked if he could come with me. I touched him on the shoulder and said, "No, I'll probably work late again and spend the night there." I saw that Mickey was looking at my hand—I'd grazed my knuckles hitting Georges Massigne. I said to Mickey, "Did they tell you I'd been in a fight?" He said, "They said you'd broken two of his teeth. That might shut his big mouth up."

As I walked along the road, I took deep breaths of the night air. No lights were on in the village except in front of the gas pumps at the garage and, farther on, no doubt—I didn't go to see—at Eva Braun's. It seemed to me out of the question that Elle would have told her mother what she'd told Boo-Boo. I was right. One night, as she lay in our bed, she'd said, "In a few days, it will be settled." That was the night before I hit her. Walking along the road, I thought, "She was hoping they would leave her alone, that she'd be able to keep you out of all of this." I was still madder at myself for beating her—I couldn't bear even to think of it—but those two bastards would pay for everything, including the blows I'd given her.

I know this won't help my defense, but I'm going to say it all the same. It wasn't the next day I decided to saw off the barrel of the carbine, it was that night, Thursday, August 5. To begin with, it was too bulky—you couldn't put it into an ordinary suitcase, and it would stick out of a jacket—but the real reason was that I knew I'd have to shoot from fairly close quarters if I was to see their filthy faces and watch them die.

On Friday, toward the end of the morning—last Friday, that is—after stopping first at Eva Braun's, then at home, to see if Elle had come back, I took the Delahaye out of the garage with the top down. I said to Henri IV, "I'm sorry, but I have to leave you on your own. I have to go out." He sighed and shook his head, but it was just so he'd look like a boss. He never really minded what I did. I drove into town without even realizing what I was doing, except that I suddenly became aware of the drop on my right, because I was nearer to it. I don't think I ever noticed there was one, except during my early driving days.

I showed the car to Tessari and his pals. We celebrated the event at the café. Then Tessari took the wheel and went off alone on the Puget-Théniers road. When he came back he said, "Don't push her too hard. Let her run in. She's like a new car." He asked me to stay for lunch at his place, but I wasn't hungry and said I couldn't. I drove in the Delahaye to Annot, then on to Barrême. At first I forced myself to listen to the engine, but it was turning over quietly, so I stopped thinking about it. I didn't want to go to Digne yet, so I turned off toward the south at Châteuredon and came back via Castellane. As I drove along the Castillon dam, I stopped to get a sandwich at a food stand. I walked up and down for a bit, the sun beating down on me, my head filled with a crowd of unbearable images. There were a lot of tourists around the lake. Suddenly I noticed in the distance a girl with dark hair, and I thought it was Elle. I couldn't help walking faster to overtake her.

I came back to the village in the late afternoon. I hadn't yet got out of the car when Juliette ran down the wooden steps toward me. She said, "They've been looking for you all over. Henri has taken your mother-in-law to the bus stop, or maybe the train. I don't know." She looked at me apprehensively, as if half scared. I felt she'd gone over what she had to say to me beforehand, but, with me there in front of her, it was more difficult to say than she'd thought it would be. "Have they found her?" I asked. I was afraid she was dead. Juliette said, "She's in a hospital in Marseille. They contacted Mlle Dieu at Le Brusquet." "In Marseille? In a hospital?" Juliette looked at me, the same terrified expression in her eyes. She said, "She's alive—it's not that. But she's been in the hospital since last Saturday. They only found out today where she came from."

I ran to the telephone. I couldn't remember Mlle Dieu's number. It took some time for Juliette to find it for me. Just as I heard the schoolteacher's voice at the other end, Henri IV pulled up at the pumps in the DS. There was a woman with him in the car, and I didn't know who it was. Mlle Dieu shouted into the telephone, "I don't want to speak to you on the telephone! I want to see you! You don't know what they've done to her, you don't know." I shouted back that she was to calm down and explain. She said, "Not on the telephone. She's asleep now—they've put her to sleep. You won't be able to see her before tomorrow. So come to my place, please. I've got to talk to you." I said, "Shit, tell me what's the matter with her!" She said, almost in a shriek, "What's the matter with her? She doesn't even know who she is, that's what's the matter with her! She says she's named Eliane Devigne, that she lives in Arrame and is nine years old! That's what's the matter with her!"

For a long time she just cried at the other end of the line. I said "Mademoiselle Dieu" several times, but she didn't answer. Finally I said, a lump in my throat, "I'll come and see you." I knew, through the waves of hate that paralyzed my thoughts and my muscles, that I had one thing to settle before leaving. I said, "I won't be coming right away. Wait for me." I hung up, dropping the receiver as I did so. Henri IV put it back in place.

They'd brought back the nurse, Mlle Tusseau, to look after old Devigne. For the moment Mamma was with him. Eva Braun had taken the bus to Saint-Auban, where she'd catch a train for Marseille. Everybody had told her to wait for me, but she'd wanted to go right away. Nobody had stopped her. She hadn't cried or seemed upset in any way. She just wanted to be with her daughter. Henri IV simply said that in the car she started speaking in German two or three times without realizing it. Before leaving, she'd asked Juliette to tell me to bring clothes and underwear for Elle, because she'd been found without either a suitcase or her bag. It was La Timone hospital. I was to bring my family record book. I said yes to everything.

I went back to the house in the Delahaye. Cognata and Boo-Boo were there, and they knew most of what had happened. I told Boo-Boo to take our aunt up to her room—I had to wash. When they'd gone up, I opened the cupboard where the guns were kept, took out the Remington and a box of cartridges, and went out to put them in the trunk of the car.

I washed and shaved, answering Boo-Boo's questions cautiously, so as not to make him more worried, and because he was trying to find out what I was going to do. I said, "I'm going to see her. I'll decide then. And you're not to open your mouth."

I went up to the bedroom and took out the suitcase Elle had left, the navy-blue one, a pair of shoes, underwear, a new nightgown. The white bathrobe took up too much room—I couldn't get it in. I packed some underwear and a clean shirt for myself. I put on my black trousers, Mickey's black turtleneck sweater, and my beige poplin jacket.

I went back to the garage. It was seven or half past seven. I said to Henri IV, "Do me a favor. Go and have a word with Georges Massigne, and ask him not to lodge a complaint. Tell him I'm sorry and I'll pay him whatever I owe him. Take Juliette with you, it will come better from her." He looked at me for several seconds in silence. Juliette was standing in the kitchen doorway, at the top of the stairs, looking down into the workshop. I said to Henri IV, "I'll wait for you here. If you don't mind, I'll take your DS to go to Marseille. The Delahaye might let me down at any time." I think he understood that I wanted to get them out of the way for half an hour or so. He's not stupid, Henri IV. I didn't want either of them to see the gun, not because they would have tried to argue me out of it—no one could do that now—but because I was afraid they might be accused of something if I got caught. He said nothing. Finally he turned to Juliette and said, "I'm taking you with me. Come as you are, we're not going dancing."

When they'd left, I parked the Delahaye at the end of the garage. I took out my suitcase and put the box of cartridges in it. I set the Remington on the workbench, and cut and polished the barrel. Then I sawed off the butt at the level of the pistol grip. The weapon was reduced to about 60 centimeters in length. It didn't handle perfectly, but with two hands, and at least ten paces away, it would be impossible to miss a man, even on the first shot. I carefully cleaned and greased the whole mechanism. I was in no hurry. I just tried to concentrate on doing well what I was doing.

At one point I heard a car out at the pumps, and I went to serve them with gas. I'd put on a big blacksmith's apron to protect my clothes. As I filled up his GS, the driver, a bricklayer who worked up on the pass, said, "I hear you've got yourself married?" I said, "Yes, that's right." I looked at the wooden stairs outside the house. I thought of that Sunday evening, the night after the wedding, when Elle was sitting next to me and I was smoking a cigar. I'd said to myself then that she loved only me, and it was true. I hadn't lost her—she'd been stolen from me, broken, and driven crazy.

I swept up the metal filings and sawdust on the workbench. I put the Remington into the suitcase, wrapped in a rag, and the pieces of barrel and butt I'd sawed off. I left the workbench as I'd found it. I washed my hands. I went and sat on the stairs outside, waiting for Juliette and my boss to come back. It was hot, as it had been all summer, but the sun had long since gone down behind the mountains, and the village was quiet.

Elle had been found on a beach in Marseille, near Borély Park. It was Saturday, July 31, only three days after she'd left the village. She was walking on the sand, in her shoes and her sky-blue nylon dress, eyes cast down. She moved away without saying anything when someone asked her if she was all right. Her hair hid her face. She looked so strange that some bathers—it was six in the evening—called the police. She had no papers on her. She answered no questions. She couldn't speak.

They took her to a hospital, then to another, La Timone, where there was a psychiatric ward. She was examined. She had no wounds except a bruise on one knee, which she may have got from falling. She was exhausted and apathetic. She couldn't be persuaded to speak. Otherwise she was docile and did whatever she was told.

To begin with she was put to sleep until Tuesday, and further examinations were made. When she woke up, she was the same. Exhausted, apathetic, silent, refusing food. The police had been looking without success for someone who had been on or near the beach and who might recognize her and say who she was. She was wearing only her dress—which had got very dirty, and which led them to think she'd fallen—panties, shoes of a popular make, and her wedding band. I'd had *F. to E.* and the date of our wedding engraved inside the ring.

She was put to sleep again and fed intravenously until Friday morning. On waking, she smiled and spoke. She did not answer the questions they asked her—she did not know why she was there—but she said she was named Eliane Devigne, was born in Arrame, Alpes-Maritimes, on July 10, 1956, and still lived there, in the Chemin du Haut-de-la-Fourche, and was nine years old. The doctor who treated her—a woman, Mme Solange Fieldmann—discovered that Arrame was now at the bottom of a dam and telephoned the mayor of Le Brusquet, Mlle Dieu.

I listened as Mlle Dieu told me all this in a strange, flat voice. Her eyelids were red and swollen, but she'd stopped crying. Her head was covered with a white towel, which she'd wrapped around it like a turban. She'd had quite a lot to drink while waiting for me, and she went on drinking.

Her house was high up on a hill, with a terraced garden from which you could see the lake. Inside it was gloomy and old-fashioned, except for one room, which she called her living room, and which she'd had modernized after her mother's death. There were books everywhere. When I arrived, she had to move a pile of books off a sofa before I could sit down. I think I drank quite a lot, too, during the three hours or so I spent with her. I can't remember much of what I did, except that when she was not speaking she bit her lower lip, and I instinctively moved my finger toward her face to stop her—I couldn't bear it any more.

Elle had confided in her, as she had in Boo-Boo, about the night I'd struck her. It was the night of July 13, when she'd come back late. I heard, almost in the same words, what I'd already learned from my brother, plus something else, which really made me sit up—it appeared that the two bastards had provided Elle with an apartment in Digne, "for her to receive men in." Boo-Boo had told me, "For them, she represents money." I'd thought only of a kind of ransom, a sum of money they would demand to leave her alone.

Mlle Dieu didn't know their names, either, but she finally brought herself to tell me what she did know—that the elder of the two had a small sawmill just outside Digne, and that the other was a real-estate agent on the Boulevard Gassendi. Elle had told her, "They are well-to-do, respectable married men, not at all the pimps you might think. If I went to the police I couldn't prove anything. Then I'd just disappear—no

one would even find my corpse." Elle had also told her, and
this made my heart skip a beat, "If they don't leave me alone,
I shall get rid of them, one way or another. Or I'll tell Ping-
Pong all about it, and he'll take care of them."

Elle had asked Mlle Dieu three times to go pick her up in
Digne—twice before the wedding, and then that Tuesday when
she was supposed to be shopping, and she was wearing her red
dress, and I struck her when she came back. Mlle Dieu had
called on her in the late afternoon, in the apartment she'd
mentioned, so it really did exist. It was on the fourth floor of
an old building, at the end of a courtyard, at 73, Rue de
l'Hubac. It was the street where Boo-Boo, during the race the
following Sunday, had seen the two men with Elle, in a black
Peugeot.

When I thought of the Tuesday I hit her, I remembered
the bus tickets Elle had taken out of her bag in our kitchen
to show me. I asked Mlle Dieu, "Did you bring her back from
Digne that evening?" She looked away and said, "No, I left
her at the apartment. She didn't want me to take her back."
She bit her lower lip and made it bleed again, then added,
"I wanted to go to the police. I was terrified. We had an
argument. She never telephoned me, I never saw her again
after that Tuesday night."

She emptied her glass. She was still looking away when,
almost regretfully, she said, "The keys to the apartment are
probably in the mailbox. It's the last one as you go in under
the first-floor archway. She didn't want to keep them on her,
for fear you'd find them, yet she also figured that if things
turned out badly, you would have to go there." I was pleased,
but I just shook my head and pretended that this information
was really incidental after all she'd told me. Then, very quietly,
she asked, "What are you going to do now?" I said, "First I'm
going to see her in Marseille; I'll decide after that what I'm
going to do."

Later she gave me something to eat in her kitchen. I'd only
had a sandwich since the night before, and I think I'd worked
up quite an appetite. I can't remember what she gave me to

eat or anything. All I can remember is looking at her sitting across from me, glass in hand, wearing a peach-colored shift of some silky material that was fashionable in the department stores some years ago. She was drunk. She started telling me all over again that Elle had been found in Marseille, on a beach, opposite Borély Park. When I remarked that she'd already told me that, she said, "Oh," and two tears ran down her cheeks.

She wanted me to spend the night there—it was after midnight by then—but I said no, I would rather drive on to Marseille. I wouldn't be able to sleep anyway. When I left, she accompanied me to the garden gate. The moon was almost full, and there were reflections on the lake. She said, "I, too, would like to see her as soon as possible." I promised to call her. Standing by her gate, her head wrapped in her towel, she watched me get into the car and drive away. She was still holding her glass.

It's about eighty kilometers from Le Brusquet to Digne, but there are a lot of twists and turns before you get to the highway. I parked on the Boulevard Gassendi at two in the morning, in front of the only place that was still lit up, a sort of discothèque, where the owner was busy throwing out the last of his customers. He explained to me where the Rue de l'Hubac was. I went there on foot. It was quiet and deserted, and I could hear my own steps on the sidewalk.

In the building that Mlle Dieu had described, the lights didn't work. I managed to find the last mailbox by the light from outside. It was a wooden box; I gave a tug on the padlock and the clasps holding it came away with it. There was a bunch of keys inside, a large, long key and two smaller ones. As far as I could see, there was no name on the mailbox.

I crossed the courtyard to the far staircase and went up to the fourth floor. The landing was lit by a large window. There was an apartment on each side, but the door on the left had no lock. Nevertheless, I set to work very cautiously on the righthand door. Every time I turned a key I stopped and listened, to see if I'd awakened anyone inside.

Once inside, I turned on the light. I shut the door behind me and looked into the kitchen, which was very narrow and painted bright red. There were two washed glasses on the drainboard, and an opened bottle of beer in the refrigerator. I never discovered who had drunk the beer. It wasn't Elle, anyway—I was sure of that. I'm telling you everything exactly as I saw it.

The main room, which was also mostly red, did not smell as if anyone had been there recently. The velvet bedspread was well smoothed out, and the closets were empty. I noticed nothing to suggest that Elle had been there. There was an ashtray on a low table, but it was clean. There was a chest of drawers—I opened the drawers one by one. Nothing.

Then I went into the bathroom. Naturally, I didn't expect to see my wife's reflection in the mirror over the sink just because she'd looked at herself in it a few days before, but there was something almost as startling, something that hit me like a blow in the chest. On the shelf just under the mirror was her Dupont lighter, with *Elle* engraved on it in a smooth square.

I picked it up and looked at it. That Tuesday night when I'd hit her and emptied out her small white bag on our bed, it had been among her things, I was sure. After that, she'd only gone back to Digne once, the Sunday of the race. At least as far as I knew. Anyway, she'd forgotten her lighter—which wasn't like her. Or she had left it on purpose, for me to find.

I went on looking. Suddenly I thought of something and went back into the kitchen. I took out a small white trash can from under the sink, the kind that is opened by a footpedal. There was very little in it—cigarette butts and an empty cracker box. I didn't know what to think.

I sat on the bed for a while, then looked in the drawers again. I said to myself, "If she thought you'd come here one day, if she left you the keys in the mailbox, there must be some message somewhere." It was long past three o'clock by my watch. I tried not to think of the cigarette butts in the trash can, of a man being there before me. I thought how careful she must have been with those two bastards, careful of everything she did. Then I suddenly remembered what she'd written on the piece of paper in her handbag: "Well, what have you gained by going through my bag?"

I'd thought the message was for me. But was it? She may have intended it for one of them. If she'd left a message for me, it would have to be in a place she figured they wouldn't think of looking but I would.

It was ten past four, the first light of day was already coming through the window. I went back to the bathroom. I lifted off the shelf under the mirror, where I'd first seen the lighter. It was a hollow plastic rectangle, and two cards had been slipped inside. I pulled them out and shook the shelf, but there was nothing else inside. One of the cards was a business card for Jean Leballech's sawmill, on the La Javie road. The other was a visiting card from Michel Touret, real-estate agent, with the addresses of his office, on the Boulevard Gassendi, and his home, on the Traverse du Bourdon. On the back of Jean Leballech's card, in a handwriting I didn't know, was the address of a carpenter in Digne, but it had been crossed out very heavily.

There was no message from Elle, just those two cards. I slipped them into my jacket pocket, put back the shelf, checked that I'd left no trace in the apartment, and left. Downstairs I hesitated for a moment in the darkness, then decided to keep the keys.

On the empty boulevard it was already quite light, and another hot day seemed likely. I went over to the tourist office and looked at a plan of the town in the window. Then I drove out to Touret's house. It was a detached, so-called Provençal-style house, like you see in all the ads. The Traverse du Bourdon was off the road that led to the spa. There were a lot of houses around his. As I drove up the Boulevard Gassendi, on my way back, I noticed the real-estate agent's on my left.

I took the La Javie road and drove for about five kilometers before coming to the gates of the sawmill. A sign that was right there indicated a village not far away, Le Brusquet. It made a strange impression on me, seeing that name, so far from the Arrame dam, and just at that moment. It was as if someone, I don't know who, had put it there on purpose, just to let me know he knew what I was thinking. I don't believe in God—except sometimes during the fires—but it did have a funny effect on me. Of course I was very tired.

In Leballech's yard I saw a black Peugeot, like the one Boo-Boo described. There was a light on in one of the first-floor windows of the house. I thought it was probably the kitchen, and someone would be making coffee, his hair all mussed, eyes swollen with sleep, like Mickey or me in the morning. The telephone wire, which went from the road to the workshop, then to the house, was out of reach without a ladder. I looked at the yard carefully, making a mental note of the distances, the positioning of the buildings; then I went back to the car.

I drove another three kilometers along the same road. Just before getting to the village called Le Brusquet, I found a path on my right that led to a wood, and I drove in there. I left the DS at the entrance and continued on foot. There were no houses around, but on the flat land were pastures surrounded by fences, in one of which was a ruined shed, probably a sheepfold. I walked over to have a look at it. There was no door, and the roof had caved in.

I looked at my watch and ran the whole way back to the car. It took me less than two minutes to reach it, reverse, and get back onto the main road. In two more minutes I passed Leballech's sawmill.

I stopped the DS for a few seconds, then drove off again. When I got back to town, I made a right turn. This led to a boulevard parallel to the Boulevard Gassendi on my left, and I stopped in a square where there was a parking lot. Without dawdling, but without running the risk of being stopped by some overzealous policeman, I had taken six minutes to come from the sawmill. There was practically no traffic on the road yet, and that would be the only difference when I had to make my getaway.

Past Les Mées, as I was taking the bridge over the Durance, I threw out the pieces I'd saved off the gun, without stopping the car. Farther on, between Manosque and Aix, I parked in a rest area and tilted my seat back for a while. I went to sleep. When I opened my eyes, there were cars and trucks going by on the road. It was after nine.

I got to Marseille an hour later. As I've already said, I did my military service in Marseille, so I know the city quite well. I found La Timone hospital easily, but the psychiatric ward was in a separate part of the building, and I had to make several detours to get to the entrance. In the parking lot I took out the Remington and the box of cartridges from the suitcase and pushed them to the back of the trunk, then locked it.

As soon as I entered the lobby I saw Eva Braun, sitting very erect on a bench, her eyes shut. She looked thinner and older. She was wearing the same cream-colored dress she wore the day she came to our house for her daughter's birthday, but now it seemed to have been made for someone else. Opening her eyes and seeing me in front of her holding the suitcase, she said, "I've given you a lot of trouble for nothing, my poor son-in-law. They found Eliane's luggage in a hotel."

I asked her if she'd seen Elle. She nodded and smiled sadly. She said, "She looks quite well. She seems normal enough. But she hasn't come back to earth yet, you understand? She keeps saying she wants to see her daddy. She wants to know why he hasn't come to see her. It's the only thing that seems to be bothering her." I saw a tear on the edge of her eyelid, but she wiped it away at once. She stared down at the ground and added, "They've put her to sleep for the time being. She has to sleep a lot."

Shortly afterward a nurse took me to the room where Elle was lying. I sat next to her bed, alone, listening to her peaceful breathing, and let the tears come that I'd been holding back for several days. She was lying on her back, her hair rolled up in a bun, her arms outside the sheets. The thick gray cotton nightgown she was wearing had no collar, which made her look like a prisoner, and rather touching. As she slept, her face seemed furrowed by pain, but she still had that little swollen mouth I loved so much.

When the nurse came back, I gave her the dresses and underwear I'd brought. I kept the navy-blue suitcase, which now contained only a shirt and underwear for myself and my own toilet articles. The white suitcase lay empty in a corner of the room. Lowering my voice, I asked the nurse what hotel they'd found it in. She said, "The Belle-Rive. It's one of the hotels around the Gare Saint-Charles. In fact, you'll have to go there—your wife didn't pay the bill." I said, "She also had a big canvas handbag." The nurse shook her head; this hadn't been brought back.

Before leaving, I leaned over Elle, kissed her damp forehead, and touched her hand. I didn't dare kiss her on the lips in front of the nurse, and I regretted it later. I still do, because the other two times I saw her, it was no longer possible.

The doctor who'd treated her, Mme Fieldmann, received me in her first-floor office. Through the open window behind her, I saw men in dressing gowns and slippers walking with slow steps in a garden surrounded by arcades. She was about fifty years old, with black hair, fairly small, fairly plump, but with a handsome, kindly face and laughing eyes that had little wrinkles around them, like Mickey's. She had questioned Eva Braun earlier in the morning. She asked me various questions, some of which I found quite pointless and others embarrassing. "If I wasn't trying to see the situation clearly, I wouldn't ask you questions," she said patiently.

She kept using words I didn't understand. She explained that my wife had been mentally disturbed for a long time, perhaps for years—since she was nine, the age she now said she was—but until the previous Saturday, she was probably the only person to realize, at certain moments, that her personality was threatened. A neurosis. This neurosis had been built up, stage by stage, after an unbearable emotional shock,

Mme Fieldmann was quite sure. But there were other things, which only the examinations of the past few days had revealed: sudden, very disturbing changes in the flow of blood to the brain. Resulting from some particularly disturbing events, these might account for the loss of consciousness or hearing—"the back of my head hurts." They might also have caused diffused lesions at the level of the little veins known as capillaries.

Mme Fieldmann said, "Last Saturday—I don't know where, and I don't know why—your wife underwent an emotional shock at least as great as the first one. But this time she was unable to remain in the world she'd made up for herself, her neurosis. Have you ever seen a building where the roof has caved in? Well, it's a bit like that. What she has done is very rare and, just a few years ago, would have left my colleagues quite skeptical. After a period of stupor, she has passed from her neurosis to psychosis, that is, to an illness that is different not only in degree, but also in kind. Now everybody else realizes that her personality has been destroyed, but she doesn't. In her mind she really is nine years old. When she looked at herself in the mirror yesterday, she had no doubt she was a little girl. She simply asked us to take the mirror away. You understand?"

I said yes. I had many questions to ask her, but I was sitting on a chair, my suitcase between my feet, in a hospital office, facing somebody much better educated than me, and I felt intimidated. I looked down.

Mme Fieldmann then removed something from a desk drawer and put it in front of me. I recognized the small tinted bottle of nail polish that I had seen, the Tuesday night I hit her, when emptying Elle's bag onto our bed. Mme Fieldmann said, "When your wife was found on the beach and brought here, she was holding this bottle in her fist. We had to pull it from her by force." I couldn't see what she was getting at. She tilted the bottle backward and forward, and told me it contained powder. She said, "Mind you, so many things are made these days. For all I know, they might produce nail polish in powder form. But it isn't nail polish." I thought it might be some drug. But as if she'd read my thoughts, she shook her head. She said, "It's a very dangerous cardiovascular medicine, Dreboludetal. It's out of the question that any doctor would have prescribed it for your wife. I don't know how she got hold of it. Anyway, she apparently crushed thirty tablets that contain a derivative of bacterial toxin—a poison, if you like—several hundred times stronger than strychnine. To give you some idea, there's enough in this bottle to kill a whole family."

I just sat there for a long time, unable to respond. Then she said, "It is possible that she really didn't intend to use this powder, either on herself or on anyone else. I've known other young patients to keep dangerous things on them—razor blades, acid, and so on. It gives them a sense of security." I looked up and said, "Yes, I suppose it does," but I didn't think that was it. I thought of what Elle had said to Mlle Dieu— "I'll get rid of them, one way or another." She'd wanted to try by herself, and she hadn't succeeded. I got up. I thanked Mme Fieldmann. She said I would be able to see my wife awake the following afternoon, about three o'clock, but I would have to be sensible, because she wouldn't recognize me. I said I wasn't expecting her to.

On my way out of the hospital I stopped for Eva Braun, then drove her to the Belle-Rive hotel, opposite the great steps of the Gare Saint-Charles. It wasn't a luxurious place, but it looked comfortable and well kept. The guy behind the desk in the hall, the daytime receptionist, could remember only one thing about Elle—her pale eyes. It was he who registered her on Friday, July 30, in the late afternoon. So she'd already been to Avignon. He'd got her to fill out the form. She had written, "Jeanne Desrameaux, 38, Rue Frédéric-Mistral, Nice." Eva Braun didn't know what this was about, so I explained it was my aunt's maiden name. They showed us the room she'd spent a night in; it faced the street. A couple of Germans were there, surrounded by luggage. My mother-in-law spoke to them in their language.

I went downstairs again, paid Elle's bill. I saw she'd ordered coffee on Saturday morning and made several telephone calls, all to Marseille. I asked the receptionist if anyone had come to see her while she was there, but he didn't know. All he remembered were her eyes, which had made "a strange impression" on him, and which were "blue, it's true, but almost colorless."

Then we went to study the train schedules, in the station lobby. Eva Braun wanted to get home to look after her husband. She said, "I'll come back next week with him, if you'll bring us." There was a train for Digne in an hour. She didn't want to go to a restaurant for fear of missing it, so we had a buffet meal of cold cuts and salad in a café near the station. Marseille is a very noisy city, and we could hardly breathe for the heat. She said, with a timid smile, "I feel as though I'm drunk."

As the train was moving out, she waved to me through the window, as if she was returning to the other end of the world and would never see me again. She may be German—or Austrian—but she belongs to the same breed as my father, my brothers, and the wives in our family. The breed of those who have to put up with everything and who, unfortunately, do put up with everything. Do you know what I said to myself, when her train had disappeared and I was walking out of the station? It filled me with a kind of contentment, almost excitement, like when I saw Mickey's red cap emerge from the mass of the other racers when he'd won his first race at Draguignan. I said that Elle and I were not like them.

I drove right through Marseille. On the way I stopped at a store on the Prado and bought some sunglasses, a red shirt, and a long plastic bag, designed to carry fishing tackle, I suppose—anyway, big enough for my gun.

I took a room at the Cristotel, in the Mazargues district, a long way from the city center. It was expensive, but it was big and modern and had a bar, two restaurants, and five hundred identical rooms; no one would ever notice anyone there. I'd seen a poster for this hotel at the station, and everything there was as anonymous as the poster had made it seem.

I filled out my form at the reception desk. I said I had to catch up on a lot of sleep and didn't want to be disturbed. The receptionist said, without ever looking at me, that all I had to do was hang the Do Not Disturb notice on the handle of my door. I followed a porter into an elevator and a corridor, but I carried the suitcase myself. There wasn't one chance in a million that he would be sufficiently gifted to see through the covering and guess there was a Remington and cartridges inside, but that's how it was. I tipped him. As soon as he'd gone, I hung the Do Not Disturb notice on my door.

I checked the gun again and loaded it. I didn't have a spare loader, and if I had to shoot twice the first time, I knew I wouldn't want to risk leaving only a single bullet for the second. I would have to reload in the sheepfold, without panicking, and wasting as little time as possible. This worried me, because I did not see myself, I could not imagine myself, in that situation.

The idea of the telephone at Leballech's also worried me. I remembered the extension of the wire, above the door to the workshop. It would be too far away for me, with a thirty-centimeter barrel, to blow it up with one shot. I would try, that's all I could do. But I wouldn't stand back from the gate to do it. Mlle Dieu had said they were "respectable married men." I didn't know how many sons and daughters would be in the house and might cut off my retreat when I'd killed Leballech. What's more, I was almost sure there was a dog there, though I hadn't heard it. I mustn't stand back from the gate.

Those were my thoughts as I lay in that room, where the fabrics and walls were blue and the wood mahogany-colored. I slipped the gun, the box of cartridges, and the red shirt into the bag I'd bought. I put the bag at the foot of the bed. I disposed of the cellophane wrapping for the shirt down the toilet. Then I got undressed and had a bath. There was a small refrigerator in the room, and I opened a bottle of beer and wrote a cross in a box on the list of contents with a pencil attached to a chain—that's luxury!

I lay in bed in my clean underwear and drank my beer, thinking I would see Elle awake next day. I imagined a lot of silly things—that suddenly she would recognize me and be cured—and I told myself they were silly and stopped. I shut my eyes. I didn't really sleep, I sensed the room around me, I heard voices in the corridor and a distant rumble outside.

I got up when my watch showed four o'clock. I put on my black trousers, Mickey's black sweatshirt, my beige jacket. All I took with me was the plastic bag. To leave the hotel, I went out through the bar. There was a crowd of tourists there. I put my room key in the glove compartment of the DS, along with the sunglasses I'd bought. Before driving out the Aix highway, I filled the gas tank and checked the oil level.

I drove on. I didn't need to be in Digne until seven o'clock, and that was about the time I got there. I parked the car on the small square I'd found that morning and walked to the Boulevard Gassendi. There were a lot of people on the sidewalk.

I didn't expect to find the real-estate agent's still open, but it was. Inside, a man was sitting behind a metal desk. He was getting an elderly couple to sign some papers. I looked at him through the windows without stopping. I crossed the boulevard farther along and went into a big café, Le Provençal. It was like being at a public meeting—people were talking so loudly. I ordered a beer at the bar and bought a telephone token.

The telephone booth was at the far end of a back room where billiards were played. I called the real-estate agent's. "Michel Touret?" He said, "Yes, speaking." "Monsieur Touret, I have some land I want to sell, just outside Digne on the La Javie road. It's a good piece of land. I'd like you to see it." He asked for my name. "Planno. Robert Planno." He wanted to make an appointment for the following week. I said, "The trouble is, I'm not from these parts. I live in Menton, and I'm taking the train back tonight." He wasn't too anxious to come. I said, "Believe me, Monsieur Touret, I'm offering you a very good deal. I need money quietly. You see what I mean? It's less than ten kilometers from Digne, there's a good piece of land and a sheepfold that needs repairing." He still hesitated and asked a few questions about the place. Finally he said, "I'll have to pop home first." I said, "That's fine, because I wouldn't be able to get there before half past eight. It won't take us long, just a quarter of an hour." He said, "O.K. You're always the same, you people." I think he meant his clients, I don't know. I asked him if he knew Leballech's sawmill. He said, in a tone almost of disgust, "Sure I do, Leballech's my brother-in-law." I said, "Well, it's three kilometers farther along, on the right; there's a path that leads through a wood. I'll be waiting for you at the entrance, on the road. What kind of car do you have?" He said it was a CX. I said, "You'll recognize me easily enough, I'm wearing a red shirt."

After drinking my beer and paying what I owed, I walked down the sidewalk across from the agency. Touret was still inside, getting ready to leave. I couldn't make out too clearly what he looked like, because of the reflections in the window, but I didn't hang around too long. I'd see his face soon enough. I wasn't thinking so much of what they'd done to Elle, him and his brother-in-law. That had become as unreal as the rest of my life. I was thinking only of what I had to do. I think that at a certain point I stopped being capable of explaining why I was there or what I was doing, let alone of considering that the sun would rise again and another day would dawn.

I went back to the DS. I left my jacket inside. I took the black bag. I put on my sunglasses. I locked all the doors and walked very quickly to the edge of town. The sun was moving toward the hills, but it was still unbearably hot. There were two traffic lights and a normal amount of traffic on the route I'd chosen for my return.

When I went past the sawmill I didn't stop, just turned my head for two seconds, enough to see that there was a German shepherd in the yard, and a boy about Boo-Boo's age with long hair. The gate was on the right side of the road, and the traffic was fast. I hoped there'd be fewer cars an hour later, but on a Saturday in August, who knows where people are going? As

I walked, I began to get thirsty. It may have been nerves, but I've been thirsty ever since.

In the sheepfold I put the red shirt on over my sweatshirt and rolled up the sleeves. I took the gun out of the bag and set it in a hollowed-out niche halfway up the wall, on the right as you came in. I checked two or three times that I could grab it easily. I put the bag on the ground just below. Then I waited until half past eight, sitting on the step. I don't remember what I was thinking about. Probably about being thirsty, or about the coincidence that Mme Fieldmann should have mentioned a caved-in roof; maybe about nothing.

When it was time, I walked toward the road. I saw a man and a woman come out of the woods. They had their arms around each other's waist and seemed very wrapped up in themselves. They hadn't seen me and walked off in the direction of Le Brusquet. Fewer cars seemed to be passing. My heart was heavy, my throat dry.

Touret was about ten minutes late. He'd brought his CX into the path, as I'd thought he would. He turned off the engine, pulled out the key, and put it in his jacket pocket. He was wearing a summer suit with narrow blue stripes, like butchers wear, and a gaudy red-and-orange tie. As he got out of the car, he said, "Excuse me, Monsieur Planno, you know how it is with women." He held out his hand. He was of average height, no more, with receding hair and gray eyes. His smile, his dynamic salesman's manner, his front teeth—everything about him was false. I said, "It's up there. Let's go and see." During the first few seconds it seemed to me I'd seen his face somewhere before, but it was only a vague impression, and I gave it no more thought.

We climbed up the path. He said, "Oh yes. I see. I've already sold some land around here." I walked ahead of him, through the field. He stopped to look about him. I don't know what he was saying to me. The words were no longer reaching my brain. I went into the ruined building first. I thrust my hand out for the gun, grabbed hold of it, and turned toward him. He broke off what he was saying and stared at the gun. He said, very quietly, "What's this all about?"

I gestured to him to retreat to the back wall. He nearly lost his balance on the rubble. I asked him, "Did you send her to Avignon?" He looked at me, his mouth open, then looked down again at the gun. "What? Avignon?" he murmured. Then he understood. He said, "Oh, that girl?" I said, "Eliane, my wife." He moved a hand in front of him to stop me from firing. He said, "Listen to me. I've got nothing to do with this business! I swear. It's entirely my borther-in-law's fault!" Since I said nothing, he made as though to move along the dry-stone wall, but he stopped when he saw me raising the Remington. I was holding it with both hands, pointing it at the upper part of his chest. Then he made a sort of grimace, which was probably intended as a smile, and said, even more quietly, as if he had difficulty finding the breath for it, "No, you're not going to do that. You just wanted to frighten me, didn't you? I sear it's all my borther-in-law's fault." I still said nothing. He must have thought I couldn't press the trigger. He moved away from the wall, saying, with sudden courage, "Come on, now. You surely didn't believe what she said. Can't you see she's cracked? Is it my fault if some bitch . . ." I fired.

The explosion was so powerful that for a fraction of a second I shut my eyes. He had stumbled forward, one hand open to deflect the gun, and he'd been literally thrown back against the wall. He was still on his feet, a gaping hole in his chest, his face unbelieving for a time that seemed very long. Then he fell forward through the smoke of the shot, and just from the way he fell I knew he was dead.

I went outside, to listen. There was no sound. Then I realized that the birds were singing in the bushes and trees around me. I went back into the sheepfold. I put the gun back in my bag. I had to look at Touret when I bent over him to get his car keys. His jacket was all torn open at the back, full of blood. He'd fallen on a pile of broken old tiles, with his eyes open.

I ran. The distance, which had seemed quite short that

morning, now exhausted me. There seemed to be no air in my lungs. By the time I was sitting at the wheel of the CX, I seemed to be breathing fire. I waited for a moment, then reversed. I waited for two cars to pass, both of which honked because I was already slightly out into the road. I drove, repeating to myself, "Be careful! Be careful!" I didn't want to think of anything else. Big drops of sweat were falling onto my eyelashes, and I had to take off my sunglasses to wipe my eyes.

I stopped on the left side of the road, just before the entrance to the sawmill. I left the gun outside the bag, on my seat. I didn't turn off the engine or shut the door as I got out. I walked a dozen or so steps past the gate into the yard. The sun was going down, a blazing red, and its last rays were falling behind me. "Monsieur Leballech?" I shouted. In the house the dog started barking. A woman wearing an apron came to the door, shielding her eyes to see who it was. I said, "Is M. Leballech there?" She said, "What's it about?" I gestured toward the CX behind me and said, "I've got something to show him—I've just come from his brother-in-law." She went to get him. The air smelled of resin, and in places the ground was covered with white sawdust that looked like snow.

He came out; he, too, was bothered by the sun. I didn't move. He was tall and thickset, a bit like me, but twenty years later. He was stripped to the waist and was holding a table napkin. He said, "What is it now?" I answered, "Come and see." I turned around and went back to the car. He shut the house door, and I heard him walking across the yard. I sat hunched over the seat, as if I was looking for something, till I knew he was quite near. Then I turned around, the gun in my hands, got out of the car, and walked toward him in such a way that no one would see me from the road.

He stopped seven or eight steps from the gun. Screwing up his eyes, he stared at it, as Touret had done, but he didn't react in the same way. He said, "What's going on? Who are you?" He was taken aback, but not afraid. His voice remained calm. It struck me that I'd already seen him, too, somewhere. Cars thundered by behind me. I said, "I'm Eliane's husband." His chest was hairy—pepper-and-salt, like the hair on his head. I think it was the only moment in that nightmare when I believed that he and Touret had slept with Elle. It was the dirty hair on his chest, his thick paws. He said, "So that's what it's all about." He was playing with his napkin between his fingers. There was a spiteful look about him. He glanced back toward the house and said quietly, contemptuously, "You poor fool! You don't believe everything she tells you, do you? I've never had to rape any woman. And as far as I'm concerned, now, you can keep her." He shrugged his shoulders and turned to go back to the house. I pressed the trigger. He stumbled, hit in the back. He dropped his napkin, but he stayed on his feet. Doubled up, his arms around his body, he made an effort to keep walking toward the house. I heard him say, "Shit!" I followed him and fired a second time. The bullet traveled right up his body and blew his head to pieces.

Almost at the same time the door opened. There was barking and shouting. I saw the German shepherd leap into the yard, and I think I stood riveted to the ground. But the dog didn't come for me. It kept jumping around its master, barking and whining. I also saw several people come out of the house shouting. I dashed to the CX. I was vaguely aware that a car had pulled up on the road with a screech of brakes between the first and second shots. I was right. A man and a woman had got of a car that had stopped a few meters up, concerned about what was happening. I threatened them with the gun like a madman and yelled, "Don't stay there! Move on!"

The engine of the CX was still running. I pulled off just as the boy with the long hair I'd seen earlier, who must have been Leballech's son, had got hold of my door. He let go after a few meters, and I drove off toward Digne at 120 or 130 kilometers an hour. I slowed down a bit before entering the town, and made a right turn. I had to stop at a red light, behind some other cars. I took the opportunity to put the gun and the sunglasses into the bag. Just before the small square, I pulled up half onto the sidewalk and turned off the engine. I took off the red shirt, used it to wipe the steering wheel and the gear shift, knowing quite well that this precaution was unnecessary, and stuffed the shirt into the bag.

When I got out of the car, my ears were blasted by the screech of police sirens from at least two vehicles. The sound died down in the direction of La Javie. I stopped myself from running to the DS, so as not to attract the attention of passers-by or of people looking out of their windows. I lifted the back seat and put my bag under it. I put on my jacket before driving away.

At the traffic circle just before the bridge over the Bléone, there was a lot of traffic, as always, and a police car, siren screeching, was making its way through. They hadn't had time to set up a roadblock, and I drove toward Manosque behind a long line of cars. At one point, two motorcyclists overtook me at full speed, crouched over their machines. I saw them later, just outside Malijaï, with some policemen. They were stopping all the CX's and GS's, probably because, despite their different sizes, the two cars look alike. Nothing else happened on the way. My heart began to beat normally, but I was very thirsty.

It was just after eleven when I left the highway, in Marseille. I drove to the Corniche. On the rocks, at the edge of the sea, I made the gun unusable by hitting it with stones and threw it far out into the dark water. I also got rid of the cartridges that remained, one by one, the box, which I tore up, and my sunglasses, which I smashed. On my way back to the Cristotel, I stopped twice more. I threw the bag and the torn-up red shirt into two different manholes.

At midnight there were still a lot of people in the bar. No one seemed to notice me. I went up to my room. I drank two bottles of beer, and had a shower, and went to bed. I was still thirsty. I thought of getting up to get a bottle of mineral water out of the refrigerator, but before finding the strength to do so, I fell into a deep, dreamless sleep. I woke up, I don't know why, in the middle of the night. I had a feeling of anxiety about something, but it took me several seconds to remember I'd killed two men. Then I went back to sleep.

I saw Elle the following afternoon, in her blue-and-white hospital room. She was standing by her bed, her hair spread out over her shoulders, her eyes paler than ever. She was wearing her white summer dress, one of the ones I'd brought her. I was glad she'd put on that one. She stood very straight, looked at me attentively with a vague, gentle smile, but—how can I put it—it wasn't her smile.

Mme Fieldmann, who had come in even though it was a Sunday, said to her, "This gentleman knows you. He knows your daddy!" Elle just moved her head to show that she was pleased. I didn't know what she'd like, so I brought flowers and a box of chocolates. She said, "Thank you, monsieur." Then she started talking to herself, very quietly, while the nurse brought a vase and put the flowers into it. I said, "Eliane." She looked at me with that smile that wasn't hers, and I saw she was waiting for me to say something. I said, "If you want something, just ask me and I'll bring it." She said, "I'd like my silver heart, and my teddy bear, and I'd like . . ." She didn't finish her sentence, but, still looking at me, she started to cry. I said, "What? What would you like?" She shook her head from right to left, still looking at me through her tears, and that was all. Mme Fieldmann, who was standing behind me, said to her, "This gentleman is a great friend of yours. He's going to bring your daddy to see you in a few days." Then Elle started to laugh while she was still crying, and walked up and down the room, repeating, "Oh yes! I'd like that. Oh yes! I'd like that." Then she started to talk quietly to herself, moving around busily but contentedly, the tears still wet on her cheeks.

Mme Fieldmann made a kindly gesture to me that I should leave her alone. I hadn't stayed more than five minutes. I said, "Good-bye, Eliane." She turned to me and smiled again. Her cheeks looked hollow. She held her head very erect I looked at her for some time, trying to imprint her image on my mind, and I noticed that they'd taken off her wedding band.

In the corridor I leaned against a wall, and Mme Fieldmann said, "Come now. I did warn you. You must try to pull yourself together." I made an effort because I was ashamed. We walked to the elevator. I said to her, "She can't stay like that, can she? It's not possible." She said, "Nothing, nothing is incurable. If I didn't believe that with all my heart, I'd be at home in front of my TV watching a program on crocodiles. I adore crocodiles. They look as though they've survived so long.'

I drove around Marseille for a bit. I left the DS on the Allées Léon-Gambetta and went into a café. I was still thirsty. At the bar I didn't know what to order. Finally I had a Vittel-menthe, which was Elle's favorite drink, and more thirst-quenching than beer. I think I wanted something that didn't exist.

Then I walked down to the Canebière, to the Old Port, letting myself be jostled without saying anything, looking at the shop windows. Her silver heart. Where could her silver heart be? The teddy bear was in our bedroom, sitting on the wood stove. I remembered seeing it before I left. I stared into the water of the Old Port, with its patches of oil, and the ships taking people out to the Château d'If. Strolling up the Ca-nebière, I stopped at a newsstand and bought the *Journal du Dimanche*, which comes from Paris, then went to read it in another café, drinking another Vittel-menthe.

There was already an item about what had happened the night before in Digne, but it was very short. The owner of a sawmill had been shot dead at his home by an unknown man. The victim's brother-in-law, a real-estate agent, had disap-peared. His car had been found, but they were still looking for him. I knew the Monday-morning papers would say more about it, but I felt nothing like fear. I felt I didn't care.

I went back to the DS about six o'clock. I decided to drive home, and to come back and see Elle the following day. I'd bring her the teddy bear—that would make her happy. That evening I would be able to talk to Mickey. I wouldn't tell him what I'd done, so as not to compromise him, but it would be a great comfort to see his face and listen to his nonsense. He would talk to me about Eddy Merckx, Marilyn Monroe, and Marcel Amont. And maybe about Rocard. According to him, Rocard is a true socialist, and everything he says is intelligent. I'm telling you, when he starts to talk like that, the only thing to do is put earplugs in.

Without really deciding, I drove toward Aubagne and Brignoles. I couldn't possibly go via Digne, so I went as far as Draguignan, where I ate a sandwich, then took the road via Castellane and Annot. A hundred and eighty kilometers.

The first person I saw when I got back to town was Vava, the boy who painted the portrait of Cognata's husband. He was wandering around the café terraces with his big portfolio, trying to sell his works to tourists. He said Mickey was at the movies with Georgette. He hadn't seen Boo-Boo. He asked me how Elle was. I said, "She's doing well, thanks." I parked the car in the little street by the movie theater, behind the old market square. Loulou-Lou was in the cash booth, but I didn't want to see her. I went into the café across the street to wait for the intermission, as I told you at the beginning.

When did I start telling you all this? It must have been Monday night, the following day. I talked to you on Monday night, and Tuesday afternoon, and it is now Wednesday. It's only Wednesday, August 11. I was surprised to see the date again just now in my diary, where I've noted down, on each page, on each day of this spring and summer, in a few words that mean something only to me, what has happened since the afternoon I danced with Elle and held her in my arms for the first time. It seems so long ago.

Yes, as I was telling you, I was looking at the poster for a Jerry Lewis film, through the café window, as I waited for the intermission, and for Mickey to come out. Suddenly I thought of my suitcase. I couldn't remember what I'd done with it. I remembered that when I was paying my bill at the Cristotel, it was at my feet. But I couldn't remember what I'd done with it since. I didn't remember putting it in the trunk of the DS, but maybe it was there. I'd been off the tracks for several days myself.

Some kids came out of the movie theater, lighting cigarettes or licking their ice cream. Then I saw Mickey with Georgette. He was wearing black trousers like mine, and an electric-blue turtleneck sweater. He was swaggering around, proud as a peacock, in his electric-blue sweater. If you haven't seen Mickey come out of the movies, swaggering around and saying to the others, "How are things, pal?" with all his upper teeth in line, like Humphrey Bogart, you can't imagine what it does to have him for your brother. It makes you want to laugh out loud— it makes you feel good inside.

I got up from my chair and knocked on the window. He saw me. He also saw a lot of things when he saw me. Georgette followed him, but he said something to her and she stayed outside, under the lamps, and he came in to join me. I was drinking a beer, and he ordered another. He asked me how Elle was. I told him about my visit the day before and the one that afternoon. I said Mme Fieldmann seemed very good, and I had every confidence in her. He drank his beer, his forehead all creased, like it is whenever he's thinking, and he said, "You look really beat, you know. We'll be putting you in the hospital soon."

We just sat there for a while, on either side of the table, without talking. Then he said that his boss, Ferraldo, wanted to see me. I'd met Ferraldo about a dozen times, just to say hi, how are things. He even came to my wedding, but he isn't someone I know well—I never think about him. Since I was surprised he wanted to see me, Mickey said, "It's about one of his old employees at the sawmill, someone named Leballech." I felt a lump rise in my throat, but the expression on my face didn't change. He added, "Two weeks ago, Elle went to see Ferraldo for information about him. He was the truck driver who brought Dad's player piano back to the village. You know, when he tried to pawn it." Leballech, Dad, the player piano—I was lost. I said, "What are you talking about? What's this all about?" I must have raised my voice, because Mickey turned his head around the café, looking rather embarrassed. He said, "I don't know. Ferraldo told me he wanted to talk to you, that's all."

I paid for the drinks. The bell went off in the theater, on the other side of the street; it was the end of the intermission. When we came out of the café, Georgette was standing alone on the sidewalk, looking annoyed, waiting for my brother. I kissed her on the cheeks. She asked after Elle. I said, "Mickey will tell you." Mickey said, "Come in with us. It's a funny film. It'll do you good." I said no, I didn't particularly feel like laughing. I watched them go into the theater. Loulou-Lou was standing by the door, taking the intermission tickets. I waved to her, then went and got the DS. The suitcase was in the trunk.

When I got home, Cognata and Mamma were in the kitchen, watching TV. Mamma was also doing some mending. She turned off the set, and I told her about my two visits to the hospital. Two or three times I turned to Cognata, who said, "What? What?" and I repeated certain things to her, articulating clearly so that she could read my lips. Boo-Boo was out for dinner. There was some leftover lamb stew with beans, but I wasn't hungry. I still had the sandwich I'd eaten in Draguignan weighing on my stomach.

I asked Mamma, "You know the truck driver who brought the player piano here, when I was a kid? Well, do you know who it was?" She said, "I even found the bill. I showed it to Elle. He's named Jean Leballech. I wasn't here that night, I was at the Massignes' because old Massigne had just died, but I saw Jean Leballech quite often, and so did your aunt, ask her."

She went up to her bedroom to get the bill, and I talked to Cognata. At first she said nothing, eyes filled with tears, thinking of Elle in a madhouse. Then she said, in her loud, deaf voice, which didn't go at all with what she wanted to say, "It was Jean Leballech and his brother-in-law. They were here, in this room, with your poor father. I remember very well. It was a Monday night, in November 1955. There was snow on the ground. They brought back the piano and they drank wine, here, in this room, and you were there, you were ten years old."

I couldn't remember. All that remained with me was that impression of having seen Touret's face somewhere before, and the same feeling, but stronger, when Leballech stared at the gun I was pointing at him. I repeated several times to Cognata, till she understood, "When did you talk to Elle about this?" Cognata said, "The girl? Two days before her birthday, when she went to see her schoolmistress and came back so late."

I sat down on the end of the table, my hands on my knees. I wanted to think but couldn't. I didn't even know what I was supposed to be thinking about. What did the piano, my father, and a winter twenty years ago have to do with this business? I felt empty and cold inside.

Mamma put a piece of paper in front of me. It was the bill she'd mentioned. I saw Ferraldo's name, Leballech's, my father's. The date at the top of the bill was November 19, 1955. My father had signed it at the bottom, on November 21. I looked at Mamma, and I looked at Cognata. I said, "I don't understand. Why was she looking for information about this truck driver? She wasn't even born then." Cognata—I'd been speaking very quietly, almost to myself—understood. She said, "November 1955—it was eight months before she was born. And she was born of an unknown father. If you can't guess why she was looking for information about that truck driver, then you're really stupid." And she sank back into her chair, staring at the floor.

I looked at the clock on the mantelpiece. I told Mamma I was taking the DS back to my boss. She said, "At this hour?" It was nearly eleven, but I had to see Eva Braun. I couldn't wait until next day. I said, "You go to bed. We'll talk about all this tomorrow." Before going out, I drank two large glasses of water at the sink.

At Eva Braun's, a light was still on in one of the upstairs windows. I knocked on the window of the kitchen door. The

moon, I remember, was so bright that I could see myself in
the glass, almost as in a mirror. I stepped back a few paces and
shouted upstairs, "It's me, Florimond." For a couple of seconds
I thought she hadn't heard me. I was about to call up again
when the kitchen light went on and the door opened.

Eva Braun had put on a light robe over her nightgown. She
was still tying the cord. Her hair was combed back and held
behind her head with a pin. She smiled broadly when she
opened the door, no doubt because she thought if I hadn't
been able to wait until the following day to come see her, I
must have some good news. Her face changed as soon as she
saw mine.

I went into the kitchen. I stood with my back against the
wall. She asked me to sit down, but I shook my head. She had
the same eyes as her daughter's, only a deeper shade of blue.
I said, "I must know the truth. I can't stand it any more. You
can see what a state I'm in. I can't go on like this. What
happened in Arrame in November 1955?"

What Eva Braun told me that night you already know. She
told you yesterday, when you went to see her in the village.
She no doubt told you the same thing, with the same words,
the same sentences she's been forming all these years, when
her daughter has harassed her with questions.

I only interrupted her once in her story—at the moment
when I understood that Eliane had thought that the Italian
who was with the other two, the Italian with very dark eyes
and drooping moustache, was my father. I could hardly get
the words out, I felt so indignant. I couldn't explain that it was
impossible. In fact, how could I explain it? It was simply
impossible—that's all there was to it.

So I said no more but let Eva Braun tell the rest of her
story. Her meeting with Gabriel Devigne on a road in Germany
at the end of the war. The happiness of a little girl named Elle,
a happiness shattered during a trip to Grenoble. I heard again
about the dog who ate scraps of meat she had given it under
the table in a restaurant—"Lucifer, like the devil." Eva Braun

was sitting on the stairs, her eyes fixed on the floor. She spoke in a sad, monotonous voice, just loud enough for me to hear. I'd drawn up a chair and was sitting quite close to her.

Finally she told me how her daughter, aged fifteen, on a forest path near Arrame, had brought on the paralysis of the man whom, up till then, she had called her daddy, hitting him on the head with a spade. She also wanted to tell me why, but she couldn't go on. I put a hand on her arm, as if to say it didn't matter. When Gabriel Devigne regained consciousness at home, he said he'd fallen from the top of a ladder while pruning a tree, and Dr. Conte probably pretended to believe him.

We said nothing for a very long time. Eva Braun stopped crying at last. My only more or less coherent thought, among the confusion of all the others, was that I'd killed two bastards for the wrong reason, for lies. They had not found Elle, who might be the daughter of one of them. She had sought them out, beginning with the clue of the player piano, and found them. My father was dead, and thus out of her reach. So she used me to punish the others.

I said to Eva Braun, "I really knew my father. He couldn't have been one of those who attacked you." She said, without looking at me, "I know, and quite recently my daughter realized it, too. The Sunday your brother won the bicycle race, and she slept here, she knew then, I'm sure. I'm sure the reason she went away was to find the one they called 'Italian.'" I remembered how Elle had been during those last few days. It was true, she was no longer the same with me. She was at once kinder and more distant, as if I had become for her, once again, the man she danced with at the Bing Bang.

I asked Eva Braun—it was nearly one o'clock in the morning—"But didn't she ever tell you what she was thinking?" She shrugged her shoulder sadly and said, "She was afraid I'd stop her. Forgive me, but I wanted to see a photograph of your father. Then on the day of the wedding—your aunt had agreed to have an oil painting of her husband done, it was a present from Eliane—she showed it to us, to Mlle Dieu and myself.

I realized my daughter had deceived me. She'd shown me a photo of your uncle, not your father."

She looked at me just for a second, and lowered her eyes again. She said, "I was very afraid, because I'm a religious woman, and you were already married. So I went to the cemetery. On your father's grave there is a photo, in a marble frame. He did have dark eyes and a moustache, and of course one forgets a lot over twenty years. But I could see very well he wasn't the Italian." She repeated, "Forgive me."

I got up. I said, "Did you talk to Elle about it the night she slept here?" Eva Braun nodded. I remembered that the next day Eliane had wanted to go with Mamma to the cemetery and, in fact, had only stayed there for a minute or two. Just long enough to see the photo on the grave. I said, "If she never told you what she was going to do, why did you think, when she'd left, that she'd gone to look for the Italian?" Eva Braun didn't answer right away. She sat motionless for a moment; then she, too, got up. She went and opened the sideboard door. From behind a pile of plates she pulled out a heavy object, wrapped in a blue-checked rag, which she put on the table in front of me. She said, with tears in her eyes, "She wanted this. I didn't give it to her."

I opened the rag. There was an automatic pistol inside, in a thick khaki canvas holster marked *U. S.*, with a belt of the same color rolled around it. I picked it up. I'm not so familiar with pistols as with rifles, but this one is so well known that even without reading what was engraved on the steel, I would have recognized it as a "Government Model" Colt .45, assigned to the American army during the two world wars. It seemed in good condition. Eva Braun told me that Gabriel Devigne had got it in 1945, when he was working for the Americans in Fulda. She said she constantly changed its hiding place so that her daughter wouldn't find it.

I put the pistol back into its holster and said, "Anyway, she certainly wouldn't have been able to use it. Did the doctor, Mme Fieldmann, tell you about the bottle of nail polish?" Eva Braun shook her head and seemed surprised. I could have kept it to myself, but I said all the same, "Your daughter found a more suitable weapon. But she can't have used that, either." We looked at each other. Like me, the poor woman was at the end of her tether. I added, "She should have talked to me about these things, and to you." I put a hand on her shoulder. Then I left.

I drove back through the village in the DS. My brother met me halfway. They'd been waiting for me on the steps of the town hall. As he got in behind me, Boo-Boo said, surprised, "You've kept the car?" I said I would need it in the morning to go back to Marseille. I said, "Go and explain to Henri IV in the morning. If he needs a hand, do what you can to take my place."

Mickey said nothing. I parked the DS next to his yellow truck in our yard, and the three of us sat there for a while, the windows rolled down. "Who did Elle talk to first about that damned piano?" I asked. Boo-Boo said, "Me. Or, rather, I talked to her about it. She didn't know we had it. It was the day of the Bing Bang, after you'd left. I asked her why you'd gone off in such a temper." So that was it! That was why she'd been so interested in me, why she'd come to the garage with a flat tire the next day. It was all because of the player piano. That much, at least, was clear.

Mickey was next to me. He lit a cigarette. I said, "What was the film like?" He said, "Not bad." That was all. I told Boo-Boo what Mme Fieldmann had said to me at the hospital. I said she was very hopeful, and she seemed to know her job. Then I said, "You know, Boo-Boo, forget Eliane's story, I've checked into it. It's all made up." He said nothing.

When I was alone, in my bedroom, I looked at the teddy bear sitting on the wood stove, with its reassuring face. I looked around a bit for Elle's silver heart. It was nowhere to be seen. I went to bed. I don't even know if I slept or not.

It was next morning, before leaving, that I noticed the Marilyn Monroe book on the bedside table. I leafed through it. A piece of paper fell out. It was a page torn from another book, folded in two. I looked over it quickly. It wasn't about

Marilyn Monroe, or any film star, but about a racing cyclist, Fausto Coppi. I was surprised, of course. I vaguely remembered having dinner in the yard, not long before Elle disappeared. Boo-Boo and I were talking about Fausto Coppi, just to annoy Mickey, and Elle asked us a few questions about him. I couldn't remember what she'd said.

I had to see Ferraldo. It was time for me to go. For the last thirty hours or so, behind everything I'd thought or done, there'd been a kind of heavy anxiety. Sometimes the image of Leballech or Touret collapsing in front of me came into my mind. I put the Marilyn Monroe book back on the table and thought no more about it.

It was Monday, the day before yesterday. I only realized this morning, after talking to you on Monday night and all Tuesday afternoon, why Elle's attitude toward me had changed in the last few days. As soon as I'd begun talking to you about this summer, I realized I'd already given you the key to the whole mechanism of this madness. She, too, was more observant and more calculating than I'd thought. She, too, in her own way, had got information about the death of Fausto Coppi—too late.

First, when I learned from a police officer what you were trying to find out, I was really annoyed with you. I said to myself, "How long have I been talking to him? Seven hours, eight hours, in all? I told him everything I knew, as it came into my head. I wasn't lying. And the only thing he thought of doing when he left me, his head full of my misery, was to go somewhere, probably to some cheap restaurant, and check the date of Fausto Coppi's death with some pathetic drunkard. What's more, if it can be found, he hasn't got it yet.

Hang on a while, and I'll tell you.

You seem to think that the snow in what I'm telling you has to do with my father, with something I associate, in spite of myself, in the very words I used, with my father. That's not how it is. My father is bound up not only with the snow, but also with the spring, and with the summer that has just ended, and with the autumn when I was walking beside him among the chestnut leaves. He's tied up with everything I'm telling you, because in everything I'm telling you, in a way—my way—I'm still suffering from the fact he left us.

As for the rest, you thought about it before I did. He had no moustache in November 1955, because he only grew a moustache out of mourning for an Italian he admired, a man who won everyone's respect, whom he regarded as the greatest You, too, could have discovered that in a page torn out of a book: "Angelo Fausto Coppi died on January 2, 1960, a few minutes after 9 A.M., at Tortona hospital in Italy."

I went down into town through the morning's great patches of sun and shade. I stopped on the square to buy a paper. I read it in the DS, with Elle's teddy bear sitting beside me.

The double murder in Digne took up a quarter of the front page, with photos of Leballech and Touret. Touret's children had discovered their father's body in the sheepfold. The information given by those who'd seen me at Leballech's was as follows: a man of about twenty-five, well above average height, wearing a red shirt or sweatshirt, *probably a North African*. The woman who got out of the car with her husband, between the first and second shots, declared on oath that I had threatened them in Arabic. They'd spent several years in Algeria. I don't know what particular race she thought I was.

Two Algerian suspects in the area were brought in for questioning, but they were released on Sunday. The expert who analyzed the bullets found without difficulty that they belonged to a sawed-off Remington carbine. Nothing in the lives of the victims could explain so brutal an end. There was talk of "cold-blooded execution," revenge of a dismissed employee, the possible settling of accounts over some property deal. At the end of the item, which continued on another page, it was pointed out that "the murderer was wearing red, the color of executioners."

I threw the paper away on the edge of the sidewalk. I drove to Ferraldo's sawmill. I was afraid of him now, but he'd asked to see me, and I had to go.

As soon as we shook hands, I realized he hadn't read the news. He was making some coffee on a heater and offered me a cup. He seemed very embarrassed. He said, "You know, my boy, I don't want to be a wet blanket. But I don't know how serious what I'm going to tell you might be. I was really worried when Mickey told me your wife was in the hospital. I must talk to you."

On Thursday, July 8—two days before her twentieth birthday—Eliane had come to see him in the middle of the afternoon, in the office where we now were. She was wearing a new dress her mother had made for her, white with a blue-and-turquoise pattern. So it was probably the afternoon when Cognata had told her who had brought the player piano back home.

She asked for information about Leballech. Ferraldo told her that Leballech had left the sawmill years before and set up his own business, on the La Javie road in Digne. He showed her his register for the year 1955. He showed it to me, too. One note, at the bottom of the page—"Pass closed, piano Monday evening"—was supposed to explain why Leballech had not come to our house on Saturday, November 19, as planned. I knew the real reason. He left Eva Braun's house with his companions, late at night, and the three of them were completely drunk. The bastards.

Ferraldo sat there silently with the register opened on his table, drinking his coffee. I thought he had nothing more to tell me. I was relieved, in a way, and was about to thank him and leave. Then he raised his almost bald, suntanned head and said, "She came to see me again a week after your wedding. On Saturday, July 24. I remember, because your brother was running at Digne the next day. She had a bruise on her cheek. She said she'd hurt herself opening a car door. She asked me something quite silly, or anyway something I thought was quite silly at the time, because I couldn't see how I would have been able to remember, twenty years later, such a detail. She asked me if there was an Italian working for us in 1955 who might have been with Leballech when he brought back your piano."

I raised my eyebrows as if I was as mystified as he was. Ferraldo didn't give me much time to think; he added, "You must excuse me, my boy. I thought I was doing the right thing. After Eliane left, I called Leballech." He was looking straight at me with his piercing eyes. At that moment, I couldn't have said whether or not he'd read the paper.

Now listen. When he went to call Leballech, at eleven in the morning on that Sunday, Ferraldo found that the page with Leballech's number was missing from the directory. His secretary, Elisabeth, swore that it was Elle, the time she'd stopped in, who'd torn the page out. Then, when he finally got through to Leballech, using an old directory, there was such a long silence at the other end he thought they'd been disconnected. But they hadn't. Leballech was still there. He asked Ferraldo, "Could you describe this woman to me?" Then a moment later he said, "I'll come see you this afternoon. It's too delicate a matter to talk about on the telephone."

That afternoon he arrived in town in his old black Peugeot 504. Ferraldo hadn't seen him since five or six years earlier, when they'd met once by chance, in Digne. Leballech's hair had turned gray, and he'd put on weight. He said, "I have to put up with the noise of saws all year. Let's go have a drink somewhere." They went to a café on the square. Leballech said, "I didn't know Eliane was married. She told me her name was Jeanne. And when she went to my brother-in-law's to rent an apartment she even said she was a schoolteacher." He laughed at himself, rather sadly, for being taken in. He said, "What a fool I was." Then, as if Ferraldo didn't have to explain it to him, he said, "It's true, she is a pretty girl." He shrugged his shoulders cynically. Ferraldo said he seemed genuinely upset, but he said nothing more to explain why.

Then they talked about that day in November 1955 when Leballech and his brother-in-law brought the player piano back to our house. Leballech said, "It's a long time ago, but you might remember. My brother-in-law, Touret, used to lend me a hand sometimes. He was already in the real-estate business, but he had no office and was always looking for a little extra money." Ferraldo asked him, "Who was that Italian she talked about?" "Oh, some poor guy named Fiero. My brother-in-law ran into him managing a bar in Marseille two or three years later, but he didn't make a go of it. He must have known too many criminals. He was killed in 1962, in the bar, two bullets in the head."

Then Ferraldo asked, "Why was Elle—Eliane—who came from Arrame, on the other side of the pass, so interested in all that?" Leballech didn't know. She'd said nothing about it to him. He'd seen her three times in all, but she'd never asked him anything about it. That was precisely what he found so difficult to explain. He thought for a moment, then said, "Listen, Ferraldo, I brought back the player piano to the Montecciaris' on November 21, with my brother-in-law. I remember the business very well. And Fiero was not with us. He did have the truck on Saturday, November 19, but I can admit to you now that on Saturday, November 19, when the truck went to Arrame, I wasn't in it. Neither was my brother-in-law."

So there we are. I don't know how I stopped myself from jumping out of my chair and shouting when Ferraldo said that. I think I had the same reaction Elle must have had when she learned the truth. I clutched desperately at the idea that it was a lie, that Leballech had lied. Ferraldo said nothing, obviously disturbed at the effect his words were having on me. I said, as naturally as I could, "I'm listening, go on."

On Saturday, November 19, 1955, Leballech went with his brother-in-law to the sawmill in Digne, which he bought a few months later, and settled some of the details of the deal. His boss at the time was Ferraldo's father, a man whose attitude toward his employees was quite different from his son's. He was a tough boss, and everyone was afraid of him. Leballech hadn't dared to confide his plans to him. That Saturday, for a sum of money agreed between them, he lent his truck and his load to Fiero, who wasn't working, and to another truck driver from the same area, a big guy with short hair named Pamier who later set up a freight business in Avignon.

It was agreed that the two men would bring the empty truck back to Leballech's, in town, on Saturday night. They didn't come back until Sunday afternoon. With them was another man, much younger, about twenty—they must have picked him up on the way. In any case, he wasn't from this part of the world. Leballech remembered his name; it was Rostollan. Fiero and Pamier claimed they'd got stuck in the snow and had to wait till the next day to set off, but the other guy, Rostollan, who was not at all impressed by Leballech's annoyance, suddenly said, "We had a pretty good time anyway, didn't we?"

They didn't bring the player piano back to our house. It was Leballech who did this, early in the evening of Monday, November 21. He had Touret with him to help him out. My father gave them something to drink in the kitchen, and I was there, but I have only a dim memory of it. I was ten years old. Life's a funny thing. It passes by without leaving any trace.

I drove to Marseille without looking at either the road or the villages I passed. I probably went via Draguignan. I don't know. I had one wish and one wish only—to get to Elle in her hospital room before Ferraldo read about the crimes in Digne and went to the police. I couldn't see how he could avoid doing that, despite being an old friend of the family.

I had to stop on the way and get gas. The *Nice-Matin* was spread out on the attendant's desk when he gave me my change. I looked away from the carefree faces of Leballech and his brother-in-law. The attendant said, "Well, there are two who won't have any more taxes to pay." He laughed. He walked back to the car with me and washed the windshield. He laughed again when he saw the teddy bear sitting next to me. He said, "You should put his seat belt on, you know. That's what the law says." I was thirsty again, and hungry, too. So I stopped farther along, at a café, to get a bite to eat and settle my stomach. I wanted to vomit. The paper was on the counter, the men's two heads turned away. The proprietress was talking about the business to one of the waitresses, who was setting the tables for lunch. I went out very quickly, leaving my sandwich.

I remember nothing of the rest of the journey to Marseille. I was no doubt still clinging desperately to the idea that Leballech had lied. The next thing I remember, I was in the hospital lobby, walking over the black and white tiles, holding the teddy bear. Mme Fieldmann came toward me. She said, "You can't see your wife now. Come back at three o'clock this afternoon." She was less optimistic than the day before, I could tell from her voice. She explained that for the past week Eliane had been given treatment to regularize her cerebral circulation, but it hadn't improved. The longer she remained in her present state, the longer and more difficult it would be to get her out of it, though she did have youth on her side.

I looked down. I made as if I understood. I was sitting next to the doctor on a bench in the lobby. People were walking past. Then she said, "A police inspector came this morning. He brought your wife's canvas bag and glasses. They'd been found at the offices of the newspaper Le Provençal. The inspector, whose name is Pietri, wants to see you. You'll find him at police headquarters." I nodded. I asked if I could have the bag. She stood up and said, "It will be handed over to you. You'll just have to sign a receipt. I'll keep the glasses and give them to your wife."

A woman in a white uniform, in an office, got me to sign an inventory, checking the contents of the bag against the list. I also signed some papers for the hospital administration and Social Security. I made several mistakes, because I'd just seen, among Elle's things, a piece of a cigarette pack bearing the name Fiero and a telephone number.

I examined the contents of the bag again, sitting in the DS, in the hospital parking lot. It was noon or a bit later, and very hot. I took off my jacket and my tie and opened the neck of my shirt. Sweat dripped from my forehead on everything I looked at. There were two things to see in the end; the rest was just the usual stuff Elle took around with her wherever she went. The first was that piece of cigarette pack. What I'd thought was a telephone number was in fact a date:

Fiero
8/18/1962

The second was a page torn out of a telephone directory. At first I thought it was the one she'd torn out at Ferraldo's, but I was wrong there, too. It was a page from an Avignon directory. I looked down the columns and saw the name Pamier. There were several of them.

I drove to the Old Port. I asked a passer-by to direct me to the offices of *Le Provençal*. I drove on and parked the car, half up on the sidewalk, at the corner of the Rue Sainte. I walked the rest of the way to the newspaper offices. I explained to the receptionist that I wanted to see the person who had found my wife's bag. It was the guy in charge of back issues of the paper. He'd gone out to lunch. I waited outside, walking up and down the sidewalk. I was carrying my jacket over my arm. It was as hot as ever. Aside from the shade cast by the buildings, there was no relief or color. Everything was dazzling.

I didn't feel remorse or anything remotely like remorse. It would be a lie to pretend I did. Try to understand. I was thinking only of Elle. What she had done, away from me, gradually became clear. Fiero, Pamier, Rostollan. Sometimes a thought came into my head that made me angry with her. Then it passed. For example, I said to myself, "If she saw Leballech three times, she arranged to meet him. She rented that apartment to receive him." I was sweating more than ever. Then I said to myself, "She isn't guilty. She's the victim. She thought she understood everything, and she was wrong. When Leballech and Touret told her, in the black Peugeot, on the Sunday of the race, she didn't believe them, or it was such a shock for her that she forgot the lighter she left for you on the shelf."

At one point—this is the honest truth—I began to wonder whether I'd really done what I thought I'd done. It was like

waking up in daylight after a feverish night: you're not even
sure what you've been dreaming. I, Florimond Montecciari,
killing two men with a carbine, really killing them, pressing
the trigger, hating them to the point of really killing them.
Polishing the edge of a sawed-off barrel, going into a store to
buy a red shirt, accelerating at top speed to throw off a long-
haired boy who was clinging to the door handle—it was just
a dream, a filthy dream. It hadn't even come out of a man's
head. It had all been thought up by the German shepherd in
the sawmill yard, suddenly barking in his sleep. Or the other
dog, the one who ate scraps of meat under the table. It took
me some time, walking up and down in the shade of the
sidewalk, to get rid of the idea that I was a character in a dog's
dream.

At two o'clock I saw the man who had dealt with Elle the
Saturday she must have been found on the beach, wandering
around aimlessly in her high-heeled shoes. He was about sixty,
a fatherly type. His name was Michelin, like the guide. He
looked up at me—he was a short man—and said, "She came
to look up some old copies of the paper. It was about this time
of day. I didn't see her leave. In the afternoon I realized she'd
left her bag and her glasses. I put them away in my office,
thinking she'd be back to collect them. I thought no more
about them, either on Monday or on Tuesday. Then, Wednesday, opening a drawer, I saw them again. I had them sent to
the police. This morning a police inspector came to see me."

He hesitated, his bright little eyes on me, and added, lowering his voice, "Pietri, from Criminal Investigation. He's at
police headquarters." He gestured for me to follow him into
a room where there were two large oak tables darkened with
age, lamps with green shades, and shelves of large books lining
the walls. He said, showing me the farther of the two tables,
"She was there, all alone. I brought her what she wanted. I
don't know how long she stayed. As I told you, I didn't see her
leave. She left her bag and her glasses."

I asked him if he remembered what she'd wanted to see.
He sighed and said, "I already showed them to Inspector Pietri

this morning. She asked me for the copies of the paper for the summer of 1962." This came as no surprise—I was expecting it. I said, "I'd like to look at them, too."

I sat down at the table where Elle had been. M. Michelin brought me three volumes bound in black, containing the issues of *Le Provençal* for July, August, and September 1962. He said, "Please don't leave the way she did. Let me know when you've finished." I hadn't brought with me the piece of cigarette pack on which Elle had written the name Fiero and the date—it was in the canvas bag, which I'd left in the car. But I remembered it was August 1962, so I turned to the August volume first.

I found it without any trouble. On August 18, 1962, between 11:30 and midnight, as he was closing his bar in the Capelette district of Marseille, Marcello Fiero, 43, was killed by an unknown man, by two pistol shots. A woman who had rushed to her window on hearing the shots saw a man run away, but could not describe him.

There was some mention of this shooting in the papers for the next few days, but less and less was said about it, and in the end it dropped out of the news altogether. I looked for a long time at Fiero's photo. It was like one of those prison photos. He'd been in prison twice, though I can't remember what for. He had the kind of face women find attractive, with large, dark eyes and a moustache that made him look tough, because without it—I don't know, this is just what I felt—it was the face of a very ordinary man who let life carry him along, and who was even rather shy. Or it may have been that I was thinking of what Eva Braun had said—that he was the least spiteful of the three.

After that I looked through the rest, page by page, for the whole of August, without finding anything else. Then I looked through the July volume. I probably followed the same procedure as Elle, with the same slow application. On July 21, 1962, in Avignon, a truck driver by the name of Antoine Pamier was shot in his garage, about eleven o'clock at night. Three pistol shots had been fired, the last of which had hit him in the heart. He'd been alone, the garage deserted. No one had seen or heard anything. One of his sons had found his body there in the early hours of the morning. A lot had been written about Pamier, too, for a few days. Investigation proceeding, and people questioned. Then nothing more was said about it.

I'd taken off my jacket again. I was sweating. And yet there were moments I felt cold. The thing that Elle could not bear, discovering what I had discovered, the very idea that she had not been able to bear and which had driven her crazy, was already in my head. I opened the third black volume, the one for September. I turned the pages one by one, as I had done with the others. I had no need to go any further. In Marseille, September 9, 1962, near L'Estaque, a twenty-eight-year-old taxi driver was shot in the back of the neck by a single bullet, at the wheel of his car. It must have been about two o'clock in the morning, perhaps later. His name was Maurice Rostollan. He, too, had his photo on the front page. He was smiling and looked sure of himself. He seemed to be saying to me, as he had to Leballech, twenty years before, "We had a pretty good time anyway, didn't we?"

I read on. Two days later, the police had connected his murder with that of Fiero, in his bar on August 18. But they never connected these two murders in Marseille with the one in Avignon, unless it was much later, I don't know. Anyway, the same weapon was used to kill Fiero and Rostollan. A .45 automatic, the bullets for which are easily recognizable. It was described, for the benefit of the readers, as "a seven-shot Colt pistol, American army issue, no doubt bought or stolen from a GI during the last war."

I sat for a long time, my elbows on the table, in front of the closed volumes. I thought of Elle sitting there in the same place ten days before. I thought of that Gabriel, whom I did not know, who lay confined in his bedroom, and of Eva Braun, who had said to me about him, "He was a man who was afraid of everything." I imagined him putting on his jacket and saying to Eva Braun, and to a little blue-eyed girl who didn't want her daddy to go away, "I'll be back tomorrow." They stood there watching him go down the path, as they did each Saturday when he went to visit his sister, Clémence. Fiero, Pamier, Rostollan: all three were killed during the same summer, on Saturday or Sunday nights. Fourteen years ago.

So I'd come to the end. I don't know what I felt at that moment—I don't know what I feel now. She probably imagined she would go home and find her father as he used to be, once those who had brought all the evil on them were punished. That's what she told him on our wedding day, when she disappeared to visit him. Mlle Tusseau repeated it to Mickey and me: "Soon we'll be the way we used to be. You'll see, I'm sure of it."

I don't know what happened inside her when she read what I had read, understood what I had understood. She held her little bottle of poison in her hand. She went and walked on a beach. She walked and walked until she reached—how can I put it? It's not a place, but it isn't time, either. It is something else. Traces that, against all expectations, the breeze might have left on the water.

I can tell you how she was when I saw her in her room, after I'd left the newspaper offices. I gave her the teddy bear and her silver heart, which I'd found in the canvas bag. I fastened the chain around her neck, lifting her hair. She laughed. She let me kiss her on the cheek. She said, "I dreamed of you last night. You were with my daddy, on a staircase, playing catch-the-cork." For several minutes she seemed to forget what she'd just said to me. She took no more notice of me. She arranged the red ribbon on her teddy bear. Then she looked at me and said, "You pull the cork with a string and I have to catch it. It's fun, you know. Yes, it's really fun."

Then she saw I was crying as I sat on my chair, and came up to me. She put her hand on my head and said, "Don't cry, don't cry," very gently. She showed me her fingers with the nails bitten back to nothing. She said, "You see, they're growing again." I wiped my face. I said, "Yes, that's good." There were circles around her eyes, which looked bloodshot and staring. I could see her cheekbones through her skin. Only her hair was the same as it used to be. She was wearing her dress with the Russian collar. I asked her, "Have they given you your glasses?" She said, "They're no good. Daddy's going to buy me some new ones. Anyway, my daddy doesn't like me to wear them."

Mme Fieldmann was there. She hadn't wanted to leave me alone with Elle, but she said nothing. I kissed my darling on the cheek. I said to her, "I'll make sure your daddy comes." When I left the room, she was sitting across her bed. She'd already forgotten I was there. She was talking to herself, or maybe to her teddy bear, which was perched on her knee.

In the corridor two men were waiting for me. The taller of the two showed me a plastic card, striped across in blue and red. He said he was Chief Inspector Pietri. He knew I'd been to the offices of *Le Provençal*. He wanted to know my feelings about what I'd read. There was an open window near us. I could hear the birds in the trees of a garden, and, in the distance, the rumble of the city. They must have been able to tell from my red eyes that I'd been crying. I said, "I was coming to see you. Two men were killed in Digne on Saturday night. I killed them."

We left the DS in the hospital parking lot. I gave the keys to Chief Inspector Pietri, but he couldn't say when Henri IV would be able to get it back. I was more worried about the car than about my own fate.

In the office where I was taken for questioning, I was allowed to telephone Mickey at Ferraldo's sawmill. I told him I'd killed Leballech and Touret because I thought they were responsible for what had happened to Eliane, and I'd given myself up.

His voice at the other end was sad but calm. He may drive his yellow truck like an idiot, but he's not nearly so stupid as I say. He knew perfectly well the night before that I'd done something terrible. When he read the paper in the morning and talked to Boo-Boo and Ferraldo about it, he understood the rest. He said, "You've done well to give yourself up. Now, until you get a lawyer, watch what you say. The less you open your mouth, the better."

In the early afternoon, with Boo-Boo and Ferraldo, he got in touch with a lawyer. "Do you know where they're taking you?" he asked me. I said the examining magistrate wanted to see me that night, and I expected I'd be taken to Digne. Mickey said, "That's what we thought. So the lawyer will see you there. His name is Maître Dominique Janvier. He's young, about thirty. But he's supposed to be very good."

I was tongue-tied. There were so many things I'd have liked to say to him. I was sorry I'd never said them, and now it was too late. I said, "Look after Boo-Boo and Mamma, and Cognata. And Elle, too. You must take her father to see her." Before putting down the receiver, we were silent for several seconds. All we could hear was the crackling on the line. Then I said, "My poor brother. If only they'd taken that filthy old piano when we tried to pawn it, none of this would have happened." After another silence Mickey said, "On Saturday morning Boo-Boo and I are going down to the bank in town, and we'll give them the serenade we always said we would. By the time we finish, they'll be sick to death of 'Roses of Picardy,' I can tell you."

Then I was taken to Digne. I stayed with one policeman for a long time, in a room in the law courts; then another policeman came to take me to my lawyer. As I got nearer, along the corridor where our steps echoed, I gradually made out a young man wearing a dark suit and tie who was waiting for me, standing by a window.

It was you.

La Fortelle
September-October 1976
April-May 1977